THE BAKERY GIRLS

by

FLORENCE DITLOW

ISBN-13: 978-1461079545

ISBN-10: 1461079543

Florence Ditlow also wrote:
"Long in the Tooth: Surviving chronic illness with a sense of humor."

The Bakery Girls is dedicated to those women who inspired it:
D, L and E

BIOGRAPHY

Florence Ditlow was born in Harrisburg, Pennsylvania. Her grandfather owned a bakery in which her parents worked. She too became an employee of the sweet place by the time she reached ten years of age.

An education in nursing took her to Washington, D.C. She worked as a registered nurse there, followed by Knoxville, Tennessee, Boston, Massachusetts and New York, NY prior to retiring in 1995. Hospitals utilized her skills as a writer in order to produce patient education materials as well as the instruction of the nursing staff. She wrote for a nursing textbook company as well.

Florence used humor as a therapeutic tool throughout her nursing career. In 1988, she joined what is now called the American Association for Applied and Therapeutic Humor. The group effectively promotes the use of humor and laughter to "enhance work performance, support learning, improve health and as a coping tool." Florence wrote some articles about humor for nurses and was a contributing author in a textbook: Nursing Perspectives on Humor, edited by Karyn Buxman. Along the way, she provided hundreds of fun programs for nurses and patients.

Her memoir, Long in the Tooth, appeared in 2002. The book discusses the value of humor in chronic illness and explores complementary health practices she has studied.

She wrote The Bakery Girls in 2011. This first novel is based on the family bakery and is dedicated to the real life bakery women who inspired it.

Florence Ditlow lives in Bonaire, a Dutch Caribbean municipality.

THE BAKERY GIRLS

The story you are about to taste is fictitious because in writing factual accounts, I ran into gaps in the timeline. I relied on the characters, often asking them the question, what happened next? All of the Stitt family characters, including the employees, were inspired by real people, though several names were changed. I based many scenes on my own interactions with Dot, Louise or Elaine. These whimsical women influenced my life, showing me the power of food prepared with love. Their ability to survive through the spirit of good humor is phenomenal. All three honed their personal senses of humor and used it as a survival skill. The reader may notice my tendency for employing some antiquated wording and this is intentional, in keeping with the period in which the action took place.

Originally, the term *lady* denoted a 'kneader of bread'. It comes from Old English *hlœfdige*, a compound formed from *hlf* 'bread' (ancestor of modern English *loaf*) and an element *dig* – 'knead' (related to English *dough*). It is a measure of the symbolic (and actual) importance of bread in medieval households that (like *lord*, also a derivative of *loaf*) *lady* came, as a provider of bread, to be applied to someone in a position of authority within a house.

Excerpt from Merriam Webster's online dictionary

1

The trolley car rolled to a stop, its bell clanging. The conductor shouted out his location, "Sixth and Reilly." The day was going slowly, and Floyd took his passengers' nickels, yawned and noticed by his old railroad watch that he was ahead of schedule. Just as he was closing the door, a face appeared at the window, smiling broadly. After the teeth, he noticed a soft, voluminous velvet hat ascending the stair, and the woman's dark brown eyes looked up as she placed a nickel in his palm. The passenger's highly piled hair was almost black and went well with the caramel-colored velvet suit she wore. Her thin wool Billet wasn't enough for the dry autumn wind.

The instant it took for her to take one of the wicker seats was enough time for the tall redheaded conductor to register a sort of excitement, an air of expectation, or perhaps unleash his testosterone. He started the vehicle and sparks flew unnoticed from upper guide wires.

She spoke to a girl in the adjoining seat, someone she attended church with, and when they left his car at the Walnut Street stop, the girl said, "Bye now, Clara."

Floyd thought about Clara for the entire day, and he paid no attention to the rollicking atmosphere in his car about the Harrisburg Senators' baseball game.

The oak leaves were a bright shade of yellow on the trolley route by the time of their next meeting. Clara had visited Pomeroy's Department Store. There she purchased a spool of white ribbon for a high-necked winter blouse. Her talent as a seamstress had been honed at Mrs. Edwards' Finishing School, but now at twenty-one, she would procrastinate at employment.

"I might get to looking for work next week," she told her mother.

Well, this was fortunate for Floyd Alexander Stitt. He had been residing in Harrisburg, Pennsylvania these two years and was planning to stay there in that Mid-Atlantic capital city. The city of 200,000 seemed a metropolis to Floyd. His encounters with women hadn't gone well. Maybe he had set his sights too high after he left his boyhood farm home. Pine Street Presbyterian Church yielded a few eligible ladies, like May Ulrich. She was gorgeous, indeed, but so cantankerous. She lured him in as if he were her prize catch of the day. After hooking him, she changed into a self-appointed critic. Finally, she attempted to eject him from the church choir, accusing him of "making the choir sound like a hurdy-gurdy."

But now, the trolley was at Clara's stop, and she was a "Gibson Girl" with some muscle, holding her satchel, which matched high-laced boots with pointy toes and spool heels. Later, Floyd called them "fairy godmother's boots." Indeed, Clara became a sort of fairy godmother, granting his farm-boy wishes. She certainly had an air of confidence that seemed like an aromatic drink, one he wished he could taste.

Clara stepped into the car when Floyd's large hand extended to her smaller, gloved one. She handed over her Liberty nickel.

"You get change," said the conductor, quietly smirking.

Her questioning expression was met with a tipped hat as "Floyd Stitt" introduced himself. He placed five new Indian head pennies in her glove.

Clara glanced at him sidelong as she swept to her seat. The pennies in her hand were hot. Floyd laughed down from his near six-foot height and added, "I would ask your name, but I already know it."

And that was the successful start of the Stitt family. It was 1907. There would soon be a President Taft, a Ford Model T, and an electric toaster.

***

Clara stood in the kitchen doorway, a little breathless. Her mother turned from where she had started the fire in the cook stove. "Dearie, you're back! Now, why don't you take off that coat?"

"Mom, I was just invited to the Pine Street Bazaar!"

Caroline Shultz's hazel eyes lit up as she sat her daughter down, helping her off with the black winter wear. "Do tell!"

"It's the trolley conductor—the tall boy with the red hair," she puffed. "He seems real sweet. I talked to him all the way home today, and I'm planning to go to his church with him on Saturday for the bazaar. He wants to drive us, and says he never takes the trolley unless he's paid to do it."

Clara had an ally in her mother—in both of her parents in fact. They didn't believe in sheltering children and approved of Clara's calculated risk taking.

"Listen," Caroline said slowly to her only daughter over her glasses. "Don't lose your head over him or over anybody. There is a world waiting for you. Keep your wits, please." Caroline's two boys were in happy marriages and Clara would find a suitable suitor.

The courtship started with visits to the church and taking rides in Floyd's dogcart, a small carriage powered by Floyd's gray horse, who he called "Gray." As the spring warmth thawed the ground, they strolled by the wide Susquehanna River, on its promenade, dreaming up a future, holding a good income for the future family.

They celebrated their betrothal on Valentine's Day 1908 in Harrisburg's Harris Ferry Tavern. In the foyer, a white-haired Negro musician at the piano played the *Maple Leaf Rag*.

Carriages passed by their window view of Third Street. A fireplace warmed them as they relaxed into their creaking oak wood chairs. "Clara, I've never been so... felt so... like I am right where I belong." His sky blue eyes were earnestly seeking his future, and he felt he needed Clara because of... of... not a socially inspired need. No sir, it was love of the highest level.

"Oh, you say the sweetest things," Clara giggled, holding his hand under the table. Her wavy dark hair ballooned under a bun, her matching brown eyes framed by black eyebrows. She seemed quiet, but her body communicated, often taking words right out of her mouth.

"Do you think about our future and working it all out?" Floyd declared with a furrowed brow. "I bet we'll have no problems with living together, even if we have to start out with your family. But you have to be prepared for changes, some good, some not so good."

They sipped a bitingly tart cider from glass mugs while their luncheon was prepared. She knew he yearned to leave his present job. He had saved to start a business. The farm had shown him that he needed a different way to earn a living. He told her of the day he had tied a hundred bales of hay. His weariness wasn't physical; rather, he had found farming unchallenging. Floyd was driving toward independence, similar to a spirited draft horse, intent on escaping his restrictive harness, then bursting through all of the fences. He didn't like taking orders and was on a search for stability.

He looked around at the bicycle trade, the fledgling motorcar, and the railroad establishment, but these were off the mark because they were big businesses. In germinating a new occupation, some enjoyment was required. No more baling for him, nor ticket taking. Ironically, Floyd found the answer would come to him inside of a cake.

***

Floyd was enjoying dinner at the Shultz residence, where Clara's father, Byron, treated him like his own son. The talk centered on the Ford motorcar, and both the men were doubtful, even afraid of these sputtering, smoking machines.

Byron said, "These motor carriages are just packed *full* o' stuff that can go wrong! You add speed to it an' well, ya just better throw yer goggles out 'n get a suit o' armor."

Floyd liked everything about horses and felt that they were a reliable, versatile and beautiful bargain. "Yeah, I was on a motorcar ride last year at the Path Valley picnic, and the tire exploded while we went down Hammond Lane. We had to get a horse to pull it from the ditch! Hah!"

The kitchen was warm with the scent of baked chicken. Caroline Shultz was a whiz in the kitchen and a superb baker. Today she had made a "Sunshine" cake, a light yellow cake, onto which she spooned honey butter. Small plates, ringed with green leaves, were a perfect frame for her dessert. The accompanying teacups were soon steaming with hot water, and she relaxed into her chair as the family dipped in Lipton teabags, unaware that she and her cake were about to become conduits for creativity.

The group quietly stirred, leaning away from this Sunday dinner in the sunny Shultz kitchen. Floyd was digesting the heavy meal, smiling, gazing toward the last course. The edge of the cake's bright wedge was toasty, which added to the aroma, and as he put the fork tines in, they became magical in that he stopped.

Putting his fork down, he took a sip of black tea. Somehow sitting with the spirited Shultzes, he had forgotten to worry about any of the thoughts that had weighed on his mind since he arrived in Harrisburg. Maybe the whole world could be viewed clearly, right inside the cells of this yellow cake!

Indeed, at closer examination, in a second or two, with his vision soft, he thought the glaze on top of the cake had formed the image of a three-tiered wedding cake.

Later, Floyd described how in that moment, the hand of God had reached him. Somehow, someway, the cows' butter, the bees' honey transcribed how God wanted Floyd Stitt to make wedding cakes, and cakes were born in ovens, and ovens lived in bakeries.

Clara, noting Floyd's reverie, whispered, "Floyd?"

He took a deep breath, sipped his tea and returned to the moment. Smiling, he said, "Yes, my dear?"

"You seemed to be daydreaming."

"You are so right." And clearing his throat, he picked up the fork and popped a bit of his cake on his tongue. "Ummm... the best cake... better than Mother's."

This honest revelation insured Floyd an ally in Caroline, his future mother-in-law, and simultaneously crystallized Floyd's future.

2

On a breezy October 1908, one year after their meeting on the trolley, they married, much to the delight of the Stitts and the Shultzes. The couple had a picture taken in a studio before the wedding, he in a starched collar with a dark suit and Clara in a voluminous white linen dress of her own design, following Godey's Lady's Magazine. Her hat from Paula's Millinery, an exquisite rendering of lace and pearls, was a crescent frame for her face. The photographer told her not to smile. She smirked at him in a controlled way and said, *"You hoo."*

The reception at St. Paul's Episcopal Church found the couple socializing for hours over a banquet of Clara's favorite treats and a ham brought from the farm homestead in Franklin County. Clara's mother made the three-tiered white wedding cake with white icing. The cake melted in the mouth, vanilla scented, and it was the center of the festivity due to the unique ornamentation on top.

Caroline had taken to heart the tradition of a bride needing to have something old, something new, something borrowed and something blue. Early in the couple's engagement, she went seeking bird feathers to fashion two small doves. That was the new, and the "old" eyes on these birds of peace she found in her jewelry box—lapis lazuli beads. Next, she would trail blue satin ribbons from the bird's cake perch. She borrowed these from Floyd's mother, Lucinda, who found them in her local dry goods store. No one was more taken with the cake than Floyd.

***

The wedding acted as a rite of passage, steering Floyd down an entrepreneurial path where his horse sense, independence and sweet tooth guided his way to success. He joined the Masonic Order, a select group of businessmen—a network of mutual value to each other. A banker in this exclusive club took to joining Floyd on Saturday trots on their horses. Their path looked through a stand of denuded chestnut trees and the wind was chilly.

Looking out over the river, Timothy Goethe said, "Just pay me a visit, and you'll get a business loan. Get down to business," he chuckled.

Floyd was about to tell Tim how he got the feeling God was plinking him on the head, daily as if to say, "Get going, get sugar, get pans, turn that oven on!" But he mumbled in a monotonous whine, "I need to get some good bakers... a building."

Tim interrupted excitedly, "Yeah, ya never did it before, but hey, you work in a trolley car, you can manage a building. Try thinking of the rides on your trolley as being like loaves of bread. It'll be the same customers. A different Goethe once said, "Whatever you can do or dream you can do, do it. Boldness has genius, strength and power in it. Begin it now"."

So, an invigorating mental shift inspired Floyd to take a different route home. It was tree-lined Woodbine Street, which was a conduit for much activity, though it was somewhat residential. He took the time to notice that there were established stores, a general store and a butcher shop, there. Women in pairs passed, and boys in short pants carried bags of groceries for an elderly lady.

He spied a vacant corner store, displaying a gold-rimmed sign saying "FOR RENT." Floyd felt an excitement that propelled him through that stage of uncertainty, of procuring the money that bought his new place of business.

He knew there were people who would like this type of

business on a nice city street. He let the world know he needed a hardworking baker who was able to come up with the energy to produce a good product. He needed to make a good impression on these families on Woodbine. Not everybody has what it takes to make the staff of life.

A miller who just happened to be in the Masonic group came to him at the next meeting. They formed an alliance that would last through twenty years and countless sacks of white, wheat and pastry flour. Meanwhile, the vision of three-tier wedding cakes spiraled through Floyd's brain. He dealt with anxious moments by singing hymns:

> *"I sit in the garden alone while the dew is still on the roses,*
> *And the joy I feel falling on my ear,*
> *The son of God*
> *Is ca- al- ling..."*

3

Spring thawed the ground as the bakery took shape. The oak wood floor shone when the sun hit it and creaked when the baker walked across it. Floyd saw shelves installed, baking pans purchased and now a heavy worktable stood in view of the front window. It allowed the room needed to do the prepping, the proofing, the panning and the bake. People who read his ad in *The Patriot News* approached Floyd: "Position available for experienced baker. References required."

Mostly, their references didn't enter into these employment dealings because Floyd was after a determined plodder. Someone clean enough to satisfy the health department, and smart enough to make it taste good and loyal. He needed a man who would appear in all types of weather, ready to work in the dark of night.

He rejected men who drank because he suspected they couldn't think straight, let alone leave a Friday night party to bake bread at midnight. Floyd made a point of looking over their horses because ill-cared-for nags indicated how men ran their lives. He was accumulating standards as well as the furrowed brow of worry. Floyd was determined to produce bread that was better than any other in Harrisburg.

In April, as Floyd and a bricklayer from the Masons were busy constructing the oven, the door opened and a thin, dark-haired gentleman entered. "Excuse me, are you interested in hiring a baker?"

The meeting started well. This young man, Richard Dan Fegley, had a restaurant job in Steelton and wanted to move to Harrisburg. He had plenty of kitchen savvy, with the ability to bake. Floyd asked him to visit at his home on the day Caroline usually set aside for baking. The youth learned about Floyd's concern for his future product, whereupon the man said, "Just let me show you... I just need the correct recipe proportions."

Clara and Floyd soon saw that he understood the process. He set out all the ingredients, warmed the yeast, then made the batter. They watched as he employed his wooden spoon with authority. The wheat and yeast left a distinct tang in the air of the kitchen, and the dough was sticky. While the bread rose under a blue kitchen towel, they ate lunch.

Clara inquired about his knowledge of baking. "I learned at Mother's knee," he started, taking a sip of milk. "We had one table in the kitchen, and Mother baked bread while I ciphered my school work. After a few years, she gave me the title of 'puncher.' She called me 'pain puncher' since she was half French—pain is the word for bread."

He made excuses with a gesture and jumped to the bread, resting in a large, blue ceramic bowl. They saw him punch the air out of the dough, setting it for a shorter rising period. Energetic folding transformed the dough. He shaped the resulting three loaves, long baguettes, covering these once again for the last period of rising. He efficiently prepared the baking pan and washed dishes in the meanwhile.

Floyd said, "You know your stuff, Dan," and peeked under the blue tea towel. The loaves had doubled their size, and he liked the smell of yeast. The baker, patted water on the bread, and made three diagonal cuts on each loaf.

"These cuts are for decoration, aren't they?" Clara asked.

Gesturing with the blade, Dan replied, "Right, but it also lets the dough expand while it bakes." Before the bread went in, he threw a handful of water in the dry oven and claimed it would make good humidity for baking.

The bread cooled on the dining table. Floyd had been impressed. Both he and Clara had learned from this demonstration just who they were hiring.

Caroline entered the room and eyed Dan. She tasted the crisp steamed baguette and smiled. "You bake like you have a reverence for flour."

And Dan responded, "Yeah, and Mrs. Shultz, isn't it extraordinary what yeast will do?"

Respect for the process of preparing food breeds a focus in the cook. Focus on the food, and it will come together in a harmonious manner, and in a bakeshop this attracts customers.

When Dan joined Floyd, the bakery expanded like a brick of yeast in the warmth of private enterprise. Dan insisted on the highest quality of grain that ever met the millstone. He would soon impress his attitude on farmers who supplied green tart apples for pies and fresh eggs for cakes. The summer saw the Woodbine Street shop sporting a dark green sign with yellow letters: "Stitt Bakery." There was now a second baker and an assistant who could do the less skilled work. In Floyd's horse-drawn wagon, he delivered to a growing number of patrons, who were hungry for their creative loaves of crusty bread.

There was news at home of family expansion too. Clara was expecting.

4

Floyd Stitt's menu was small in 1909. The bakers made the baguettes today and a dense wheat bread tomorrow, alternating until Saturday, their day of rest, when their hands stopped flouring, and they were off their feet at last. This schedule made them a good name from their good intent as well as their superior wheat. It grew on a Lancaster farm, and if one concentrated, the sun came through its taste... yes, right through to the wheat germ.

A new assistant meant there would be time to bake cakes. Fridays found Dan producing a yellow batter, rich from freshly laid eggs and creamery butter. He balanced the sweetness with the white icing, sweet from sugarcane grown in Louisiana. To Floyd, he said, "I wish these ladies who buy our bread each day will stop making cakes—like they stopped making their own bread."

Through creating variations, he got his wish. Using his buttery icing as a sort of canvas, he applied shaved lemon peel or orange peel at Christmas. If citrus zest was in the air, waiting customers were entranced. Black walnut topping pleased a woman who bought a birthday cake. Later on, Floyd tried apple schnitz successfully. Autumn apples were plentiful, so he dried wine sap apple slices in a slow oven, then incorporated them as schnitz into the yellow batter.

***

Meanwhile, at the home of the Shultzes, Clara confronted a major tragedy. Like all new mothers, full of expectation at the birth of her son, she was also on the edge of the unknown.

Things went well as she carried the baby to term, then after a six-hour labor, the midwife and Caroline delivered a five-pound boy who, sadly, was a cyanotic blue. He suffered a congenital heart condition for which there were no treatments in 1910. Mercifully, he died and the unforeseen torment seemed unbearable to Clara. She had never known depression, but now it seemed this feeling sat on and on—like a guest who wouldn't leave. Her appetite declined, and often she subsisted on breakfast food. Caroline took to making her toast over their fireplace, taking it to her in the dim light of the bedroom. This was the heavy wheat bread, dense, and nutritiously chewy. The toaster, Caroline, used a long metal rod with a claw on one end to hold a slice over fire; the handle was a wooden grip, comfy to the hand. Caroline sipped tea with Clara as her daughter tearfully and repeatedly lamented, "I loved him so!"

Floyd certainly mourned too and told her to quiet her heart, reminding her that she was young and strong enough to try again. He insisted she sit in the sunny backyard, away from noise, near the flowering raspberry vines.

Finally, after two months of dark moods, Floyd convinced her to attend her church at St. Paul's. He accompanied her there by carriage, and on the way, they hummed *Bringing in the Sheaves*. Before the service, churchgoers enjoyed a rendering by the organist. Clara's effervescent sister-in-law, Tinnie, came over and began to whisper womanly advice into Clara's ear . "Get the heck out of that house, girl, what you need is a magnificent distraction. Take a respite from thoughts of babies."

On their return home, Floyd saw a little more color in his wife's cheeks and sighed with relief.

"I plan to go to tea at Tinnie's tomorrow," vowed Clara, with some strength.

They stopped by the bakery so Floyd could show Clara the latest bread. It was baguette dough, but round, something Dan called a *boule*.

"Now, this is really beautiful." She admired the heavy loaf because it had a high, flour-dusted dome.

Floyd said wide-eyed, "They found a way to speed up the process, and it happened to improve the taste."

Clara nodded, took a boule and a cake for tea. On the way out, she noticed a new a sign: "Get your just dessert—A Stitt Cake!"

5

L *ow and behold, low and behold, how do I get out of here?* This thought ran through Clara's mind when Tinnie revealed what she had referred to as the "magnificent distraction."

There were two friends of Tinnie also present, and the subject of discussion was women's right to vote. A red-haired woman of about forty poured Clara's tea and said, "I know it's wrong to keep women out of the voting booth. We will get the right to vote, and I want to live to see it." Her freckled nose wrinkled.

"I like the idea. Beyond the officials, there are the ordinances... laws," said Tinnie. "You remember me trying to get into Kirkwood College? Then I wanted to work in the railway office. Both times they refused to take me," she seemed to breathe fire. "'Oh, it's only men here; women don't work here,' they said. We need new laws!" she growled slowly, leaning forward.

"Clara," said the blue-eyed Bess, who was a recent graduate of Wilson College, "we plan to meet with about one hundred women's suffrage groups in June. We've tried to get through to various elected officials," she said, smoothing her blond braid. "To no avail. We really have to make noise and alert other women by getting into the newspaper."

Cutting a slice of her Stitt's "just dessert," Clara thought a moment before replying. "I can't picture myself at the marble steps of the Capitol. Floyd would be embarrassed."

"We do this so lots of women can enjoy life more," Tinnie countered. "What you do now will change your opportunities *and* those of your daughters."

They continued their afternoon debate related to justice. Slowly, Clara saw the need for change, and the distraction had worked in the sense that now, her future occupied her thoughts. By the time she left, she had decided not to march; instead, she would make the suffragettes a sailcloth banner and hope they came out of it unscathed. By the time of the women's mass assembly on the Capitol steps, Clara was carrying her second child.

I feel different this time, she thought as she swept the walkway at home. *My back hurts less this time...* And she hummed to herself, "It'll be a girl." Perhaps the thoughts of her daughter helped to press her into service of the suffragist cause. She mused over this while making toast, which, by Clara's recipe, employed butter then brown sugar. Her doctor was glad of her prenatal state of health, though she craved the toast, crunchy pickles and occasionally pickles on that toast.

The door opened, the sun streamed in with Caroline, who took a seat after finishing the day's laundry. She washed sheets, put them through a ringer and hung them in the sun to dry. They had talked that morning of the women's protest at the nearby State Capitol Building, preceded by a quarter-mile march on Third Street. The parade was fronted by those carrying Clara's banner. They were dressed alike in leg-o-mutton blouses, long skirts and straw hats.

Clara's toast crunched as she spoke with her mouth full, staring at *The Harrisburg Patriot News* front page, showing unnamed women holding her banner. "Well, Mom, they got their news story and a picture with the mayor. He had to do it—Tinnie kind of twisted his arm. She told him to think of them as prospective voters."

Laughing with glee, Caroline whooped, "It's high time somebody moved that dusty old coot! She's right! If women get the vote, it'll double the number of voters. They won this skirmish. Watch out Washington!"

"You're excited! Do you expect they'll get the vote?"

Staring intently at her daughter, Caroline said, "*You* will and we all will; it's a matter of time. Things change, why my mother didn't have a ringer for clothes washing, that ringer has saved me so much energy. Ideas do change the times."

6

Clara was making a christening dress when her water broke. Four hours later, April 26, 1911, Dorothea Caroline Stitt arrived. She yelled, she displayed moving parts, and she was perfect. There was a watchful midwife, her grandmother and the family doctor welcoming, while Floyd fervently prayed in the backyard, sitting by the raspberry vines.

"Alleluia!" he sang. He rushed to Clara's side and saw quite a different scene than he had the previous year. She and her daughter were lively in spite of the birthing travail.

"It's a girl! It's a girl! It's a girl!" he sang to the tune of the hymn Alleluia. He told Dorothea, "We will celebrate you and Mother."

Caroline took the child as Floyd made a dash for Woodbine Street, where he found Dan, who was baking cakes. The employer told the crew as he leaped into the air. "Hold everything! It's a girl!" After shaking a few floured hands, Floyd told them to finish the work at hand. They would spend a couple of hours producing pink iced strawberry cupcakes—the cake was white—in Dorothea's honor to pass out to their walk-in customers.

***

When you celebrate, there is sure to be cake. Dorothea's birth may have fueled a consciousness of cake or the business may have naturally expanded. No matter, cake was there, in a tender triumph of taste. The cake menu featured more varieties. Leftover milk chocolate combined with white, giving birth to "marble swirl." Customer requests were encouraged; records kept. Two years passed, the demand grew, and the housewives on Woodbine Street clamored for cupcakes.

"They fit nicely in Timmy's lunch pail," said one.

"My father takes two to work in his lunch," said a woman waiting in line.

A charming matron declared, "Tea time is made for these Stitt cupcakes."

***

It wasn't too long before Dan ran out of chocolate for the second week in a row. When Floyd's wagon pulled up after lunch on Monday, Dan informed him excitedly, "We sold out of cake by ten this morning, and the cocoa bin's empty."

This demand for chocolate cake and cupcakes got Floyd thinking about larger cocoa quantities. Customers became mesmerized now by the chocolate cupcakes with bittersweet frosting was as heavy as fudge and supported, barely, by the cake underneath.

He sat down at his desk. Staring about his tiny windowless office, he saw that business was good and the budget balanced. He stared at a wreath on the door entirely made of bread dough, woven into a circle. Empty cotton flour sacks were stacked on a chair in a pile, and in the air was the aroma of the crusty hard rolls with the soft white centers just out of the oven. Leaning on the blotter, he reached for a fountain pen standing next to the photograph of Clara and little Dorothea—nicknamed Dot. He wrote a business letter to a millionaire.

Dear Mr. Hershey:

I own a bakery in Harrisburg and it benefits from Hershey Cocoa. I would like to arrange an appointment in regard to a standard automatic shipment of cocoa. I do not want to be without it. Please meet with me,

personally, as soon as it is convenient.
  Sincerely,
  Floyd A. Stitt

Two weeks later, Floyd was sitting in a much larger office of the president of the Hershey Chocolate factory. A secretary welcomed him with a steaming cup of cocoa in a white porcelain cup. There was a tall bookcase filled with maroon notebooks labeled by year. A globe sat on the heavy oak desk. Cacao grew in a tall pot, soaking in the sunlight of a recessed window. A man with a dark moustache sped into the room and tossed a bowler hat onto a waiting peg. Extending his arm, he motioned Floyd to a wing-backed chair.

"Floyd Stitt, how can I help you?"

So, this was Milton Hershey. He had become a millionaire by making caramels! By the time he was fifty, in 1907, his chocolate factory had expanded so that a town had grown around it.

Floyd filled him in on the state of the bakeshop, about how he was having a hard time keeping up with the demand for chocolate cake. Milton listened from his seat at the desk. He had only a fourth-grade education but was a valedictorian in sensibility.

He smiled, thinking amusedly of the early days in the caramel factory, and said, "Your trade has stepped up and you'd be smart to get more help. Go small with that chocolate cake. They! Want! Cupcakes! Go with the demand and make fewer large sizes."

Floyd felt the old pangs from the tugboat of change; it pulled from him the words, "Maybe I could use a manager to make it work out."

Milton added, "What about other small-sized items? Can you make other cake variations?"

"I could indeed." Floyd pictured one measuring four inches with two layers, white icing separating the layers.

Milton speculated, "Try a test week of smaller cakes and keep records." Then he laughed about the caramel trade. "I'm at home here. I really like chocolate, you know. Ha, ha... it goes down easier than caramels too. A woman working in the caramel factory once bit into a sticky piece and lost a front tooth!"

The meeting congenially came to a close, and Hershey had the last word. "My assistant will see to your order. If you have doubts about going small, think of the Hershey Kiss. He handed Floyd a coffee-colored tin of chocolate kisses labeled "Hershey Cocoa."

Out on the Hershey Road, Floyd returned home by horseback while the Hershey factory emitted the intense aroma of the roasted beans turning into chocolate. Floyd had felt the presence of a genius. He would attend to these thoughts of miniature desserts, now looming as though they were real. Small cakes for lunch trade and cookies incidentally; he had a good feeling about cookies. As for an assistant, well, he really resisted giving someone else the power to make decisions, but it was a risk he would have to take.

He told his horse, Gray, "I've done it before, yeah, I can take another chance." Then he broke into his unique rendition of "I love my sweet soft soda crackers." The laughing horse felt a curiously better mood had taken over their spirits.

"The man who has plenty of sweet soft soda crackers
And gives his neighbor none
Shall not have any of my sweet soft soda crackers
When his sweet soft soda crackers are gone."

By the time the State Street Bridge came into view, Floyd knew how to manage the baking. As for interviewing new employees, now he needed to talk that over with Clara.

"Put the word out at your church," he said, and I'll tell the people at Pine Street Presbyterian. They had remained faithful to their separate religious affiliations. "I'm looking for help, personally. Try to think of any people who could help me run the shop better."

"Okay," said Clara absentmindedly as Dot, teething on a crust, squirmed in the crook of her right arm. She stirred a huge pot of chicken corn soup with her left hand. Caroline and Byron came to the table. He set it for dinner, while she took the baby on her lap.

Floyd reviewed his encounter with Milton in the town of Hershey. "To get you an assistant? This brings only one person to my mind," said Caroline, "not a manager, but a good baker just the same... a girl."

"Naw," Floyd whined. "Women have no place out going to work at midnight."

"Hey! Give that Dan a promotion and get a new person to bake bread," interjected Byron. His voice got high when he was excited.

"What exactly do you want the new person to do?" asked Clara as she salted her soup.

Floyd said thoughtfully, "Relieve me of the baking decisions, so I'm free to do the paperwork and some deliveries."

"She could do it, she's pretty smart," Caroline said to herself.

"Out of curiosity, who are you talking about," said Floyd with irritation.

"Sarah Fegley. You don't know her. Just graduated high school."

Maybe Dan knows her, his name's Fegley too," mused Floyd. "I'll have to see about a news ad if I can't get the assistant by word of mouth... goodness... this is great sunshine cake, Caroline."

7

Dan smirked when Floyd asked whether he knew Sarah Fegley. Yes, she was his younger sister, and yes, she was adept in the baking arts. Though she hadn't yet worked for a living, she baked for the family, relatives and the church bazaars, which is how Caroline came to appreciate her skill.

"Why didn't you tell me you had a sister?" Floyd asked.

Dan said, "You never asked."

Floyd interrogated Dan more specifically and discovered that his kid sister was highly organized, with good grades in school; he said she was the only one in the family with good penmanship. Aunts begged for her cake recipes, but then they couldn't seem to duplicate her desserts. She had saved some money selling her baked goods, featuring tall, layer cakes topped with gaspingly good icing, sugar and spice cookies—the hit of the church bazaar. The cookies were like small circular road maps: leading down the road to crunch town. All of this was good news. Floyd pictured her as his future cakemeister. Still, he balked at the idea of a woman assistant. He would go to meet with her.

Floyd was digesting this small *slice* of data about Sarah when he was presented with an entire *cake full* of information. Dan, ever genial, went on to say that he had two brothers, and that they worked at the Jefferson Bakery!

The day after these revelations, as the workday ended, Floyd and Dan rode in the delivery wagon over to Jefferson Street. It wasn't every day that this sort of miracle happened, and Floyd, in full business expansion mode, was ready. God had spoken before through Caroline's cake, now through Caroline and that clear message was, "Get a hold of as many of the fantastic Fegleys as you can!"

8

Herbert Mince, a sixty-four-year-old entrepreneur who had learned about expeditious food transport in the Army, owned the Jefferson Street Bakery. Retirement bored him, so he built the bakery, two adjoining apartments and a stable. His was a sweet operation, you might say, since it was a dessert-driven, breadless haven for the sweet tooth. Thanks to Edison, electric lit the workroom, powered a huge fan and a spiral mixer. The walls were lined with tables sturdy enough to support a mill for mixing pie dough and large enough to mix cake batter. A huge cylinder on one table could roll out slabs of dough, soon cut into circular disks for piecrust. Stacks of metal baking sheets four feet in length were stored beneath the work surface. Bins in the entryway held the requisite flour and sugar. Perishables such as lard stayed locked in an iglooish room with blocks of ice. A single light bulb hung over the huge black gas oven, positioned against the back wall.

The "crumb crew," as the cake bakers referred to themselves, had gone home, leaving the two Fegley brothers to the pie packaging. Dan made the introductions. The tall thin Bill Fegley smiled and said, "I'll get the flour off my hands," while tipping his white cap.

George Fegley, at five feet six, looked up at the red-haired stranger saying, "Mr. Stitt, we get dirty, but we sure do have a lot of fun."

Floyd had had an exciting first impression. He hoped to convince all the Fegleys to join him and decided on a business meeting at his house. They would accompany Sarah, and in the meantime, Floyd had a few days to organize his thoughts.

That night Floyd had a dream about all of the change before him about to unfold. In sleep's deep rest, he felt released from the turmoil of going small with cake, choosing a manager, and the prospect of luring the Fegleys away from the Jefferson Bakery. He dreamed he was standing in a bread- packing box, a green one with yellow lettering. He held on to four horses by leather reins, harnessed to the box. Their rumps strained forward in an attempt to pull their passenger. A white mane tossed, a yellow tail twitched, a chest leaned against his harness, a special dark horse whinnied and yet they went nowhere. Dreamy oddness allowed the animals to have skins of cookie and cake textures.

Floyd puzzled over how such a tiny vehicle could be stuck, and twisting to see behind him, he saw a fat man, well dressed, sporting a pork pie hat. This oaf was holding on to the box, impeding his forward movement. After an endless period, a toddler came running with outstretched arms. She wore a white dress and lace bonnet. She sprang up, bouncing onto the broad back of the white horse. The fat man disappeared, releasing the four animals into a lively trot.

"Gracious me! Dot… that was Dot!" said Floyd, waking with a start.

"ZZZ… what?" Clara mumbled.

"Uhh, nothing, go back to sleep," said the disturbed Floyd.

9

The Stitt Bakery, as it would exist in 1914, served the neighborhoods north of the Capitol Building. Two horse-powered wagons went to several general stores and the Broad Street farmers' market at Third and Verbeke Streets. The bakery sold freshly baked goods at its own store too. The work night saw the one gas oven loaded with bread and rolls, then pie then cake.

When these items cooled, the cakes were frosted and the pies were "dumped" by hand from metal pans onto thick, white paper plates. The wares went to markets by wagon. These baked goods rode on three-foot long metal trays placed inside of drawers inside the wagon. Customers wished to see these offerings, so they were wrapped in brown paper bags only after purchase.

Stitt Bread had a crusty exterior and air made it crustier by the hour. An inventor Otto Rohwedder, then residing in St. Joseph, Missouri, was on a course to change bread usage forever by building a bread slicer. He quietly attempted cutting loaves by machine, then employed long hat pins to keep the slices together, thus having less exposure to the air. Otto repeatedly went back to the drawing board because of the effect of air. To slice a loaf of bread successfully, he decided that one must be prepared to wrap it. Paper failed as wrap because it was porous and not transparent. Mr. Rohwedder's determination was tested because during his trials to invent a slicing-wrapping device, a fire destroyed his work. He diligently experimented as Floyd's bakery business grew.

Thomas Edison's least known invention was wax paper, which he made in 1872, at age twenty-five. "Paraffin Paper" would wait almost fifty years to be widely used for bakery packaging. Meanwhile, the brown paper bag offered protection for shoppers in 1914.

***

Herbert Mince appreciated pie and all it stood for. He had wisely concentrated his Jefferson Bakery business resources on producing pies for every taste. The ingredients were affordable and the results weren't only appetizing, but fortifying. He thought about this, in part, because he was a veteran of the Spanish-American War. He thought about soldiers and their need for food in the field. They needed energy-rich nutrients that could be carried miles, and mess kits for field meals. Maybe the war in Europe triggered his thoughts, reminding him that "an army travels on its stomach." Like Otto Rohwedder, his mind was on the packaging and preservation of comestibles.

Coincidentally, the Fegley brothers came to confront Herbert. They worked for two years at Jefferson, receiving a wage of sixty dollars a month. George was curious of his own value to the operation, while Bill anxiously wondered if they could get better wages. Then they suggested that they needed more lighting in the shop.

"Boys," said Herbert, "I'm convinced that you deserve better wages... and more light bulbs too. Let me tell you my side now. I have done good work here with your help. I have an ambition now, to change businesses and go into packaging. There's food to transport, and I can find ways to do it."

"Where are you going to go?" George wanted to know, rubbing his chin.

"I need a smaller office," their boss mused. "So I'll have to look for a buyer for this building."

Bill and George were thinking the same thought at that precise moment. "Maybe... we can help you." Bill said cautiously, glancing at George. With these words, they began a new era for both Mince and Stitt.

Herbert Mince went with the Fegley brothers to meet Floyd and to see his building. Mince encountered Floyd at his desk. That day, daughter Dot, who was visiting, sat on the desk in her yellow pinafore dress. The two bakers related to each other as a lock relates to a key. Herbert looked at the baked goods and sensed the thought that was behind the basket of loaves in the window. He was impressed by the appearance and aromas issuing from the trays of chocolate cupcakes just out of the oven. Floyd curiously asked about Herbert's bags, boxes, even bins for transporting pies. The next meetings in Floyd's office culminated in a project allowing them to trade their deeds, Herbert taking the Woodbine Street location, and Floyd taking over the building on Jefferson Street. Thank God for the bank and Caroline! The ball was rolling now, just like a glazed donut honing in on a dunk in a cup of black coffee.

***

Floyd conferred with the Fegleys numerous times in order to match the team to their logical aptitudes. He had a shop with lots of possibilities now. He promised them a raise for Christmas, when sales would exceed those of the old location. He employed two skilled bread bakers and two dessert experts: Dan and George, Bill and Sarah. Floyd encouraged her to take on a role of cakemeister and tested her managerial abilities by asking her to requisition the supplies. She was placed in charge of orders for everything from aprons to apples.

Sarah found her first obstacle to be the nighttime hours, that left her eighteen-year-old brain mired in an inept sluggish state. She explained this clearly to Floyd, and they saw how to overcome the apparent snag in her routine by allowing her more daylight hours. The cakes would be the last thing in the order of the day, with George overseeing baking and Sarah handling cakes. All her other responsibilities could wait until dawn.

She ordered not only new light bulbs but shades to direct more light to work surfaces, shiny wire baker's racks with wheels and steel tables which took less time to clean.

The Fegleys' jovial mood could not help but improve their product. There was an atmosphere of collegiality now that Sarah and Dan joined Bill and George. Floyd knew less about the baker's art than the Fegleys, and he told them so. Though Floyd was just a few years older, he seemed patriarchal to the Fegleys, perhaps because they had lost their own father.

10

"Put me down, Carrie! Come on! Let me down!" Byron yelled over his wife's salt and pepper head.

"No!" Caroline exclaimed. "Think about it!" She stared up at her husband, whom she had deposited on top of the icebox in an effort to display her strength.

He pleaded, looking down, "I don't want you running in a ditch in the mud... these tin lizzies are nothin' to play with."

Silence. He exhaled, continuing, "I love you too much, that's all." She looked up at him for a minute and finally stepped back, smiling, so Byron seized the chance to leap to the kitchen floor with his arms winging in the air.

"Dear, you'd best relax because I already took some driving lessons from Floyd."

As if in pain he responded, "Ahhh, Floyd. *He had* to go'n get a motorcar."

"You have to take risks sometimes," she had told him that over the years, and now she would drive a motorcar, pretty much like she drove the marriage, and no man would convince her otherwise.

Byron shook his head, but smiled, hiding his concern as she took off down Boaz Street with Clara holding another of her suffragist banners. Luckily, Byron would sit with Dorothea and play until they returned. *That's all I need,* he thought, *them endangering a little kid.*

The kid surprised Byron then when she yelled, "Mamaw! Drive carefully..." Dot waved toward the car, a Model T, being occupied by her grandma and cranked by her mother.

Clara directed her mother to a church meeting hall where one of "the rabble rousers," as Byron referred to the women's voting rights group, was to speak. This would be Caroline's first visit to these kindred spirits of hers. Pedestrians stared as the two chugged toward a stone edifice near the river. When a couple riding horseback trotted into the street, Caroline put on the brake, then couldn't find second gear, so she went the rest of their way in low gear. They emerged from the vehicle, Clara with her banner that proclaimed, "Votes for Women!" and her mother carrying a yellow bakery sheet cake decorated with the mint green letters: "Welcome Carrie Catts."

The two latecomers sat in the back of the room. The meeting hummed with an excitement that was different from the previous session at Tinnie's place. Clara spotted Tinnie and Bess, the blond girl with the braid.

The speaker projected, "…liberty and justice for all. Who is that? All of the men?"

Now here was a woman so well dressed, she reminded Clara of some actresses. She had a black Billet, plus a hobbled skirt displaying her ankles, and the hat was a beauty. It was gray, the short brim decorated by a black polka-dotted lace veil.

She spent some time telling the audience how she had met hundreds of women and corresponded with hundreds more. She boiled it all down to three points: the care of ourselves, the care of our families, and the care of future generations.

She spelled this out in a way that they could repeat to their "sisters" at home. "We need a voice, and it will come by way of the ballot box. The prohibition of alcohol is a higher priority each day. We cannot allow drunks to get behind the wheel of the motorcar."

Caroline whispered to Clara, "I'm glad your father isn't here."

Mrs. Catts's voice projected, "Our daughters need to finish high school, to make a better life for themselves and the family. We need laws allowing marriage licenses at eighteen in every state. I urge you to write your congressmen, not to *ask* for the vote but to demand what is yours. Dear friends, voting is the bread of a democracy. Today we women haven't any of that bread."

Clara's eyes widened. Votes like slices of bread. The audience listened intently and gave up a sigh of approval. They had stepped out of their routines long enough to see that women needed to elevate their positions, be it on the farm or in the city. Applause became a crescendo of cheers.

The cake was sliced and enjoyed while the women circulated and conversed. While much feeling was exchanged by housewives, mere girls and matrons, the esteemed Mrs. Catts seemed to have disappeared. But she soon reappeared with the red-haired woman Clara had met at the tea and asked that the hundred be seated at tables so that she could meet everyone present. Her strategy was to get the women united in their common interest. In a short while, the whole group had planned a letter-writing campaign.

When the speaker came to the table, a spirited Clara reached out to shake Carrie Catts's hand. She said, "My sister-in-law told me women's equality would be a magnificent distraction in my life. I really didn't take it seriously then. Now my head is clear, I see voting as a voice, and I am part of this fight."

By no coincidence, a member of the church choir exuberantly caught the spirit of the moment and decided that the group should close with a song. She quickly had to choose something everyone knew. A hymn? No, no not a hymn… too solemn… a war song? No, no, too militant.

"Ladies!" she yelled over the din. "We women will send Carrie to her next meeting with an unusual rendition of *Row, row, row your boat*. However, in keeping with the moment, we will say *vote* instead of row!

"Ready," she said, pointing to the group.

"Vote, vote, vote your boat gently down the stream, merrily, merrily, merrily, merrily, life is but a dream."

Caroline and Clara sang it all the way home, and as the gears engaged, their spirits rose.

"Dot will appreciate this effort when she reaches voting age."

"Clara, today I feel about twenty-one." And Caroline laughed from a place of finding a new sense of accomplishment. That night she celebrated, and as she broke out a bottle of homemade dandelion wine, she wondered how the temperance movement would play out.

11

Though the First World War had been in progress in Europe for two years, the America of 1916 maintained its neutrality. Pennsylvania's population expanded due to the immigration of Europeans. The Harrisburg Suffragists and Women's Christian Temperance Union quietly continued to write to Washington to get their voting rights and to prohibit sales of alcohol. Clara's second daughter was born July 26, 1916. Her name was Louise Ruth.

Concurrently, under the newly painted sign, "Stitt's Better Made Bread," the Fegleys did, in fact, make it better. Fermentation was their life, at least among the bread bakers. One could witness them mechanically mixing batter, and later, folding dough at their floured workbench. They had a room near the oven for the final rise called "the proofing room." The fermentation process finally stopped inside the oven when the dough reached one hundred thirty-eight degrees, so one could say that as the yeast died, the bread was born.

Yeast reacting with sugar yielded gas. Dan expertly picked up fifty pounds of cream-colored dough and folded it on top of a floured surface. He had learned not to remove all the gas, just enough to make a superior loaf. Every time he folded it, the strands of gluten became uniform, which strengthened the dough. The bread was shaped and proofed. When proofing was complete, Bill scored the dome of the loaf with a sharp knife so that it could fully expand in the atmosphere of the dry oven heat.

The Stitts lived in an apartment one flight of stairs over the bakery store. Little Dot, now five, woke up to the heated atmosphere of this better made bread. The child grew taller and had natural brown curls, laughing eyes and seriously thin lips. Early on, Dot had a sense of justice and was quick to point out injustices. Clara's small kitchen had a new toaster, a rust prone A-shaped affair, powered by the gas stove. The drying bread slice had to be observed carefully for doneness. She toasted, keeping her other eye on the baby in the cradle. While she rocked the bed with her foot, she and Dot sang, "Rock a bye baby on the tree top." Dot's doll sang along—Dot named her "Caruso Singer," though no one knew where Dot had heard of opera.

"Uh-oh... burnt! But only on one side." Clara scraped off crumbs of carbon and buttered it. As the bread had come out of the bakery oven recently, it somehow retained an acceptable taste. She inserted a new slice for Dot and told her soberly, referring to the carbon, "This is good for the health of the liver."

"Ahh- ah- ah- ah- HA, HA, HAA. I will only take light toast!" sang Caruso Singer, who had a piece of stale bread tied to her wrist as she sat on the kitchen table. Dot chewed her toast and offered some to her doll with her left hand. "It's good for you." An autumn breeze blew through the kitchen. She was reflecting on her first week of school.

"The teacher was so mean. She said I have to write with my right hand!"

In order to whip lefties into shape, the teacher demanded they use the right hand. Dot found this awkward, dared to use her left, and her punishment was to sit on the floor, using a chair as a desk.

Clara listened and said, "I'm sorry, dear, but they say it's better to be a right hander."

"I was happy to go to school till now," Dot pouted.

Clara left the cradle, took her daughter on her knee, and gently put a fat, eraserless pencil into her right hand. She wrapped her right hand around Dot's and printed "A."

"See? You gave yourself an A."

Then Clara took the pencil and made an A with her own left

hand. "Well, it feels peculiar, but it will come with time. Why, here are your crayons! Make a picture of Louise and use your pencil and right hand."

Dot began a shaky line drawing saying enthusiastically, "Okay."

Clara waited, and when she finished the portrait said, "Take your Crayolas and color it with your left hand. You'll learn to use both of your hands." Clara knew Dot had creative abilities the day she observed the child eating her bread in a new way. Each day she nibbled her bread into the shape of a different U.S. state! She dotted butter on them where there were mountains! Added jam for lakes!

By the end of the school year, Dot was able to use pencils, chalk and spoons in the right hand with dexterity, but when she breezed through the shop door at 3:30 in the afternoon, one could say sinisterly, she went left.

Bouncing into the empty bakeshop, she went to their newest product—the cream puff. Its custard cream was encased in a light pastry shell. Holding on to the fat, powdered sugar shell with her left hand, she ran upstairs, opening the door with her right.

"Hi," she breathed, hugging her mother. The bow in her brown hair was askew. She had grown an inch taller and was learning to be ambidextrous.

Clara asked her, "How was school?"

Swallowing some of her snack, Dot answered, "We talked about Leonardo Vinci and guess what? He was a left-handed artist!"

"So he was, and quite a famous inventor too."

Baby Louise had crawled under the table and shrieked, "Dot!"

"Hee-hee!" laughed Dot, placing a piece of puff in Louise's toothless mouth.

"Now, Dorothea, you really did well in school," Clara declared.

"Umm, umm." Dot was still chewing.

"And you are soon going to the second grade."

Dot sat high in her chair. "Yeah, maybe that teacher will be smarter."

Clara said, "I know it was hard… to become right-handed, but you overcame that, and it shows you're a very strong girl."

Dot went to her mother, hugged her large, aproned waist and said, "YOU were my handwriting teacher. I was so mad at Miss Quill, I couldn't pay attention."

Clara beamed at her precious daughter, smiled and told her, "That is one of the nicest things I've ever heard. Let's celebrate tomorrow! We'll ride the streetcar to the park, and then we'll take a tour of the museum."

"Ohh. Okay."

Clara went on, "We'll drop Louise at Mom's. They will be so happy to see us!"

12

The morning found them climbing aboard the eleven a.m. trolley. Under her straw hat, Clara was thinking of how she had gotten on this very car only seven years ago and now... mother of two. Time flies when you are raising daughters. She sensed the percolation of change. Why, these children would be voting, driving cars, and they may drive to jobs. Clara wrote a number of letters asking for the vote. She wrote some to her congressman and some to Mrs. Woodrow Wilson, only to read of Mrs. Wilson's death.

A young man in an Army uniform talked to the conductor about the war in France, saying the U.S. Army would be involved. He said, "It's not if, but when."

Lunch was somewhat greasy. They munched at chicken drumsticks while sitting on the Capitol Park grass against a mammoth chestnut tree. "This is a 'barky' chair," giggled Dot. School was out now and the June heat of the sun filtered through the canopy of leaves. They ate some small, juicy strawberries and drank lemonade.

Entering the museum on Third Street, Clara said, "Just look at these statues, now. This is kind of like Mr. Da Vinci's work." The gray marble figures posed in abundance as part of the wall and entry.

The two visitors saw rooms full of paintings. The collection was dominated by a wall-sized rendition of the Battle of Gettysburg.

"That happened in Pennsylvania?" Dot queried. "Why did he paint it so big?"

Clara stared up at the carnage and replied slowly, "He

wanted us to see how bad it was. It was too big to explain, so he made a picture."

"Dead soldiers can't say how it was," said the little student.

Clara whispered, "No," and thought of the Army private on the trolley.

They went on to view Pennsylvania Indian artifacts. The tools of early Indian cultures proved that they made lots of bread. An exhibit of Paleolithic artifacts showed Dot and her mother that the Indians had made ovens for transforming grain and water into bread. Dot craned her neck to see inside the reconstructed clay oven. Three feet in diameter, it was a dome of yellowed clay, bleached by fire—or the ages.

"You see, all kinds of people like bread. It looks different in other countries, but it's still good bread," Clara exclaimed. She read on about the mixing of water and grain, how together they can produce bread over a wood fire. Ovens similar to the one before them dated back five thousand years before Christ. Egypt, Syria and the Balkans all had their version of the oven. The fire heated a flat stone holding the grain and water mix. Eventually someone placed a bowl over the bread to contain the heat. This began the invention of domed ovens.

"Ladies would have to work hard for a loaf of bread," Dot reflected.

"Yessiree," Clara answered, while she continued to read that the Roman armies carried bread. An obscure Roman goddess, named "Fornix" was their spirit of bread baking.

An old Dutch sign at the exhibit illustrated just how intense the creation of bread is. It read: "Hij is in zijn vak door kneden," which translates to, "He is kneaded into his work."

"Are you Mrs. Stitt?" a museum guard queried as they turned from the crude oven.

Clara smiled and nodded. He exclaimed, "I guess this exhibit makes you proud to be a baker."

"Sure enough, it… bread is basic."

Touring the gas-lit museum was now tiring, and Clara

decided to go home. She sat on the trolley, her arm draped over Dot's shoulder. The art of the State Museum of Pennsylvania had come down to marble statuary, war and bread, an unlikely combination. Little did she know how big a seed she had planted in the mind of her talented daughter.

***

Floyd liked to eat the evening meal at about five-thirty. That was because his workday began at three a.m. He had met with Herbert Mince while Dot and Clara toured the museum.

Floyd laughed over a bowl of chicken soup, "He was full of questions about biscuit making."

Clara answered, "But didn't he want a packaging business?"

"Right," said Floyd. "He is going to work on a container contract for the armed services... K rations. He'll help to package hardtack. But that is no sweet soda cracker or biscuit. We make baking powder biscuits. I told him I never made hardtack, but the secret of it *is* in the packaging."

"Hardtack is biscuit for soldiers," Clara said while feeding the baby.

Floyd said, "See, as long as hardtack is dry, it's edible. Any moisture will ruin hardtack, so it has to be hard. Soldiers eat it with soup or coffee. So he's making hardtack tins."

13

Woodrow Wilson could no longer stay out of the war in Europe, and by 1918, American men were "over there." The impact on the Stitt Bakery was slight because the men who worked for Floyd didn't enlist. Bill Fegley called Wilson "half-baked" for involving Americans. "The war to end all wars? Humph! What became of neutrality?"

Byron Shultz worked on the railroad and reported a war-related event to the family at Sunday dinner. "Two-hundred Army recruits done took off today, them in their doughboy uniforms. It was a heck of a sad scene with a weeping crowd on the platform singin' *Pack up yer troubles in yer old kit bag*"...

Clara and Floyd joined with "and smile, smile, smile," while frowning.

While the war was a terrible strain on families of the Army recruits, another scourge was about to tip the scale; it was called influenza by the British, la grippe by the French, but Byron Shultz would have even more words for the flu.

The influenza symptoms of body aches, sore throat, or cough were unusually debilitating. The illness was unusual in the numbers of vigorous, young people affected. Infants and elders commonly died of diseases such as diphtheria and typhoid fever, but this was an unusually virulent new form of illness. Weeks of bed rest actually was detrimental to those who were sick. Lying in darkened, unventilated rooms often led to pneumonia.

October of 1918 alone saw the inconceivable number of 195,000 persons dying, and that was just in the United States. Many more would die in Europe and Asia, Britain estimating 200,000, France 400,000. The final toll was recorded at twenty to forty million. Ironically, this illness, which knew no borders, helped end the war: after all, war required participants, and thousands of men were lying in infirmaries fighting la grippe.

Into this mire stepped Floyd and Clara. The hospitals warned the populace to beware of ill soldiers returning home, and they urged immunization of civilians. Clara dragged Floyd to the hospital for immunization, as neighbors were taking ill.

The immunization was believed to prevent disease by injecting a small version of it. The diseases targeted then by the immunization were typhoid, yellow fever and diphtheria among others; there was no effective flu vaccine, as the offending organism hadn't been identified. Humans naturally become immune when they build antibodies by enduring an illness. The exposure to vaccination bypasses the body's first line of defense against illness, the skin and mucous membranes.

The immunization of servicemen was the first in history. The camp physicians hoped to prevent epidemics so they injected fourteen to twenty-five attenuated forms of the above diseases. To complicate things, the hospitals had already sent their best practitioners overseas, leaving the populace at home to suffer for the lack of seasoned physicians and skilled nurses.

The congregation of men in service camps was suspect in driving the influenza outbreak. They were at the peak of bodily strength yet under the stress of new environment and a life-threatening mission, they succumbed to the illness. Allied leaders overseas propagandized rumors of germ warfare. Doctors pushed for and got improved sanitation in service camps, but out in the trenches, sanitation took a backseat to survival.

The illness operated strangely, beginning with the common flu symptoms, but victims experienced rashes, fevers and racking cough. Pneumonia followed, presenting doctors with ashen-faced patients who would die directly from blocked lung passages or unremitting diarrhea. Some soldiers died soon after enlistment, in camp, in an apparent reaction to the mass vaccination. Never before had humans been intentionally exposed to so many, albeit minimal quantities of disease. Some had mentally related reactions, which prompted physicians to label them as shellshocked, even though they never saw action.

Civilian flu victims reported sudden weakness, leaving them prostrate on the spot. A group of four middle-aged ladies played their weekly bridge game one evening and three died hours later.

Stitt Bakery closed, as did the schools and churches for all the month of October 1918. Fearless general store merchants provided food, blankets and home remedies until their shelves were empty. People crept through the streets wearing surgical masks, for a sneeze was purported to be a lethal weapon. Forget about doctors, they were at the hospital—a place you would go only if you wished to enter a large morgue.

Clara and Floyd succumbed to the sickness, so they spent their tenth anniversary in bed. It was not romantic.

"Well at least we're together. If I were well, I'd be down at the farmer's market."

"And YOU would be there all alone," Clara shot back.

His face resembled a crumb pie, thought Clara. It was mottled and dry, so dry. They had never been sick at the same time and Clara prayed for strength. "Please get me out of this bed so I don't have to look at that, hear the coughing, smell stinking linens." Then the horrible truth struck her that she hadn't looked in the mirror for the week they had been sick. How must she look? She had forgotten to care. She could only drink water, eat dry toast and be grateful for indoor plumbing.

The children were at her mother's, a few blocks away and missing them, she was, through her ache, beginning—only beginning—to see the light at the end of a scary tunnel. What about her parents, suppose they got it? But they were holed up at home, living on recently canned jars of sausage, tomatoes and corn.

She shuffled to the telephone, picked up the earpiece and dialed her mother.

"Hello there, honey!" said Caroline. "You sound stronger.

45

Yes! We're doing okay! Byron's reading *Alice in Wonderland* to Louise, and Dot helps me make flapjacks with the milk Byron got."

Breathing deeply, Clara coughed.

Hearing this, Caroline launched into a repeat of her earlier instructions, boneset tea, soup, rub your chest with goose grease and… and get yourself a hot bath. Byron will bring you some food tonight."

Clara thought, *She doesn't know how… weak I am… people die of this.*

Clara went out the door of her kitchen to walk on the roof over the bakery. Red maple leaves were falling, sparrows chirped and the air was dry. She slowly walked the roof perimeter, coughing and feeling her wheezing chest muscles expand. She decided she had no choice but to endure until the "Grippe" unhanded her. The handkerchief tied on her wrist, embroidered with cross-stitching, was now decorated with phlegm and sweat.

Hearing the teakettle rumble, she went inside to partake of boneset tea. It steamed her face and with each sip, her head and throat soaked it in. Her fingernails had a blue tinge, yet gratefully, they could hold a tea cup.

That day was one of miraculous proportion. Clara scrounged for something edible and made oatmeal for Floyd, who first refused, then relented with the addition of cherry jam. She dragged him to the tub and forced him to bathe. This exhausted both of them, and as they lie sweating on the bed, the doorbell rang.

Thinking it was Byron, she went down a flight of stairs to admit him, only to find a strange woman. She wore the uniform of a Red Cross nurse, but Clara had never seen a Negro nurse. Of course, she wore a white cotton mask. She seemed anxious.

"Hello, ma'am." She nodded with a large black hat. "I'm Cecelia Scott, with the Red Cross. I am distributing masks and taking down names of folks who need food or blankets."

Clara invited her in, and they shared steaming cups of Lipton tea and horehound cough drops. The woman seemed out of breath, revealing, "I'm the only person covering north Harrisburg. I thought I was doing good till…" she inhaled, "I found a whole family dead."

Clara gasped "Where?"

"Division Street. I just came from there," she shivered, briskly rubbing her elbows.

The nurse recovered after an unusual sort of lunch consisting of fruitcake, which was the only thing Clara found down in the bakery. "I know we in Harrisburg're lucky," said the nurse, shaking her head. "I was told Chicago has no sheets in the stores because they used them all for to bury the dead! And nurses—two hundred died, and that's only in the Red Cross."

Clara shuddered and replied, "This week I look less like death."

Cecelia later proceeded to take vital signs and tell Clara that her heart was normal, though her lungs "too wet." She took a look at Floyd, who was somewhat delirious. He was a different story. She helped Clara change the linen. She rubbed goose grease over the backs of the ailing couple and Clara's skin hurt so much that she was on the verge of tears.

"I'm going back to the office now, keep him warm and make him drink liquids, okay?"

Grasping Cecelia's hand, Clara whispered, "Be careful and bless you."

Before long, another masked man was at the door—Clara's father, toting a soup kettle. He served that chicken soup to Floyd in bed, then he sat a while with Clara, who recounted the tale of the Red Cross nurse. In his search for milk, he had found that the trains would soon resume a regular schedule, so he would go back to work wearing a mask.

The troops were hobbling back with battle wounds and a few coming home to die on their native soil. The railroad employees were urged to take the vaccine, since they would be exposed to the hundreds of people traveling. Byron had quietly told his superior why he thought the shot was a bad idea.

He chanced to ride the train with a sick doctor who had said the Army typhoid vaccine was a weakened form of salmonella typhosa, which this particular doctor knew he didn't have. The physician said the germs of typhoid were entirely different from influenza. Byron went on to say the doctor believed more in chicken soup than vaccines. Thanks to the events of 1918, Byron became quite shy of needles.

He mumbled to Clara, "I'd sooner have a bloodletting."

***

Germans hid influenza casualty statistics from the world. The war had been drained of its human resources. The armistice called in November of 1918 led to the Treaty of Versailles, officially ending "the war to end all wars" by spring of 1919.

For Floyd it was touch and go. A record consumption chicken soup had him dreaming of gardens full of garlic. His wife prodded him repeatedly to take a seat on the roof, then to consume unusual things like red raspberry leaf tea and dandelion wine. Clara feared spreading the flu to the children and wouldn't see them until Floyd returned to work—the Christmas of 1918. Weeks of tending Floyd had Clara forgetting that she too had been ill. Maybe the pots of steaming soup had wafted into her brain, for she paid more attention to her mate than she had ever focused on anything in her thirty-two years. She was able to do it through blind determination and scanty general store provisions. She sensed her personal victory over the epidemic one evening when Floyd broke into his rendition of *Down by the Old Mill Stream*:

Down by the Ooold street car
Where I first met you
With your eyes of brown
And you didn't frown

48

The Bakery Girls

Ooh it was there I knew
That you really loved me too
You were twenty-one
My sticky bun
By the old street car

14

The sticky bun is Pennsylvania's own contribution to world cuisine. Cousin to the cinnamon roll, these yeast buns are baked, cozily touching each other on a sheet pan, atop a gooey mixture of butter, sugar and pecans. The cooled pan is inverted, after the bake, revealing the tops stiffly caramelized while they retain a soft body. Enjoyed by the British and Dutch, sticky buns found a permanent home in Germantown, PA about 1680.

Bavarian and German immigrants to Philadelphia established Germantown and Bavarian bakeries. Bread was an early food of convenience since it could be created early in the day and safely consumed later. It afforded a sense of freedom from food preparation, ease of transportation, and it was simply a necessity.

Conversely, the sticky bun was a cheap thrill. That, paired with a cup of coffee or tea, could make the morning great. Stitt Bakery made their many selections well; after all, they had proclaimed on their trucks, "Better made Bread." The unassuming yet caramelly scented sticky bun was in a major league; so good that its fans forgot about war and the flu plague and drove on toward the roaring twenties.

It was during Floyd Stitt's recovery from the flu that Clara took a turn managing the office. She relied heavily on the Fegleys, but successfully took large orders, signed checks and answered the phone in the morning hours. Dot returned to her class in the third grade, but spent several Saturdays taking special orders for cakes.

She was the unlikely engineer of a huge sticky bun sale due to the customer's hesitation in making up his mind.

"Well," she said. "You could get sticky buns."

***

In the year 1922, a memorable event occurred when Dot was eleven years old. Her elementary school had a fair in which the class showed off special projects they had made throughout the year. Her project was from art class when the students learned to make red clay boxes and decorated them with glazes. Her contribution won easily, as it looked like the teacher might have made it. The clay was smooth, glaze shone on its surface and the lid fit snugly. A blue ribbon prize lived proudly in Dot's bedroom.

The women of the family were amazed, even sister Louise, who had never seen a blue ribbon ceramic before. Floyd was glad for his daughter, but really didn't fathom how it was that his Dot edged out other equally talented children. Her ability to concentrate on details, coupled with total immersion into the production of the piece had made it happen.

Dot, like any girl in 1922, was breaking new ground, like a dark red rose bursting through... well, wet clay. Girls in that year seldom chose work over marriage and society expected them to behave accordingly.

Women for the first time viewed other women in silent films, heard women sing songs on the Victrola, and read news about women voting. Post war celebration and renewal changed the status quo. For Dorothea, this era seemed to call for her own unique expression. She tolerated the usual school activities so that one hour a week, in art class, a way was open for her to revel in artistic endeavors. This contrasted starkly with her bakeshop home, where goods were also made with creative precision but were soon consumed.

Schooling of the 1920s usually ended at age eighteen. Women who wished for employment as a teacher or a registered nurse were required to attend the appropriate higher education institution. Industrializing cities attracted office workers, clerks and unskilled labor. Work was generally unregulated and women received lesser wages than men.

Dot had within herself a rainbow of spirit while she believed the Stitt realm was a world based on chocolate and vanilla. Art class was basic, with a traveling teacher, pushed to serve four schools. Yet this teacher, Miss Rose, was able to help the students to make inner discoveries on that two-way avenue going from the brain to the hand. At her urging, simple materials converted the imaginary into minor masterpieces. The combustion of adolescent talent usually yielded emotion as a byproduct. Slowly, Dot began to idolize Miss Rose, secretly dreaming of working as an artist.

The influence of fashion added electricity to the roar of the twenties, and it wasn't lost on the willowy Dorothea. It seemed that the war in Europe scarred the landscape as well as the mentality of the populace. Women were ripe for change, and the twenties called for a life-affirming sort of woman to take on the challenge. Thanks to Coco Chanel, they never turned back. The voluminous skirt, corset and wide hat made way for the flapper era. Dresses became less fussy and tubular silhouettes with bras and undergarments called step-ins were the foundation for a knee covering tube, a flapping necklace of beads and the cloche hat. Hats became sleek to complement the rest of the radical ensemble. Cloche, the French word for bell jar, was also slang for "going wrong." It often appeared as a soft version of the ancient helmet or a cylinder pulled to the eyebrow. No one knew whether tight hats triggered short hair or short hair called for matching hats.

Long hair was getting in the way of working women, who took the opportunity to shingle it, vamp it or bob it, which relieved them of tedious hair care. Dot had taken years to grow her hair long, and kept it that way, wearing it in a chignon at the nape of her neck. She twisted it into a figure eight and clasped it with a ceramic of her own making. Clara welcomed the new fashion style as a practical way to scale down laundry drudgery, and so she supported Dot's fashion sense.

Clara certainly had a poor opinion of her body and her tendency to put on weight; hence tight corsets continued to be indispensable. Dot constructed new school clothes matching the tube dress to long scarves. She caused a stir at her mother's church, Easter 1926, when she moved like Chanel herself over the carpet to the pew sporting a white lace Garbo cloche, a white jersey tube with horizontal tan stripes and a string of pearls. Clara and Caroline followed, dressed in a looser version of the tube, but keeping last year's Easter bonnet. And there was Louise, wearing a short yellow cotton frock with capped sleeves. She had a short bowl haircut set off by a headband of cloth daisies. She was instructed by her elders to respect the sanctity of the church, but to "let it out" during the hymns.

Dot enjoyed assembling artistic projects. There was a converted toy chest full of things she was proud of: party hats, window decoration for the bakeshop store and stalls, Christmas ornaments and a fruit basket of papier-mâché grapes. They had emerged like brainchildren!

For her sixteenth birthday, she received a Kodak camera. The dull black and white images it produced were small. She brought one of the photos to art class, so she could make a large sketch from it, and added watercolors. She impressed everyone except her father with her talent. Longing to find her niche and make him happy drove her to make a twelve-page calendar of sketches. That summer, she took rolls of pictures of people and bread. She thought, *If the people in these photos could talk, they would say, "Here's my favorite food."*

Dot took shots in the bakery, in the bright light at the window or had her subjects come outside for better lighting. January's sketch was of Dan eating a glazed doughnut. She asked him to wear his coat over his sleeveless shirt and pose, leaning easily against the brick front of the bakery. His graying hair was poking out of a black beret. Dan looked shorter, or maybe Dot was taller. His backache was an occupational hazard, but according to Dan, he had chosen "the right line of work."

Dot felt as though the camera began to act independently. Her finger clicked the shutter all right, but there was a moment where she stepped into a stream where the spirit took over. She followed this stream gleefully.

February showed Bill taking a pie out of the hot oven with a peel. The peel acted like a shovel for dough exposed to high temperatures and the flat wooden scoop had a long-handled grip that protected Bill from burns. His white apron contrasted with the blackened oven door. The flour dust in the air had irritated his lungs, but he wasn't complaining.

March featured a smiling George poised over a three-tiered wedding cake, about to affix the topper, the tiny bride and groom. Dot instructed him not to grin as widely to hide tooth gaps. George had a gift for producing flavorful products in an economical way. He mixed cake batter in a huge mixer he found difficult to rinse out, so he would begin with white batter, move on to yellow, then to milk chocolate, ending with devil's food. He got the color and flavor desired, yet washed it only after mixing all the batter.

For April, she herself was the subject. Louise snapped one of Dot, wide eyed, clutching a bag of molasses cookies in one hand while she held one out as if to say, "Have a bite!" She left her hair loose with a ribbon and bow. It took a few tries for Louise to keep the camera still. Louise said, "Go take a picture at the farmers' market-- you can see all the stuff people like at our stand." The ten-year-old had the same brown eyes as Dot, round cheeks, one with a beauty mark. Her straight, heavy haircut like Clara Bow—Louise wished for curls.

Her sister replied, "But honey, I only need one person to hold one item... but I'll think about it." Louise's English class was reading Ralph Waldo Emerson. One quote stuck in Louise's mind: life is a series of surprises. Well if that were true, she said, Dot could just build surprises into the calendar.

May showed a bakery deliveryman, Rodd, stacking bread

into his truck. Dot angled the photo so that the words, "Stitt's Better Made Bread" were included. Dot avoided a close-up, as Rodd was inclined to get his hands dirty. Today she saw purplish ink on the back of one hand, powdered sugar on the other. Floyd had to lecture Rodd about tidiness.

In 1927, there were six trucks serving three farmers' markets and numerous groceries. The grocery stores had small refrigerators so they traded in the less perishable items such as apples, jars of applesauce or apple pie.

After taking an hour to compose the photo, Dot captured the flavor of the market for the month of June. She placed a sea of blurred cupcakes in the foreground. Mary, the clerk at the farmers' market, stood near the cash register in a white apron with her arms open, as if she was a real model in an actual advertisement. The focus was sharp enough to catch a fly that happened to buzz by.

July starred Louise in a white apron, icing an éclair. Dot took the shot in the sunny shaft of window light and used a hidden lamp. The artist and her subject soon cut the éclair in two and consumed it, standing in hot fan-generated air.

August followed with another icing activity by Sarah, applying white icing to a round devil's food chocolate cake. The cake was so fresh that some cake crumbs migrated into the icing. Sarah gave her requisitioning duties to George long ago, who seemed to be the one person with his hand in every bakery "pie." Sarah's moods were increasingly unpredictable and she tended to enjoy working alone, usually building layer cakes and icing cakes.

September seemed a portrait-still life of "Mamaw," her grandmother, standing while holding a boule loaf of round sesame, pointing the pinwheel-cut top at the camera. She appeared a youthful age sixty-three. Dot positioned a sheet over an outside wall that reflected more light on Mamaw.

October starred Byron with sticky bun in hand. Dot's setting was in his backyard, where she had dragged a rocker and had handed him the sweet on a plate.

After the picture was taken, Byron pushed the plate away and began, "This is a pretty big deal, all this work. Do you like it?"

"More and more, I do."

Hoarsely Byron continued, "You said you enjoyed drawing too."

"Pawpaw, I need to draw and paint. The whole color box of paints looks like me. I hope there is a way to be paid for being artistic."

"Well, Dorothea, you have my vote." He savored the bun delicately.

The November selection was her mother sitting next to a shiny electric toaster. Yes, she had to have the three-slice Toastmaster because it not only browned bread, but also ejected it! Incidentally, one had to stand ready to catch it a la baseball's catcher, Smokey Burgess. Her knife was poised over the toast as if applying butter. Clara giggled all the way through the exercise as though the thought of featuring toast was a silly whim. "Honeybunch, you sure know your way around a camera."

Seeking affable Santa, she snapped her father, the breadwinner, wearing a suit, tie and fedora on his beloved horse, Gray. He held a brown bag full of long loaves of hearth bread as Dot instructed him to smile broadly. The caption read, "I'm loafing around."

She was propelled through the months by what force she really didn't care, and the matter of the cover was solved on a day when Dot was in Sunday school. The class was over and the exuberant kids had been still for so long, that they were like tiny tigers screaming and springing from a jungle. Someone sat at the piano and played the Charleston. Dot wasn't surprised to see Louise dancing in a corner, not missing a step.

Later, Dot appealed to her, "Louise could you pretend you're doing The Charleston for the calendar?"

She said, "Yeah, while I balance an angel food cake on my head?"

Dot screamed, "Ha-ha-ha! Maybe I've taken this thing too far." And she couldn't stop laughing at the image her sister had given her.

The sisters' knock-kneed joy unleashed by the Charleston came through on the cover, the dancer being Louise wearing an apron with the words "Stitt Bakery" painted on the bib.

15

In spite of prohibition, the Stitts' summer of 1926 was never more intoxicating. The economy had recovered from wartime and Coolidge sat in the White House saying things like, "Never go out to meet trouble, chances are it won't find you."

Floyd planned to move to a larger home. Dot, nearly as tall as her father at fifteen, and Louise, destined to be shorter than the rest, were both told that they would spend July at the farm home where Floyd grew up. That meant a trip to Aunt Ruth's farm! Wearing bibbed overalls! Amid the familiar relatives and cousins to play with, the girls whiled away the hours doing farm chores, climbing trees and petting the family of peachy colored cats.

On July 8, the party line rang. It was Floyd wanting to speak to his daughters.

"Girls! Guess what!"

Sharing the earpiece, "Hi, Father," said Dot.

"Hi ya," said Louise.

Floyd cleared his throat and said, "Louise, how would you like an early birthday present?"

"Okay, what?" said Louise.

Floyd smiled. "We have a little sister for you."

"What?"

Floyd continued, "We'll bring her home from the hospital in a week or so."

Both girls were astonished and listened next to Aunt Ruth conversing over the line. When she hung up the phone, Dot said to her aunt, "Gosh, you already know about it."

Louise responded as if in a trance. "A little sister named Elaine."

The girls were in the dark about this event owing to Clara, who tended to gain weight and then hide it under shapeless garments. It was a trouble-free pregnancy, in spite of the fact that Clara had reached forty. However, they welcomed their sister and couldn't wait to see her.

The surprise addition of Elaine had Louise feeling quite grown up at ten. She had puttered around her bakery home countless times helping Dan and kibitzing while sampling cookies that were broken. She was right at home in the bakery store, at the front of the shop, where people lined up to buy the crunchy indulgences that caused the air of the neighborhood to waft friendly aromas— hard to resist. Her forte was coming to the fore.

Dot loved her new sister, but in the space of three years, they were destined to be parted when Dot would leave for higher education. The thought of college became her adolescent obsession, even more fervent than hers for Douglas Fairbanks, star of *The Thief of Bagdad*.

The calendar sketches were complete. Dot added watercolors and the faces came alive in a sense that the people were more recognizably real. The original photos were paper clipped to each month's rendering. The days of the month were calligraphies in black ink, and the pages added to small rings with a cord to display the "baker's dozen."

When she presented it to her parents at Christmas, it caused a stir. Passing through the hands of relatives, one uncle remarked about the workmanship and went on to notice an advantageous detail.

He smiled, simply noting, "I look at this shot of Dan with his doughnut, and I feel like eating a doughnut too." It seemed Dot had found the crux of advertising inside a playful message.

But Floyd missed or ignored that point, even though he never denied her artistic talent. The calendar spent the 1927 New Year's week in the living room until Dot hung it on the wall of Floyd's office. There! Now her abilities had been presented to the world, even if it was a small world.

"Breaking out" is a term often associated with the acne of adolescents; that was what Dot wanted—to break out. She needed to free her mind and spirit, and they were as disrupted as her blotchy complexion. By taking black and white drab reality and then sketching and adding color, she was creating an improved life experience. Movement toward her future self gained momentum by taking her grandfather into her confidence.

He quietly urged her to ask questions, learn what she could from the art teacher and take risks.

Dot began to seek an imaginatively playful way of being and an avenue that would free her from the structure her father had set up.

***

Meanwhile, Otto Rowedder of Chilicothe, Missouri had spent years now perfecting an electric bread-slicing machine, a device that changed most bakeries in 1928 by making it possible to slice loaves of bread and immediately wrap them in wax paper. Floyd read about it in a newsletter, which credited a baker, Mr. M.F. Bench, with testing the machine at his Chilicothe Baking Company.

"Sandwich sales will go through the roof!" Floyd vowed, pointing to an unsliced loaf of hearth bread. "This is a small miracle."

Clara, who sliced six pieces of bread that day for their lunch, said, "I'd think it would help bread fit inside a toaster too."

Floyd and Clara had been ready to move into a larger dwelling for a long time, but this suddenly seemed a lesser priority than sliced bread. Instead of moving out of the apartment, they invested in the Rowedder bread-slicing-wrapping machine.

***

Floyd brought the mail to the kitchen table, as he did each day when he came to have lunch with Clara. Among the bills was a business letter from Philadelphia addressed to Miss Dorothea C. Stitt.

"I see Dot has friends at the Art Institute of Philadelphia," Floyd fumed, shaking his red hair.

Clara looked at the envelope saying, "She hopes for a good school to go to... like I did, long years ago."

Floyd looked surprised.

"You didn't have that option, did you?" said Clara quietly.

"I thought running a business was self-taught. Well, where Dot is concerned, she's making a turn down a rocky road. What can they teach her that will get her a job? Painting? Whose portrait?" He had grown accustomed to controlling his daughter, but he felt the girl might just bolt!

Clara just looked at him as he sizzled. "Try to remember she's just a kid."

There was a growing rift between Dot and Floyd, opening ironically by power; his was waning as hers gathered momentum. Fueled by excellent marks in school, mentored by Miss Rose, Dot dreamed of exploring a new life, hopeful in all its mystery. She branched out as she was breaking out by taking on the 1928 high school yearbook, doing most of the drawings required.

Dot drove the Model T without a chaperone now, she was newly licensed. Lanky in the jersey dresses, she grew her hair longer, often wearing it braided. She wore makeup but mainly concentrated on her perfectly penciled black eyebrows, which framed a pair of intense brown eyes. "I'll use Anna May Wong as an eyebrow model," she promised, looking into the bathroom mirror. Anna May Wong had starred with Douglas Fairbanks in *The Thief of Bagdad*.

She earned an allowance by working in the plain but sunlit bakery office doing filing, answering the phone and putting things in order, work she saw as a temporary grind. In summertime, Louise helped Sarah in the store, in winter, she put the cardboard boxes together by the hundreds, boxes intended to package cupcakes and lunch-sized items en route to grocery stores.

Dot and Louise savored Saturday, when they could blow their earnings in town and free themselves. Dot wore a clinging long-sleeved dress with "Chanel" pearls. Louise enhanced a plaid dress with lip pomade and a new ring made of Bakelite in gold plastic. First, they stopped at the Blue Swan candy store—nothing but candy. The spacious place had lots of windows and an ancient hardwood floor that creaked as soon as you stepped inside the glass door. The two widowed crones who ran the store were also a bit creaky. On the right side was a long glass case displaying a sea of homemade confections—chocolate-covered tidbits of every description. Small white boxes were being filled as they entered. An elderly woman in hat and gloved church attire was ordering one for a friend. Dot and Louise turned to the opposite side for the penny candy and scored a bag of Mary Janes and a bag of red licorice whips. This fuel would get them through the matinee movie.

They sometimes thrilled to the cowboys. "See Hopalong Cassidy singlehandedly save the town from desperadoes," the movie poster would promise. They preferred the Our Gang comedies because the gang was full of boys and a girl or two. This mindless rib-tickling fun became their habit. It was movie stars who inspired the girls; "darlings," or "dahlins," their mutual terms of endearment, they borrowed from Greta Garbo and Talulah Bankhead.

To top off the day, they visited the drugstore lunch counter, which was a fanciful treat. They looked up at the wall for the drink menu.

Louise recited, "Let's see... how 'bout a lemon phosphate..."

"No," said Dot.

"Egg Cream?"

"Not today."

"Two cents plain?"

"Think again," Dot giggled.

Face to face in unison they shrieked, "Banana Split!"

Karl was behind the counter in a white uniform, his apron dotted with the cherry juice spattered from a recent sundae. Karl wanted to get to know Dot better, ever since the day he sat next to her in the school cafeteria; however, their class schedules differed.

Louise ordered, "A banana split, vanilla ice cream—two spoons, please."

Smiling Karl responded, "Commin' up," and added an extra scoop of ice cream on the ripe banana. He took pains to top it with Hershey's syrup. He put a doily on the heavy white plate, set the banana-shaped glass dish over it, slowly pushed it toward Dot and said, "Sweets for the sweet."

Louise, noting the trance Karl was in, insisted, "Kiddo! I asked for two spoons."

The poor boy turned to get their spoons and Louise whispered, "He's thinking of spooning, not about our spoons. Do you know him?"

Dot smiled and thanked him for the spoons. When a new customer beckoned, he moved down the counter.

"I don't know," whispered Dot, "I only saw him once before."

Now Karl had a new order for a creation called a "Dusty Road," and the girls watched as he put a couple of scoops of vanilla in a sundae dish. To that, he applied chocolate sauce like a maestro and then a sprinkling of Hershey cocoa powder, finally carefully arranging a handful of chopped, salted peanuts.

Dot mused, "Well, he can build good sundaes," while she chewed a banana slice.

Returning, Karl came over to Dot and, straightening his white cap, said, "We should talk… maybe you could look for me Monday in the cafeteria."

Dot looked into her bag as she hurriedly paid for the sundae and replied, "We'll see."

They walked home, which was a bit of a hike, but one had to discharge such a day from the system. It was enough to see a show that they had sandwiched between virtual meals of sugar, but then to "encounter" the attentions of a soda jerk—well, they had to walk it off.

"How do people act on dates, dahlin'?" Louise wondered.

"Ha, heh!" Dot responded, "I'll know when I ever have a date."

"Yeah, girls wait for the date."

Dot interjected quickly, "We decide if we want to go too."

Clearing her voice, Louise replied theatrically, "Say no, I don't want to go. Or yes! I'd be delighted."

Dot went on, "I've been thinking about dating. You gamble. He might look nice but be a bum. But! He might be plain-looking then turn to acting like a prince. How can you know?" She thought and answered, "Try, I guess you try."

Louise continued the guessing game. "Try to what?"

"Watch what happens. See how you feel."

"How did you feel back at the drugstore?" Louise went on.

"First confused, then like escaping," she sighed. "Yeah, like running." She gestured with her small beaded handbag.

Louise declared, "To run or not to run, that is the question."

Dot dug into her intuition then with, "But if you are running away 'cause you don't like him, you can also say, 'No dahling, I do not want to go out with you.'"

The two sisters continued ping-ponging their budding knowledge about the opposite sex until they found themselves in front of the bakery door.

The bakery was quiet on Saturdays because the town didn't do business on Sunday.

When the girls came to their home over the bakery, Clara was cooking dinner while their father listened to the radio. Baby Elaine sat on the floor, teething on her sleeve.

"Hello girls," he greeted, lowering his newspaper.

Louise went to her father's chair, looked over his shoulder and read to herself, "Germany's stock market hits all-time low."

Dot gave her mother a kiss and swayed to the voice of the woman crooner on the radio.

The tune wafting out of the polished maple radio belonged to Alberta Hunter. Now Dot was about to acquire her second teen idol, after Douglas Fairbanks.

"Wait just a New York minute," she whispered, took a seat near the radio, and she listened to the voice sent all the way from New York, a voice that seemed to be the essence of a kindred spirit. Dot lifted Elaine into her lap and bounced her.

"Ain't nobody's business... She sounds like she's either got a megaphone or a big, big voice... *Ain't nobody's business if I do,"* she zipped along, imprinting another yen for freedom in Dot's ear.

The Stitt family dined in the small kitchen and the girls related their day's highlights. The parents listened and Clara enjoyed hearing of the candy store lady, the silent movie and the drugstore, although Karl was kept out of the conversation. Clara saw their Saturday smiles as proof of the girls' initiative and happiness.

Floyd waited for the right moment to broach a seemingly unrelated subject: work. "Both of you, it's time to talk about work." He stared at each of the girls. "Louise, I'd like to promote you from helping in the store. She looked up from her dessert of pound cake. "I want you to run the store when not in school."

"Hmmm..." said Louise, swallowing. "Do Sarah's job?"

"Yes, after school, three-thirty to five, and all day in summer. Twenty-five cents an hour."

"I guess I can do it. Now we have a freezer, so I don't have to worry about ice."

You already know everything except about cleaning the freezer chest out."

Louise digested the promotion easily. This she understood; she saw herself selling bread to a mother and handing a cookie to a child. Dorothea meanwhile braced for what she felt would be bad news.

"I got a notice from school, an invitation," said Floyd sternly.

"Oh?" Dot had a look of surprised anxiety.

Her father worked at neutrality, but what a lost cause! "It seems we are invited to meet representatives of the state colleges next week."

Strongly sighing, Dot declared, "I want to go to art school, you know." There, she had said it, no more hinting, though she had a sort of begging tone to her voice.

"We need to remember a few things about art. It is a luxury for people who have extra cash. It's not like... bread," Floyd replied authoritatively. "People need bread."

Dot loudly exclaimed, "I'll find a way to do it! I need to be an artist."

Riveting blue eyes stared over his glasses. "Just calm down. Let's meet these school representatives and see what they have to say. As we go, remember how many poor people live right here on Jefferson Street! I don't intend for you to be one of them."

"Do the colleges teach artists?" she gasped.

Clara neutrally replied, "They are mostly teachers' college representatives. Maybe you could be an art teacher."

Tiring, Dot glared at one parent then another. "Okay, I'll go with Father. But that's just to listen to the program."

***

Monday's October sunlight illuminated the John Harris High School cafeteria. Dot had been combing her brain for ways to get enough artistic skills to make a living. She didn't need a lecture from her father on starving artists.

She saw Karl at lunchtime, but she was hiding, camouflaged

behind a Halloween haystack, so he never found her. She could draw, she could paint and she was especially good at painting glaze images on ceramic plates. This could make money if you sold enough of it, but Floyd was correct in the sense that one ceramic plate could do for life, while one's better bread on a ceramic dinner plate had to be made fresh daily. Dot would hope for a way to break out of the drab bakery, to find her undefined but surely colorful way of making a living.

16

Monday evening Dot went dutifully with her father to the "College Night at John Harris" program. When they got into the car, they talked about Dot moving from Harrisburg, and she calmly noted, "I'm almost the age you were when you decided to leave farming."

Floyd gasped, quietly recalling his escape to Harrisburg. He knew in that minute precisely what drove his daughter to want to become an artist, and yet the very notion of Dot in a Philadelphia art school was out of the question. He decided he would support only a professional education and that did not leave room for producing art.

Students and parents assembled in the auditorium and the audience buzzed with excitement. Their interest centered on the ten people on stage, those who represented colleges of the state of Pennsylvania. The attendees heard about courses, facilities and settings of the individual schools and throughout the evening Dot heard much, maybe too much, about teaching as a profession. However, there was among the schools a standout, and one Dot could not ignore—Lock Haven State Teachers' College. Curiously, their representative made a point of giving a small speech, and then turning to a tall, young woman sitting with him, who he introduced as a recent graduate of Lock Haven.

"Good evening, students and parents," she began, looking at Floyd. Dot liked her blond bobbed haircut. I come here to give my impression of Lock Haven, from the horse's mouth, so to speak. I have been in your shoes, wanting an education and insisting I have the best future I can… in this uncertain world."

The audience sat at attention.

"I found the right start at Lock Haven, and now I am grateful for the lessons of professors, the help of the staff and perhaps most of all for the campus which provided me the right atmosphere to learn and even excel at teaching as a career."

People, impressed by her charismatic presentation interrupted her with questions, which she obligingly answered.

"I went to the school to learn to teach high school students, but my course took a turn when I signed up to learn to jump horses. I loved the horses and the satisfaction of being out of doors; I knew I had to work outdoors. Now I teach as a corporal in the U.S. Women's Army Corps, and I am the first woman to be a member of the U.S. equestrian team. We expect to win at the '32 Olympic Games."

Well, the audience was stunned by the willowy girl, who at twenty-fivish had "jumped" into a man's world. Dorothea was entertainingly distracted from going to Philadelphia, and Floyd gave a standing ovation.

Clara was curious about the meeting when they returned home, and Floyd hurriedly answered as he had stayed up past his usual bedtime of seven-thirty.

The girls gathered around the kitchen table, covered by a yellow tablecloth decorated by Clara's cross-stitching of fruit baskets. The biting apple cider they drank was thirst quenching.

Dot surprised Clara as the excitement of the evening came through. She said, "I went to the Lock Haven recruiter, and I said, right in front of Father, 'I have artistic talent and I want to work so I can use it, but my father says I need a profession where I can get… regular paychecks.'"

Louise sipped and Elaine chewed an apple slice.

"He said that the schools hire Lock Haven graduates to be art teachers. But! There aren't very many jobs for art teachers. He said getting a teacher's certificate would mean I could teach any subject in public schools. He had me sit at his table where he showed papers on Lock Haven. He said, 'If I were you, I'd get the college degree. Practice the drawing and painting in your spare time. If you need help along the way, we have good professors of art.' That's what he said. He thought I should see the school and meet there with an advisor."

Clara patted Dot on the back, saying, "I know colleges have major studies and minor studies. Let's maybe try for art as a minor."

Louise tugged at Dot's arm. "Have your cake and eat it too," she smiled.

Clara laughed, "Tonight, your father was in the best mood I've seen in a long while. Let's go visit the school and then we'll know more."

17

D ot was indeed frustrated as her brain tried to grasp the concept that she would soon be leaving home... and thinking of herself as a teacher. She had school on her mind as she applied red lipstick and tossed a feather boa around her neck. She sighed, expelling the mental turmoil of the unknown, and she turned her attention, gratefully, to the "Harvest Dance," a big event at John Harris.

Many of her friends were eager to go, even though few had dates. Girls wore their frilliest, flounciest dresses, the trend being toward longer hems complemented by higher heels. Boys borrowed their father's suits and pomaded their hair.

She arrived at the gym that Saturday evening, delivered by Floyd, who was happy to see Dot in a social mood. Every instinct told him his eldest daughter would marry well, in spite of her lack of suitors.

After Dot helped arrange a huge pot of fall foliage, dried flowers and gourds, the school band, with more verve than talent, began playing a medley of catchy tunes, starting with *Basin Street Blues*. Dot chatted merrily with a friend who had attended college night. They pretended not to notice two boys who were staring at them. The boys eventually trouped over, jokingly introduced themselves and pulled the girls out to dance. Dancing the foxtrot worked up to Charleston tempo and Dot noticed she had left her ponderings a time out.

Thirst lured kids to the punchbowl, now bubbling with an unknown orange concoction. That was when she heard Karl say, "Having a nice time?"

Karl took that opportunity to get Dot's attention, first guiding her to a seat among the wallflowers, then when the band got frantically loud, out in the chill wind of November.

"Feels good outside," Karl sighed, and Dot noticed how sweat trickled down his chin, as they were both about the same height.

This encounter went smoothly, both dancers benefiting from a breather, but then he unknowingly made a mistake that turned her punch sour. They were comparing notes on dancing and music when he offered her a taste of bootleg gin!

"How's this for spiking your punch?"

Dot, taken aback, replied, "Not for me, thanks."

Tipping the flask to his lips, he answered, "Well, I don't mind tellin' you, it helps me talk to girls."

She had been at family Christmas dinners when alcohol was on the table, but otherwise it was a mysterious potion, and illegal at that. They rejoined the others, resumed dancing, and Karl stumbled a few times, though he did talk a blue streak.

Dot had enjoyed herself tremendously. Karl, feeling little pain after imbibing half of his gin, started to whine, but Dot interrupted, saying, "I had a swell time, Karl, let's be friends. I'll see you at the drug store." This post-dance parting took place on the sidewalk, just as Floyd drove up to collect Dot.

***

Sunday dinner turned out to be a more heartening occasion for her. Byron, her grandfather, inquired about the school situation, and Dot spilled all the frustration, angst and longing regarding her future, and there in the quiet of their backyard, Dot began to become "her own parent."

"There really is nothing stopping you from going to an art school. You could work to support yourself and take fewer classes. Your father would just have to accept it."

Dot determined, "Pawpaw, he is so set against my art school idea—he'd never forgive me. He would be angry, *even if I succeeded.* I thought it all over, and I don't want to be some sorta' black sheep of the family. If I went to Philadelphia, there would be hell to pay!" She saw his bushy eyebrows lift at her swearing admonition.

Byron sighed, saying, "You have proven abilities, and now what? You will teach? But," he soothed, "they say people teach what they most wish to learn."

"Oh?" Dot went on. "That man at college night is probably right about me learning to teach while I produce my work on the side. And I keep on having such a good feeling about Lock Haven, so swell, almost like it's a sure thing... I was surprised at that."

The senior year of trials would begin to smooth out now, and Byron credited his granddaughter for thinking ahead, for looking prior to leaping.

18

The family visited Lock Haven State College on a Saturday in early November. The mood was frivolous in the backseat, starting at the city limits.

The girls' rendition of *On top of Old Smoky* quickly changed to:

> *On top of spaghetti,*
> *All covered with cheese,*
> *I lost my poor meatball,*
> *Whenever I sneezed.*

Then Dot told a joke: "A man went to the doctor 'cause he felt bad. The man said he thought he was a bridge. The doctor said, 'Well, what came over you?' and the man said, 'A truck a car and a bike.'"

With that, Floyd told the girls to sing hymns as Elaine harmoniously screamed, "I like my sweet soft soda cwackrs, Fadder!"

The car navigated well the fifty miles of main road, but when Floyd entered what amounted to a country dirt path, there commenced so much bouncing that Clara had to yell, "Floyd, you're going to slow down now, or Elaine'll be thrown off my lap, just like a rubber ball!"

Indeed, the three year old's arms continued to bounce, even though the Ford, on balloon tires, slowed to a stop. They took in the wooded hills and Clara told Louise and Dot to jump out to stretch their legs.

"Dahling, your school seems like it'll be quiet," Louise mused.

Dot nodded, "Uh huh."

Floyd said, "We are close to Lock Haven, so let's hope the road is better up ahead."

Although the college buildings were nothing to write home about, the campus was alive. A manicured lawn and huge oaks protected the buildings; gently whooshing sounds of wind nurtured their ears as the Stitts walked about. The horsewoman had said the school promoted excellence, and now Dot felt impressed after viewing the classrooms, including the art studio. The studio was currently showcasing a display about Georgia O'Keeffe's work. She was a tonic to Dot; she painted flowers, had achieved a reputation and, as a coincidence, was female.

Dot excitedly agreed to study at Lock Haven. In doing so, she had finally accepted the stability of teaching and had broken away from the world of the bakeshop... or so it seemed.

Her parents felt relieved, as her father was standing in opposition to Dot's first choice, what he believed would be a poor choice without a future. To Clara, art was what was in the Harrisburg State Museum. She knew Dot was capable of doing similar museum pieces and yet she thought Floyd had a point about the unlikelihood of being paid adequately for creating works of art.

***

The work of bread baking was bringing in more money due to the ability to slice and wrap. This was fortuitous because just as Dot was off to her studies at Lock Haven, the economy fractured, and that led to October 1929's infamous crash of the stock market in America.

The country's impoverished thousands, those obscured behind the Charlestonesque post-war climate of the twenties, suddenly became visible, and by the thirties, economic depression was the norm.

Floyd breathed easier for two reasons: his daughter Dot was, to his mind, in a "haven," and sliced bread was at hand. Now that was an art, he chuckled knowingly, to bake, to sell loaves of sliced bread wrapped in waxed paper! More restaurants were ordering Stitt's Better Made Bread, not only because it was better, but also because it was faster. White bread was in style and restaurants promoted its use. One such restaurant added sliced bread to the menu by making French toast for breakfast, club sandwiches for lunch and bread pudding for dessert.

So, the company survived the economic downturn thanks to Floyd's belief in the bakery, the tirelessness of the Fegleys and the products they all became known for.

19

Families grow in close proximity, making survival more likely. Family business by extension happens though closeness; it also supplies cheap labor. Sometimes elders justify the situation with statements like, "Through work they will know the value of money," and undeniably, the times we live in will shape our work.

Louise at thirteen felt surprised by the change in the life she led, but then, life *was* full of surprises. She was five feet tall, with dark eyes and a beauty mark on her left cheek. Now she was the eldest child living at home, and home was at a new address, 2232 North Sixth Street. Floyd could finally afford to move a few blocks from the bakery into a row house on a busy street. Louise had her own room on the second floor with a window from which she viewed pedestrians on the sidewalk, motor vehicles and the far fewer horse-powered carriages. She missed the continual wafting of baking bread and now had to contend with leaded gasoline fumes from the nearby service station. Surprisingly, Clara seemed to relate to her more seriously and even more shocking, how her father treated her as a business partner. The Stitt girls would show no interest in the actual baking. Dot had not needed a baker's white linen apron, as hers had been office chores; now Louise went in a different direction, borrowing one of Clara's embroidered bibbed aprons.

When Louise was little, Caroline made her first doll from a rugged piece of linen. She clipped hair from Floyd's horse's mane to make its stuffing squeezable, and the embroidered face had a whimsical cheekiness. This was a doll on the move, not one to languish in a cradle or get lost in a toy box. Its hat was lifted from a lidded basket that Caroline brought with her when she emigrated from Germany. The doll had a small shoulder purse, tinkling with pennies, for the doll was rich. Louise called her "Saley."

"Saley wants to buy Cracker Jacks," Louise irresistibly announced. Saley accompanied Louise on tours through the bakeshop, where the doll regaled Dan with tales of how she had helped Louise buy new shoes. At Sunday school, Saley prompted Louise to ask, "Now, if Jesus fed the five thousand on two loaves of bread, why didn't he ever tell us the recipe?"

When Louise went to her first day of school, she returned to tell Saley, "You didn't miss much," and proceeded to explain that her schoolbook was free.

Louise learned a few things from Saley: put on a happy face, enjoy the marketplace and step to your own music. Her music teacher taught Thoreau's line about how if one cannot keep pace with one's companions, perhaps one hears the sound of a different drummer.

Louise met with fewer obstacles than Dot had, simply by being right-handed. She enjoyed all new words, possibly because at five she could read well. Her grandfather spent hours reading to the children, and one day Louise began reading Sunday comics to him. She wrote short postcards in crayon to her aunt and uncle in Spring Run. She could count out change in the bakeshop store. Her respect for confection came from Caroline, who loved the baking arts and had ingenious ways with textures, flavors and fragrances. Memories of Caroline's kitchen were fun and loving, containing a wave of excitement erupting from her enjoyment of the molding of the simplest ingredients into revitalizing victuals.

Elaine and Louise sat at her table, in a new rapture over chocolate fudge. It seemed that what Caroline focused on bloomed and the girls learned from her to trust themselves.

Caroline thought aloud, as she added vanilla, "You'll never please everybody, but you can please yourself."

The two onlookers watched with delight as she poured the hot, thick concoction onto a blue and white platter, and the bittersweet aroma filled their heads as they waited for it to cool.

Caroline modeled her own sweeping brand of freedom, not that she feared for them as growing girls in an era of the Depression; rather, freedom exuded from her as a matter of course.

"Where does this fudge come from?" Elaine asked.

"Lots'a places," Caroline declared. "I could go on, child..."

Louise turned to her sister, explaining, "Fudge is candy and candy is sugar that you get from Mississippi."

Caroline nodded, "Yeah, the farmer sees to the sugarcane plants and then the trainmen move it to the mill to make sugar. Oh, think of the sifting, bagging and then we buy it. But every other ingredient is important... like butter from cows and chocolate is another fascinating story, why we have to get cocoa from hills in... in Central America. You see how grateful I am to get to make fudge?" Almost to herself she said, "You can't count the people responsible for a piece of fudge."

Indeed, knowing about sugar was primary to young Louise's existence as manager of the bakery store. At a tender age, she recognized the darkening effect sugar had on crust and how it attracted moisture in bread, how it dances with the yeast. She already had so much sugar in her own diet, she had a number of teeth with dental fillings, yet still there was something irresistible in the Stitt selections, holding Louise's interest in food and keeping the patronage of their customers.

One Saturday, she was wiping the bake store cases clean. Yesterday, the children had smeared white icing on the glass. She had been to a church social where there were ice cream cones, and she thought about doing the same here at the store. Would Father agree? The vision of creamy treats in the freezer chest kept her attention until a stream of customers appeared. As usual, they were after bread, but one asked for shortcake.

"Sarah," Louise called into the bakery, "do we have a shortcake?"

"Believe it or not, we do!" Sarah cautioned the customer while wiping her sugary hands on her apron, "We usually stop making shortcake after Labor Day."

Well, Father liked Louise's ice cream idea "Just cones!" he exclaimed. Cones and napkins, minus packaging. She was allowed to sell ice cream, bottled Coca-Cola, in addition to baked goods. Her 1929 school schedule included geometry, and here Louise's bakery background worked to her advantage. Just about the same time as the ice cream appeared, she did a unique promotion in the disguise of a geometry report to the class.

She was finding the area inside of an ice cream cone, which she computed on the black board and then with the assistance of her teacher, passed out small cones to everyone.

"You are eating four point five cubic inches of vanilla ice cream. If you want to try other flavors, you can come up to Stitt's Bakery, 2463 Jefferson Street." We can safely say it was a memorable report, for she got an A and several kids became ice cream regulars, bringing their parents in tow.

Food surrounded the Stitts like the cherry syrup in a cherry pie, so it wasn't a surprise that Louise was developing a certain reverence for the dessert realm as well as serious versions of food. She was weaned on sunshine cake, graduated to cream puffs and now as a fledgling store manager, it was all about homemade ice cream. Oddly enough, the prohibition of alcohol in the twenties gave rise to ice cream establishments— teetotalers' taverns. The creamy components were seen churning electronically each Saturday morning, with Louise stopping to wait on the entering customer. Today she was elbow deep in a pink tub of strawberry when her math teacher walked in. The teacher picked up a birthday cake and added ice cream after she saw the familiar smiling clerk.

"That was a grand report, Louise." The teacher was getting inspiration as she inhaled the sugary air.

"Thanks, Miss Rule."

The teacher had seen an elusive sort of talent, but what

exactly had she seen? "Do you have any special interests?" she asked the diminutive clerk.

"A few," she replied, while about fifty wisecracks went through her head. She might have said, 'Oh, I'd like to run the church Easter egg hunt, or play piano for Glenn Miller or peel grapes for Mae West.'

"How long have you been working?"

"I used to be running around here or riding my wooden lion on wheels. One day, somebody showed me how to make a cardboard cake box, and when Father noticed the finished boxes, he gave me all his loose change and that was the start. I really like to make ice cream though."

"Louise, I think you could help me out," she said, drawing closer to the glass case. "I have a section at school that is repeating... you know the section on graphs? Could you come to my classroom, Monday at 11:30 with an apple pie—large size?"

So they worked it out that Louise did a similar demo using a pie to calculate fractions and make pie graphs. It was partially because Louise was a child that the lesson was of interest to other children, but it was also because Louise was Louise.

She started by putting the problem on the chalkboard, then the class laughed when she used a large knife as a pointer. She declared, as she waved her knife, "Your sharpest instrument is right here," and pointed to her head. What would happen next? When they had successfully worked out the problem, she turned to Miss Rule and whispered, "I need an assistant."

"Tom." She selected a boy who had slept through the first class on fractions, and now, he was about to shock everyone by acing the exam.

Tom cut the pie into twelve thin slices and a tall girl in the front row helped share them with the class. With a mouth full of apple chunks, he said, "Hmmm, never had apple pie."

Squinting, Louise said, "You've been leading a sheltered life."

20

The aroma in the store was of chocolate—baking chocolate slowly warming on the stove. Louise placed a tray of small chocolate cakes topped with vanilla cream and a dollop of chocolate on display. These were Sarah Fegley's interpretation of the eye of Popeye the Sailorman, a popular cartoon star.

"Popeyes," she whispered. Next, she displayed heavy sweet rolls, loaded with raisins and coated with vanilla icing; the bear paw with almond claws. It would satisfy the appetite of a bear. Floyd taught her to watch that display case as though she were a first-time customer. Empty trays were off limits! Consolidate half-empty trays! Broken cookies: save for the undecided customer who couldn't make a choice! No tolerance for flies!

The ice cream/pie incidents made Louise a reputation for ingenuity by the time she was fourteen. She expanded her vocabulary thanks to a good Latin teacher and her interest in reading. She was reading a Redbook Women's magazine during a slow hour in the store and she looked up to see Tom enter.

"What cha readin'?"

She turned the article toward him, and he whispered, "'Women must learn to play the game as men do,' By Eleanor Roosevelt. Well, what's the game?"

Louise said, "What do *you* think it is?"

"Aw..." he smiled, "to look like they're smarter than girls? Yeah, a man is supposed to be smart'n if a girl is too smart, why a man can't..."

"What? Can't what?" she said quietly, inquisitively.

"Can't run all over her?" he replied, as though it was news to him.

Louise was silent for once as the words settled over the room. Glenn Miller music floated in from the garage.

Louise thought aloud, "I think you're right, and smart enough to see it. I bet the woman who wrote this is living in the game because she knows from experience. Probably she's been a housewife and then left her house to make life better for women. But once she saw how politicians are used to having their own way, she had to explain it... loud."

A woman entered, a light green hat tilted, showing the face of a dignified woman with dark skin. The crown-like hat caught Louise's eye, and the stranger seemed familiar.

Tom went on, "Look, Louise, I really came here to say thanks for helping me. It's not that I didn't get fractions; I just lost interest in school. You and Miss Rule sort of woke me up."

Louise smiled so that her eyes laughed. "When the teacher asked me to do it, I was surprised, but I'm glad now, and I learned from doing it."

Tom replied lightly, "You can make ordinary things funny!"

Two small boys entered, which speeded Tom to pay for an apple pie.

Louise nodded to Tom. "I'll get you a large so you can divide it again with your mother," and she went for a bag.

"My momma died in the flu epidemic."

Louise and the woman gasped in unison. "That's too bad," said Louise, handing him her largest apple pie.

Tom thanked her and was out the door.

The woman motioned for the boys to order.

"Two Popeyes, please," said the smaller boy as the other handed Louise a nickel.

As they scampered out, the woman said, "I was here in the flu epidemic, when the Stitt couple was so sick."

Louise tilted her face to the side. "In 1918. I'm Louise Stitt, their daughter."

"I'm Cecelia Scott. Oh," she said heavily, "I was working for the Red Cross as a nurse. Your house... the bakery was on my roster, and so I met your mother and father."

Louise said, "They were so lucky to live through that time," she said, motioning for her to sit in a chair.

"Many didn't make it," ...and she told the grim story of the flu in the neighborhood.

"Umm, Cecelia," said Louise insistently, "I was just reading about women. How they ought to be as much as they can be, and not let men.... rule the world."

Cecilia rolled her eyes, "Land sakes!"

"I'm just hoping I do my best. Do you... have any ideas about women making a good life?"

She thought and answered slowly, "You have good parents, like me. They help you learn to care for yourself. Now how could I be a good nurse if I didn't do that? I remember Mama said, 'You need to know how to do something real well, so you can earn a living.' I went and got my diploma in nursing, and having that made me a success."

Louise said, "But I don't know what I'd like as much as I do making ice cream."

"You have time now, dear, just don't ignore your heart's desire. Now, time flies, so I'll take my cake, marked 'Scott.'

Louise found it. "Happy Birthday, Cecelia."

Louise ventured tentatively, "But, how 'bout men? Eleanor Roosevelt says women should play the game men play."

Cecelia mused, "I lost my husband in the war. He was a treasure. Not to be replaced. But to your point, I think one thing's luck—just crossing the path of a treasure is luck."

Louise nodded.

"And another thing is truth. You can't live a life built on falsehood."

Louise handed her the boxed cake, tied with red and white string. "Thanks for everything."

21

Dorothea's life revolved around visual art and now, dance. Floyd may have distracted Dot from moving to Philadelphia, but he could no more take the art from the girl than his own mother could take the business driven mentality from Floyd.

Clara and her mother were lunching at the Harris Ferry Tavern on Caroline's birthday. While they drank cider, Clara opened a large business envelope which was stamped "Lock Haven, January 12, 1930." The envelope displayed a large sketch of a hand, index finger pointing toward the names "Mr.& Mrs. Floyd Stitt."

> *Dear Mother and Father,*   *Jan. 5, 1930*
> *How are you? I miss seeing you but don't miss Harrisburg. The food here leaves a lot to be desired, and I won't even mention the bread. My teachers are wonderful, and I enjoy everything but studying regulations of school operation.*
> *My modern dance class requires choreography, and I love it. They have a swimming pool—I've been to a few times—imagine me swimming in the dead of winter!*
> *My roommate, Lillian McGill, is one character who knows it all. I said she ought to get herself on the faculty, and she thought I was kidding but I meant it!*
> *Well, it's time for lights out so I wish you love,*
> *Dot*

Caroline and Clara agreed: life is too darn short for bad

bread. So, Floyd himself set out in a truck with fifty loaves of sliced white bread bound for the office of the school cafeteria manager and persuaded him to change bakeries. Lucky for Dot, the school liked the "better made bread," and continued their patronage beyond Dot's graduation.

Lillian McGill was not easily impressed. She had come to Lock Haven to get a diploma, but in truth, she was a born authority. As a toddler, her first word(s) were "Well, well!" Most of the time, Dorothea was aghast at her opinions, and she definitely had them on everything from politics to penis size.

By the time they had shared a dorm room for a month, Dot tacked a biologically inspired poster on the wall indicating symbols for man, woman, birth, death, and infinity. She captioned it, "Lil's brain." But irritation always gave way to mirth in that room. It was almost lights out time now, and they had been quietly doing homework. Lillian broke the silence.

"You would be a great one to join us on Saturday. My new friend Franklin and I will be going hiking and maybe he could get Paul to join us."

"Yeah? Who in the world is Paul? I don't think much of blind dates." She was on the spot now with a minimal social life and had been looking forward to having the pottery studio all to herself.

"He's in my English lit class. He's tall, brown hair, polite but quiet, and he's a friend of Franklin. Well, if you're not coming, do you happen to have a blue sweater I could borrow?"

Dot stretched. "I'll decide if I'm going in the morning, kid."

***

The late winter, Saturday hike for four started out nicely, on a note of high adventure, with the gear stowed in the rumble seat of Franklin's Ford. Dot brought ham sandwiches and a jar of pickles. Lil was planning to get cake from the school cafeteria until Dot reminded her how tastelessly dry it was. "Inedible," was how she described it. Therefore, Lil brought bananas because they came in their own package and were "appealing." The men brought a thermos of coffee and a blanket.

There were the introductions and then a decision made to walk a trail to a look out on a mountain where they would picnic and proceed to retrace their steps on the same trail. There was small talk ended by Lil with a discussion about how the recent opening of King Tut's tomb was to be a Pandora's box of trouble for the world.

The tension between Dorothea and Paul heightened when he attempted to help her scramble over a rock by taking her hand, then not letting it go. Later, he offered again, she refused and she quietly said, "Please don't touch me."

It seemed to Paul that she was playing "hard to get," while Dot really decided that Paul was getting hard to handle. As the group pulled into the doorway to the girls' dorm, and all the passengers exited, Paul dared to grasp Dot's wrist and without blinking an eye, her fist came down on his wrist in a maneuver not unlike karate, which instantly freed her. Dot sped off to her room, leaving Paul sheepishly apologizing to Lil as he cradled his hand.

Lillian bid Franklin farewell, then sought out her roommate, who had taken refuge in the ceramic studio. When discovered by Lil, she was standing at a workbench over a mound of porcelain clay with white dust forming small clouds as Dot worked the elastic substance.

Lil approached, apologizing by proxy. "But I feel worse than you because I thought he was nice... and boy, I was mistaken."

Dot replied smartly as she rhythmically leaned into the clay, "What if you were wrong about Franklin too? What if they decided to throw us off the cliff? Think!"

Lil went silent, her blue eyes clouded, which was a rare experience. When she finally spoke, Dot was rolling out a slab of porcelain to place on a mold. "You are my friend. You're worth ten Franklins. I have decided to talk about this to him so he remembers it, whether he stays friends with me or not."

Dot expected evolved behavior from people who had plans to teach others. From that encounter, her behavior changed. She began to value herself as her own mother valued her; she liked better the woman she saw in the mirror. Intense hand building of ceramics served to ground her frayed nerves. Group outings in canoes didn't hurt, for thanks to vigorous rowing, she lost all her baby fat. Dorothea was becoming more herself.

22

In Harrisburg, Louise was simultaneously delighting in what was to become a lifelong friendship with Ginny Murr. Although Ginny was two years younger, the pair became inseparable in their high school Latin class.

Latin was a prerequisite to higher education, and Louise followed it as a stab in the dark toward the future. Ginny knew she would go on to a liberal arts college.

Their amusement with Latin began when the teacher, Mr. Dedlingue used his magical attention-getting scheme. He was adept at throwing out certain zany phrases, which were memorable.

The first day, in the midst of defending Latin as a base for other languages, he taught them, "in mari, meri, miri, mori, muri placet," which means, "it pleases the mouse to die in a sea of wonderful wine." These silly phrases stunned the class and were irresistible to Louise.

"It pleases the mouse to die in a sea of wonderful wine" was translated in unison by Ginny and Louise as they walked home from school, stopping by the bakeshop. Often the drivers coming to cash out their receipts could hear their hysterics.

The girls got cooled molasses cookies, small green bottles of Coke, and then ran upstairs to see Floyd in his office.

"How was school?"

They greeted him with a duet of "in mari, meri, miri, mori, muri placet."

Floyd could not hold on to a professional stiff upper lip, dissolving tension in their silly atmosphere.

The girls got A's on vocabulary tests and B's in declining

verbs, all the while cementing a friendship bent on having fun. Oh, the frivolity of shopping with Mother, when Ginny would meet them at the movies, and then Saturdays at Ginny's house when Louise was occasionally invited.

Mrs. Murr related most of all to Louise and Ginny's sense of style. They were somehow naturally building an unusual flair for uniqueness and transcending a dark atmosphere of economic depression.

"Louise, you are fifteen now, what do you want to be when you grow up?" Mrs. Murr smiled.

"I'll figure that out next year. I like Mr. Dedlingue's class because of the word play. I like Home Ec because..." she pondered, "of trying new recipes." Suddenly a serious face declared, "I guess I want more than the job I have now."

Ginny said clearly, "I'd like to meet a nice guy, and schools have lots of them."

Mrs. Murr demurred, "You, dear heart, will find the right one, but school—and what you learn—is forever faithful... and men, well, there's just no guarantee."

Louise practiced finding the fun in work and school, so finding it elsewhere was as easy as pie. Five fun seekers met at the candy store en route to the movie, *Ruggles of Redgap*. There Clara and Mrs. Murr got a small box of milk-chocolate-covered creams, golden-haired Elaine, then nine, clutched a Cracker Jack box, while Louise and Ginny chose an assortment of penny candy.

"Come on," Elaine implored impatiently. "I love Zasu Pitts!"

"Coming, honeybunch!" Clara paid for the treats and bustled out into the car at last.

Louise drove Floyd's car to the Senate Theater, where Mrs. Murr bought tickets. There were so many laughs in the throats of young and old that they couldn't consume their candy!

If it seemed a rollercoaster of frivolity before they took their seats, the movie put them over the top. Zasu Pitts charmed the audience simply by rolling her huge eyes, but what tickled

Elaine was her way of saying, "Oh dear. Oh, my." Each time she said those wavering words, little Elaine started giggling, and it started a chain reaction that erupted in a full house howl.

The wide-screen appeal of the leading lady wasn't lost on the Stitt women. Dot modeled her makeup after Mona Maris, inspired by the chic fashions she wore. Louise came out of a Mae West movie, with hand on her hip, breathing at Elaine, "Peel me a grape."

She replied wide-eyed, "OH, dear... oh, my."

As the sisters mimicked screen idols at the Senate Theater, they were transported out of the Depression.

Clara had attended finishing school, and in spite of the fact that she earned no wages from it, she was certain of its value. It polished social skills, her organization improved, and the under girding of a shot of self-esteem didn't hurt either. So, when Dot went away to college, Clara began grooming Louise for higher education. It was an even less clear road than Dot went down because, as you see, Louise was enjoying too many things.

Floyd confided to Clara, "She knows people and our products well, and if she were a man, she could supervise the bread truck routes." However, that meant working the night shift, and he didn't think it best for a girl to supervise men. Better to encourage her in the store as it fostered responsibility and taught marketing and math.

During the depressed years of the early thirties, people bought fewer baked specialties, but their need for bread never wavered. Whether folks were working or not, somehow they bought, bartered or begged for bread. Floyd brought in a few workmen he had found standing outside the Broad Street Market holding signs scrawled with the words, "Will work for bread."

Above those who were desperately hungry, everyone felt the pain of shaky businesses, crops failing and the rise of crime in big cities. The woman on any Harrisburg street would tell you, "We just *make do* with less."

The Roosevelt administration counteracted the country's

economic depression by offering relief and restructuring to farms, industry and transportation. Floyd felt that in order to insure the survival of family and employees, he must reduce the price of sliced bread. He began in earnest when a competing bakery imported Wonder Bread from out of town. Wonder Bread had the distinction of making white flour whiter by bleaching the flour, pumping in air and making up for bleached out nutrients by adding vitamins. He tasted it with the Fegley brothers circled around and pronounced, "The only thing I *wonder* is how anyone can stomach it." Seeing its glue-like texture, George impulsively took the whole wax bagged loaf in his hands, forming a sticky baseball, and tossed it into the trash barrel. Stitt Bakery finally produced a better-made and better-priced small loaf for eight cents and a large Pullman loaf for twelve cents.

23

Dorothea was accumulating college credit toward a degree, and not at all depressed. She cherished interpretive dance as inspired by Isadora Duncan, and she proceeded to choreograph a dance unlike anything seen in recorded history. Bread and Dot had commonalities: they each were predictable, reliable and durable.

She named her piece "Self Risen" because it honored bread as a metaphor for growth. She had thought of everything, down to her ballet shoes, which resembled hot dog buns. Oh! She had it organized in minute detail, working in partnership with the stage manager. It was gratifying also that her family, including her grandparents, were in the audience.

In the opening number, she quietly interpreted the mixing of ingredients so that the audience felt a clockwise stirring and witnessed Dot, in gossamer white gauze, making undulating spirals. Primitive percussion instruments simulated mixing the components. Finally, she ran in one of her large spirals to an oven where she took up a large wooden mixing bowl, holding it heavenward. Throughout the number, flour was "sifted" without a sound from above her head.

The second segment employed wind music, reaching a crescendo as she rose from a large dough board on the floor. This was the most difficult, the interpretation of expansion. She achieved it though, by briefly flitting behind the looming cardboard oven, during which she was fitted with a ballooning ivory cape. Her arms extended, then her legs, in a powerfully wide grand plier position, and even her cheeks blew out as the light shifted. It almost seemed that Fornix, the Roman bake goddess, had taken Dot over.

The finale left the audience awestruck. She danced freely in her white gauze, leaping expansively to a gay Gershwin rhapsody that hushed as she "entered" the oven. She disappeared for a full minute so that a freshly baked loaf of bread was put before an offstage electric fan, providing the audience the aromatic setting needed. They inhaled the scent of caramelizing crust!

The audience stood and yelled for more. Dot made her exit from the oven, smiling in relief, wearing a stiffly standing crusty cape and toasty hat to depict oven browning. Amid heady bravos, Lil McGill presented her with a sheaf of wheat tied with a ribbon.

The feeling in Dorothea's heart was freedom in its purest form.

***

It was Dot's third year at Lock Haven, and it appeared that she had hit her stride. She would have liked more immersion in the visual arts; however, she found a ring of truth in her father's efforts to prevent her starvation as an artist because America's cities were teeming with the unemployed. By December 1932, prohibition of alcohol was no longer in force, which meant that usual college mixer dances mixed in keg beer. Dot was social but careful to sidestep the men she referred to as "wolves." They frequented the mixers under a gin cloud repulsive to her.

"Hey," said Lil one week after the ballet program, "somebody wants to meet you."

Dot quizzically raised an eyebrow, "Yeah?"

Lil continued, "Nice boy in my math class. You'd know him if you went to football games. He said your dance—the last part—reminded him of a football play."

"Ha!" laughed Dot. "A ha-ha... football player was watching ballet dancing? Oh, it strikes me funny!"

Nevertheless, the introductions took place in the cafeteria, where it was chicken corn soup day, a welcoming of warmth to a student after walking a campus covered with a four-inch snow blanket. Lil was waiting with Dot as the "somebody" appeared carrying a book of football plays.

"Chris Hammaker, meet Dot Stitt." He was as tall as Dot was and squarely built, with brilliant blue eyes and curly brown hair.

"I'm so pleased to see you again," he said, looking at her through wire rims. Dot regarded him through her own wire-rimmed glasses. He helped the girls off with their coats, while Lil went for three bowls of steaming soup.

"I heard from Lil that you saw me dance."

He excitedly answered, "Yeah, that was a real lulu... I hadn't gone to any of those shows, but you sure knocked the socks off everybody. How 'bout it?"

Dot clearly enjoyed this critique saying, "Thanks, Chris, it was... the most... the happiest day of my life."

"You don't say! Call me Christy... my friends do."

Lil sat quietly while Dot was explaining what the art of dance meant. "Christy, I step into the techniques and movements for starters, but then I lose the mold so to speak. I get inspired mysteriously and poof! I become a real live dance!" She leaned forward "I *am* the dance."

He had tasted what she meant when he witnessed the sight of her spirals on stage. He seemed entranced by her talk of molding, her feel for festivity, and how she spoke the word "Christy." Dot meanwhile noticed how easy this meeting seemed to go, and she suddenly asked him how he felt when he was in his own element.

He gestured, using his soupspoon like a baton. "My job as lineman is to help the team gain ground toward the goal. If I get the space, I can move anyone back. Last season we gained ten yards and I intercepted the ball." Here he almost came out of his seat, wide-eyed. "I jumped over the only man in my way and flew to the goal line. I got the fuel to do it out of nowhere. When

I stopped, I was so high I… it was like I got taller."

They hurriedly slurped their soup because the class bell had chimed one p.m.

Christy urged, "Okay, now you've got to come to my performance. Please."

He found two tickets in his sweater vest and handed them to Dot. Here was a presence Dot had never known, and she was glued to his blue eyes for a moment.

"And how!" She exclaimed. "You can count on it."

24

The bakery girls' success in the midst of the Depression stemmed from their association with the bakery business, built upon the foundation of a loving family. The three enjoyed each other's company, even though their ages spanned fifteen years. For reasons known only to Clara and Floyd, their first living child was born when Clara was twenty-five, their last when she reached forty. Each of Clara's daughters received motherly and grandmotherly attention plus that of associated women like Aunt Tinnie. This spacing of the children created three inimitable "only children."

"My father owns a grocery store and in it he sells... 'P.'"

Louise sat with Ginny wearing wool sweaters on the steps to the bakeshop store, warmed by the November sun. Elaine and three of her friends listened intently as they tried to win the prize of a free ice cream cone. What grocery began with the letter "P"?

"Potato?"

"No."

"Pickles?"

"No."

"Popcorn?"

"No."

"Popsicle?"

"No."

"Pop?"

"No."

"Peaches?"

"Polywogs?"

Louise giggled, "Polywogs! You're disqualified."

The seven-year-old boy in suspendered short pants said, "Hey, you can't do that!"

Louise said, "Come on, ragamuffins! Somebody guess a three-letter word."

"Pie," said Elaine, nodding and swinging her gold braids.

"Remarkable!" yelled Louise, leaping to her feet. She made them all cones in her newly created flavor, tangerine sherbet.

The flavor came to her as if it was straight out of the pocket of the dairy angel when Louise ate a dish of vanilla ice cream one day. Ginny peeled a tangerine and gave a section to Louise, who accidentally dropped it on top of the vanilla bean flecked oval in her dish. She enjoyed the coldness of the citrus flavor enough to turn it into a selection at the store. The color enchanted her, so next Louise had her mother create a delicious dress of tangerine for her birthday, and she impulsively complemented it with an unfashionably pale orange lipstick.

Her beauty seemed to be a secret only to Louise, and though she received numerous complements, she expertly deflected them with a haughty, "Sez who? Yeah?" Or the softer "Really, dahling." She could bounce a complement as easy as Babe Didrickson could drive a golf ball.

She had reached the height of five feet three inches in high heels and her well-proportioned body had somehow weathered all of those cream puffs in her diet.

The money she earned went into Louise's "look," and that featured her hair. For her sixteenth birthday, she had her hair permed, and after that, she would attach herself to "the parlor," as she referred to it, for the rest of her life. Yes, she thought only a seasoned stylist was qualified to make her hair presentable—thick, dark brown and straight, yet she did not want straight locks. Her stylist came to know Louise better than Father Waggenseller at the church, and he saw her nearly every Sunday.

She made the claim that she could estimate brainpower in a stranger by inspecting his hair. So one can only imagine what went through Louise Stitt's curly head when she told her stylist

Frieda, "I'm going red. What are your shades?"

Going deep rusty red created an initial shockwave at home. Her mother hyperventilated, frozen for a few minutes, saying of the russet do, "It's not... ugly, I don't think. But until that henna washes out, you could be taken for a floo-zy." She pulled on the word floozy as if it was hot taffy.

Floyd came home, did a double-take at his siren daughter and judged, "Well, that's better than that red hat you have. Clara, her hair'll grow!"

Elaine, observing from her vantage point at Floyd's elbow, was curious. She had long blond braids of good hair, also requiring some timely upkeep.

Louise bent down, put her arm round her sister and asked, "What do ya think, kid?"

Elaine rolled her eyes and pronounced, "You're prettier than Lucille Ball."

"Out of the mouths of babes," whispered a stunned Louise, who accepted that complement.

***

Floyd may have been a strict disciplinarian, but his daughters had qualities that occasionally left him under their spells. One lazy Sunday afternoon, Louise and Elaine played "unbirthday," a game of songs, invisible guests and equally invisible gifts. During the course of this giddily imaginary party in the dining room, Elaine served green bread, actually sliced white bread with a piece of lettuce on top.

"It's green bread," said Elaine. "With green meat."

Louise answered, "Let's hope it's from a green goose."

Then Elaine imagined, "Hey, why don't they make green bread?"

Louise thought a minute and replied, "Wheat is sort of tan, and it doesn't come in many other shades."

They jumped to Floyd in his chair by the window, where he

read the Sunday paper. They said, "Father, can you make green bread?"

He took off his glasses, explaining that although God's plentiful wheat was brown, man had made green food coloring and said, "Yes, bread could be turned green, blue or pink."

Elaine frowned when he said, "Would you like matching mannaise?"

"No, I want *mayonnaise*," she pronounced.

"By George, those girls of mine..." Floyd, who was in favor of variety on his customers' shelves, made small orders of tinted bread for Christmas and New Year's 1933.

George Fegley had gotten bald and somewhat shorter in the span of time at Stitt's, but he certainly grew in wisdom. "Personally, I like bread as is, not camouflaged, but here's your green," he said, staring at an oven full of loaves headed for the slicer, "And there's your red."

He nodded toward an order of loaves due for the oven that were a dark pink.

Floyd wanted to see the public response to the bread so he could decide how many loaves to produce. He asked a caterer to experiment with his colorful loaves. It happened that a wedding reception coincided with the experiment. The caterer made finger sandwiches Neapolitan style, arranged in green glass platters reminiscent of holiday wreaths. Why, the wedding guests had never seen such colorful tidbits and the bride had a photo taken of her and the groom holding the tray of green and crimson sandwiches.

Louise soon found herself at a teen dance with Ginny at the church recreation hall. They were surprised to see triangles of more Stitt red and green bread at a buffet table. The girls had to admit it was a novel way to eat sliced bread.

Louise's dance card was often filled with the names of "kids" in her class, but this time a tall stranger approached for a slow version of the waltz. The Victrola played Billie Holliday's *If You Were Mine*.

Boys didn't easily snare Louise, but this was not a boy. His name was Ted, and he exuded confidence, unlike the perspiration of the boys. He was blonde with curly hair and that's where she got caught, though neither knew exactly what the hell happened. He had a cloud of scent that seemed to spill from his hair, and what it did was arousing. His hair was clean, but he couldn't wash out an earthy vanilla odor, which captivated Louise. She left the dance with Ginny, starry eyed.

"Who is he?"

Louise lit a cigarette in an effort to wake herself up. "Tom, or was it Tim?"

"Why are you sniffing your hand?"

Louise extended her hand to Ginny's nose, asking, "What does this remind you of?"

Ginny inhaled saying, "Candy. No, vanilla. Vanilla."

Louise hypnotically added, "Or vanilla cream soda. What an unusual scent."

Ted came to the store the following Saturday wearing a stylish, shoulder-hugging sweater and asked Louise for a vanilla cone.

"What a surprise," Louise said evenly, although she expected this visit from Mr. Vanilla. She followed him to the window seat, and they sat behind a basket of chewy baguettes.

"Ummm. Bread's so good." Ted inhaled the bread aroma, and Louise repeated what Floyd had said to her.

"Bread is our first convenience food, you know."

Ted replied, biting into the creamy cone, "I guess the cavemen had bread."

Louise sighed, "Made by cavewomen at cave ovens. Father said that the pyramid builders of Egypt did all that stone moving by having food that was able to be carried in a pocket."

"Bread." Ted popped the last bite in his mouth, gesturing toward a Coca-Cola clock on the wall. "Would you like to go for a walk when you get off work?"

She tried not to gasp, saying, "Okay. How 'bout seven?"

The pair walked to the nearby park called Italian Lake, and walked around the lake, finally sitting on a park bench, where Ted took Louise's hand, told her she was more beautiful than Claudette Colbert in Cleopatra, and kissed her. Between the bodily contact and the heavenly scent of vanilla, she found herself mesmerized. She could barely think and her body took on a consistency of liquid—even her bones felt liquid. She had never been that passive and never would be again. He was visiting a relative in Harrisburg, he claimed, and said that he worked at a Philadelphia radio station. To Louise, it felt excitingly natural, this new love, and she wanted to stay on the bench but opted to go home.

They met again the following day, strolling to the lake at a more entrained, synchronized pace. The raw energy of this vanilla bandit overcame reason. This time they forgot the time and found themselves in a missionary position on a bed of grass. After that pivotal experience, Louise thought she had grown in many ways; however, all the delicious expansiveness of first love would come to a screeching halt.

He told her he would be at the store the following Saturday, but alas, he did not show up. She felt angry and sorry simultaneously.

Louise told Ginny, who reflected, "Mom says men aren't guaranteed, that girls are not equipped to handle the boys our age," mused her friend. "You believe you know a boy and then you see his true colors. I'm sorry too… for you and Tad or was it Toad?"

Louise fretted, "Toad. When *is* the time, then? How else can you learn if not by experience?"

Ginny added, "She says women are more logical as they get older. She says men are wild and out of control in their twenties. Their hormones steer them to you and then you, the girl, mistake lust for love."

Louise grudgingly sighed, "Like Mr. Dedlingue said, I need to find harmony in discord."

"Concordia discors," Ginny said softly.

25

Dorothea was a bit of a perfectionist. She completed the coursework to make herself eligible for a teacher's certificate and went as far as she could in the art department at Lock Haven. Her artistic forte in the end was producing ceramics and painting them decoratively.

Lil was thrilled that Dot hit it off with Chris Hammaker and took it upon herself to encourage and coach her friend as they made their way to the football field.

"Don't be too available, Dot. Keep 'm guessing. Play hard to get," warned Lil.

"Hey, kid, I'm not one to play games. He doesn't put pressure on me, and he likes my 'common sense.'" Dot raised her penciled brow.

Those football game tickets had seated Dot and Lil near the players' bench. Christy waved when he spotted them. Lil spoke nonchalantly, noting Dot's confusion about the rules of the game, saying, "It's a ball game, so they move the ball, take the ball, try to keep it and score. They look scrambled because the ones who don't have the ball, play to get it."

Dot replied quizzically, "Simple. Oh yeah, like the moving ahead of play time, the hitting after play time and the yelling at the 'damn referee.'" Lil explained that these were penalties.

The game ground away. Dot saw Christy moving his offensive line forward and seldom losing ground. Lock Haven won by a score of 12 to 6. In spite of Dot's lack of interest in watching the game, later, she did enjoy his explanations of the plays. Rather than attending a victory dance, they walked to a drugstore and sat in an oak wood booth sipping Cokes and enjoying the blue plate special.

Dot felt as comfortable as if the booth was the most cushy she had ever had and Christy, not given to gab, gave her dissertations about how the game looked to be a violent clash but was equally a mental challenge. She listened and loudly laughed over his serious speech on tackling efficiency.

"Center of gravity is my tackling secret. If I keep my pelvis square, crouching, and aim toward the opponent's center of gravity, well my weight has to work an efficient tackle. I'm a bowling ball and he's a pin! Hee, hee, hee, hee!" He slapped the table for emphasis.

He had no use for art and was unaware of that whole realm of self-expression. He was just now reaching for a symbolic doorknob, which seemed to open an avenue to the mind and heart of art itself. His large calloused hand fit the doorknob. The hinges were well oiled and the surprises began as he stepped into the world of Dorothea.

For the first time since he had been admitted to Lock Haven, Christy was developing an interest outside of sports and his intention of learning to become a coach. The beauty of bouncing an opponent off his route toward the goal line was now comparable to the unpredictable swirling motion of Dot's new mobile, made of red tin. He had lifted lighter weights than Dot's customarily hefted stoneware clay, which she milled herself. Yes, Christy appreciated her art and placed her on a pedestal.

Just as she followed him to the home games, he also witnessed her artistry.

"Surprise!" Christy entered the ceramic studio to say hello and found Dot, alone and painting a design on a porcelain plate. Peering over her shoulder, he said quietly, "This is just like painting a barn. Only I had a bigger brush."

She put down her brush, laughing, and he cradled her elbow, kissing her on the cheek. She planted her kiss on his lips with creative enthusiasm. They had become friends, learning about how family businesses operate in the city versus the country. He had grown up on a farm in Holidaysburg, the youngest of nine children. He related well to girls, as he had lived with six of the species. Now in their last year of college, he was spending much of his time coaching the Bald Eagles in preparation for his coaching career. The head coach wanted him on the staff, not only because he utilized physics to win games, but for his uncanny way of building endurance into the team.

26

Floyd Stitt decided to make the weekly bread delivery personally to Lock Haven on a sunny February day and to take that opportunity to meet with Dot. Floyd strolled toward the cafeteria singing as he toted a green bin labeled "Stitt's Better Made Bread" plus a large brown paper bag.

Dot was catching up with him on the path and loudly sang out, "When his good, sweet, soft soda crackers are gone." They embraced, the protective father and his eldest artist daughter. He believed he had kept her safe. She adapted her creative nature toward teaching, but that detour had taken her to a place where she was learning to discharge her anger and now, her heart was open. Christy stood by the cafeteria door.

This planned meeting left the three of them smiling, and it actually changed the course of their lives. They say two's company; three's a crowd, but not these three. They met and talked, and the whole thing felt synchronized. Floyd didn't believe how much harmony he felt with his daughter after years of awkward skirmishes. She had changed, it was true, but there had also been a force working to provide a powerful catalyst, and that was in the unassuming person of Christopher Hammaker.

After lunch, Christy asked what Floyd had in the large bag at the end of their table.

Floyd offered, "Please look inside." And he did.

The aroma of sweet and crusty things took over the table, and they were some of Dot's favorites. He pulled out a round loaf of raisin bread—a new experience for him.

"Do you mind if I taste it?"

Dot pushed a butter dish his way as he tore off the tender crust. A raisin fell out on the plate. "It's so fresh, I don't want to put anything on it," and he took a bite.

As the unforgettable cinnamon on yellow bread hit Christy's senses, Floyd felt an onrush of pride in his product and company. Why, hundreds of customers had this same reaction each day of the week! He felt what philanthropists feel when they feed masses of people.

Christy declared as his eyes rolled, "Dorothea told me so much about your bakeshop, but I didn't really know it until..." He paused, smiling, searching for a way to shout it without shouting. "Better than homemade!" He said it with his mouth full.

Dot broke their reverie by warning, "Well, pal, you might go into a tailspin when you get a piece of that shoe fly pie."

That Dorothea had attracted Christy seemed to impress Floyd more than her perfect report cards. Perhaps he felt surprised by the effervescent sight of the happy couple. Maybe he could lose the habit of underestimating his daughter, and one knew the weekly shipments would always include tender raisin bread.

27

Young Elaine never really attached herself to a doll. She herself *was* a doll. Her most cherished toy of childhood had been her toy car; a four-door Ford sedan she played with as though she could drive it. "Let's go awaayy!" She laughed, rolling it down the dining room table. Her family doted on the charming blond child, and the Fegleys all but adopted her. They never tired of repeating the story of the bakery truck driver who chewed tobacco. Elaine met him when she was four, saw his asymmetrical face and pronounced, "Father, something is wrong with his face!"

The driver responded, "Well, kiddy it's a chew'a 'bacca."

Elaine looked at him quizzically, "Are you chewing tobacco?"

Now Louise found harmony readily enough. She spent her summer holidays working and shopping with Elaine. Downstairs in Bowman's basement where they discovered racks of dresses, prices newly reduced, they were having the time of their lives; or so it seemed to the saleslady.

"Eeek!" said Louise. "You've got the figure for it, but not the height... why you'll trip over that hem!"

They were staring into the dressing room mirror, and now it was Elaine's turn. "Who are you trying to impersonate, showing off your knees? Shirley Temple?" Then giggling, she added, "Subcula tua apparet!"

"What?" Louise gasped.

Outside, the saleswoman had to snicker too because the Stitt girls were howling.

"Ahem." She cleared her throat. "I hope I can be of assistance?"

Elaine said, "I just said, 'Your slip is showing.'"

Elaine yelled over the mirror, "Yeah, come in, and bring some shears and a magic wand."

Louise was silent but her look of exaggerated astonishment gave way to miming punching at her sister.

Wearing a jersey dress adorned with Chanel-inspired pearls and a measuring tape, the woman entered the changing room wearing a smile. "Are these clothes you're trying on for an event?"

"How'd you know?" Louise replied. "Our father is taking us to Philadelphia."

"That will be fun," she said, bending to pin Elaine's hem and then let out a portion of Louise's lemony shirtwaist dress.

Louise's figure appreciated the yellow dress, with its Joan Crawford shoulder pads and thin belt. "I think I'll take the dress, and Mother will let out the hem.

"The alterations are free, so save your mother the trouble." Addressing Louise, she said. "You may be interested to know about our new shipment of bras. They have sizes for cups! Brand new."

Elaine said, "I'll keep that in mind." She stared at her future hem, riding below the knee. "Much better, and I love the colors." Navy with polka dots on the sleeve and pocket. Elaine excitedly continued, "I hope to go to the Philly stores and eat at the automat."

Louise just grinned, looking forward to sharing the drive down Route 22 because she had never driven a car outside Harrisburg.

28

"Father, why don't I just go along with you to the bakery convention?" Louise asked. "Mother and Elaine are going shopping and visiting the Liberty Bell... how 'bout it?"

So, Floyd and Louise stepped through the revolving door of the Latham Hotel. The displays of the vendors were what attracted Louise, while her father headed for a business meeting.

She strolled down a line of displays by millers, bakery truck manufacturers, and a new bread slicer company. A low whistle turned her head.

"Hey, cupcake, come over... I've got something for you."

Louise smiled but kept walking. By the time she turned toward the next aisle, the whistler was standing right in front of her, pushing a brown bagful of pecans into her hand. "Hey, what's yer name?"

He was old, at least twenty-five. She didn't like his smarmy way of whispering.

"You're nervy," she said as she walked through him.

"C'mon, sis, what's your name?"

This time he was behind her, close enough to her behind that she felt his polished shoe against the white heel of her three-inch spectator pump. She wanted to swat him like the flies that harass iced buns at the farmers' market. Saying nothing, she stopped, he lurched forward as she instinctively raised her heel, bringing all of her leg's force down on his big toe. She stood on it as he wailed.

A policeman and three of the vendors ran toward the scene as pain drove "Gourmets' Choice" best salesman to push Louise away. But she twisted her heel harder and jumped off the foot.

The man finally sat on the floor, gripping his foot.

"What's all this?" said the large policeman who heard the commotion from the street.

"Officer, I'm sorry. I offended this... girl." He was contrite. Convincingly contrite.

The officer pushed his cap back, saying, "Now, may I ask what happened?"

A woman in a suit and small straw hat, out of breath, appeared. She puffed, "I saw it from across the room. Why, he's a masher! He pushed his, his nuts at her. She should be congratulated. He's a menace!"

The beaten masher, in a new whisper, said, "I'm sorry, miss."

"Nuts," Louise whispered, dropping the brown bag of pecans on the floor near his depressed shoe.

She stood tall in her new yellow dress. "Thanks a lot," she exhaled, smiling around the circle of onlookers.

The straw-hatted Mrs. Amanda Smith from Pottstown and the officer stayed around the place where "cupcake" had rejected the masher and his nuts. Then the woman invited Louise to the hotel's restaurant for breakfast. Louise learned more that day than she did in her senior year at William Penn.

"I think you could enter the Olympics with reflexes like yours."

Louise waved her off, saying, "I did it by instinct."

Mrs. Smith was a product of the Depression, a woman who had had children to raise and who turned her flaky pie dough into... well, into dough, the spendable kind. She regaled Louise with her stories of the kids plucking cherries and how she transformed fruit into cherry tarts. It all started in a home kitchen and now her pie bakery served entire counties.

She watched Louise eating cinnamon toast. Louise breathed in the ground cinnamon thinking, *I want my life to be like this cinnamon toast*. She bit into the white toast with its exotically sweet taste.

"I hope your father appreciates you. I'm sure you are a real asset to the business. But you must consider *your* dreams. Do you like the job you do? Search your heart for your true calling," Mrs. Smith implored.

Licking cinnamon from her lip, Louise replied, "Well, I like to read, to dance, and I like selling baked goods. I like buying *and* selling. Is that any clue to find my way to a good job?"

"That, my dear, is a good start." Mrs. Smith smoothed her salt and pepper bangs. "Buying what?"

Louise laughed, "Dresses, dishes, dominoes, da limit."

"And selling?" Mrs. Smith queried.

"Our bakery sells bread, buns, biscuits... you name it."

Hmm, thought the older woman, of the buying and selling as a cycle. Then she advised. "Today, I would like to study the cooking arts, but I'm just too darn busy working with the bakery. Take my advice, Louise, get an education before you get married. Education and freedom are like twins. And don't let anyone talk you into doing anything you don't want to do."

The memory of her artist sister prompted her to say, "Per aspera, ad astra!"

Mrs. Smith's eyebrows shot up. "What?"

"Through difficulties, to the stars!"

She left Louise with, "Invest in yourself. Learn. You'll be wiser when you're older."

29

Dot's formal education ended with a flourish. She envisioned a position in a school where she could be an advocate for kids. Her dream scenario featured herself in a print dress set off by one of her ceramic pins on the collar. She carried a satchel full of tricks... er projects. How to: paint, draw, paste; from there make masks, hats, flags and musical instruments. The creative satchel, full of ways to experiment, express and enjoy. Smiling, she said to herself, "Why, a person could earn a living creating art projects."

Meanwhile, Christopher Hammaker had become a football coach at Lock Haven. Like yeast in dough, the love of Dot and Christy bloomed in the meantime, through the transition to gainful employment. Dot applied to various schools nearby and was rejected, as one principal said, "Not by me, but by the Great Depression," for there were no jobs. She went home to Harrisburg, where she secured a job as a substitute teacher in the public grade schools.

***

"Marry me." Dot opened her first telegram; two words sent a week after she came home. She entered a reverie of sensual memory. Their courtship had reached a point where she felt limitless affection. It happened on a Saturday that the team went to an away game. A player ran out of bounds and his momentum met Christy's knee. This was enough to get Christy carried off the field on a stretcher, then on home to the school infirmary.

He lay there a while before persuading the nurse to phone

Dot. Eventually, she appeared in the doorway wearing baggy pants, sweater and a beret.

"Oh dear, what will we do?" she exclaimed, thin brows frowning, yet relieved to see him.

Propped on his elbows, Chris answered, "Well, I just have to stay off the leg, use crutches for a while."

The leg was on two pillows and the knee packed with ice. Dot leaned over the bed, gripping the football hero's shoulders. They kissed as lovers do when longing goes on for too long and something has to give. It was magnetic and suddenly overwhelming. The beret rolled to the floor and Chris' eyes scanned her face. They turned to the sound of clunky-heeled shoes approaching, then parted, warmer breath coming fast and Christy's hand holding the back of Dot's head.

The nurse had come to say she was going to get dinner for her patient.

"Hey," Chris implored. "Could you get one for Dot too, and say you'll come back after six?"

Indeed, she returned after sex, and sex was intoxicatingly lovely. His knee had to be spared so it was Dot who covered Christy like a warm blanket in motion. All the tenderness of their friendship had created an amorous dam of friendly feelings. Interlaced fingers squeezed, their bellies kissed and the dam broke, moans pushing against equally urgent kissing. In the midst of this, she broke out of her kiss of longing, stopped then found a whole-brain-buzzing kiss. Their eyes locked in, in a two-way beam, "I need you," she said, "and I like life with you included."

Dot's memory thereafter stored his immortal words, "Football and sex on the same day—it's heavenly!"

She was to say this again and again to the man who had captured her heart like a football, hugged to his chest in the game of life.

30

L ouise returned from Philadelphia—a city known for love and liberty—from an excursion that galvanized her. Taking a wise cue from Mrs. Amanda Smith, she set a course in her mind. It was sketchy, but she worked at making it real.

Louise was smart enough to know what she was not. She was not a flaky crust aficionado. That is to say, not amused by any sort of manual labor—no, she achieved more when surrounded by people, people who were in the market for a Stitt fruit envelope, or pie. Pie, like Louise, contained juice, was lively and rewarding, but to find it one had to see through the crust.

Though the Stitts were less depressed than most of their neighbors of the thirties, one could not ignore the mood on the street. It was in the air of the jobless men, desperate women and little kids, still wearing the shoes they had outgrown. Floyd's business kept several good souls working, and Clara gave to the church's relief charity, but that monotonously desperate air of hunger was in everyone's head.

Louise held Elaine and her mother by the hand as they exited the trolley, conveying them home from a Saturday movie. "Wow," said Elaine. "Myrna Loy was sooooo glam!"

Louise intoned with drama, "Why, she's the bee's knees!"

Yes, they went to escape the Depression and found themselves mesmerized soundly by the leading lady. Clara said, "That gal has some real class. She's no Mae West."

Class, so sought after by young people, was difficult to define, but it seemed Myrna Loy had hit the mark and hence their escape from the mundane was a success.

***

The next day, the two girls rehashed all the costumes worn by Myrna Loy while working in the bakery store. "I'm expecting a few friends from school to come in and chocolate is their fave'," Louise said as she added today's batch to the freezer.

Elaine, whose job it was to clean the Venetian blinds, mumbled to the floor, "I'd just like to *grow up!*"

Louise heard the exasperation of her kid sister and said softly, "Dahling, why?"

"I want to do what I want. And I don't want this job... I really can't stand it," she answered, her hands vigorously wiping the blind's slats.

Then Louise's queried, "Well, what would you do if you were grown up?"

Elaine's hands went still. She tossed her long blond hair over her shoulder, staring though the Venetian blind with unfocused brown eyes. "I wish I could solve mysteries... just like (and here she batted her eyelashes) Myrna Loy," exhaling a big sigh.

"Dahling, you have that same star quality, ya know, you do!"

Then Elaine's coffee-colored eyes flashed. "I wish I could solve crimes like in the *Thin Man* movie, going to exotic places with a steady guy by my side." Elaine went on about observation, interrogation and hard-won clues, all the tantalizing elements of mystery.

Louise asked, "As an actress?"

"No. I mean it would be swell to be able to know how to solve mysteries. I can't."

Louise, intrigued, replied, "Well, how do the detectives do it? They puzzle it out—is there a detective school? They do a lot of lookin' around and questioning people."

There they were, giggling their way into the prospect of their mysterious futures.

"Okay, let's puzzle out my future," Louise said hopefully.

Elaine screamed, "Now *that* is one for Charlie Chan!"

They laughed in shrieks, slapping each other on the knee. The slaps seemed to trigger the laughs and their humor was a release valve, opened to the maximum.

Louise sighed, "What do I know, besides this job?"

Elaine said, "How to dance, how to sell and you're real good at kidding around..."

This brought them another round of belly laughs, with Elaine saying in a whispered laugh, "You weren't voted 'Wittiest girl in your class' for nothin'."

Waving her away, as if to reject all complements, Louise replied, "I was born that way."

"You seem to like people coming in here," Elaine observed.

"Yeah," said her sister, "I love the customers."

"Oh. If you could dance and get paid for it, you'd have work and play."

They went into another cascade of laughs that echoed out into Jefferson Street.

31

The miserable years of the Depression in Harrisburg sank to an all time low as spring flood waters from the Susquehanna rose in March 1936, washing out the bridges to the West Shore.

Floyd Stitt sat across from Pennell, the driver who delivered for the West Shore of Harrisburg, as rain slid down the office windows.

"Ha, ha, ha... what boat?"

"Well I got out my row boat..."

"Wha ha, ho, ho..." Floyd bent over now, in near hysteria.

"I piled in the bread..."

"WWWax wrapped," Floyd wheezed.

"Well, sir, people need bread."

"Nee-hee-hee-hee-need need..." Now Floyd was slapping Pennell on the shoulder.

"When I got to the West Shore, people were standing in wader boots ready to help me. I sold most of it right there. A policeman drove me to the market house, and the rest was gone in a half-hour."

Floyd said, "You've got powers beyond mortal man."

The bakery had continued to endure the Depression. Floyd's bread was made from scratch, bagged by machine and shipped within a fifty-mile radius. Perhaps his biggest accomplishment since creating his business came in the early thirties when expenses were going up.

Floyd told Clara and the girls at breakfast, "Everyone's costs are higher. That tells me I've got to *lower* the cost of a loaf of bread. Lower it below my competitors' prices."

Clara said, "Good idea," as her toast popped up. She spread

on some tangy apple butter.

His blue eyes focused toward the future as he replied, "Ten cents is like going backwards, but by making that loaf slightly shorter, I could do it."

32

"**H**un" was Marlin Hunbert Allen's nickname. His father employed him at their family grocery on Walnut Street, where Stitt bread was popular. Louise stopped in one day with a carton of white bread and a large tray of cream puffs, so fresh that a gust of wind could blow their powdered sugar into the delivery girl's hair.

"Miss, can you tell me how it is that these thin cream puff shells are made?" It was Hun's introduction to the young woman whose hair smelled like she had just had a permanent wave.

Looking out from under a Veronica Lake tress, she replied, "Very carefully."

Louise never would give Hun a straight answer, and in his world of bacon, eggs, dollars, and cents, that was fine with him.

"How'd you come to be so smart?" Hun wanted to know.

Although that she would never reveal, saying simply, "Sugar, Sugar," with a Tallulah Bankhead straight face.

Marlin declared loudly, "You do have ready access to that. Well, *then* I guess bakery food is brain food."

Louise posed a question to her counterpart. "Don't you ever get tired of standing and handing out pork chops all day?"

"Miss Stitt, I'd rather be here than in some school." He laughed. "Look, I get to meet people like you."

He and Louise met again at The Sunset Grill, located in a tree-lined suburb of Harrisburg called Paxtang. The years under Prohibition had been a boon to the Coca-Cola Company, and the grill attracted teens like Hun, who came to dance and consume fountain cokes.

The joint was sandwiched between a grocery and a grade

school, both closed at night, allowing music from a huge radio to drift out into the street without waking the neighborhood. The walls were adorned with an assortment of small Navajo rugs, neatly stretched, and the occasional full-length mirror. The interior was divided between a dance floor and a grill, a fountain tap and cozily arranged tables and chairs.

Now, Louise drove to the grill after the sun went down, after a day at the store and after her father had fallen asleep. Her mother warned her to be careful; she herself had visited the grill on rare occasions and trusted that Louise would keep her head and not get carried away. "NO bootleg gin! Or else!" Clara admonished, with a hand on her daughter's shoulder.

Louise seriously reassured, "No distilled liquids."

"What a Dagwood sandwich!" Hun said as Louise motioned for him to have a seat.

"I like assortments," Louise said, referring to the club sandwich stuffed with layers of meat, cheese and pickles, pinned together by toothpicks.

The radio played dance music from the popular Lucky Strike Show, and Louise, gesturing toward the sound, said, "I like so many bands, it's hard to choose a favorite."

Hun was not one to brag, and unknown to Louise, had won a couple of dance contests. Maybe all of that time Hun spent standing at work had stored up the right kind of energy in his dancin' feet. The loose swing beat discharged any anxiety and the dance provided a little world in which to secrete them away from the Great Depression.

That night was memorable, brimming with a newly born bouncing rhythm, so far from usual uncertainties, in a surrounding of friends, while glasses of carbonated Coke fizzed.

Hun said, as he cut the rug, "There's somethin' special about that Benny Goodman."

Louise grabbed his hand, leaned toward his face and, perfectly synchronized to the song on the radio said, "Goody, goody!"

Hun put down his drink, guiding his partner between other dancers. "I know a guy who makes white lightning, and the stuff tastes like motor oil until you mix a Coke into it."

Louise said, "Bleah! The strongest thing I ever drank is Mamaw's dandelion wine."

The banjo clock on the wall read twelve-thirty as the *Lullaby of Broadway* filled the room, and Hun asked her longingly, "Let's meet here next week, okay?"

"Why, sure," said Louise with a smile.

She drove home in her father's Packard, surprised by her feelings of delight. Today, she had worked, played, doing both with a certain flair that was about her coming of age. This Hun was a good person who did not threaten her. He genuinely liked to shmooze, and that set Louise at ease.

And where *was* Louise going? Didn't *she* get tired standing, selling and scooping? Soon her parents would notice that she had no plan, not really. However, her spirit presided over the space around her, as if it had commanded her: *play*--play all you can.

33

Christy was soon to marry the art teacher and love of his life. Dot continued to hunger for creative pursuits while occupied with the challenge of Harrisburg's school system, which could only employ her as a substitute teacher. Incredibly, her father urged her to run his office. At first she thought, NO! Not on your half-baked life! Floyd was desperately seeking help—even worse; this search was being driven by "Tillie the Toiler," his malodorous secretary.

Her name was really Thuly Ann Cluge, and soon after her hiring, she abruptly stopped bathing, which made her an obstacle to those who breathe. "She smells worse than the whole farm," Floyd shouted, pleading with Sarah to complain to Tillie about her body odor.

Sarah described the secretary's attitude as "sweet but kind'a stupid," because of the comment, "I ran out of soap." Sarah raced to the storeroom, and then slapped a bar of Lava into Tillie's hand.

Next, Floyd complained to her that, "This uh, *odor* (he said the word through his nose) will lead me to fire you, so take care of it." Still, after two months, the office remained unbearable, even with its windows open. The truck drivers mumbled about how she smelled like a goat farm. Louise had a habit of exclaiming "nocens nidor"[1] in a high quaver. Elaine came up with a nickname for the secretary that stuck so well it remained in their memory long after the bakery closed its doors: Tillie the Toiler. Ironically nicknamed after a chic cartoon character who

---

[1] Bad odor

was a hard-working woman, sought after more because of her beauty than the brain in her head.

Floyd felt so exhausted by dealing with Tillie that he stayed away from the office, and now he was frustratingly overcome with paperwork. He met Dot's refusal by talking about her meager teacher's pay and his vibrant appreciation for her eye for detail.

"I didn't go earn a degree to work in this place," she declared, stamping her feet so her curls bounced and her Chanel pearls swung.

Seeing her there, he felt an outpouring of loving compassion, born from his own memories of his escape from farming, but now he was desperate for help, and it all seemed to hinge on Dot. Floyd promised her an apartment and office furniture.

"No."

"You can paint the walls!"

"Nope."

"Put your plates on the wall and make it artsy."

"Nnno- HA!" She had to laugh, first Floyd saying the word "artsy," then at the thought of the grayish bakery office as some sort of creative universe. Also, at the incongruous state of affairs; for she was her own ace in this card game. The standoff went on. That week Floyd fired Tillie the Toiler, to the relief of everyone. Floyd minimally ran the shop, cut corners and hoped, while a new respect solidified for Dot.

***

The family gathered for Dot's twenty-fifth birthday, and they looked forward to a visit from Christy as preparations for the wedding began. Caroline, Clara, Dot, Louise, Byron and Elaine gathered at the rectangular dining room table, and Dot had pulled back the curtains for maximum April light. Floyd and Christy sat together. Each had been pondering their occupations, but chatted about bakery trucks, ball scores and Roosevelt's re-election.

Before the birthday cake regalia, Christy made an announcement that fell like an ill-thrown football hanging over a player destined to intercept it.

"I've lost my coaching position for now because of the school budget," he said apologetically.

Floyd swallowed a bit of water as Clara moaned, "Oh! And you were so happy there."

Christy continued, "I'll have to hope they rehire later but," he sighed, "the outlook for the economy isn't too good."

Dot held her breath, knowing she couldn't be the sole breadwinner.

"Ahem," Floyd snapped into action. "We want you to coach, but while you're waiting for your chance, I'd like to help. How'd you like to work for me? Pick any job except baker!"

Dot stared at her father then at her fiancé.

Christy looked at Floyd as though he had removed a heavy helmet. "I could see more of you," he told Dot. "I'll think it over."

Imagine Dot's wish as she blew out her twenty-five candles.

34

The park called Italian Lake was a peaceful place. An elderly man walked a terrier by some tulips. The only sounds came from a flock of ducks on the water. Christy took Dot by the hand and strolled around the water. He knew Floyd had a good business mind, coming through the worst economy the country had ever seen. Christy's forte was not business, it was teamwork, and now Dot was Christy's biggest concern. She was depressed inside the Great Depression, it was true, but smart enough to see the big picture. She didn't try to conceal her joy at the prospect of her lover joining the family, even though she faced her beckoning bakeshop occupation with unwilling trepidation.

"Hell..." Dot gasped.

Christy implored, "You could be in Philadelphia now—I know."

"I'm a victim of circumstance. It's funny-peculiar," Dot sighed. "I'm glad I found you and that's what really matters." She shook off a layer of frustration. "I wanted a stimulating, creative life; I got you. Now you're going to be a slave to this... this yeast mill!"

Christy jumped, "Hey, don't run down the hand that feeds ya', please. You think this is bad, what about these dirt-poor farmers or these guys digging ditches to put food on the table? How many years before bad times end? Buck up, sister." He had a brown bag full of stale bread and spun a slice toward the lake like a discus.

Dot's face softened. "I know Father is smart. Maybe he did save me a world of pain. Maybe this offer to work in the office will be better than me waiting for the art teacher to quit her job."

Christy added, "You could do worse than to run Stitt's office. You *know* what bread means to people." He passed the bread to Dot, she threw a slice to a duck, who hungrily caught it.

Well, one thing Floyd could take credit for: the wedding proceeded on schedule. Floyd's kin from Path Valley, Christy's Hammaker side, including eight brothers and sisters, the bakery employees and other well-wishers appeared to celebrate.

Dot had a delightful time custom designing her cake, and the bakers said they had never actually attended a wedding where they could eat the cake that they baked a few hours before.

After creating a cake ornament of cavorting cupids made of sugar and cornstarch, she lost herself. "This is what I need," she mused as she fell into the momentum of creation.

Yes, she was in her element, all right, but something else had been stirred in, a strange ingredient that she could not identify. She shocked her mother by insisting on having a marble cake.

Dot insisted, "I look at marble and see two. These two are joining, just like a wedding."

"But it will look... not elegant."

Dot pressed, "Swell. Hee, hee, swelegant!"

"Swirligant, I know," Clara smiled.

Elaine and Louise would attend Dot. Louise giggled as they dressed for the wedding, "You be *sure* to catch the bouquet, dahling. I'm not planning to marry."

"What? You can't mean that!"

Louise, with a faraway look in her brown eyes, continued, "I'll work in the store, make enough money to pay for clothes, and tickets to dances... and repairs on high heels. My church shoes and dancing..."

Incredulously, Elaine asked, "You don't really want to find a... a husband?"

Her sister's silence gave way to a sidelong smile as she affixed a rosy flowered cloche to her head. "What, and ruin a perfectly good life?"

Elaine suddenly had to forget her assumption that Hun was a

serious beau. She replied, "Oh, dahling, you must really want to be a sales girl!"

Now, Louise was a prominent force in the setting up of her sister's wedding reception. And, while she cleaned the church meeting room, while she counted the folding chairs, and while she decorated the door, she pondered *her own future.*

The reception saw the Stitts and the Hammakers greeting, praying, eating, laughing and undeniably swirling. The cake was after all a fitting centerpiece. Dot asked master baker George Fegley to make a toast. George presented an unusual figure, dressed in a navy blue suit, but he seemed excited to speak. He smiled a gap-toothed grin that belied his limitless brain, holding hundreds of recipes.

"You know, I supervise these wedding cakes, and as I baked this'n, I thought about why a good marriage is like a cake baked with love. You put it patiently in the oven, take care not to let it fall and you're proud of it. I was thinking that when I attached these three tiers and piped on the decoration. I wish for Dot—she's been like a daughter—and Christy, our new family member, a lot of love."

35

Hun and Louise were dancing to *Begin the Beguine* at The Sunset when Louise announced her plan, with an unusually proper tone. "I'm going to college."

"Heck!" exclaimed her partner, who took her out to the parking lot, embraced her suddenly and kissed her thoroughly enough so that when his lips parted from hers, he had absorbed all her lipstick.

She laughed, "Ruby Red... the name of your lipstick!"

His clown lips said, "I probably can't stop you. What would it take to make you stay?"

Louise took his hand, saying softly, "Mother says girls need to learn skills. I need to go away. I need a change of scenery and now's the time. A great lady told me to get an education. She knew how bakeries are. They pull you in, moving your whole body into the bread or whatever they're baking. Before you know it... just look at the Fegleys... your lungs are floury and your knees are tougher than stale biscuits."

Hun looked abandoned and could only sigh. When he left the Sunset, he went directly to his private store of gin and proceeded to get numbly inebriated. Louise promised to write.

When Ginny Murr heard news of Louise's plan from Louise's cousin, Jane, she was in the midst of changing her own life gears.

"Louise! Ginny here," she barked into the phone receiver. "You plan for school, Jane told me. Well, I want to come over and I want to bring Jane. Yeah. I have an idea."

The idea would become the legendary "Cuba-duba caper." Ginny was embarking on higher education, and she had contained a burgeoning wanderlust throughout the year 1937. While dancing at the Hershey Ballroom, she had serendipitously met a man who owned a plane. Well, one thing led to another and it seemed that there were three seats available in that spring of 1938 on a roundtrip flight to the fashionable island of Cuba.

The ball started rolling quickly on the adventure when Cousin Jane got a job as a dance instructor in the YWCA. The manager respected the twenty-year-old girl for her knowledge of dancing and her ability to teach it. He recognized the growing interest in Latin dance and offered Jane an all-expense-paid trip to Havana to learn it at the source. This coincided with Ginny's penchant for travel and Louise's plan to go to college. The Havana School of dance would teach Jane the essentials in two weeks' time.

All the parents recognized the three as young but also responsible, hardworking adults and gave their approval. Clara trusted her daughter, but she gave Louise a hard look and said, "Stay clear of 'demon rum.'"

Louise queried, "When did you join the WCTU[2]?"

For the trio of travelers, Louise, Jane and Ginny, the trip would mean learning while they simultaneously enjoyed themselves "out of this world." The voyage began on the plane, a ten-seater. The passengers sat five on each side and the aircraft filled with Cuban men of various descriptions. The girls telegraphed their excitement to a pilot.

"So this is your first airplane ride?" he chuckled.

Jane responded, shifting in her seat, "Yeah, I'm scared to look down."

"Take a deep breath, he said. "You've probably been on a higher mountain. We're going a bit higher than Clark's Summit."

"What did you take onboard to Harrisburg?" Ginny wondered.

---

[2] Woman's Christian Temperance Union, an organization dedicated to the abolishment of alcoholic beverages.

"Sugar. Coming from Cuba."

"To bakeries?" Louise asked.

"Nah," answered the pilot. "To a good customer." He didn't reveal that the sugar was bound for a distillery. He went on, "Now, in Miami I get a load of Florida oranges."

The trio noticed that the men, who wore white suits and straw hats, were a friendly, energetic lot, speaking Spanish between themselves, and only as they neared the Havana airport did any of them approach the girls. A rotund man of about fifty noted Jane had a problem with heights and got the stewardess to bring her "café his way," an espresso loaded with sugar. She smiled, sipped and was jolted prematurely into a Cuban reality. This served to distract her from the landing, fast approaching. From their vantage point in the sky, Cuba looked like an overgrown caterpillar.

It was warm under a stand of gentle palm trees as the three grounded themselves. A turquoise cab, a Ford, approached at top ambulance speed.

"Por favor," said Ginny to the cabbie. "Hotel Habanero."

Their driver replied, "Gracias, amiga," and jolted into high gear. Certainly, the road was not a Pennsylvania city road, for it was rutted, patched and dusty. On the highway, Louise swore he hit eighty miles per hour, skimming a sidewalk at seventy and upon entering the town, never slowed for stop signs. Rather, he lurched from 30 mph to stop at intersections.

Louise said, "Could you slow down?"

Ginny said "Lentamente, por favor."

But the cabbie looked ahead and said forcefully, "No, it is a sign of weakness!"

Sighing with relief, the three were welcomed to their hotel by a bellman. The lobby seemed to go on and on, a dim cavern under woven ceiling fans. They passed a bar and dance floor to their right, a restaurant to their left, sparsely populated at the hour of five pm.

"I feel like I'm in Spain," Ginny said with wonderment at the high-ceiling Castilian architecture.

They registered with a clerk called Ramon, who proved as slow as to be the opposite of their cabbie. Ginny asked to see their room before any money exchanged hands. It was as if she had asked for a rare gem, and then Ramon proceeded to take his sweet time mining it. The indolent clerk rummaged through a pile of keys and left. There was not a clock in sight, still, thirty minutes passed by Jane's watch and she remarked, "I think the only fast service here is our cab driver."

They laughed weakly. The trio inspected Ramon's three rooms before they found a quiet one, not facing the mescal bar. One had to be rejected as it was directly over the hotel bar and had spiders in the bathroom.

Ramon chatted aimlessly. "This hotel is two hundred years old," and, "we have a good reputation, señorita."

Ginny focused on the lethargic Ramon, retorting, "Your rating would improve if you speeded my way to the lodging I called in a month ago."

Jane added, "You must get tired of people asking the time. Couldn't you put up a clock?"

Ramon's eyes widened as though enchanted, "A clock! Que buena idea!"

Finally, installed in a large room, the traveling trio plopped onto their beds in unison.

"Cuba-doooba," Louise sighed. They would sleep like loaves of melting sugar.

36

By the strands of daylight coming through the bamboo window shade, Louise could , see that it was a nice accommodation. Pink stucco walls were adorned by two oil paintings of a man and a woman dressed in traditional costumes. Originally vibrant, the paint had been dulled by years of tropical heat. A French door opened out onto an iron balcony over a garden one floor below. The tiled garden was inviting, filled with tables set for breakfast. A woman swept the tiles and Louise realized the sound of her swishing broom was what had awakened her.

Before you could say "que buena idea," Louise, Jane and Ginny were sitting in the garden sipping coffee made from beans grown just ten miles away. The aroma filled the courtyard as white-attired businessmen occupied matching linen draped tables. Jane was to put in a full dance day at the studio, which included a two-hour lunch break. Ginny and Louise wanted to shop. They would shop at fruit stands, dressmakers, cigar factories, leather tanneries, bakeries and souvenir shops.

That garden brought in a worldly breakfast bunch. The lazy air felt charged by the verve exuding from the hotel's patrons, such as the cigar buyer from Madrid, a jute merchant, a coffee manufacturer and several in the sugar trade.

Through the staccato of Spanish, the diners overheard a repeating theme, one they had heard in English at home: Hitler was going out of control. Clara Stitt worried about a repeat war in Europe and took to referring to der Fuhrer as "that barbarian." Hardly a morning in the garden went by without newspaper accounts of a German Army above the law and rumors of a manipulated German population.

Ginny whispered, "In the States, we have the Depression, and that's all the bad news I can handle!"

"Think about this: a strong-armed dictator with an army above the law. Now this is pretty bad news for Germany," Jane answered. "The government would tell you how to live. Can you imagine?"

Louise swallowed her black coffee, saying, "I really didn't like the high school principal. So I'd have a hard time with a dictator."

Hitler's activities could alter Cuban trade of their biggest crop: sugar. The growing of cane was economically crucial on this agricultural island.

Jane moved toward the dance studio, trying to recall what mambo steps she knew as her friends adjusted their broad-brimmed straw hats and ventured into the Havana sun. They strolled to the central marketplace, a series of wooden stalls shielded from the sun. Tropical fruit stands were full of limes, bananas and coconuts. Ginny picked up a plantain, cousin to a banana, asking the clerk about it in Spanish. A small mountain of green plantains rested in the stall of a woman with black braids named Maria, who told Ginny it was not a sweet, but used as a vegetable. She then offered the girls a sample of plantain chips—salty as thick potato chips. "Truly exotic."

The two scouted the neighborhood, stopping to inspect the colorful offerings of the even more colorful vendors. They viewed yellow pineapple candy, then jewelry made from seashells and watched as a man sculpted castanets, wooden hand-held implements associated with the passionate flamenco dance.

Jane joined them for lunch in the cool, palm-shaded garden, exclaiming, "The instructor treats me like Carmen Miranda! He saw that I knew mambo steps and started flipping me around the studio."

Louise asked, "How old is he?"

"Old… at least thirty."

Queried Ginny, "And about the class?"

"Well, we have three couples, and the instructor explains new steps by taking different partners to demonstrate."

"Hmmm," they replied.

Ginny wondered, "That sounds great so far, and now, you know the mambo."

Jane did a sinuous shoulder mambo, "Sort of, and Mr. Baile said I should go dance at our hotel because it's a good place to practice."

Louise whistled, "You don't say!"

Jane continued, "And how's the Havana shopping?"

They gave her an account of the market and a brown paper bag of plantain chips.

"It's remarkable!" Louise exclaimed. "In twenty-four hours, I met several nice people and enjoyed their wares. It seems that the Cuban economy depends on sugar, and we saw farmers selling sugarcane in the market too."

37

After sunset, their hotel world cooled enough so their heads cleared, and the "gringitas," as Ramon referred to them, ventured into the restaurant. While dining, they noticed the band assembling, and as they consumed the last of their caramel flan dessert, a guitarist began. The song was sweet at first, but soon he began a crescendo of thumps on the wooden body of his instrument and the band came to life with a trumpeting, drumming wave that started everyone's toes tapping.

The trumpet was a clear and melodious strain that they had heard before, but the conga drum was new to them. It was about three feet tall, with a goatskin drumhead, cylindrical, narrowing to a conical base, supported by a metal stand. The sound was metallic with deep tones, alerting their temperate ears.

As the maracas peppered the warm night, Jane assured herself, "So this is Latin rhythm."

Ginny replied, "Seriously tropical, dahling."

People came to meet the music. The spacious area soon held a small crowd of dancers. Women wore bright cotton dresses, men usually the traditional white. The youth seemed tireless as they spiraled around, but Louise noticed that the most accomplished, fluid teams were the elder dancers. It differed from the Sunset Grille, a magnet for the young. Here were the young at heart.

When the band finally rested, a charming couple in their sixties took the table nearest Louise, who then complimented the woman.

She spoke English better than her husband, and said with a giggle, "Manuela is my name and dancing is my game! It is good for the soul." Her silver earrings shone against brown skin, and she asked about their vacation to Cuba.

Jane informed her that she was in town to learn Latin dance at the source. Ginny added that it was her first big vacation and first international trip.

"I'm with them," Louise gestured with a tilt of her head.

This banter continued until the band came back to life. Manuela's husband, Pepe, was a bit of a clown, listening intently and chewing on an unlit cigar. His animated facial gestures seemed inspired by the women's frequent giggles.

"Pepe speaks no English," said Manuela and launched Pepe into impersonations of James Cagney: "You guys!" or "Why, you dirty rat!"

Jane exclaimed, "He's good," and then it was as if they joined an angel with a dirty face. When he learned that Jane wanted to learn Cuban dance, he invited her, proclaiming, "Josè! Baile es pipiolo.[3]"

Maybe Jane was experiencing the effect of practice or maybe it was the rum or maybe Pepe was indeed an expert dancer, but it seemed as if she floated on the Havana night air. She really picked up the vibration of Cuba that evening and would do well when she taught it.

Manuela advised seeing Morro Castle, which had protected the Havana harbor since 1589. Louise told Manuela about bakery life, and that prompted another suggestion to see a sugar plantation. "A piece of cake will have greater meaning," Manuela promised prophetically.

---

[3] Greenhorn

38

The rickety brown bus was supposed to resemble a cigar—a stogie, not a Montecristo. The passengers chuckled when they saw how the tail pipe appeared altered so it would look like a smoking cigar, and then they climbed aboard the "Seguro Cigar" tour bus.

Louise wasn't thinking of sweets on that fateful trip with Ginny and a handful of Floridian tourists en route to the plantation and factory. Sugar had always been that sandy, free flowing commodity that came out of the big bin in the bakery near the huge mixers. She saw vast fields of sugarcane, most of it twelve feet high, from the bus window. Men wore protective gear as they cut the plant by hand. They had gloves, hats and it was a necessary defense against spurting cane juice, badly aimed machetes and the burning sun.

"That's not farming, that looks like torture to me," Louise groaned to Ginny.

Ginny answered, "Well, it's like cotton. It was a product of slave labor. The slaves were brought here years ago to work in sugar. The sugar went back to Europe for flavoring food. The manufacturing of coffee and rum interact with sugar; you even need sugar to make your yeast bread."

Louise mused, "That was trading—real trade in goods, not money exchange for goods, as we're accustomed to."

They went from the field to a large mill under a canopy where after washing, giant wheels ground into the still hot cane, separating woody bark from cane juice. The group followed the cane extract to a tidier kitchen, with white-garbed employees, where an old man explained in Spanish and English how sugar starts as cane, grown for about two years. Next, workers added ten percent water, and then lime, to precipitate out colloids. The resulting mix was next centrifuged to pull out molasses. Further heating of the resulting brown sugar, followed by centrifuging, will yield a wet substance that becomes white sugar after it is filtered and dehydrated.

The visitors found the tour ended at a gift shop decorated with jute bags stretched over white walls, and these bags, predictably, were stamped: "Sugar CUBA."

They were greeted by a young woman who gave them small glasses of "café con leche," as it highlighted sugar, or was it the coffee? There were authentic representations for sale of Cuban sugar in tiny jute bags, coffee beans or bottles of rum.

The bit of caffeine got Louise's mind moving, and underneath all the Hispanic chatter, she noticed that the woman had a quality she had seen before. She saw a person who looked tired, even worn, but had retained her dignity. Louise bought a bag of coffee beans and spoke to her. It seemed that she ran the gift shop, an occupation uncannily similar to Louise's: long hours of selling and managing the store. She had wed an immigrant from Spain, and they had two children. The woman was grateful to be working and had a seemingly holy respect for sugar.

When their stogie bus pulled out of the sugar plantation, the humbled Ginny and Louise quietly agreed, "Cuba is one big sugar factory."

On the day before their return to Pennsylvania, Louise went from the beach down a different street where a family produced pies in their kitchen. The pies themselves were about as exotic as Carmen Miranda; however, it was the *way* they were sold that got Louise's attention.

The tiny store had a pair of large Dutch doors and with the bottom halves closed, the opening became a framed window and on the sill sat a number of steaming vegetable pies. Crunchy plantain crusts, filled with meat and topped with cheese drew customers toward the aroma. A pan of ice on the sill became a frame for coconut cream pie, small fried chocolate pies and tart lime pies.

The wafting scents wove their way into the nose, bending the brain and overpowering the bakery girl. She had never eaten a fried pie or a chocolate pie, and now sitting on a curb, she regarded the folded crust envelope, quite like a crisp crepe. The sugary bittersweet chocolate filling was a surprise, and she liked the dusting of cinnamon. One who knew Louise would agree that she had a resemblance to pie: heavy with sweetness- but with a sarcastic crust!

The scent of baked goods, she thought, the smell of this dough: one of the simple pleasures that helps you to live a little. Louise needed her rarest of vacations and now restfully smiled at the Dutch door display. She had to focus on school and leaving home.

There was an air of festivity on the plane home as the three rehashed their social life in Cuba. Jane had learned a lot. She had also taught José Baile where he could put his hands. He used certain dance moves in order to take liberties, to José it was sensuous, but Jane found it obnoxious. She felt his right hand on her bottom, and she elbowed his arm away. When he exceeded her limit again, she dug her manicured crimson nails into his bicep, saying, "No me gusta!" stomping out of the studio post haste. She danced at the hotel every night and never needed to buy a drink.

Ginny sighed, "I guess Harrisburg will seem mighty quiet after this. That Ricardo was so smooth! Oh! I almost lost my senses... till I got close enough to get a whiff of him."

Jane said, "Why, you could be engaged right now..."

Louise interjected, "If she wanted to be a captive for life on that island."

Ginny quoted, "All he wants is for me to help him get a liquor license."

Jane added, "Like you're really cut out for running rum."

Ginny shrieked, "I couldn't bear to kiss him; he reeked of cigars!"

Louise, arching an eyebrow, said straight faced, "A small price to pay for unlimited wealth."

Louise's Cuban dance partners spoke little English, and that was good because what came out of her mouth would have made their heads spin.

39

She was not taken in by Latino men. She really was not captivated by any particular type of man, but she deftly employed her antenna, keeping the suspect ones at bay. Her radar was sensitive to men who were kind, smart and particularly men switched on to life. It was a complex shield Louise wore that had dispatched men who never knew what hit them.

"Okay," she had said when a gentleman offered her a Cuban cigarette after a dance in the hotel. When he gestured toward his shiny 1938 auto, she said, "No, I only ride in busses shaped like cigars."

At the beach, a dirty old man who worked as a policeman sidled up to Ginny and Louise to make friends. When he got too close and insisted on following them, Louise whispered to her friend, "How do you say scorpion?" She turned to the man slowly, as if ready to dismiss him, gasped and brushing off his uniform epaulette, yelled, "Alacran!"

The policeman sped away, brushing himself about the neck.

Some days later, when they were accosted by a Spanish-speaking, amateur musician in the street, Louise declared, "The loudness of your voice is only exceeded by your costume."

The musician took her matter-of-fact tone as encouragement.

Next, Louise loudly insisted, "Take your maracas away! Go." Ginny was giggling too hard to translate when coincidentally, the officer of their recent acquaintance came around the corner, giving Louise the option to yell over her shoulder, "Police!"

As Ginny and Louise sped to the hotel, the rejected ones commiserated, reminiscent of whining dogs.

40

The trio spent their layover in Miami by having lunch and discussing their future plans.

Ginny and Louise agreed to share any research on colleges, while Jane would return to the Y and teach her hotly spiced dance steps to the next class. They looked refreshed in tropical themed short-sleeved dresses, small straw hats and crocodile heels.

Meanwhile, a man had recognized Louise in the airport and followed, summoning the courage to introduce himself. Now he approached their table with a pitcher of Coke from the fountain. "Please excuse me, are you one of the Stitt girls?"

Louise snapped to attend to the sound of a northern accent with a hard 'R.' "Yes, yes I am!"

His suit was of a new fabric, cream-colored, with a blue polka dot bow tie that went well with his hazel eyes.

"My name's Harold Simon," he cleared his throat. "I come with my mother to the Broad Street Market, but you wouldn't remember," he said sighing.

Ginny pulled out a chair for him. He was around thirty, had quite a smile, and a haircut like Clark Gable, a lock falling on his forehead.

"We eat a lot of that poppy seed hearth bread and get birthday cakes from Stitts."

"You do?" Louise said. "What brought you to Florida?"

"I'm employed by Alcoa Aluminum, in Pittsburgh. They sent me here on business. I brought my mother. So, for fun, Mother and I visited relatives in Miami."

Louise skimmed over events of the vacation, then surprised

everyone by giving a preview of her near future. "I work in the bakery. I'll have to stop soon because I'm looking for a school."

Harold asked, "To study what area?"

Louise mumbled, "Food." And she added, "Food is my subject."

The surprised girls chorused, "And then what?"

Louise snapped, "How should I know?" Then she sighed, brown eyes wandering to her friends. "I'm not one for paperwork. I like to sell food. I like getting a cookie for a kid. I like to suggest egg custard pies to grandmas with no teeth. I guess that's service, and you know how much I like the feel of stores."

Harold suddenly stared with his eyes doughnut glazed. "I've been to the Stitt market stand at Broad Street on Saturdays when it was so busy a boy couldn't squeeze through the aisle. People would wait five minutes to buy those sticky buns," he salivated. "When *you're* serving, the line goes faster, you call the regular customers by name, you tie string around the white cake boxes and you never stop smiling." The appetite place in his brain regarded the Stitt stand as sanctified, but he came back to the problem. "About a school, my cousin is a graduate of the dietetics school of... of the school in Ohio... Lake Erie College for Women.... dietetics... that's it."

Ginny said thoughtfully, "Food."

Harold grinned. "Provisions, in depth."

The flight home found Mr. Simon standing in the aisle, arms crossed, next to Louise's seat. Somehow, from the cockpit, the pilot's radio played *Moonlight Serenade*. She learned that he was an expert on the production of aluminum.

"I went to Miami to attend a meeting. The Pentagon is producing more... of everything really, and I went to advise a few generals."

She learned that he enjoyed the movies. "Have you heard about that book *Gone with the Wind*? Well, they're making a movie out of it—in color! Can you believe it?"

And she met Mrs. Simon, his mother. Mary Simon wore a black suit with a broad brimmed hat. "Pleased to meet cha'," she said, peering over tinted glasses, extending a gloved hand with which she effectively pinched Louise's nails to the exclusion of her hand. Mrs. Simon did not say too much owing to the farewell party that went late the previous evening.

Harold had had his eye on Louise ever since he saw her, elbow deep in hard rolls, but he was too shy to try to start something… until now.

When Louise exited the plane, Mr. Simon boldly said, "I don't want to stop talking to you. Can we meet next week?"

Louise agreed with a thrill, and her lizard heels fairly skipped toward her father and mother, who had come to collect the gang of three. For the first time in a long while, the way ahead seemed clear. Floyd had not worried about Louise. She could take care of herself as long as she had a car and a beautician. His wrapping machine was broken now, and he had to face a huge debt to get it wrapping the jellyrolls again.

41

Hun missed Louise in the meantime and decided to take comfort in Southern Comfort, Canadian gin and a woman named Inez, in that order. Hun was a man who could imbibe so gracefully that he had been referred to as "a man who knows how to have fun," when he really was so drunk, he couldn't see straight. Many of his acquaintances never knew about his nightly nightcaps. "I can hoooold my liquor," he told his father, smirking after he smashed the family Packard into an old iron hitching post.

"Sure you can," sneered his father, "but the question is, can you hold on to a steering wheel?"

Louise sensed Hun's painful situation and did her best to be understanding, but after all, she understood her pal was a lush. She had developed a clear intention to educate herself, and that focus saw her through the ensuing months.

A typical Saturday morning would find Hun on the phone pleading, but in a deranged tone that Louise had not heard before.

"Hi." A small word, which seemed to echo through stale air.

Louise could sense that his perpetual hangover was not clearing—not today.

"Remember all the fun we had? Ya' danchin' fool!" Hun's voice was getting louder. "Will ya remember me when yer... God knowsh where... with yer head in a book?"

Louise answered, "I'll remember. Hun, you sound trashed."

In a singsong reply he retorted, "Gosh, ya sound like my dad. Know what? I want thish gin... to to be my college. 'S right."

"Hun, you're out of your ever-loving mind. I'd like to pour a little milk on ya and throw ya out."

"Jush go study… see if I care, but before ya leave jush throw me out." And he hung up.

Louise thought about her Latin teacher, who once said, "Absentem laedit cum ebrio qui litigat: to quarrel with a drunk is to wrong a man who is not even there."

42

The Lake Erie College for Women accepted Louise into the class of '38. Painesville, Ohio, two hundred-fifty miles northwest of Harrisburg, was to be home for a while. She enrolled in the School of Home Economics. The letter of instruction from the school informed her of her schedule, the house rules, including dress code and the eight-hundred-dollar tuition.

"Gasp! Such a lot of money." Louise shook her head and gazed at Harold Simon across a table at Pomeroy's Tea Room.

He found himself attracted by her sparkle and independent nature, but he noticed she also had a way of underestimating herself. He gestured with a butter knife. "You've found a school with a history of believing in women. These schools are rare. That money is an investment in your future, and it'll be there always to make you a better life."

Louise replied, rolling her eyes, "Yeah, I'll be an educated cake monger. That'll really help me through the Depression."

Harold looked at the ceiling first, then responded, "You don't take anything seriously, do you?"

"Ha," she replied, keeping her face straight, her voice down. "I'm seriously thinking of asking you to go dancing tomorrow."

Harold, with woe in his voice, said, "I'll have to take a rain check, chickadee... I'm headed back to Pittsburgh." Placing his hand over her smaller one, he said, "I'll make it up to you, and I will find a way to visit."

Louise found Harold captivatingly smooth, a worldly man who had not been educated beyond his intelligence. He retained common sense in a world of growing confusion.

He was privy to government information; there were signs that the war in Europe was soon to expand. Harold informed her that the rumors of Hitler's plunder, bullying and conquests were all true. Remembering the newsreels at the Senate Movie Theater of Hitler's army engulfing other countries, Louise said. "My sister, Elaine thinks his name is 'Heil Hitler.'"

***

Life depressed proceeded, regardless of worldly tensions. Due to a subsequent auto repair problem, the couple found themselves in the bakery in its off hours.

"So," said Harold, entering the garage door, "this is where my bread is baked. Funny," he said, staring at stacks of large cotton sacks of flour, "how you eat something every day, and take it for granted... how it was made for you by people you never meet."

Louise sat on a stack of white flour sacks. Harold bent his head toward hers and kissed her cheek. She stood up again, placing her hands on his chest, kissing, kissing, *kissing*. Their breathing blew motes of flour in a cloud, and then her lips paused and her eyes flew open. Footsteps clicked on the stairs.

"Dot!" Louise sensed her sister's approach. Now she was a married working girl, living over the shop. Louise and Harold dusted themselves off, and exited the front of the garage. Dot came out the office door, picking up the Saturday mail.

"Dot," Louise shouted, towing Harold toward her. "I'd like you to meet Harold Simon."

After the introductions, Dot insisted they come to her place, and as Harold was seated in the small living room, he remarked, "Is that the smell of... sharp cheese?"

Dot and Louise came out of the kitchen with a macaroni casserole and three place settings.

"We already ate lunch at Pomeroy's," said Louise.

"Na! Ho! Nobody walks away from my macaroni!" Dot

spooned out wedges of creamy pasta with a crust. Harold was most impressed with that topping.

Dot explained, "I take hard rolls, butter, salt and cheese. It does have a nice crunch, doesn't it?"

Then the conversation turned to aluminum. Dot said sadly, "We just spent $10,000 on a new wrapping machine, so the shop is in a lot of debt."

Harold said reassuringly, "The situation in Europe is quite unstable, and I expect next year our country will start rationing metal, ladies, so be grateful for purchasing your machinery—to slice—it'll keep the place going."

Louise, popping a noodle in her mouth, asked, "Why should we ration metal? And by the way, are you a big cheese at Alcoa?"

Harold answered, "Not really. Now macaroni excepted, your sister is a bigger cheese in this establishment," he gestured toward the bakery. "The need for metal is to build up our army—all kinds of weaponry."

Dot and Louise laughed briefly at the thought of the bakeshop compared to Alcoa Aluminum, but Harold smiled quietly and responded, "You must realize that bread is a necessity and cake… well, cake makes life worth living."

"Pie? What is pie?" urged Louise.

Harold turned to Louise without much hesitation. "Pies are to Thanksgiving what prayer is to a church."

Dot whistled, and Louise declared, "I'm telling Reverend Waggenseller."

43

The school-bound Louise was smiling when she bid the bakery farewell. Incredibly, the Fegleys were still turning out baked goods after twenty-five years.

Sarah gripped her arm, saying, "Now don't you go marryin' the first man you meet."

Louise winked and thought of chocolate cupcakes. She felt Sarah was synonymous with cupcakes.

Bill said, "We sure will miss you, girl."

Louise nodded, choked by separation.

George rounded out the send off, smirking at Louise, who was like his kin. "If you intend to get into home economics, remember if it contains sugar, you know it, girl, like the back of yer hand."

Louise felt homesick and momentarily stunned by George.

"Yeah... sugar," she said, her vision blurring and heart full of bittersweetness, and nodded. "Sugar is sweet and so are you."

***

According to plan, Louise proceeded west to Painesville, Ohio, via the Pennsylvania Railroad, in the fall coolness of 1938. She appeared determined to the conductor who had collected her ticket, in her no-nonsense navy blue suit. The shoulder pads accentuated her waist, which had disregarded every Coke, creampuff and bonbon she had consumed. As the car rocked, she read in *The Patriot News* about Germany's new ally, Japan. There was also the news of Germany annexing a portion of Czechoslovakia. She alternated doing a crossword and gazing at leaves in the Allegheny Mountains that were turning a pleasant yellow, and this foliage hypnotized her. The train stopped in Pittsburgh for a half-hour and Louise exited the car, looking about the platform for a familiar face.

Harold ran from the stair waving with new emotion and finally catching her by the elbows. He steered her to a bench where they squeezed each other so hard that Harold was breathless. "I feel so glad just seeing you."

Louise laughed out of delight and exclaimed, "Oh, you kid!"

He looked into her brown eyes with his own. "I missed you... too much."

"I love you more than the smell of Wisteria."

"Who is Wisteria?"

Hugging him tight, she murmured, "I'll write, I promise."

"I'll be visiting when it's allowed," he said as the conductor yelled the final warning and the engine revved.

Louise shouted, "Yeah, come up and see me sometime."

Harold stepped back saying, "Cram for the quizzes and you'll do better in the finals..."

That was a lot of intensity to pack into a mere half-hour and at the twenty-eighth minute, he walked her to the car, kissed her cheek and pressed a brown bag into her hand. His imposing figure gave a wave as the train pulled out, and Louise's gloved hand returned it.

Back in her seat, she recovered her breath and then gloated in a sort of way where she was just fine, but something about the meeting had bothered her. True, it was a tiny nag, but a concern of her heart. Why did she want distance between herself and Harold? He was the perfect gentleman, he adored Louise and... and now what was the scent? The familiar odor of oven baking filled her senses—the aroma coming from the bag. She was delighted to find a small pie in the bag labeled "Quiche Lorraine." The accompanying note read:

Dear heart,

Can't wait until we meet again. Here is a bite of nutrition to get you in the mood for school.
Love, Harold.

When he might have given a box of chocolates, he had chosen pie.

She felt again a mixture of love, and it was as true as the accompanying confusion. She tasted and immediately approved the cheese tart. After a few more hungry bites, her estimate of Harold had improved immeasurably ("not only smart, but packs a great snack!") And then, her tooth met a stone. The man sitting across the aisle eyed her as she fished a tiny chain from the crust, and she faced the sunny window, putting the remnants of her snack on her lap. In the light of the train window, she pulled the chain up and finally saw that it was a necklace, suspending a sizable pearl. Louise gasped, cleaned it of piecrust crumbs and hooked it around her neck.

44

A bout that same moment, in Berlin, Hitler would munch on a "Berliner"—a jelly doughnut. He gloated gleefully over the engulfing of Austria. The "expansion" as Harold had referred to Hitler's pugilistic inclination, moved ahead. The German people, now groomed as the rightful leaders of the world, were taking Hitler's dictation well. Twist the truth, build up the military, expel undesirable citizens, and seize land in an effort to preside over Europe.

FDR had expected as much ever since his envoys had told him early in his second term of "an unnatural massing of war planes."

U.S. companies involved in producing war materiel were alerted to plan for the impending entry of America in a fight against Germany.

Harold Simon, with his position of assisting those in charge of the aluminum company, had his work cut out for him.

Though she was an avid newspaper reader, Louise faced away from politics and the Depression and was happy to have found her place at Lake Erie College. The grounds were encompassed in green lawns and ivy-shrouded buildings, framing a school, giving fortunate students the tools to better themselves, in spite of the Depression. The faculty of men and women were often hired from nearby Cleveland.

An early experience revealed to Louise what a sweet education it had been to live inside the sugary confines of Floyd and Clara's bakery. Home Economics provided training in the construction of clothing, the processing of food and considerably less about home economy. Ahh, but on a deeper level there was chemistry, physics and studies of fabric strength, the heating and cooling of comestibles and then record keeping of all types of proceeding experiments.

Louise was minding her own records in the food lab, assigned to make and analyze the condiment, mayonnaise. She was entering her findings into a composition book when a rotund girl in a plaid dress sidled up to her, peering into the bowl filled with mayo.

"Well, this looks tasty, very tasty. My name's Tina, Tina Garfinkel."

"Greetings," said Louise, who was entering the last of the data.

Then Tina, fresh from the class on smoking meat, showed Louise the contents of her lunchbox. The aroma of smoked ham emanated as the tin opened. They exchanged pleasantries. Tina had led a luxurious life in Cleveland where her father managed a department store. Louise noticed Tina's textbooks were book-marked by crisp ten-dollar bills. "They come in so handy."

"I'll bet they do," quipped Louise.

While growing up, Tina had missed a few of the basics and this astounded Louise. Thereafter, the two bonded, awed by their differences. At Lake Erie, Tina learned many skills, among them, ironing, making her bed and building a sandwich.

"This smells great," Louise exclaimed. "Do you have any plans for this meat?"

"What do you mean?"

Louise laughed. "We can make our lunch out of our school projects."

"Okay!" Tina watched as Louise applied mayonnaise to four slices of rye bread.

"I like this because of the caraway seeds," said Louise, then asking Tina to wash her hands and cut up the sizable slab of ham. Lettuce completed the sandwiches, and Tina stood mesmerized by every step.

"I've never made a sandwich," Tina announced.

"What?"

"I have a maid who cooks at home," she continued.

Louise was smirking, yet there in her face was astonishment. "Who's cookin'? This is what's called 'throwing our lunch together.'"

Tina took a bite, getting mayo on her chin. "Oooh, delicious," and asked, "Where did you learn to 'throw it together'?"

Louise looked at the sky, saying quietly, "At Mamaw's knee."

"You're so lucky, Louise. Ya think ya could give me the recipe for this?" She said it gesturing with the crust as if it were a magic wand.

Thus, as their lunch hour ended, Tina entered the recipe into her notebook, complete with a smudge of grease. She titled the entry: "Louise's Sandwich Recipe."

45

The dormitory, College Hall, was home to one hundred and nine students, the whole of the college's student population. Freshmen lived in the upper, smaller rooms. When Louise arrived in her room, she opened a letter from Harold.

> *Dear Louise,*
>
> *I trust you're finding yourself at home there in Painesville, but I miss you. We are even more involved in producing war materiel. It seems like the Army wants more, ever since the U.S. gunboat "Punay" was sunk by Japan last year. I don't think the U.S. can stay neutral the way things go in Europe. It's getting difficult for people to get out of Germany. It's a dictatorship, after all.*
>
> *Well, I will see you in a week at the dance. Please let me drive you home for Thanksgiving. I'd like to take you to New York too.*
>
> *Until then,*
> *Harold.*

Louise whistled, mumbling, "Harold Simon thinks big." Next, she opened an envelope decorated with the watercolor image of a model in a sailor suit. "Wonder who this is from," she whispered, knowing Dot was the artist.

> *Dear Louise,*
>
> *How's school? Here I am in the office, taking a lot of orders for Christmas wedding cakes. I don't get much work as a substitute teacher; you'd say my career's iffy. I*

got a week of teaching music, and Elaine was in the class! She didn't want the kids to know we were related because they would kid her about it.

I was very amused to read of your class on piecrust. What was the topic of your essay? "The Allure of Baked Goods?"

Christy and I have the cabin finished at Silver Lake. It is beautiful, and I'm happy to hike around there.

Well, the drivers are coming in and I have to get shakin'.

Love,

Dot

46

"The Allure of Baked Goods" essay caused a stir, the reason being Louise's statements about pies. She put forth the position that the pie had become a necessity for the American homemaker. While bread is the staff of life and cake is for the special occasion, pie, with its high-calorie textures is home itself! Furthermore, since the young women of the country were tapped for jobs outside of their homes, the pie was set on a similar course. It would soon be made en mass in bakeries, owing to its labor-intensive nature. Then she went on to select Amanda Smith of Mrs. Smith's Pies as her prototype of things to come.

Hermoine Crum, baking aficionado and Louise's instructor, responded first by marking the paper A-. The instructor had then penned, "You have a creative theory which requires more data to support it." She assigned Louise to make five pies and endeavor to prove her statements regarding labor intensity.

Louise's moaning was like fuel to an engine. She began making five different pies with different crusts. *I wasn't meant to sweat over a hot stove*, she thought as she made fruit filling and created piecrust. She found the crusts required an average of thirty minutes, filling, forty minutes and baking another forty-five minutes. Her second paper did not focus on these numbers, but rather upon the shopping for ingredients, cost of gasoline, oven heat and the *value* of the homemakers' time. Louise concluded that these costs alone would justify the purchase of a bakery pie. Beginning with the selection of the fruit and other ingredients, all the way to the slicing of one apple pie, with all its cinnamony goodness, a homemaker would need three hours to make this pie.

The oppositional Crum was hesitant to concede her point, and though herself a busy tenured professor, found room in her schedule to make and time a pie. While rolling out the pie dough, she gasped. She had been basing her personal stand that a pie could be baked in seventy-five minutes on the use of *canned filling*. Crum was not in the habit of miscalculating! She, as a busy career woman, had inadvertently proven Louise's thesis.

Meanwhile, Louise cajoled the school secretary to permit a phone call to George Fegley at Stitt's. She asked him for the time required to bring a pie into the world.

Gripping the receiver with an oven glove he declared surely, "Hey, hon, well, based on the doin' it all by hand, I'd say, two hours, fifty minutes. If you knew what you's doin' that is."

47

Autumn Oomph. This was the theme of the Lake Erie harvest dance. As Louise was a member of the Drama Club, she helped decorate the gymnasium.

In the midst of this, she and two club members became inseparable friends. The three hung innumerable "leaves" overhead in an elaborate plan to cut the strings during the dance, and so, engineer a leaf fall on the dancers.

"You see how straight my hair is?" said the perspiring Louise. "I've got to get to the beauty shop—now!"

Mary Lane chuckled. "I cut my own hair, and I guess it shows," she added, adjusting a large copper barrette at the nape of the neck.

They took Mary's car to a church bazaar and purchased Indian figures made of corncobs. They used Rose Marco's tempera paints to disguise the punch bowl as a huge inverted Pilgrim hat. This last escapade would become a highlight of their college years. Year after year, just for a laugh, Rose wrote to Mary and Louise on her Christmas card, "Remember when Louise spelled out OOMPH in ice? What a punchbowl!"

***

Louise's friends were impressed by Harold Simon, and predictably, Louise made light of her relationship with him. "We met in the Miami airport, but he says he worshipped me from afar."

Mary asked, "Afar from where?"

"Across the market aisle, over the display glass. See, the glass protected the sticky buns. He smelled fresh sticky buns and thought if I sold such a great treat, well, that made me okay."

Rose interjected, "Louise, he doesn't love you for being a bakery girl. He loves *you*."

Mary laughed, "You are the treat."

Louise clucked, "Well, dahling, we shall see."

And there he was at the door, a man of the world, sharply, distinctively dressed, as suited a college social event. He speeded to Louise and guided her outside behind a tree for a discreet embrace, a hug likened to aluminum foil surrounding a sticky bun—one with nuts.

Harold whispered, "I missed you so much."

"A likely story."

He stepped back, his eyes narrowing. "Did you miss me?"

"Well I wrote you, didn't I, kid?"

"Oh yes, yes, a poem—in Latin—and I don't even know what amare…"

Louise cleared her throat and quoted, "Amare et sapere vix deo conceditur. It means: it's difficult to love and be wise." She took his arm and reentered the gym. The clarinetist commenced to play *The Sheik of Araby*, and the room's occupants synchronized. Hands clasped, bows bounced, and pumps pumped.

Rose and Mary had been dancing with Case men, that is students attending Case Western, in Cleveland, and nobody stopped for a half-hour. Even the wallflowers twirled, holding punch cups extended.

At intermission, the six revelers claimed a table where the Case men monopolized the conversation, bragging how as athletes, they could dance all night.

Rose responded, "We have no trouble draggin' our hooves, man."

"Yeah, she's an equestrian, man!" said Mary.

Harold asked, "A rider? In shows?"

Rose answered that the L.E.C. Equestrian Club went to shows and won numerous ribbons.

The Case men turned the subject to horse racing, and Louise

got irritated, mostly because they were inebriated. She smoothed her hair and said, "She doesn't *race* her horse, she is a good rider and she's helping train the club members."

Harold turned to Louise, smiling. He was polished, she thought, next to these so-called "men."

The men got up in unison to refill their punch cups, which they looked into and yelled, "You're too small!"

Harold waved his hand through the air, as if clearing the alcohol out of it. Over her shoulder Louise stated, "In the good old days, children like you were left to perish on windswept crags."

Rose laughed. Encouraged, Louise kept a straight face and went on, "In meri muri miri mori. The mouse dies happily in a sea of wine."

Rose and Mary whispered, "We'll dance the punch right out of 'em." Indeed the two from Case had chosen partners who had planned and set up the dance for a good reason. They had their hearts set on having a ball, and they were not going to let anything stop them.

Louise and Harold discussed the world of aluminum manufacture, and Harold took her hand. "We're bracing for the president to stop the export of munitions. Europe is crumbling as the day goes by."

The band beat out the tune, *A Tisket a Tasket*. Faster than you could say, "I lost it," Rose leaped on the bandstand and sang the lyric.

"She's got it, she's got it," Louise sang along. Harold, still holding her hand, stood up and guided her to the floor. The social whirl escalated to the point that the chaperones lost all their somberness as the swing fest progressed.

One of the Case men lost his partner because the equestrian trainer, a quiet redheaded man, grabbed Rose for the next dance.

The leaves fell on cue, just before the band closed up for the night, by playing *Cheek to Cheek*. The dancers had come away from their studies and employment to let every worry cease. They had visited a dance haven called "swing."

48

Louise and Harold spent a long weekend in New York City. She had lots of laughs; Harold valiantly conducted a campaign to capture her heart. What he couldn't know was that she did not wish to be contained. She had been suspicious from the start because he seemed to have an ulterior motive and that, simply stated, was marriage. Harold was not prepared for what would transpire.

The low point of their trip happened in the Lincoln Hotel ballroom. There had been a quiet, candlelit dinner for two. After a cheese rarebit appetizer, Harold passed Louise a small black velvet jewelry box.

When opened, a large amethyst shone in the dim light of the dining room, and this widened Louise's brown eyes with a seemingly violet reflection. After sliding it on her left ring finger, Harold tentatively ventured, "Well, I... had hoped... you'd... consider it an... engagement ring."

Louise smiled at the flattering proposal. "Dahling, you really shouldn't have. I'm in school now, and can't think about this."

Harold pressed for ten minutes, "Later—after graduation..."

They sipped a sweet wine, ate dinner and Louise digested his words as she chewed a parker house roll. She smiled, explained that she was not ready, and he continued pressing her. By the time dessert disappeared, Harold was still urging her to reconsider.

"I said no." Louise exited the room, following a corridor to the service elevator. She went out, feeling the damp of November on her long-sleeved dress, walked a couple of blocks and breathed out her sense of discomfort, relating to who would control her future. After pacing the sidewalk, her high heels halted. She whispered, "He behaves like he owns me!"

Then she returned to the hotel service elevator, where a woman of color stood in a full-length fur coat. The woman stepped back, and they both boarded the elevator.

Louise detected something familiar in the exotic woman's café au lait face. Where had they met?

"Excuse me, are you from Harrisburg?"

Turning, the woman displayed heavy makeup, pearl earrings and a smile, "Philadelphia."

Louise said, "I'm from Harrisburg and thought I knew you."

The door opened and the woman observed, "You may've seen me here—I work here."

The ballroom level buzzed with preparations for the evening. Harold joined Louise and thankfully turned his topic to the assembling band.

"You know, we should have a nice evening, listening to Artie Shaw... and I hear he's got a good singer too."

Soon the band played a rousing introduction, *Begin the Beguine*, and as the tune came to a supposed close, the female vocalist made her entrance. Louise gulped her Coke, gasping, "I just came up on the elevator with her!"

"You did?"

"Yeah... now I know... I saw her picture in the lobby. Billie Holiday. We spoke!"

"Why all the excitement?"

Louise rolled her eyes and as if answering, sang along with Billie's slower version of *Begin the Beguine*.

Then, Louise found herself with Billie once more. Billie pointed a garnet lipstick as Louise entered the ladies' room. "Oh, Miss Holiday, I have to thank you. You did a lot for my mood. I had a sort of disagreement with a boyfriend."

Billie turned to Louise saying, "Love's like a faucet, it goes on n' it goes off."

Louise said thoughtfully, "Why, sure."

The singer asked, "Now what is it you want? I mean what did you look for to happen tonight?"

Louise said certainly, "I came to New York to have fun."

"Well, what cha waitin' for? Go have fun."

"Hee-hee." Louise was charmed and ventured, "And what did you look for... coming here?"

Billie blurted out "Money... well that's just really to get myself on stage. I came here to sing."

Louise added, "This is a great hotel."

"Like I said, I'm here working with the band. Colored folks don't stay in hotels."

Louise took this in with a start. The undisputed star of the show wasn't allowed to sleep in the hotel she worked in. Her picture stood in the lobby, but she didn't dare stand next to her own picture. That was probably why they had run into each other in the service elevator.

"Yeah," Louise quickly changed the subject. "I'll go have fun, now."

Billie slowly added, "You know, I will too."

When Louise related that "Lady Day" was only permitted in the hotel ballroom to Harold, he had remarked that, "It's just the way things are."

"Humph." said Louise. Then she thought about money. *Why, I don't have enough money to stay in a hotel, but if I wanted, I could do it because I'm white.*

She pondered over the events of the weekend. She had slipped out of Harold's clutches, and yet he insisted she wear his ring. She looked forward to resuming her studies, thankful that she didn't have to pay tuition.

On the trip home, she would experience a few flashes of insight. Billie Holiday and Louise had something in common: they had worked half of their young age of twenty-two and didn't have much in the way of money. Saying this to Harold brought him to add, "We are in a depression, kid."

Louise snapped, "Too bad I have no talent."

Harold steered with his left, put his right arm around her stiff shoulders, saying, "Oh I wouldn't say that." Then, her talents, he thought, were myriad and nameless.

49

Mary and Rose met Louise at the train. On the way through Painesville, back to school, in Mary's Dodge, they rehashed the holidays. Louise said with a sigh, "He wants to tie the knot," and flashed her deep purple stone.

Her friends cooed, "He's a real catch."

"Well, are you engaged?" Mary asked eagerly.

"I told him no. And I found out something. I'm not ready for that. Even if I weren't studying. I don't need to be keeping house now." Louise's friends acted disappointed, then, she changed the subject.

She went on to describe how much she had needed to have fun. City excitement, dancing and seeing those creative, Manhattan store windows had been a tonic. "I rubbed shoulders with Billie Holiday."

Rose whispered, "She sings *Pennies from Heaven!*"

Louise replied, "Yeah, and she sang it." Then she related just how she met the singer.

"She's beautiful and did a good show. We talked a little about love," here Louise smiled. "How it's like a faucet... it goes on and it goes off."

Rose and Mary went uncharacteristically silent, then Rose sang another tune recently heard on the radio. "She sings, *Night and day, you are the one...*"

***

Nineteen thirty-eight saw the opening of the next semester at Lake Erie. Louise found a note in her mailbox in a neat handwriting. Miss Hermoine Crum asked her to come to the office.

The Marcel-coiffed Crum sat and offered Louise a seat. The instructor looked over her wire rims. "Miss Stitt, I have not been happy with your performance for the first semester. You, of course, are still immature in the world of home economics. Based on your lack of tidiness and organization, you'd probably get a C. However, you have come up with... ideas that have promise, and they cannot be ignored. I've given you a B minus."

Louise murmured, "Thank you, Miss Crum."

The instructor continued, "I appreciate your insight on the working woman and the sale of pies. Perhaps you'll follow in the steps of Mrs. Smith and her pies." She managed a smile.

Louise digested this and went on, "Miss Crum, I don't need a job in a bakeshop. Why, I grew up in a bakery."

Surprise overtook Hermoine Crum. "Oh!" And a strange, instant truth dawned on Crum, that here was a student who had more firsthand bakery experience than her zealous instructor.

"These... these pie selling ideas are not new ideas. They are... facts of life. And the life of a bakery girl isn't easy. I'd have to say no to running a bakeshop like Mrs. Smith does."

"Okay," replied the instructor slowly as she stood up from her desk chair. "I see how you've benefited by your years in the production of pies. Here is the outline for the next semester. Pay attention to the study of desserts and baked goods. Next time, the grading won't be so lenient."

Louise backed out of the office, smiling, "Happy New Year."

***

The Dessert Study was the subject at lunch. Louise happened upon Tina Garfinkel in the cafeteria. Tina felt taken aback, when after scanning the study directions, Louise belted out a huge laugh, and then Tina a few of her own laughing blasts. Tina read,
"Dessert Study-

Take your knowledge of home economics further. As graduates, you will be applying your skills in industry. Your assignment is to take the product you have been studying to the public. Describe the process. Tabulate the response of the public to your product. Will you sell or distribute samples? For instance, a church bake sale would record the setting of the sale, the patrons and the type of product sold. Any money exchanging hands would be recorded. Note: do not use a church bake sale for your project. Half of your grade depends on this assignment. "

Louise, weak with laughter, squeezed out in a whisper, "She wants me to peddle my pathetic pies in Painesville!" She laid her head on the table, pounded it, then heaved out more derisive laughs.

Tina responded, "Well, how could you do the assignment otherwise?"

"It has to be done here. I don't have any connections in town."

"You've got the students, faculty, workers. Of course you can serve pies here."

Louise's eyes lit up suddenly. "Workers at the Knox and Austin Houses. Why, there are droves of laborers coming to work there."

"Hey! Tina queried, "My project in meat preservation could sure use your help! What if we help each other?" And that was the beginning of the inimitable meat preserve/pie peddling project.

Louise now was imbued with enough enthusiasm to speed herself to the Kilcawley Library. Its dark paneling was reassuringly calming. Thinking with her nose, Louise recalled the roastingly hot Stitt pie oven and, well, an olfactory dictionary of scents. She ran them by her mind. For flavor identification, the top piecrusts were stamped A for apple, B for blueberry, C for cherry. Cherry. Yes, cherry is a good, friendly flavor. Some research about flavor revealed that human sense of smell plays a large part in how a flavor is perceived. Dietetic schools of the East Coast found apple to be a favored flavor. West Coast schools favored cherry. Louise thought she had sold more cherry pies at work.

But after you have baked that pie, what's to be done with it? Taking product to public? Could be sale... could be taste test... incorporate sense of smell. Louise pondered the pie predicament.

***

February saw a deep freeze on the romantic sector of Louise's life. She felt a sense of love for Harold and yet did not wish to see him. Her brain—tentatively—said yes to Harold, while her heart said, "Go out and make pies!" Winter, along with the inevitable assignments, had invited her inside, like a cat attending to catnip by a fireplace. Meanwhile, unknown to Louise, her beau inspected Pennsylvania steel mills.

Louise opened her mail to discover that Dot made her a large, white valentine with red lace, signed by the entire family. Enclosed was a photograph of the bakery truck fleet, numbering nine. Louise recognized all the faces behind the wheels, including her own.

Elaine sent a letter, typewritten on company stationery:

> *Dear Louise,*
>
> *Wasn't Dot's valentine a dilly? I miss you. Let's go to the movies when you get back! Have you been to any dances?*
>
> *I wish I were glam. I want to cut my hair-oh it needs so many bobby pins, but Mother won't hear of it. Mother and Mamaw have kept their hair long for too long and tied into a bun it's so old fashioned.*
>
> *Mother was sick last week, and I tried to help by doing the laundry. I even added starch—Mother liked it okay. Mamaw said I should not have starched the*

underwear.

Pawpaw and I ate candy and broke our Lenten pledge.

I earned $8.00 by wrapping crumb pies. There were so many of them, I don't want to look at another pie!

Love,

Elaine

Bethlehem, PA

April 2, 1939

Dear Louise,

I hope you're doing well in school. I do think of you, but feel at times like a fireman fighting for my life. As you know, Europe is sliding underneath the Third Reich. The worst I heard this week from my uncle, who is Jewish and got his family out of Germany. He told my father that now, Jews are having driver's licenses revoked, they can't get into movies and are being fired from government jobs. I hear Nazis want to take over Poland!

This is bad news. I don't see this country staying neutral.

Well, hope to see you in summer

Love,

Harold

The Home Ec test kitchen's radio kept a swingin' rhythm. Benny Goodman's clarinet was playing *Louise* as Louise and Tina stuffed sausage. Tina's meat preservation study had evolved. Now she had dropped her plans to preserve mainly with chemicals and focused on packaging. She got ideas as she talked and talked. Louise changed the subject.

"Father heard Milton Hershey got rich by going small with the 'Hershey Kiss.'"

Tina exclaimed, gesturing with a sausage link, "You go with

little pies! Maybe I'll make finger sausage!" Louise rolled her eyes in disbelief; yet knowing small links would have eye appeal.

Louise's study met with skepticism by Hermoine Crum. She proposed to sell small pies to workmen during lunch hour and do a survey to see why they bought or did not purchase the pie. She knew she had to make the test pies herself because Tina, though well meaning, admitted she was a "bird-brained baker." Louise taught her to roll out piecrust though and lay it on pie tins. The baking, she knew from her father, to be best on night shift.

The "pie study store" had to be close to the customers. Louise bartered with the foreman of the carpentry gang—five large cherry pies for a small amount of scrap lumber, from which he fashioned a tidy closet-like structure with a Dutch door. It held a chair, an electric hotplate and fan with an extension cord.

From the recesses of her mind, Louise reproduced the Cuban bakeshop of her summer vacation, with headier aromas. Analyzing the sensual experience of dessert, she felt, would make her grade. Tina's responsibility was pie transport from the kitchen and surveying of customers after the sale.

The week of sales to the public began with cherry pies cooled by the fifty-degree spring weather. However, a pot of cherries sat on the hotplate so that the sugary aroma wafted beyond Louise's booth by the fan. Louise wore a white-bibbed apron and a red beret, coincidentally, resembling a pie. She accessorized by pinning a bunch of cherries on her apron—made of plastic Bakelite.

I'm glad my permanent wave still holds, she thought, sighing.

She put a few pies on the shelf of the Dutch door at eleven a.m. Workmen were already alerted by the foreman, who had shared test samples, the previous week

A stream of men came out to the pie sale. Some brought lunchboxes or brown bags containing sandwiches. Tired but grinning, Louise greeted them as if she were back at home, bagging up bread in the store. "May I help you?"

"Sure looks good," said a white-haired carpenter.

"Haven't had a piece o' pie since I don' know when!"

"I'll have two, please."

As the pies were consumed, Tina approached, explaining it was a Home Economics project and would they answer a few questions as to why they paid for this particular pie.

The two students closed the portable bakery at one o'clock. They sold twenty-four pies to all the twelve workmen as well as to four passing students. The team carted the electrics back to their rooms and fell into bed, asleep before head hit pillow. Night shift was approaching.

Back in the kitchen, brandishing a tin pie plate, Louise sang out, "Produce we must!"

"Yeah," the bedraggled Tina said. "I guess you think we'll bake more than twenty-five tonight."

Help arrived when two faces appeared at the door. Louise yelled, "Rose, Mary! How'd you know we'd be here?"

"You cherry queens! We saw what you made," Rose whispered.

Mary added, "Yeah, the kids from drama club shared a taste of your pie. We were eating lunch and you were the topic of conversation."

"Ooh," Louise laughed. "With whom?"

Mary answered, "First just the two from the club and us..."

Rose interjected, "And we were a bit loud and your instructor came to see the pie."

Tina gasped, "Crum? Looking over your shoulder?"

Rose giggled, "Crumbling."

Mary became serious now, "She had this look... impressed and disappointed."

Louise straightened her apron. "Let me guess. She liked the pie, but she didn't want to give *me* credit for it."

Rose replied, "Well, I'm anxious to hear what she says to you because what she said at the cafeteria was, 'I'd like to see the recipe.'

That night's work went easily enough with double the bakers and a cutback on labor. Louise decided to make crunchy streusel topping, sprinkled over the top of the pie, allowing cherries to shine through the center. Pies baked, and the process resumed. The week was hectic, and as the word got around, pies disappeared. Tina's survey was gratifying.

She read the responses to Louise in her dorm room: "The most common reason to buy pie was, 'I was hungry,' and 'I ate it yesterday and I'm back for more.' Then, it was 'Nice mouth-watering smell,' next 'Good memories of pie eating at home,' then, listen to this, 'The bakery lady was sweet.'"

"How many said that?"

Tina said, "Nine. In some way they refer to you as part of their decision to buy."

Automatically, Louise laughed her self-deprecating shriek.

Tina corrected her, instantly... knowingly. "Louise, try to be serious for me. This is an appropriate response. The saleslady has a value. Think of the shops where you trade. The salesman can make a big difference as to how the product is perceived."

Louise smiled, raised one eyebrow and whispered, "Yeah?"

Tina continued, "Remember, my family has a store. I know all the people selling there and not one has as much of what you have."

Louise chuckled, "Oh, I have *it*. I am the 'it girl' of Broad Street Market."

Tina sighed, looking her in the eye. "You laugh. Belittle yourself, but I'm telling you, this is a genuine finding. If a shopper is given any choice, he'll return to places where he's helped the most. They like to shop where it feels comfortable because spending money can be painful. Choosing and finding products isn't always easy, and salesladies have a position of," here Tina grabbed Louise's arm, "influence in a sale."

While this *it* is difficult to define, Louise had *it*, whether she sold or bought. She came by the ability honestly, for Floyd was a salesman's salesman, and Clara was the ultimate customer. No matter which side of a market counter Louise found herself on, she was at home.

Finally, Louise's Dessert Study submitted that her sale succeeded due to a close proximity to customers, a high-level product produced on the day of the sale and customer assistance. The factor of sensory impact was addressed, based on the survey. First, the customers *heard* about the availability of cherry pie. Second, they *saw* the booth and the pies on the shelf. Third, they *sensed aroma.* Finally, fourth and fifth, they *held and tasted* the dessert. Based on their taste approval, they returned for more of the same.

Louise carefully submitted costs against profits, which happened in the presence of free labor and the cafeteria being the only competition.

Hermoine Crum read Louise's paper and reread it. She wrote in red pencil: "Original!" Then she put on her spring coat and left her office to find a cherry pie in Painesville, at the Gartman Model Bakery.

50

No shots were fired when Germany took over Austria. Hitler referred to it as annexation. Hitler and Eva Braun subsequently visited Vienna, strolling surreptitiously down a side street. They were wearing plain clothes and aviator sunglasses, but he really could not disguise the moustache, so when he opened the door of a shop labeled "Konditorei," the owner removed his chef's hat nervously.

"Adolf, let us have some of this cake!" Eva enthused.

His eyes shifted, never leaving the desserts. "Coffee and..." Hitler pointed toward...

"Black chocolate tea cake. We make it with black tea," prompted the baker.

Eva requested, "Sachertorte please."

The two slices of chocolate cake, dusted with sugar, were served. The coffee was steaming from glass cups. Hitler didn't need caffeine, as he was already sweating from the effects of amphetamine. He sipped nervously.

Eva had always had a calming effect on Der Fuhrer. "Edeldolph, y' must try our cake. Don't be afraid," she cooed his pet name.

"Cake?" he said, shoveling a huge hunk between his lips, then speaking with his mouth full. "Why should I be nervous about cake?"

Eva stirred cream into her cup and looked over her shoulder toward the baker. "Edeldolph, y'need to take a rest from... annexation."

His moustache twitched as he barked, "Why- should- I- be nervous? This week I expanded the navy—bigger ships! Sixty-nine of them over two oceans!" He brought his coffee cup down with a pounding crack, and it smashed, sprinkling glass onto the floor.

***

Louise spent her summer break in Harrisburg, where the bakery continued to persevere through the Depression. Floyd employed eight people in the shop and four drivers, who sold the baked goods to stores. Dot had not been able to teach and continued to manage the bakery office. Similarly, Christy, her spouse, was also a Stitt employee, who now knew the work of the entire place from the ovens to the wrapping of cupcakes.

Adolescent Elaine was getting tall, and as she grew, her blond curls turned a mahogany brunette. The family certainly doted on Elaine, even though she showed no interest in the business of baking. One Saturday in June found the three girls strolling to a downtown movie theater. Elaine was flanked by her sisters.

Dot aired her frustration, shared by many that year. "Work *is* scarce, but there's not one opening for a teacher. Still, I have an income, but Father makes me kind of do the work of two."

Louise said, "You're miffed, I'm confused. Why am I studying? To what end?"

Dot asked, "Dietetics isn't enough, kid?"

"Nah, I'm not cut out for the world of Dietetics, kid."

Elaine added, "I'm hip to that." Although she felt impressed by her father's ability to produce bread for a dime a loaf, she was already seeking a path away from the bakeshop on Jefferson Street.

They went to several movies that summer and each began with a newsreel. They saw vivid accounts of how the Roosevelt government got Americans back to work, sports heroes' accomplishments and a growing discord in Europe.

Dot complained, "It seems that every time I see a newsreel, another country is taken over or being threatened!"

51

When Louise returned to Lake Erie in the fall of 1939, she did not know it would be her final year of higher education. She pursued the Home Economics curriculum, as it was the course of most interest. She finished the academic year, went home and elected not to return. Rose Marcos and Mary Lane became her pen pals for life. Her relationship with Harold Simon died for lack of Louise's attention. He earnestly wanted to place Louise on a pedestal, but she found the air up there to be stiflingly unreal.

Miss Hermoine Crum did not agree that Louise turn her back on higher education. She summoned Louise to her office after she heard Louise was to leave Lake Erie. Her marcelled waves trembled. "Why, you're casting aside a perfectly good record... career... future!"

Louise thought it odd that her instructor now seemed to value her so much. "Thank you for being interested in me," she smiled. "I'll miss you. But the truth is: I don't like analyzing food. I'd rather eat it."

Miss Crum then launched into an impassioned plea for Louise to come back to her senses. Without either of them realizing it, Louise had become Miss Crum's inspiration!

She clutched her own elbows in a vise grip, in her intended effort to sway the maverick student. "I didn't want to reveal this, but I have some good news, and I want you to hear it first. I'm engaged to be married," she inhaled.

Louise offered, "Congratulations!"

"It's no small feat for an old maid schoolmarm. And I do believe it's because..." She paused, then rapidly spit out,

"Because I've put 'm on a diet of cherry pie. Homemade."

Louise gasped, stifling a shriek.

"We want to open a bakery. I had hoped you'd be the one to train the staff as to sales." She advanced toward Louise. Her posture had shifted from pleading to begging.

Louise said, "I'm not interested in teaching."

Louise was surprised and she imagined what it would be like to report to Miss Crum as part of a gainful occupation.

Hermoine pressed on, in some sort of cherry stupor, "The crumb topping, the olfactory impact, the color red! Why it all makes perfect sense. Won't you reconsider?"

Ironic, is it not, when the shoe is on the other foot? More accurately, a work shoe, sturdy and white was ready in Crum's plan, waiting for Louise, but true to form, she would return to Harrisburg in spectator pumps. The war soon provided a new set of shoes for the unsuspecting Louise—also white.

52

World war loomed ahead of the populace, a fight every citizen, even those in Germany, hoped would not come to pass. However, Hitler was a monster with an insatiable appetite for countries like Czechoslovakia and Poland on one end, insuring a gargantuan pile of waste at the other end. Now Japan was posturing for war, with Hitler's support. Great Britain was in peril and the League of Nations ineffective.

Meanwhile back at the Stitt Bakery, the summer's heat was cool compared to the indoor atmosphere near the oven, where George had the fans going full tilt. Work proceeded as the radio played Glenn Miller. Louise didn't stay idle for long because after all, a new summer dress and hat required income. She settled in and a year flew by.

Louise ate lunch in Dot's apartment, which adjoined the bakery office. They were having leftover baked macaroni.

"Kid, I haven't had this in two years," Louise gestured with her fork.

Dot had been glad to have her sister back, though she wished Louise would finish her schooling.

"I'm working here because I can't get the work I want. But you... you actually like working here!"

"I guess I am at home here. Even more so since I spent the school years collecting information about food, writing papers... I just lost interest in working at my desk."

Dot grimaced. "I work ten hours a day at menial office tasks and my... my yen for painting or pottery just gets buried."

Louise declared, "Oh, I'd never be able to accomplish a secretarial job." Then, impersonating Shirley Temple's finger snapping determination, with hands at her waist, she barked, "Wrapping sugar cookies for freshness—now that's a better use of *my* skills."

Dot threw up her hands. "Aaagh. Hey, I've got a couple sheet cakes that need to be taken down to Shafer's Restaurant. How 'bout we go together?"

Louise took off her apron, combed her shoulder-length pageboy hair, clipped-on pearl earrings and applied red lipstick. The two wore print shirtwaist dresses that were fetching, although Louise referred to her clunky shoes as "ad absurd."

The vehicle Dot loaded with special order sheet cakes was a small Austin Healy truck, and it would take them to a restaurant close to the Susquehanna River, on Second Street.

The two delivery girls cruised by the sale windows of Pomeroy's Department Store.

Louise was developing a dislike for her figure and remarked, "When I shop for a dress I'm in my element, especially if when I look in the mirror, the waist looks smaller."

Sarcastically, Dot answered, "Stepping into a dress shop, now that's adventure!"

"Really, dahling," Louise denounced. And they parked and proceeded to unload the Austin Healy.

The service entrance at the back of Shafer's Restaurant opened with a flourish. "Dorothea Hammaker! Well, I wasn't expecting such a handsome delivery team!"

Edward Shafer met them at the service entrance of the restaurant. He wore a starched white shirt, vest and bow tie. He was a youthful looking manager, but he made up for that in his professional manner. He instructed the dessert chef to collect the cakes while he paid the bill.

"I haven't had the pleasure," he said, grasping Louise's hand. He squeezed the finger wearing the amethyst ring and his brown eyes both winked. His light brown hair was neatly combed, and it had some sort of pomade in it that strangely reminded Louise of peacocks.

Something powerful happened to the college escapee right then, she couldn't explain it. It may have had life-changing impact. He insisted they have a seat in the unoccupied large dining room, where he snapped fingers and a waiter appeared with a coffee pot and a tray of accoutrements.

Edward brought them various sandwiches of homemade pumpernickel bread, which he referred to as "pumps," then he joked, "I'm waiting for Charlie Chaplin to come in and order a tongue sandwich."

He took the seat closest to Louise and proceeded, deftly, to discern her availability. Dot told him Louise was back from college and working in the bakery.

"You are youthful for a college graduate."

Louise smiled and adeptly lied about her age, "Oh, I've skipped so many grades in school. By rights I should be in the eleventh grade!"

Edward was soon to learn that Louise had a knack for exaggeration. "Ho, ho right. And I came by my nickname honestly. I'm not twenty—not really."

Louise laughed, "What *is* your nickname?"

He whispered, "'Babyface.' But if you tell anyone, I'll stop doing business with Stitt Bakery."

Dot sighed, tiring of the unfolding flirtation and said, "Someday we'll look back on this encounter in wonder. Louise, Edward's nickname is 'Eddie.' Now, we need to get back, kid, before the truck drivers come in."

Then, faster than you can say jellyroll, Eddie insisted Louise go to the Saturday matinee with him, to a cartoon called *Fantasia*.

On the way back to work, Louise said, "Why, I haven't been this excited since... since I tasted that chocolate pie in Cuba."

In the days until Saturday, Louise felt a heady sense of elation. She hummed a bit of music from the radio, recently playing the music from Fantasia. She knew it as "The Nutcracker." After that movie date, the two were buoyed, floating on whimsical mutual admiration. There was none of the suspicion with which Louise met her other suitors. For Louise and Eddie the "Depression" ended early.

***

For the country at large, Roosevelt's plan to get the country moving had worked. The Civilian Conservation Corps, Works Projects Administration, The Tennessee Valley Authority were putting Americans to work, usually in a good way. Now Roosevelt's administration was urged to aid the European Allies in order to rein in Hitler's dictatorial activities.

Roosevelt's latest speech at University of Virginia called in essence for young people to converge in the armed forces with the full support of the U.S. population. America was supporting the Allies already with munitions. The government worked behind the scenes establishing an Air Defense Command against a possible attack by Germany. FDR really did not have to add that it was all in the defense of freedom. American newsreels showed in brutal black and white how the Third Reich forbade freedom of speech, assembly, religion and equality.

53

L ouise pulled the Austin Healy into the State Street Parking
Garage somewhat late on a Friday. She helped make acres
of chocolate sandwiches filled with vanilla cream. This was a
ten-hour day in which she machine-wrapped those half moon
cakes, provided lunch time breaks for the Stitt sales ladies at
Broad Street Market and then, after bringing forty empty cake
trays back to Stitt's, proceeded to go shopping for a dance dress.

There was a young man in the garage ticket booth who came
out and motioned for her to stop. He could have made a standard
impression, with a medium build dressed in Levi jeans and a
wool sweater. His face was one big smile, transforming his
image as it focused on his customer. The close-cropped shiny
black hair framed eyes of deep forest green. He extended his
hand and pulled the gloved Louise out of the driver's seat.

"I'll be about an hour," Louise said matter-of-factly.

"No, I guess it'll be longer. You said that last month—that
it'd be an hour and it was three hours."

"Well shut my mouth!" Louise exclaimed.

"Heh, heh," said the attendant, climbing into the truck after
handing Louise a ticket.

Louise felt somewhat anxious when she saw how fast he
parked her truck in that narrow garage.

The dress sought by Louise quickly surfaced from a sale rack
at Mary Sach's Store. It would match her Cuban alligator shoes.
She did not want to see the rascal parking attendant again, but
there he was, smirking as she turned in the ticket. This time he
said less but smiled as he turned "Big Band Radio" station lower,
but still, the tune *Tangerine* echoed against the garage walls.

Louise said seriously as she stared at the clock in the office, "I hurried."

He replied, "You don't say," as he stamped the ticket.

Louise smiled and added, "Yeah. I have a date. How much for an hour?"

The green-eyed man smiled and replied, "Oh." He passed her the keys that he pulled out of his jeans pocket. "That'll be a dime."

"Only a dime?" she queried.

"Yeah, it's the truck rate."

As Louise drove out of the garage, he motioned for her to slow and handed her shopping bag through the window. "Don't leave your shopping bags lying around. And have a nice date."

Puttering down Third Street, passing the State Capitol Building, Louise whispered, "Whew what an oddball." But she noticed something strange in the truck interior. It seemed to have been supercharged, just like... about like sitting and hearing Billie Holiday sing *Having Myself a Time*.

54

E ddie and Louise seemed to anticipate each other and months passed in an effortless way. Watching them was like watching Astaire dancing with Rodgers, and they virtually seemed matched as well as the two even layers of a cake. She became a regular at Shafer's after lunch hour.

"You've got a real penchant for having fun," a smiling Eddie observed, joining her at the counter.

Louise shot back, "But maybe I'm having fun 'cause you're around."

"Nah, you don't know what a bad day is."

Louise pouted, saying, "Maybe I *just look* happy. Maybe I like restaurant coffee."

Eddie kept a straight face, gripped the coffeepot and filled her cup. After a minute of staring at her brown eyes, her lips and smirking cheeks, he thought her beautiful and declared. "You never take sugar."

"No... I get enough o' that from you."

This banter carried them on to dance dates, Sunday lunches at 2232 North Sixth Street and into the comfy backseat of Eddie's 1937 Chevrolet.

Here Louise often quoted a randomly catchy movie line, "I'm trying to be a lady," or something to that effect.

While Eddie's movie recall was less reliable, he could impersonate Walter Pigeon, one of Louise's favorites: "Shall we disrobe, my dear?"

This elicited gales of laughter that heightened the intimacy.

They squeezed a sane world out of one that was going to Europe in a hand basket. Often when they waltzed at the

Hershey Ballroom, they swirled right through the other dancers' thoughts and prewar angst that eerily resembled cold fog. But dance they did, and they had the effect of sinuous white icing wending its way through a glaze of devil's food.

She glided, her hand resting lightly on his shoulder. "Father wants us girls to choose the new bread bags."

"How nice."

"We like the new thinner cellophane."

"Why?"

"It's quieter than the old squeaky kind."

That evening did not want to end. They stopped at Shafer's, now closed. The male housekeeper waved them a "goodnight." Eddie made brandies in snifters and they sat at the counter, sniffing and sipping. First, it was toasting each other, joking around, but then the gravity or reality seemed to surface.

"I feel... when I'm with you... in my element," he exhaled.

She sipped, swallowing the heat. "I'm happy with you, and when I'm away from you, I'm still with you!"

His palms cradled the glass. He stared into the sweet liquid, searching for words that would work, for words good enough to be meaningful to Louise. For a seemingly wise woman, she certainly could deflect complements and positive observations. She lost some of his early complements like she was tossing off dirty laundry.

"I wanted to, " now his hand covered hers, "...ask you to be mine forever, darling." When Eddie referred to Louise as 'darling,' he meant it. "But now, I expect I'll be joining the Army. I just can't ask you to get engaged in this type of situation."

Louise sighed. Mixed emotions converged in her complex heart. She didn't like hearing that Eddie was going into harm's way, yet she didn't feel at all comfortable when she heard the words—or the sound of "being mine forever."

55

December 7, 1941, Japan attacked Pearl Harbor due to the U.S. embargo on oil supplies to Japan. The reason for the embargo was that Japan was invading China, a supposed ally of America. The U.S. embargo cut into Japan's resources, which crippled her economy and military. Japan hoped they could bring America to the bargaining table to negotiate expansion into Asia. Various failures to communicate led to the bombing of Pearl Harbor in Hawaii.

There was a black table radio in the central work area of the bakery. The casing was of Bakelite plastic, and it sat on a shelf, away from flying soft shards of trimmed pie dough. Christy Hammaker had now become an efficient pie assembler, and he usually operated the machine used for producing bottom and top crusts. That groaning, wailing machine made about a dozen medium circles of piecrust per minute; even more when two bakers were available. Christy was having difficulty concentrating, as were George and Sarah. He shut off the motor and turned up the latest news:

"...two thousand military casualties are estimated. The United States is at war. We have joined our European Allies and we have launched our Pacific Fleet against Japan."

George rubbed the crumbs off his palms, saying only, "Whew!"

Sarah spit out, "We're not gonna take this sittin' down. Those damn Nazis have been askin' for trouble. Now they'll get it!" She stamped her white oxford hard on the wooden floor so a splotch of dried chocolate icing bounced off the shoe.

Christy took off his apron early that day and went down to

the Navy recruiter. He emerged from the office as a naval recruit, soon to join the Seabees. He would leave in March of 1942. Meanwhile, Navy Rear Adm. Ben Moreell, Chief of the Bureau of Yards and Docks, requested the establishment of construction battalions, officially named the "Seabees" on March 5, 1942. Christy later used many of his skills as a football lineman, only instead of pushing 300-pound linemen down the field, he quickly hefted tools or bridge timber.

***

Christmas of 1941 was lacking its usual frivolity for the Stitt family. At 2232 North Sixth Street, the focus was on the year to come. Their neighbor, Mrs. Brown, came over with some canned tomatoes, probably put up in World War I. The most intense conversation was between Eddie and Christy, who had enlisted in the service. The rectangular dining room had holly at the snowy windowsills while the air was heavy with the aroma of Caroline's sweet potatoes.

"Did you hear FDR has been entertaining Churchill?"

Christy replied, "Yeah, what about that?"

"The two met with the commanders of the Air Force and the U.S. fleet. Strategizing."

Christy added, "Admiral King and General Arnold, I read."

Clara pronounced, "Where there's smoke, there's toast."

Floyd interjected with a laugh, "Churchill? I heard they had to bring in lots of extra bacon and eggs, plus cold cuts just to keep him in a good mood at breakfast!"

Dot added, "He's roundish for good reason."

The meeting was truly crucial to the Allied cause. Luckily, for the free world, no one got wind of Churchill's heart attack, as it was kept from the public. Sir Winston, perhaps hampered by his inebriation, had tried to lift the window of his White House bedroom. The excessive pressure taxed heart vessels and though the angina was painful, the coronary did not do him in. This was a blessing for the Allies.

Louise and Elaine played an old game of Caroline's called "Stem Halma." Elaine squeaked, "Gotcha" as she captured various marbles on the board. "Come on, pay attention, before I win."

Louise seemed to have matured since the war started. The citizenry had plowed through the Depression and now its youth was poised to join the Allies. There was a marshalling of force born out of the attack on Hawaii. What began as chaos was solidifying now toward a new reality.

American women were doing things that their grandmothers could not when faced with the First World War. Thousands of women went into the service and women took the job positions vacated by their brothers or husbands. Military mattered more these days, so resources went to munitions factories. Clara regularly stood on tin cans, flattening them for the smelting, as did neighbors. Fabrics went into soldiers' uniforms, thus Dot, Louise and Elaine's future dresses would be inches shorter. In 1942, Caroline and Clara bought only thread for mending and food. The butter and sugar they consumed were inside Stitt baked goods, and Floyd encountered many sleepless nights, or endured nightmares of rationed sugar, wondering how a bakery could prosper on a low-sugar diet.

Elaine and Louise abandoned their board game and helped themselves to dessert. Caroline had outdone herself this holiday, baking a new crusty cake, with honey, featuring crunchy almonds and dried apricots with candied ginger.

Louise listened to Dot, lamenting the upcoming loss of Christy and Eddie. She soothed, "Mmmaybe it will all work out. We just have to do our part."

Elaine put down her fork and said, "A few of the senior boys at school enlisted."

Dot sighed.

56

Dot sat uneasily on a bench overlooking the Norfolk, Virginia docks. She and Louise drove to the naval base to see Christy off. Louise had left them to their extended goodbyes and found herself strolling in an older part of Norfolk known as Ghent. She wandered through a commercial area and on a whim walked into a beauty parlor, and spying a movie poster on the wall, requested, "I'd like that, can you do it?" It was a close up of Ingrid Bergman in the embrace of Bogart. The hairstyle had a part, curling in a shoulder-length pageboy.

The owner of the shop was an old woman who had dyed her hair black with marcelled waves. She said, "Sure thing, sugar," and a teenage stylist appeared with comb in hand.

Louise chatted with the two women regarding the enlistments of Christy and Eddie.

The proprietor said, "Oh, we miss our Norfolk men. We even said goodbye to Harriet last week... she washed my customers' hair for me. Now she's a WAVE in the women's Navy. She makes more money there and said they want her to be a photographer."

Louise hastily paid for her new look and sped back to her morose sister.

Dot put away her monogrammed cotton handkerchief. Louise hugged her as they sat and watched the ship ease out to sea. "They really aren't leaving."

Louise queried, "Not yet?"

Dot answered, "They have to do their practice run, I guess..." And then her tears interrupted.

The sisters had designated that day as a way of sending

Christy off to his assignment. On the return drive to Harrisburg, they purged themselves temporarily of the strain of war, even getting in a laugh or two. Dot remarked, "You got your *hair* done?"

Louise glanced at herself in the rear-view mirror, replying, "Yeah, it kind'a got me through this business of sending Christy off."

Dot noticed, "Well you do have that Bergman look."

Louise didn't believe she looked even vaguely, slightly, remotely like Ingrid Bergman. She sang out to Dot, "Here's looking at *you*, kid!"

57

L ouise sensed the stir created by the entry of her country into war. People surrounding her were propelled by many years of witnessing Nazi Germany's quest for power at the expense of thousands of innocent citizens. The American reaction to Pearl Harbor was to forget about local problems and to fight abroad while supporting that effort at home. Now as she drove toward Harrisburg, it seemed clear that she needed to do more than collect tin cans or buy war bonds. But what?

Glenn Miller's Band played *Pennies from Heaven* on the Stitt bakery radio. Louise's constructing of cardboard boxes had filled a large worktable. Louise whispered to herself, "Two hundred... that could be enough..." She was looking forward to the weekend when Elaine came in. Elaine had become taller than Louise, and her heavy hair had gone glamorous. She and Louise went upstairs, where Dot had just finished with the last of the deliverymen. They wanted Dot to join them at the movies.

Dot had abandoned the hope of teaching art. Now she accepted her role as office manager, and she did clerical tasks quite efficiently. Her creative inclinations mostly materialized as great home-cooked meals in the face of all the wartime rationing.

Now her younger sisters walked into the sunny office just as a bakery route deliveryman, Mike, was speaking with Dot about a recurring problem.

The three young women listened curiously. "I goes into Jake's Grocery in Steelton. I used to never take any cakes out'ta there. Their customers likes our cakes. Well, this week three cakes was bashed in."

Dot showed a round marble cake to her sisters. Dot sighed.

"It was bashed in all right."

Mike said angrily, "The other two was flattened on top and I gave 'em to a stray dog."

Elaine observed, "Looks like it was not accidental. No, a dish or something made that damage."

Mike said, "The grocer didn't make these dents. It's probably the salesman from Stroop'n they serve Jake's Grocery too."

The small grocery stores sometimes traded with two bakeries at a time. Stitt and Stroop both supplied goods to Jake's Grocery Store.

Dot felt the destruction as a waste of everyone's time. Fuming, she said, "Here we have to work with rationed sugar, and we pay countless people to produce a cake. Then some other idiot bakery destroys it!"

Floyd entered from the back stairway, and Dot gave him the news.

He sighed. "They have some driver who just wants the business and wants us to go away."

Mike said, "No real proof of that, Mr. Stitt, but this," he said gesturing to the cake, "was done in the store." They all stared at the pathetic marble circle exhibited on the counter, nearly cut in half by a dent.

Elaine asked Mike whether he ever saw the problem in any other place. "No. Not like this… done on purpose."

Then Elaine felt intrigued. She wished she could defend Stitt Bakery goods and was curious enough to become—she imagined—a detective.

***

The three bakery girls did get out to the movies, and that was a tonic for their myriad stresses. They found a great bargain at the Senate Theater for ten cents. The show began with a Disney cartoon, followed by a newsreel covering recent wartime events in the Pacific, and a great fashion show of women's clothing remade from tablecloths and men's unoccupied suits. Soon, actress Betty Grable persuaded, "Ladies! Our Civilian Defense Volunteer Office needs women to build a wartime work force!" Then another impassioned pitch for war bonds by Bob Hope, and finally they viewed the main feature.

They chomped on rock-salted pretzels that Dot had bought at Zimmermann's. During this lighthearted movie, after their initial relaxation, the minds of the three sped on to other thoughts. Elaine began by unraveling the problem besetting Nick and Nora Charles, on screen, but secretly she yearned for some way to tackle the person who had damaged the Stitt cakes.

Was it a coincidence that Elaine craved a mystery? She adored Myrna Loy and eagerly awaited this newest movie—*The Thin Man*.

During the newsreel, Dot caught a glimpse of some actual Seabees and wondered what Christy was doing. His letters detailed stories of men loading ships full of building supplies, followed by a mission by sea to England.

The CDV pitch for aid piqued Louise's curiosity. They needed women; but what were the particulars? After the show, the girls took the trolley car home, knowing gas was soon to be rationed.

***

Louise finally had to face the separation from Eddie. The pain felt like a spear she had to pull from her chest. They disappeared together for a weekend to an isolated cabin near Pine Grove Furnace. It was heartrendingly bittersweet. They built a fire, then were consumed by their mutual passion. This togetherness seemed again to solidify their relationship, girding them for their upcoming responsibilities. For this moment, there was purely pleasure of skin close to skin, unleashed passion and frustration, leaving a need for nothing at all. The very air was safe and supremely peaceful.

Eddie said, "Think about marriage when all this is over."

"I don't care about anything except you getting home safely."

He replied, "I'm not that athletic like Christy is, but I am probably smart enough to survive."

"You know, next week you'll be off to Europe. Well, I don't want to be on the front lines like the WAVES, but I'm going to do volunteer work."

This was a recurring theme now. Women took the jobs men vacated and civilians formed their own cadres of support groups.

"What would you like to do?"

Louise sipped some lemonade from a heavy blue tumbler. "I'm going to work at a veterans' hospital in West Virginia— Newton D. Baker. I'm soon to be a nurse's aide."

Eddie gasped then whistled out a long high note.

***

Louise took Floyd's car into town. She gripped the wheel and thought of how it would be without the use of a car, then she dismissed the thought as selfish. She had to get a few toiletries to prepare for her relocation to Martinsburg, and soon she was at the downtown parking garage.

A woman, loudly chewing gum, appeared to park her car. Louise suddenly realized the absence of that young, somewhat handsome stranger.

Louise took her ticket. She said, "The man who used to work here…"

The attendant interrupted, "He joined the Navy. Hey, are you… Miss Stitt?"

Surprised, Louise answered, "Yeah?"

"Well, Bud was here and said, 'If you see Miss Stitt tell her I've gone to the service.'"

Louise sighed, "Well, he and every other able-bodied man. Thank you." She walked briskly to make her purchase.

But then, in the drug store, there he was. He had just bought shaving soap. Now he wore a black sailor suit, with a white cap tucked into a belt loop. This military image made his appearance taller, neater. Louise blushed, genuinely surprised to find the former attendant, and he appeared groomed, as though he'd just stepped out of a barber shop.

He excitedly sensed her confused attention and asked, "How 'bout a little drink at the fountain?"

She joined him for soft drinks as he explained that he was due on a train to Newport News, Virginia.

Louise listened as the new recruit explained how he was saying his family goodbyes and yet was eager to be part of the anti-German movement. "We'll soon be givin' 'em hell. I'm not supposed to say where I'm ordered to go, but for now I'm in the North Atlantic."

Louise felt from Bud... what was it? A zest for winning and a sort of devil-may-care tone that she had heard before when Christy and Eddie departed.

He pulled an address book from his pocket. "Would you mind if I wrote to you?" he said with a childlike hope in his green eyes. "I don't have anybody's address here except my two aunts. It would be very... nice to hear from you."

Louise smiled and said, "Anything I can do for my countryman..." and penned her address on Sixth Street.

"Great!" He read, "2232 North Sixth. I'm sorry I have to go, but I can't tell you how swell it was to see you. Why haven't you come around the garage? I thought maybe you changed jobs due to the war."

"Well, you're right!" Louise, still a bit taken back by the man, said, "I'm going to be a nurse's aide in a military hospital."

Bud responded, "Well, you don't say!"

Louise smiled at his exuberant state. He asked, "I have got to go now, would you let your countryman hug you good bye?"

She squeezed his shoulder. "I hope it all goes well."

He put one arm around her, his ear to hers. Already he smelled like the ocean.

198

Clara Shultz circa 1903

Dan, George and Bill Fegley. Baking, circa 1917

Stitt Bakery, 2463 Jefferson St., Harrisburg. Apartments to left, circa 1920s

Louise Stitt celebrating marriage of aunt Ruth Stitt and George Hammond, 1921

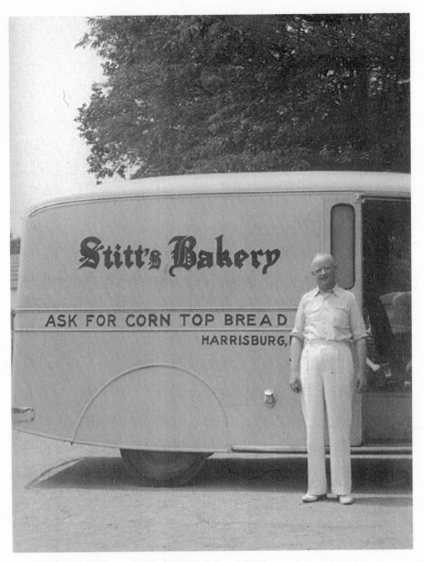

Floyd Stitt, 1936

Floyd Stitt (Left), neighbor and employees 1936

Elaine Stitt at Bakery Store entrance, 1938

*Jane Shultz, Ginny
Murr and Louise
Stitt, touring Morro
Castle, Cuba, 1937*

*Jane Shultz, Louise
Stitt shopping
intensely, Cuba 1937*

Dorothea Stitt, 1932

Louise Stitt, 1936

Elaine Stitt, 1942

Christy Hammaker,
1933

Bud Ditlow, U.S. Navy, 1942

Bud Ditlow, as delivery supervisor, Stitt Bakery

58

Eddie's outfit was stationed somewhere in England. His letters to Louise were garnished with codes as to where they might have advanced. "I'm enjoying some Earl Grey tea," meant: "I'm in England." "I had a lavender tisane you'd like," meant: "We're in France."

They were part of a raid on a Nazi submarine base in St. Nazaire. The Luftwaffe had proceeded to bomb many towns in England, which was anxiety producing in its damage, yet the Germans' use of force would only appear to work. The common bond of the Allies together with the resistance of the populace had already marshaled tremendous resources.

Yet the Allies did not know that the opposing dictator had started to unravel. Hitler's fiery speeches were fueled by methamphetamines. He twitched so much that he needed more drugs for sleep. He was in the habit of going into tirades where he threw bottles of schnapps at his generals. He got so agitated that he once twirled his torso into a drapery, fell down damask-ensnared in a tantrum and screamed, "I only ask you for... it's like I ask for a Horsh Cabriolet Sedan and you give me a... a bicycle!"

Certain generals took to nicknaming him "Herr Carpet Biter."

***

Spring bloomed in the mountains of West Virginia. Louise stepped off the train in Martinsburg after only a short briefing in Harrisburg. She expected to receive on-the-job training, but first she found a big welcome.

Louise and about twenty-six other women filed into a classroom in Newton D. Baker Hospital. The woman in charge of orienting them was dressed in a Chanel suit with a knee-length skirt. Louise didn't recognize the face, but her hair was pinned back with a familiar copper barrette. She knew! It was her friend Mary Lane from Lake Erie.

Mary incredulously saw Louise's name on her roster and then Louise in the flesh. It was like old home week, and they hugged each other, rushing to the hallway and hushing their voices.

"Louise! Did you bring any of your oomph?"

Louise screamed, "A shopping bag full. Hey, before I commit to this circus, there's something I've gotta know."

Mary said, "Well?"

"Is there a beauty parlor in walking distance?"

Mary squealed, "A very chic one. But if there weren't, I'd drive you!"

Louise, recovering her breath, said, "I think I'm gonna like it here."

59

Mary Lane was now an employee of the U.S. Public Health Service, working in the administrative office of the hospital. She introduced the trainees to Esther Allen, the superintendent of nurses. The welcoming speech brusquely reminded the women what a tradition they were upholding, caring for the sick and injured. But their colonel tested the audience with grim reality.

Miss Allen looked like she had seen a few battlefields, but in truth she was only thirty. Born in the District of Columbia, she had become a nurse, then joined the Army. She was vigorously true to her rank of colonel, which not many of her cohorts had attained. When she said the word "men," she usually referred to her patients, whereas "women" was a code word for the nursing staff.

"Welcome to you, women. We have participants from five states here today. This morning, at 0600 hours, we lost a man to typhoid. Unfortunately, we have had our share of communicable disease. I say to you, disinfectants are not to be rationed! We will ask you to do work you may never have done, and we work long hours. Luckily, we've got good staff members, and we have nursing and medical experience built upon the previous war. You may be assured that we welcome your help, and we will endeavor to win our war against illness. Welcome to Newton D. Baker."

The new inductees applauded politely, though many were having second thoughts.

The nurse's aides wore green cotton dresses, shortened to below the knee, topped with starchy white aprons; the uniform was completed by cotton stockings with heavy white oxford shoes. At least the Army helped prevent foot strain.

The day shift began at six a.m., going for twelve hours, and night shifts were six p.m. to six a.m. Their quarters were dorm-like with four women to a room. The bathroom down the hall had a few showers and one tub. The cafeteria provided hot food three times daily, and though most of the food was overcooked, Mary Lane said it was fresh, from nearby farms.

The buildings in 1942 held four hundred men. Sunny wards, large rooms lined with high-mattressed hospital beds, could accommodate thirty to fifty patients. A desk and linen closet formed the entry to a ward. This desk was for record books, pens and ink and a chair, in which the nurse sat to record. The treatment room had a table, chairs, bandage-type supplies, disinfectants and a locked medicine cabinet. From Louise's dorm, it was a few minutes' walk to the hospital and a few more to the cafeteria.

There were many things for the women to learn, but the numbers of staff were few and most of them were obliged to pick up experience from the seasoned volunteers already on the job. Bed making was usually done daily for the bedridden men, so Miss Allen made sure each nurse's aide spent a morning practicing the art.

"Women, the idea is to en*vel-op* the mattress," she pronounced. "Just as you would a package." Then she whipped up the linen so that it clouded down just in time for an "Allen attack" on the four corners, and she assaulted the linen so fast that the group could not begin to understand the maneuver.

Again, she demonstrated, but the nurse was overcome within a zone of mechanical linen lashing. She could not do it at a slow pace. If her superiors understood this sheeting craft, they would have doubled her salary and left her to the enveloping only. However, she would continue to spend her life disinfecting, recruiting and inspiring.

At the end of this bed-making session, a slim woman from

North Carolina raised her hand and asked, "Is it true y'all can bounce a quarter off o' these Army mattresses?"

Miss Allen took a dramatically deep breath, saying, "Why, yes, but if you do it my way, you all can bounce an Alka Selzer!" She then produced a tin of the tablets and spun one over the linen.

The Carolinian exclaimed, "Ah, I swan, jus' lak' a skippin' stone!"

As Miss Allen's starch sped down the hallway, Louise whispered, "It's no surprise she has acid indigestion."

Louise's mentor had only arrived at Newton D. Baker Hospital shortly after February. Nurse B. Davis was a tiny redhead who wore it in a long braid, coiled in a figure eight under her cap. B. was a recent graduate of a hospital nursing school in Maryland. She had been recruited by Miss Allen, who felt confident in B., and so delegated authority to her.

It was during a lecture by the medical director that Louise noticed how B. dramatized her life. The doctor was preparing the medical and nursing staffs for a large contingent of wounded. As they filed out to the wards, B. said to Louise, "As Miss Bette Davis says, I like a good director."

Nurse B. showed Louise how to lighten her workload by explaining how laundry and kitchen deliveries are made. She and Louise rigged up a shower in a bathtub so independent patients could bathe themselves.

The wounded arrived, fifty-five men who were now veteran pilots of the latest British-American mission. Most were suffering shellshock and exhaustion. Of these, Mark Gordon stood out in Louise's mind. He later told her, "I went over German lines, re-conning, helping get a bead on the best targets." He ran into some Messerschmitts, took a few bullets and was happy to make it back to base in England. He survived a head injury but lost the vision in one eye. As he "…hauled ass to base, bleeding into my goggles, my damn blood sugar hit bottom. Know what? What kept me goin'? Hershey Bars!"

Louise found herself impressed by Mark, who had a spirit that never wavered, and soon Mark would be indebted to Louise. Mark's family sent him a lot of candy. Let's say, Mark's bedside stand usually resembled an Easter basket in a box. If Mark, behind a curtain, sensed Louise approaching, he would say alluringly, "Come here, little girl, I have *candy*."

Louise observed that Mark's cubicle was a small Mecca for the walking wounded in that ward. Their extra efforts of dragging painful limbs down the ward were rewarded by sugar as well as sociability.

Louise heeded Mark's candy call one day, and reaching his bedside, found Nurse B. and José Santiago, a patient, sitting in chairs. B. popped a Hershey kiss into her mouth while José drank his own care package gift: a cup of Puerto Rican coffee, while he leaned on a cane, chuckling at Mark. Frivolity could reign right in the midst of war. Mark displayed a believable German accent and had an invisible moustache:

"So, Hitler was speeding through the countryside, driven by his chauffeur. Near a farmhouse, they ran over a pig, killing it. Hitler told the chauffer to apologize to the farmer. The chauffeur soon returns from the farm bearing a gift basket of champagne and sausages.

"Hitler asks, 'What is all this?'

"The chauffeur says, 'Well, all I said was, Heil Hitler the pig is dead!'"

Mark continued, "Then the one about the two Jews before a firing squad. Suddenly the Nazi gunman tells them they'll be hung instead.

"The Jews scream back, 'The Reich is so stupid, it's run out of bullets!'"

José added, "Goebbels, Goering and Hitler are sinking in a lifeboat. Who survived? Germany!"

Nurse B. laughed the hardest. She finally sighed, "Miss Bette Davis says, 'I don't take the movies seriously, and anyone who does is in for a headache.' Well, the same goes for my job. I can't be serious."

What began with Hershey Kisses culminated in pies. Louise found her way to the kitchen on her day off, the following Saturday. The baker had done something different. He had made cake doughnuts for the staff breakfast. Louise begged the baker for the remaining holy treats. She enlisted José in the patients' ward to get some coffee going, then cut the doughnuts in half so everyone could have some dough to dunk.

Now, the nurse's aides often had difficulty getting late rising men to move. But on that Saturday, José and Louise did it mostly by walking by the beds with the aroma of roasted coffee beans wafting, although there was some toe tweaking. Nurse B. believed the men, especially her surgical cases, should not rest in the daytime. She moved them in order to circulate the blood and tone the muscles. Nurse B. chewed a doughnut and assisted a man with a lumbar shrapnel injury. With her doughnuts delivered, Louise returned to the baker to report her success, hoping he would make doughnuts the following Saturday.

In the quiet of the kitchen, she approached the baker, who now was removing hot rolls from the oven. She was impressed by the cracking sound of the crust as it met cool air. George Fegley taught her as a youth that the sound promised a good crust.

She did not have to explain to the baker the allure of baked goods. He answered, "I will be happy to serve the men. But, not until after July fourth. I'll be too busy with holiday pie making."

Louise said her thanks, then as an afterthought, she stopped, turned in the doorway and said, "What if I help you bake the pies?"

60

Elaine and Floyd attended church together; his church—the Presbyterian Church. Elaine left the St. Paul's Episcopal Church for a very good reason. At the tender age of ten, she dropped her offering, a dime on the hardwood floor, breaking the silence. This sound of one mercury dime rolling on pinewood could have been a nondescript event of childhood had the rector been ministerial. Instead, he flew into a rage, admonishing her for interrupting the service. And when that silver mercury dime connected with the rector's shoe, it was as if God had pushed it. Feeling the sting of public embarrassment, she knew the rector was unfit to preside over her Sunday mornings, let alone her spiritual life.

Now nearly as tall as her father, her added height made the Sunday summer dress hem short. She had a neat straw hat with a pink linen rose and she wore wire-rimmed eyeglasses. After the service, they drove toward Loper's Drug Store.

Floyds Packard hummed, but over the motor, Floyd's hymns belted out of him:

> *"Oh! He walks with me*
> *and he talks with me*
> *And he tells me I am his own..."*

Elaine usually sang along; however, now she was consumed with Stitt cake sabotage. She had paid no attention to the church sermon, intentionally following her week's observations. Elaine had been spending mornings at the store where the cakes in question had been damaged, with Jake's permission.

"Father, don't you think it's strange that since I've been sitting in Jake's Grocery, there hasn't been a single smashed cake?"

"Maybe that's it. You're there as a witness and whoever does the damage keeps his distance."

"But I can't be seen! The owners let me sit there, kind of invisibly. They're the only ones who know my... surveillance point."

Elaine had thought intensely about the cakes that had sustained the mysterious dents, which made them unfit for sale. She took it upon herself to go to the problem grocery store and look around. She got Jake's permission to sit behind his sealed pickle barrel, distantly, yet close enough to observe her cake display. The baked goods were shielded behind a glass frame to keep curious customers' hands off, but the frame was open in the back of the counter. She saw the passing customers, deliveries, including those by Stroop Bakery men. Mostly the same deliveryman appeared. He had the name "Butch" stitched on his shirt, over the pocket. When the store finally closed out her first day and the Stitt cakes were intact, her data collection had begun.

Elaine went home and reported to her father that what was needed was a separate cake case. "If you bring the store a nice new case, marked "Stitt Bakery," with a sliding back door, it'll protect our cakes and make them look special," she said thoughtfully.

Her father had complied, and it appeared to be a good solution, but then summer came, bringing buzzing flies along. So the grocer's wife added the Stroop cakes to the case "Just for sanitation."

This in turn allowed the Stroop driver access to the case and with it a few more dented devil's food cakes. Of course, the Stroop cakes all sold. Floyd complained to Jake, and he was informed that if there was room in the case, the grocer would put in cakes other than Stitt's. For a time, the frustrated Floyd would not deliver anything to the store, but he soon lost enough business and returned—this time accompanied by Elaine.

Then she was deep into *The Thin Man* movies and mysterious goings on. She reasoned that if the Myrna Loy character could catch a thief, so could she. First, she placed a bell inside the case, over the cakes. A large hand would have more difficulty sneaking in. She brought a mystery book to read, and seated herself within a good spying view of the case. She perched on a three-legged stool, hiding behind a sealed barrel of pickles.

The Stroop man came, saw that the case was full of Stitt cakes, deposited his own cakes on the counter and left them with Jake.

"Humph." Elaine sighed, thinking of her summer vacation wasting away. Well, detectives had to do the work required of them, and she continued to survey the activities at Jake's Grocery Store. The only thing she had to go on was the Stroop delivery time: eight or eight fifteen a.m. Butch returned at about three-thirty to collect trays from the grocer's wife, plus money. It was on one of these late calls that she detected an intriguing clue, and that propelled her through the summer.

She had been watching Butch like a patient mountain lion on the eight o'clock delivery, but paying less attention at three. She noticed something that was right there each day as the man sauntered up to the cash register. Carefully, Elaine watched as the transaction took place. The woman passed him two sticky trays and then smiling, opened her register, *ding,* and she handed him an envelope. She smiled, he laughed. What was it about the laugh? Why, he wasn't doing it in the morning. What she first dismissed as her imagination proved to haunt her dreams.

61

Nurse B. Davis closed out the day shift on her ward of thirty-six men. Today four of them rode back to base, ready for another tour of duty. Louise was washing her hands at a sink where the Army soap smelled like turpentine, and maybe that was just what it contained! Nearby, a poster on the wall showed a leaking faucet and the caption read: "Don't be a drip—Save our water." The day shift exited the wards and made a beeline for the cafeteria.

Louise and B. joined a queue of N.D. Baker workers, mostly wearing green or white starched uniforms. They planned to have their chili, then go into Martinsville.

Sitting at their table sipping the notorious Army coffee, Louise remembered she had received mail. A lively postcard from her mother indicated that Christy worked with the Seabees on a Canadian project. Clara had sent a box of molasses cookies to Eddie, Christy and soon to Louise. The other envelopes bore return addresses of Army and Navy.

> *May 5, 1942*
> *Dear Louise,*
> *Miss you lots as usual. Don't work too hard on your job! We are drilling, practicing skills and parading in Britain. You won't see us in the news. If you read about General Giraud, I was there when he made it home. He was a war prisoner in a fort with a moat in Germany. He got away with a map, civilian clothes and disguised boots. He told us he spent months making a rope long enough to get to the moat then to freedom. He might have*

been caught by Germans on a train, but his fluent German saved him.

Had some great stew and even a pint of ale. No danger at the moment. Regards to your family.

I rehash all my time with you from the first time you brought in the sheet cake. I want the powers that be to move faster, so we can win, and then return.

I adore you,
Eddie

Louise sighed. Eddie was too good to be hurt. Louise kept him with her, yet she purposely did not dwell on the man who wanted to marry her. Across the table, Nurse B. took a gulp of coffee, whispering, "Battery acid."

Louise said, "My boyfriend, Eddie's in England." Then she stared at the other piece of airmail: it was stamped U.S.N.

May 9, 1942
Dear Louise,

I send you greetings from on board a cruiser. I hope you're fine. I work with a good crew and the oldest is thirty (of the enlisted men). We are told the British Air Force won the last attack. Hooray for the Allies!

You know, I worked at the garage because of I was injured on my job in Maryland, so just as I met you, the war started. Sorry we didn't talk more. I spent my childhood on a farm in Lower Paxton and never expected to go in the Navy.

Between you and me, I wished I could be a gumshoe, you know, a "G. man" who could catch crooks like darn Scarface Capone. I'm a pretty good shot with a rifle. We practiced helping the gunners here in drills. That isn't what I was assigned, though.

Know what? Ha, ha, ha, I work as a ship's baker. We follow orders from the cook who has most of the recipes in his head. You could do much better at bread baking than me. I make mostly bread, every other day cookies and if we have time, we make birthday cake. Don't you know we spend lots of time cleaning the kitchen to pass inspection.

Well, now I put your letter in the mailbag. Write if you can.

Sincerely yours,
Bud Ditlow

Louise looked over at B. "I'm writing to the kid who parked my car. I ran into him as he shipped out. He's young... twenty-two."

B. asked, "How old is Eddie?"

Louise giggled, "Even younger. Hey kid, we better get going if we're gonna dance tonight."

Soon they motored into Martinsburg in Mary Lane's car.

Louise, B. and Mary Lane made quite an entrance at a popular Martinsburg hangout. Unfortunately, no one saw them enter. Dino's Grill served Italian food in a comfortable atmosphere. As the three entered the quiet bar, the jukebox played Billie Holiday: *The Way You Look Tonight.*

Mary Lane had her blond hair coiled and pinned neatly and a blue evening dress matched her eye color. Louise had just had a permanent and her dark hair fell to her shoulders in waves. She dressed up her Sunday navy blue dress with large earrings and an ornate multicolored necklace of pave aquamarines. B. wore black, and it complemented her long rusty hair. Louise was astounded by how the color black and heels had transformed B.

B. responded in her best movie star's voice, "I often think that a slightly exposed shoulder emerging from a long satin nightgown packs more sex than two naked bodies in bed."

The three femme fatales swept into the place and looked across the windowless room. The jukebox played Glenn Miller's rendition of *In the Mood*, moodily stimulating prewar memories.

Mary exclaimed, "Why it's empty—unusually empty." But that wasn't exactly so and a voice immediately pointed that out. "Yeah, exceptin' fer us, girls. You must be Breck Shampoo models." Mary saw a table of four elder card players craning their necks and adjusting their bifocals.

Mary whispered, "I know him. They're World War I vets."

The three walked over to the card sharks and exchanged pleasantries, then took their own booth. Dino came out of the kitchen and soon was at their table with a pitcher of beer.

"The gents over there said this is for your efforts at Baker Hospital."

Mary waved thanks toward the vets.

The jukebox went quiet. Louise groaned, "Our young people are overseas."

B. agreed, "Right you are. We're rationing everything—even men."

Mary sighed, "This 'do' cramp what's left of my style."

Louise suggested, "Okay, I'll just dance alone."

"Or with those vets," Mary offered, settling down, staring into her beer foam. Louise responded by tapping her nails on the table as she sang, "Don't keep me waitin' when I'm in the mood."

The conversation turned to B.'s career path; it was winding toward something new when the war beckoned her to serve the military. "I wanted to learn physical therapy, and that's what I'll do after we win this war."

Mary said, "Oh, you will easily find work in that area."

The jukebox played swing and Louise jumped up to "cut the rug." B. joined her and Mary sat sipping another beer.

When the dance ended, out of nowhere, Louise took B.'s shoulder, looked her in the eye and asked, "Hey, is dancing physical therapy?"

"What do you think?"

Enthusiastically, Louise began, "Whew, I worked up a sweat! I last danced with Eddie, months ago and… whew."

B. replied, "Exercise is certainly a big part of it. Strengthening moves. Balancing… to the rhythm."

Mary added, "People dance to feel good too."

Recovering her breath, Louise went on, driven by some unknown spirit. "What about cooking? Is that exercise? Or is that occupational therapy?"

B. and Mary bent toward their friend, and B. demanded, "What's all this about exercise?"

Louise stared at B., "Now, you helped me with the Saturday doughnut routine. It went well. It was sort of physical therapy."

Mary recalled, "I know it was a distraction from all those aches and pains. They had to drag their asses out of bed and walk to a treat… on canes n' crutches."

B. declared, "They do it on Saturdays and my, have they picked up speed—especially Corporal Bob, that time he walked without crutches and without complaining."

Louise paused, staring through B. "They got involved, er, Mary says they were distracted and the coffee and doughnuts is kinda' well… homey-homelike."

Mary laughed, "Sure. If you're a bakery girl."

Louise's eyes flashed, "Yeah, and I don't know anybody who doesn't like baked goods for some reason."

Mary inhaled, "Doughnuts rolled in cinnamon." B. smiled, thinking of homemade bread as Louise pressed on.

"I think I'm gonna do it again, but it will be bigger and better."

B. demanded, "What do you mean… I'm dying to know!"

"It has to do with July the Fourth…"

"Yeah, there will be a party… fireworks," Mary promised.

Louise, posing as an authority, used her more proper voice. "Well, I have been thinking how very nice it would be to involve the 'walking wounded' in the pie baking."

Silently her friends absorbed the mental picture of patients at work in the kitchen. What? Holiday baking of cherry pies? They tried to picture the men, who had recently survived plane crashes, crimping piecrust with slinged arms and watching the oven with an eye patched. It was the height of incongruence!

Louise continued, "It happens that *I* am very well versed in pie baking. I thought if the men got moving for a doughnut, they would get more mental stimulation by rolling out dough. You know, some of these *men* are little more than boys, and I feel like they need nurturing desperately."

Mary laughed, "Well, if it happens, I want a picture!"

Nurse Davis' brain lit up, its wheels spun and she felt it was not just an exercise for bored patients. The truth was that B. felt a droning monotony descending on the Baker Hospital, another wartime side effect. This creative idea involving beautiful cherry pies was inspiring to her.

B. finally answered, shaking her head excitedly. "You'll get your wish, God willing. God being Miss Allen."

62

Harry Loper of Loper's Drugs was a friend of Floyd Stitt. Each Sunday he cheerfully hosted Elaine and Floyd when they dropped in for a Coke.

He had heard bits of their conversations over the years, but lately it wasn't the usual small talk; there was a whole new tone, whispered... well, reports.

Elaine took off her straw hat. Her brunette hair was too long, but Mother thought it would be a shame to bob that shiny heavy, mane. As they settled into their booth, Elaine was reviewing the results of her surveillance of the Stitt cakes. Her father cocked his good ear in her direction as they sipped chocolate Cokes.

"Three weeks of watching over these cakes..." Her eyes rolled as she tapped her drinking straw against her straw hat. There haven't been any cakes damaged in three weeks and it's taken me that long to figure out why."

Floyd said, "You protect the cakes by your presence in that store..."

Elaine interrupted, "Yeah? By gosh, something has struck me as real funny."

"Hah! Hah!" Now, Floyd was amused by his daughter, and he secretly had begun to think of her as "the thin woman," his own private eye.

Elaine reported, "We believe the Stroop delivery man is the one responsible for damaging our cakes. Now, this same man has been walking in every weekday and the cakes are untouched. What I've seen is the man comes in to deliver in the morning and collects the trays 'n money around three."

Floyd nodded seriously.

"He doesn't damage any cakes because... he's being tipped off that I'm in the store!"

Floyd blurted out, "By the owner!"

Elaine whispered over her drink, "No, his wife."

"Nina. Hmmm," Floyd rolled his eyes. "That is quite a charge."

Elaine swallowed, "Let's see, Monday was when I saw him cozy up to her."

"Why," Floyd sputtered red faced. "They have a... a..."

Elaine added, "Yeah, I know it. At the money pick up time, she starts combing her *hair*."

"The plot thickens—woo woo!" Floyd said. "And you don't hear a thing over there behind the pickles..."

"Hold on, Father. In the mornings, I never see the man stop to talk to Jake, but in the afternoon, he sure has a lot to say to Nina. He leans over the counter like he's got all day... she calls him a nickname..."

Now Floyd was intrigued, "What's that?"

Elaine whispered slowly, "Bread boy."

"Bread boy!" Floyd gasped, inhaling his drink. "Ha! You're betting that she tells him you're there so he won't get caught."

Elaine whispered, "I saw her looking over at my hiding place... while he stands there just like, like a gangster in a Stroop uniform. He's going to do damage again, but I really want to catch him doing it."

"Catch him in the act..." Floyd raised his brow, remembering his shiny little devil's food cake, his product, baked with care by George, artfully iced by Sarah. So many others worked to produce it and so quickly it was rendered to garbage. "I want to get him too." He rapped hard on the tabletop.

63

Nurse B. Davis whispered to herself, "Pray to God and say the lines." She had read it in a movie magazine, quoting Bette Davis. She cast her eyes to a small poster on the wall of Rosie the riveter with the caption: "We can do it."

She had requested a meeting with Miss Allen a week ago, and she had told her of the Saturday doughnut treat and had emphasized how well the men responded. However, something led her to avoid talking about pie baking, thinking, "I will let her digest the doughnuts."

Now her smiling superior whisked in and took her seat behind the desk. "What may I do for you, Miss Davis?"

"Miss Allen, it goes back to the doughnut idea."

"Yes, yes," said the superior, while gritting her teeth.

"Miss Allen, Fourth of July holiday is coming. A nurses' aide has quite a nice idea for the men."

"Hmmm."

"It will boost their morale... and provide occupational therapy."

"Lord knows they need that. Well, say it!"

Nurse Davis brightened, "We'd like to bake cherry pies for July Fourth... and let the men help."

Whoa! She conjured up a scene of battle-scarred men, used to shouldering rifles, now armed with spoons and rolling pins, "You are asking for trouble. Trouble for the chef. Trouble in the form of untrained food handlers—it could be an infection issue!" She stood up and walked to where Nurse B. was sitting. "You nurses have enough to do just patching up these soldiers. I think it is too risky."

The diminutive B. sighed, took a deep breath and stood. Her starched white cap shook a little as she said, with blue eyes meeting Miss Allen's piercing black ones, "I don't believe surgery and pills are the real cure. The determined mind is what got them to the battlefield, and their minds are ripe now for mending."

Miss Allen shook her head. "Still, no. But you have a good head yourself, Miss Davis."

***

Louise took the news well and started to wonder whether some alternate activity could be used to celebrate July Fourth. B. Davis was downhearted for some time, and Louise took to smothering her friend's moodiness with wit. "Don't take it seriously," Louise cautioned. "Anyone who does is in for a headache."

B. Davis would express her frustration, "But, Louise, I had it all worked out..."

Louise interjected, "You have a good script and you are a great director."

"But it could've worked out..."

Again Louise chimed in, quoting Betty Davis, "We will not retire while we have your legs and my make up box."

A week later, in an uncanny stroke of serendipity, Miss Allen received an auspicious phone call. It was from the new armed forces newspaper, *Stars and Stripes*. The editor was asking whether she had any inspirational events going for July the Fourth. He wanted to highlight the veterans. Miss Allen very much wanted to be in this new edition. Her friends were slated to have their picture in the *Stars and Stripes* because they were beginning basic training in the first detachment of Women's Army Auxiliary Corps!

Not wanting to be outdone by her friends, Miss Allen answered the editor, "You know, we have a great nursing staff and they are involving the men in a... a Patriotic Pie Party!"

64

As the newly created Newton D. Baker July Fourth Committee prepared for their celebration, back in Harrisburg, Elaine moved boldly toward catching a cake saboteur. Another Sunday found Floyd and Elaine strategizing at Loper's Drugs. The clues Elaine had collected pointed to deliveryman Butch and the likelihood of morning cake sabotage. She decided that tomorrow would be the day to catch him.

They planned for Elaine to enter the grocery surreptitiously. She knew the routine well and would sneak into the grocers with a crush of school kids who always spent their milk money on freshly baked vanilla drop cookies. She planned to squeeze under the cake display. This would allow Butch a seemingly unattended tray of cakes to damage. When he put his meaty fist into the cake case, he would ring the bell. Then she planned to alert the owner, sitting by the cash register. This strategy may have worked if Butch were just a wayward vandal who disrespected frosting. All too soon, they felt his darker side.

The next morning as Elaine slid under the wooden grocers' stand, her shiny hair met a cobweb or two. She lie on her side, caught her breath and propped her arm in order to have a headrest and some view of the cake culprit. Minutes crawled by. She heard Mr. Jake say, "Morning."

Elaine could hear only the sound of work boots entering the store and turned her head to identify them. The phone rang, and as the proprietor answered, Butch moved quickly to the case above Elaine, which held two Stitt cakes. She could see how dirty his socks appeared from her vantage point. He went to the case, opening the sliding door. She heard his breath over the case and a sliding sound. Then the glass slammed tight, yet the bell was silent.

Elaine froze, waiting for her cue, the bell. But then she thought, *He has no business near our cakes!*

Butch stood in the front of the cake case, and a devious chuckling sound escaped from his throat. Elaine, fueled by weeks of suspicion and the sudden sense that she had to corner her prey, reached for his foot. She wrapped her fingers around the boot top and screamed, "Stop! Stop!"

Jake moved into the aisle where he saw Elaine being dragged on the floor by the deliveryman, while she clutched Butch's shoelaces like a vise.

Jake yelled, "Hey, Elaine, let go!"

She would not.

The scuffling intensified when Jake attempted to hold the deliveryman's arms. Butch flung Jake, wailing, into a mountain of Maine potatoes, and he had some trouble getting to his feet, but then yelled over his shoulder, "I'll call the cops!"

Elaine screamed at the cake cutter, "No, Butch!"

He grappled with her. It was like kicking a sack of wolverines as she clawed and screamed, "Butch!"

His head spun as he looked down at her. "Who told you my name?"

"Nina."

Elaine felt the exasperation of a simple cake vandal who had had some cheap thrills at Stitt Bakery's expense. He caved in for a second.

Elaine somehow felt she had taken the upper hand. "Please, Butch."

Butch calmly said, "Take that!" And he dumped cookie crumbs from a tray onto her head.

Butch faked a laugh, "Aw shut up. Leggo my leg!"

Elaine craned her neck to see out the nearby door, and she lost her grip. There were sounds of a car engine outside and distant police sirens.

The car belonged to an unusually tall young man who bent his head to exit his recently waxed black Chevy. How luxurious. He had just spent the morning shining its finish and now he planned to buy some doughnuts at Jake's. He was about to be delayed in a most extraordinary fashion.

The young man heard shouting and sighted Butch quickly jumping into his bakery truck, then begin to back up in his direction. He shouted from the open window, "For the love of Ike!"

Elaine watched the Stroop panel truck slowly barreling backwards, and Jake shielded his eyes from the sun, saying, "Oh, he better stop now." But in spite of wailing police sirens, Butch backed into the Chevy like a loaf of stale bread smashing against a pound of butter.

Gripping Elaine's shoulder, Jake exclaimed, "That's it!" as the truck made impact. "Whew! I hope you're all right."

Elaine could only whisper, "Yeah" as she leaned against him.

At the scene of the collision, one policeman pulled Butch out of the truck while the other officer questioned the driver of the Chevy. The young man's first words were, "If I wasn't here, I'd never believe it."

He was young and so tall that he had to fold himself to get out of the car. His wavy hair shone with sweat. He mopped his brow.

The officer noted, "Your name?"

"Bill Foster."

65

The Harrisburg police force took pride in attending to detail. They questioned their surly suspect and charged him with reckless driving, disturbing the peace, and damaging private property. The assault with cookie crumbs was not charged. Across the road with his arms folded, the youthful Mr. Foster leaned against his car, which had come through the fray with a crumpled fender. He shouted, "Whoever you are, you'll pay for this."

Jake waited until the police completed their questioning then faced Butch and said, "You caused a hell of a lot of trouble damaging baked goods, 'n now disrupting my business. I'm damn glad we caught you."

Butch hung his head.

The officer asked him, "Why would you cut up a perfectly good cake?"

After a moment, he shrugged, kicked the dirt and said, "I was sick of being poor, flat foot."

Elaine walked over, looked Butch in the eye and spoke from the depths of her heart. "You think you just smeared a competitor's cake! Instead, think about workers just like you, who worked hours to produce something valuable and beautiful. Why, our bakers worked on cake after cake, my father bought this *rationed* sugar and then, my sisters sold these cakes. Then YOU cut them up!" With a tear welling up, she yelled, "You… you destroyed not just food!" She cast about for the right word while unconsciously stirring with an invisible spoon. Louise had used the word. "You destroyed *culinary art!*"

Suddenly Elaine was momentarily stunned. She was shouting

at a man for damaging cakes. She wondered as though from her Myrna Loy brain, *What was he really up to?*

The police offered to take Elaine home. Before she got into the car, Elaine stopped then she ran back to the Stroop truck. Jumping onto the back bumper, she whipped open the double doors.

"Holy crumbs," sighed the exhausted policeman. "Now what?"

Elaine pulled out the drawers inside the truck, searching. Cupcakes, cookies, loaves of bread. She looked through every drawer as the quizzical officer watched, amused.

She kneeled and opened the lowest drawer. It held an empty beer bottle, a few loaves of day-old bread and an old cardboard cake box. She pulled out the mottled box and opened it in the sunlight.

"Officer!" She handed him a heavy parcel. He pulled out the contents, exclaiming, "Ration books. Gas coupons and a few tokens too." The two police deputies started laughing and slapping each other on the back.

Elaine couldn't believe her eyes. Butch was a counterfeiter!

Mr. Bill Foster had been shocked, his car violated by a runaway truck, and now he understood that this was about black market activity! He blurted out, "That will put this punk behind bars!"

Promptly the policeman added, "Plus a big fine."

66

B y the time Louise heard about Elaine's capture of the cake saboteur, it was nearly July 4, 1942. Her work kept her busy. The nursing care concentrated mainly on servicemen recuperating from traumatic injuries, and usually the survivors required rehabilitation. Sources said the war in the Pacific was not going well, the activity in Europe promised to beat Hitler in the air, but now German troops were in the USSR, moving toward Stalingrad.

> *Dear Louise,*   *June 11, 1942*
> *I'm in a British Army camp with most of my original unit. We are safe, but close by a town that gets its share of air raids, so I haven't been sleeping well.*
> *Working with the paratroopers, servicing planes.*
> *To say I miss you is like a whisper when I want to broadcast it on some station, but only to your ear. I'm entertained by your letters and have your picture in front of me now. Remember the time we drove up to your Aunt Ruth's place? We laughed about my customers who drank too much and then the time on the farm when you showed me the tree you used to climb—we had such a great day.*
> *I'd like to help win the war, but miss you so much.*
> *Love you so,*
> *Eddie*

"What brought me here?" Louise asked herself as she chewed a Stitt cookie. Dot sent the spice disks stacked into a coffee tin, "tres ingenious," Louise exclaimed of Dot's packaging.

Perhaps she knew nursing would be a way to help herself to live through the war. She was part of the civilian war effort. She enjoyed the feeling of satisfaction that accompanied nursing. The hospital had a feel of urgency stemming from the needs of the patients and the pace of nurses anticipating those needs. The resident physician or his staff made appearances in the mornings after breakfast. Nurse B. Davis had run the unit so well; it was like a box of Cracker Jack with unexpected surprises. She used her basic knowledge of sanitation and passed this and other practices on to her staff. She had proven over and over that keen observation could prevent problems such as surgically related infection. Doctors relied on Nurse B. as their trusted colleague, largely because the medical and nursing staff communicated clearly; and Nurse B. depended upon Louise, who fueled her spirit just like rationed gas fueled an ambulance.

Louise was more fortunate than most of her peers, who toiled in other hospital units where the usual tone of the workplace was somber. She was well aware that B. was the reason that her job was enjoyable. Both Louise and B. worked better if they had something keeping them excited, driving them toward their current goal, but excitement had run out. Where would they find it? Like many civilian Americans of all ages, Louise was now doing her part, as a nurses' aide. However satisfying nursing was, nursing was not her passion. She was not so passionate over pie baking either, but the making of significant pies for the holiday became synchronized right along with the stewing cherries.

Louise had planned well enough to procure the baking equipment by July 3, with the help of the cooks. Her counters clear, pie pans stacked, utensils for her bakers readied, plus four extra fans had been found. There was even a slab of dark gray marble for rolling out impeccable piecrust. They would need large quantities of sugar for the patriotic pies, but there had been no trouble getting it for the Army, in spite of the rationing limits.

A few sparks lit Louise's creative fire, which in turn served to fuel the baking. A small parcel arrived by special delivery. Dot had found and sent hundreds of miniature flags on toothpicks. "Perfect garnishes!" gasped Louise. While Louise inspected the kitchen, a doctor came to her. He was carrying an oak, cranking ice cream maker.

He asked, "Would you mind if we have ice cream along with your pie? I've got volunteers."

"Oh, dahling, thanks loads!" she exclaimed, clapping her hands. Louise suddenly felt everything was going to fall into place.

Thanks to the July Fourth committee, the community of Martinsburg was going to be a large part of the celebration. There would be speeches, group singing and the high school band was to perform a few of their favorite patriotic marches. Louise hoped the men would find her intended occupational therapy amid all the encroaching folderol.

***

The oven sparkled and Mary Lane had placed a small flag above the oven as she had patriotically done with red, white and blue bunting in the parking lot. There were a number of stands ready for the celebration.

The patient/bakers were outfitted with starched white aprons and close-fitting chef's hats. Miss Allen, nervously treading uncharted waters, seemed to have had one too many coffees. She made much of watching the men wash their hands and grabbed a soldier who failed to scrub for a full minute. She insisted the newsman from the *Stars and Stripes* newspaper stay at the hospital two days. She treated him as she would have treated a visiting Edward R. Murrow. In return, she prominently appeared in most of his photos.

The nurses, the corpsmen and a few doctors had ushered a

dozen "bakers" into the kitchen. They put down their crutches and canes and they armed themselves with spoons, knives and rolling pins. Louise had also made a large poster depicting pie prep, she explained what they were to do, then the cook demonstrated.

"Look at this!" exclaimed Corporal Bob. He stood at the marble slab with some effort, and with his floured rolling pin, had eased the dough into a large oval. Louise turned the dough for him, and with her own marble rolling pin, demonstrated how to make the sheet of dough round, the base for the soon-to-be cherry pie. Quietly, she had propelled this group of survivors into kitchen rehab by intending that they all had to "live a little."

Now she found herself in the vanguard, losing herself to the marvels of baking. Mark Gordon was in charge of inserting prepared soft dough into pans. He accurately trimmed piecrust circles with a sharp knife. The dough-lined pans went to a group from another unit who filled the dough with a delectably cooked concoction of sugar, whole sour cherries, cinnamon and a dollop of cherry jam. Then Mark applied the "lids," pinching together the upper and lower dough, and finally he made a vent for the escape of steam. A sudden bolt of creative juice told Mark to make a star for a vent. He was recovering from the loss of one eye, so Louise told him, "You have an eye for décor."

He smiled, "Oh yeah, I have an eye. You know what? It seems like I see different today. I forgot about the accident. I feel strong, and is it because of making pies?" He said it as though it was a big surprise.

Miss Allen shone as the photographs were snapped in the kitchen, posing with the intent of her own good publicity. Louise giggled as the pies went into the ovens while Miss Allen, a leader who kept herself and everyone else on a tight rein, posed in a chef hat. *She reminds me of a Frigidaire ad*, Louise thought as hot cherry filling bubbled from pie vents.

Louise was touched by the patients who had no baking experience, yet got such joy out of the exercise. Bob laughed like a drunken hyena! She had never seen Corporal Bob relax; never heard such an unleashing of laughter. He egged the others on.

"They really achieved something outside of themselves." Mary Lane briefly sat with Louise on the wooden stairs at the back of the kitchen as they rested in the aura of wafting cherry air. They made signs to each other about Colonel Allen but felt good about the baking. Louise mused, "I'm *not* cut out for teaching, but I sure had fun today."

"There is something big going on here, Louise. You teach by example, and people decide to emulate you."

Characteristically, Louise rolled her eyes and said, "Dahling, I am *such* a role model."

Tomorrow was coming fast and promised to be quite a party. The newsman approached the two as they rested on the stair, and Louise had to be restrained from ducking the interview.

Mary explained, "She's humble."

But the man pressed on, "So this was your idea?

"I am merely trying to serve my country, now if you'll excuse me..."

Mary said, "Yeah, she's the brains behind it."

Brown eyes popping, Louise said, "Sir, this woman is the real party planner. She made the meetings and set all this up... the red, white and blue too."

The newsman sat down next to Mary, mumbling, "How am I supposed to report the facts?"

Louise said, "Facts. Well just send the message 'over there' that we care. We want the ones here to get well and those overseas," now she visualized Eddie—it was just like he held her hand for a moment, "not to get hurt."

After the man walked through crusty, cherry air, back to his reportage, Louise returned to check on the pies, leaving Mary, who came to know Louise's sense of compassion as a force to be reckoned with. She saw that what Louise inspired in people was something impossible to describe in a newspaper.

***

The Newton D. Baker July Fourth Celebration of 1942 was historic in that it would be remembered on every succeeding Fourth of July. Men who could not speak specifically of battles to their children, proudly, patriotically reminisced about pie baking as they recovered from various battles.

The high school band played *The Stars and Stripes Forever.* Girls in red and blue dresses twirled white flags. The World War I veterans whistled like teens. The stomping of feet sent vibrations through the ground. Then there followed speeches, like rough carbon copies of Roosevelt's. The chief surgeon, a man who had survived Verdun, generated applause from the town's people. He proclaimed that Hitler would lose to the Russians. More worrisome to him was the Pacific Area, as it was now crucial to stop the Japanese. Our men in the Mediterranean gave him hope to beat General Rommel. He dramatically pointed to Germany and Italy, where we worked now with the British to defeat the enemy by land and air.

Colonel Allen made a short statement in which her worthy team of nurses were given credit for relieving pain, saving lives and motivating men to reenter the fray. The nursing staff stood and took a bow. She didn't surprise anyone when she dared to take credit where it was not due.

"I love a good piece of pie,"

The crowd cheered.

"I saw how there was a need among the men for that taste and the smell that comes of baked goods. I felt good when I realized that rolling out pie dough is a powerful feeling. And now I invite these men of uncommon valor and all of you from our community to join together to celebrate this great American land!"

The chief surgeon jumped up, led a round of applause and kissed the colonel on the back of her hand. When he whispered in her ear, people wondered. What he said had nothing to do with pies.

A trio of trumpets sounded a fanfare as the bakers paraded trays of sliced cherry pie. Each slice held a tiny waving flag, so that the desserts appeared from a distance to move. It was going to feel like eating a bite of the United States of America.

The crowd perhaps had sat too long, for the sight of cherry pie, ice cream and lemonade had an invigorating effect, catapulting them to a normal life, where gas rationing and fear of the enemy didn't exist. The marching band jammed, the twirlers danced with kids from their school, and little boys in short pants marched around the parking lot.

None of this was lost on the newsman, who snapped a picture of an overjoyed José Santiago that later won him an award. Jose had a paper plate in his left hand, holding his pie. The right hand was open to the sky, where José had just tossed his cane! That was really freeing for José because whatever had traumatized his knee had vanished, just like the cherry pie down the mouth of a ten-year-old.

White uniformed Nurse B. Davis was striding past the speaker's podium, sandwiched between two corpsmen. She found the green uniformed Louise, finishing pie a la mode.

"Louise, let's dance! The band's starting again."

So the four went and swing danced, swinging until they were spent. A patient from another ward took the megaphone and sang *Pennies from Heaven*. They draped themselves over their folding chairs and relaxed. "He has a touch of Sinatra," B. decided.

The corpsman agreed, "He has the same gestures and hair."

Nurse B. noted with the concern of a caregiver, "His uniform hangs on him."

The second corpsman said, "Frank Sinatra should stay home, I hope he doesn't join the service."

Louise wistfully added, "Teenagers here need him."

The band played, people brought picnic dinners, and folks let their concerns rest as tension eased. It had been a worthwhile effort for the patients and genuine therapy for body and mind. The townspeople sighed as they were served a piece of pie by a man in a short leg cast or sporting an eye patch. This community event appeared empowering to service people, but their fellow Americans went home with the distinct perception that they were soldiering too. The sun set with three wide bands of color in the western sky: red, white and blue.

67

Two months after the Patriotic Pie Party in Martinsburg West Virginia, there was another patriotic party happening, a gala in Berlin. Black Forest Pie was at a loss for taste compared to the West Virginia cherry pie. The weather had cooled, there was a full moon, and the Nazi's imagined themselves kings of the hill—wolves howling at the moon.

They were behind schedule in Russia, and the German casualty rate was rising, even as their factories turned out more artillery. The Mediterranean and Middle East areas now were fought over by the Allies, and the Axis would hope for better news in the Pacific. Perhaps the Reich spent too much effort and money corralling the ones Hitler blamed for all German difficulties: the Jewish people. The truth, the spiraling downward of the dictatorship, was kept from the newspapers.

Hitler said his sleepless nights were due to an over indulgence of knockwurst at "afternoon teas" which he held at 2 a.m. But it was less a dietary problem and more a chemical reaction. To appear dictatorial, Hitler needed at least twenty tablets and injections, but chemical crutches to wake and to sleep had unfortunate side effects, causing concerned advisors to worry.

Der Fuhrer became a spoiled fanatic who was inclined to believe his fiendish schemes had worked when in reality the army was depleting, the government was disjointed and the ordinary citizens of the Fatherland were feeling more like orphans.

***

Elaine at sixteen had witnessed the Jazz Age swinging, the turmoil of the Great Depression and now, a world war. In her home, FDR's fireside chats were heard while she followed, scanning a map and she saw her mother reading *The Patriot News* each morning. Today Clara ate toast made of day-old bread smeared with apple butter. Floyd was now accustomed to reducing his product's sugar content and using more molasses.

"Well, it seems like Germany lost to the Russians," Clara read the story aloud.

Floyd testily replied, "Hitler is a damn crazy man."

Speaking of Germany, Caroline was a German immigrant, who had been an American citizen from the age of eighteen. Now, Byron and Caroline, Elaine's grandparents, instructed their granddaughter about rationing of food efficiently, wasting nothing. Armament manufacturers collected their tin cans with pick-up trucks labeled: "Beat the 'Pans' Off the Nazis." They remembered much from World War I and steeled themselves for the long haul. Stuffing was created from day-old bread and soup was made from potato peels or bone marrow. Caroline planted a victory garden and Byron tended it, trading various commodities with neighbors.

Elaine was working along with Dot in the bakery office. High school kids were quitting to work in industry. Now workers were scarce, as the few young men employed in the shop had enlisted in the service.

Elaine was involved in the war effort at home. She tolerated this job, knowing times were tough and out of loyalty to Floyd. Elaine thought over her interest in the new automobiles. She craved driving, so Floyd allowed her to drive in out of the way places to practice, prior to earning a driver's license.

It was curious how she had managed to get a hold on the cake-slashing Butch. Sometimes in study hall, she went into a reverie, secretly wanting to become a detective or to solve more mysteries. Did Myrna Loy need a stand in?

These ideas caromed around her brain as she dressed for a date. Her encounter with Bill was a fortunate coincidence. They introduced themselves on that fateful day when his Chevrolet was smacked by the deranged deliveryman in the gigantic panel truck.

The two young people had connected through the encounter involving them in police work, while filled with adrenalin after witnessing the careless Butch. Bill was stunned by Elaine's assertive ferreting out of the evidence. He had felt a sense of wonder, not only for Elaine the sleuth, but for her as a person.

Dress up, but not too much, she thought. She looked at her figure in the mirror, in a white-collared, long-sleeved navy dress. It had shoulder padding, which gave her the illusion of a tiny waist. As she threaded the matching belt into place, she thought, *Finally, I'm going on a real date, not a silly dance or a birthday party—a date with a boy who is seventeen!*

Elaine introduced Bill to her family, and then they went out to a movie in his recently repaired car. Byron said Bill was the tallest man he had ever met. The two went to see *The Long Voyage Home*, starring John Wayne. They thought it would be a tale of war, but John Wayne was working at sea instead.

Elaine brought along a bag of large pretzel sticks from the Blue Swan candy store—another place not immune to the rationing of sugar. Bill bragged about the amount of work he had put into the car, and Elaine found the leather seats and interior impeccable.

They met a few familiar faces in the Senate Theater lobby, but were more interested in discovering each other. They whispered through the newsreel, but not about FDR, who was in fact speaking about them. He said that schools should allow students time off to help in the war effort. Bill planned for Elaine to drive the car home.

Elaine had become a good conversationalist and listened intently to what Bill said, which seemed to be about his sacred auto or airplanes. It was clear that Elaine understood cars nearly as well as Bill. He had noticed a problem with braking, whereby the stops were not very smooth. Elaine felt that the wheel in question was the left rear and told Bill, "Speak to Joe Pozoic, our bakery mechanic, he knows brakes."

Bill murmured, "Well, if you move a truckload of cakes, you'd best have good brakes."

His mind was not on cars, and he wished he could leave a good impression as Elaine pulled the black Chevy in front of 2232 North Sixth Street. She handed him the key, saying, "Whew, that was fun!"

Bill said, "I wrote a poem for you," which was not true. He cleared his throat and quoted "Spilt milk" by Bishop:

"Brooding upon its unexerted power, deep in the gas tank lay
the gasoline
A waiting the inevitable hour
When from the inward soul of the machine
Would come the Call. Ah, hark! Man's touch awakes
Th' ignition switch! The starting motor hums;
A sound of meshing gears, releasing brakes!
The call of Duty to the gas tank comes."

Elaine laughed replying, "For me?" She jumped out, but he quickly met her over the driver's door, leaning his chin on the doorframe.

"Would ya' like to meet me on Wednesday afternoon? I need to go back to see the Air Force recruiter."

"Well, you have to come to the bakery. I work there, you know."

He escorted her to the door. He waved, pulled a pretzel from his pocket and chewed it like a cigar.

68

Stars and Stripes ran the story of Newton D. Baker hospital, featuring the photo of José Santiago on the front page. It celebrated Miss Esther Allen as though she had magically engineered the Fourth of July celebration, with front-page photos of her making a speech and pie baking with the patients. She looked like the cover of a cookbook, edging out the WAACs featured on page seven.

That very week, another colonel made all of the American newspapers. He was a Marine, decorated for service in the battle of Guadalcanal. This man was multitalented as Marines go. He was decorated for not only doing his part on the front line, but he also spent many nights in thought as to inventively outsmarting the Japanese.

Named for a president, Colonel Chester Arthur's communications with local Solomon Island natives built up a contingent of "coast watchers" who alerted Marine allies of Japanese naval approaches. He also managed to save Marine lives when the coast watchers shared their homemade mosquito repellant with him. New to Corps doctors, it was later found to contain oils of lemon grass and citronella. Their odoriferous outfit was not immune to malaria or dengue fever, but very few soldiers lay in sickbay.

When Colonel Arthur incurred a shrapnel injury at the Battle of Guadalcanal, he was flown to Hawaii for recovery. His superiors valued Chester Arthur, counting on him for the Pacific campaign. They did not expect complications.

To his superior officers' dismay, Chester had found himself falling into a mire of depression. His pain from an arm infection was manageable, yet he was really immobilized by his mental state. There were no nightmares or flashbacks, but he sat with glazed eyes, not noticing what was before them.

The head surgical nurse had never encountered the situation. She complained to her superior officer. "I'm not making much progress now. The trauma of the arm injury is improving by the day. His mind is somewhere else, Major. He isn't like any other shellshock I've seen. I'm out of ideas."

Major Jane Perkin responded by scratching the hair under her starched white cap. "You take him out in the sun, I've seen. You had the psychiatrist in there, I know. Let me take a look at him."

The major had uncommon way with men in shellshock. She had only visited him a few days before, and he seemed to be less clear mentally. She took his hand and asked, "Colonel Arthur, how can we help you?"

His face was gaunt and somewhat frozen. He blinked and whispered, "I wish I knew."

She returned later, determined to find a connection, a spark to help him recover. This did not seem to be shellshock, she surmised, but something akin to amnesia. Major Perkin walked Chester around the grounds, and he stayed in the same sort of mental quicksand until…

"Woof-woof."

Ah ha! thought Major Perkin as Chester stooped at the fence to watch a boy playing fetch with his dog. And it was the dog that Chester followed, his brown eyes transfixed with interest. The major introduced herself to the boy and invited him inside the gate. This was promising. Chester started to awaken, and the Dalmatian dog wagged his tail, laying a wet ball on the patient's lap. He rubbed the dog's back and threw the rubber ball!

Major Perkin could hardly contain her satisfaction and promised the boy a treat if he would come to the gate the next day. She asked the boy to bring his mother and promised to explain her situation. She returned to the ward to make a detailed note in Chester's chart about the change.

The following day, Lucky the dog and his owners waited in the sun at the gate as planned. Major Perkin approached with two men—one on each arm—Chester and Dr. Edmond Witts, the resident for psychiatry. She needed a medical witness to her situation. She wanted to involve him because he had been a researcher and was a keen observer of human behavior. He was a rather short fellow, but with attractive dark features and a knowing way of saying, "An apt observation."

The patient had been talking about his encounter with Lucky to nurses, even regarding his doggy scent. Witts explained to the boy's mother, "Sometimes in cases of shock, a sensory memory will jump start the brain—just like starting a motorcycle." The mother was happy to help the Marine, as she had lost a brother in a Navy cruiser incident.

The reunion of man and canine was, well, joyous. Lucky licked Chester's cheek, and they played on the grass. The boy and Chester played catch while the cavorting dog ran between them. Play worked like medicine for the chuckling war hero, opening the door Major Perkin had intended to find. Then she tripped over another sensory door. The nurse rewarded the boy with a freshly baked pie from the hospital kitchen—coincidentally, it was cherry.

The boy exclaimed as he opened the paper bag, and bit into the crust. "Hey, it's a cherry pie."

Chester Arthur looked at the boy, whose mouth was smeared with red syrup.

Chester blurted out, "Gee whiz! Just like Mom used to bake." The nurse and physician were stunned not by his words but by his booming voice quality. He was momentarily back, thankfully, to his senses.

News of the war hero's new attitude traveled around the hospital. The psychiatrist, Dr. Witts, attached a magazine ad for Mrs. Smith's Pie to Chester Arthur's hospital bed. Part of his treatment was to *imagine* the pie. He felt the patient may have damaged the area of the brain relating to taste. Just the thought of cherry pie infused Chester with more energy, safety and a will, not only to live and eat pie, but also to get back to work. The consensus of his physicians was to plan for his furlough prior to his return to the Pacific.

Major Perkin objected, as he had been an only child who had lost both parents in an accident. Plus she wanted to insure that he did not back slide into his former state. She lured the family with their playful dog to the hospital as much as possible and insisted the mess hall offer cherry pie.

For amusement, Chester read and his friends took him off the base to the local USO in Oahu. The United Service Organization was created that year for service members, offering entertainment, refreshments and fellowship. One evening at the USO, he picked up an older copy of *Stars and Stripes*. The cover story read, "Nurse Celebrates the Fourth by Baking at Baker." The face of Colonel Esther Allen gazed down at a patient holding a rolling pin. Chester thought her face resembled paintings of the Madonna, her chef's hat imitating a halo.

"This is ironic," Chester told a friend. "This hospital in West Virginia knows what the doc knows here."

"What? Do tell!" exclaimed his friend.

Chester explained, "I've recovered. Don't you think it's slightly peculiar that my medicine was playing with a dog?"

"Naw," said his pal. "Not really. I miss my dog."

Chester went on, "I can't prove anything, but I know something good happened when I patted that dog."

His friend laughed, "Well, you needed a taste of pie, you said."

"Yeah, after that I started... to be myself, somehow. I don't have a sweet tooth either, but that pie certainly... was part of my getting myself together."

A cascade of events was triggered after the *Stars and Stripes* was shown to Dr. Witts. He saw an opportunity then to study the brain/taste connection, and he jumped at the chance to connect with physicians at Newton D. Baker.

A fact-finding mission was arranged for Witts, who wanted Chester Arthur to accompany him so the doctor could observe how his patient handled travel stress, meet with Colonel Allen and have his patient's furlough.

The trip went as planned, and the Chief Medical Officer received the two, personally guiding a tour of Newton D. Baker. Colonel Esther Allen found herself unprepared for what she herself had created as publicity. She met alone with Dr. Witts, who soon overwhelmed her by insisting she "had a duty" to continue pursuing knowledge of baking as occupational therapy.

"This was a *party*, dear doctor. You surely know how we are in the business of giving care to the sick and injured."

"Colonel, what you found was by accident. It's as if you had searched for a needle in a haystack and found a gold coin by chance. Congratulate yourself. Because of your efforts, you have healed others and given me a more meaningful occupation."

Esther Allen became impatient. She wished to be managerial, overseeing usual work, not researching and merging patients with floury, sugary baking. The psychiatrist insisted he didn't come across country to meet a dead end. He had already met similar indifference from the medical staff who wanted to focus on critical care, their specialty.

Dr. Witts urged, "You have met serendipity…"

"Who?" Miss Allen began wringing her hands, becoming more disarmed by the minute.

"Serendipity is a word for finding something of value by chance. In your hospital, baking was a serendipitous stroke of luck."

She exasperatedly threw her hands in the air. "Please know I want to complete this wartime mission. We have to have an understanding. You cannot depend on me… nor should you… because I put the story out for publicity. Doctor, I confess I'm not a baker and don't even enjoy pies. I will introduce you to the baker. She will be able to answer your questions."

Edmond Witts gasped and replied skeptically, "I guess one

can't believe everything in print."

She cleared her throat and said, "I'm sorry I misrepresented myself, however, the baking was a grand and glorious achievement. I will help you more by introducing you to Miss Stitt, a nurses' aide. She's a baker's daughter."

69

Floyd Stitt had been asked a favor by Harrisburg's City Council. There was a new USO club for enlisted service people in the railway station of Harrisburg, Pennsylvania. The council implored him to supply some baked goods. What surprised him was how enthusiastically his sweets were received by men and women who frequented the USO.

"They have had their fill of K rations!" he laughed, referring to packaged Army provisions.

Dot delivered her trays in the small Austin Healy truck at first, but she soon needed a larger truck. She selected items that qualified as finger food, and monstrous cookies were at the top of her list. Soft molasses, harder sugar cookies, red spice cookies with sugar in their crevices and near Christmas, the silver-dollar-sized cinnamon sand tarts. Men who piled off the train on leave gobbled up Dot's wares. Dutiful recruits often embarked toward train platforms holding a small pie wrapped in plain newsprint paper.

Floyd had worked around the rationing of his materials, but there was a distinct shortage of manpower, and he remedied this by recruiting Elaine. He wanted to give her a full time job, which meant quitting in her final year at John Harris High School. When she protested, he imitated FDR, "This is war!"

Finally, she entered the Distributive Education program, and that allowed students to work in office environments for part of the day. She did relieve some of Dot's load and eventually earned a diploma. Shuffling her paperwork, she daydreamed about Bill.

He had been stunned by the truck crash, and then by a heart

to heart sort of collision with Elaine in their abrupt initial meeting. He felt that her love of mystery and adventure set her apart from other girls his age. And Elaine took him seriously, drawn to his good looks and uncanny knowledge of machinery.

The Army Air Corps of 1943 had him in training for their surveillance program. He had already gone to California and trained in a PT Steerman open cockpit aircraft.

He returned to Harrisburg periodically, arriving on the Pennsylvania Railroad; and then Elaine was eager to work at the train station stand.

He strode up to her counter, saying, "Hey, good lookin.'"

And she would tilt her head, flip her hair and reply, "Hi, Bill!" She was a "dilly," a divine sight in her frilly blouse and straight skirt. She handed him a slice of jellyroll, which he made a show of eating out of her manicured hand.

He smirked, "Hi doll. See, ya' got me eating right outa' your hand."

Closing the bakery stand was an energy-intensive, sticky business, but Bill helped Elaine pack up the few rolls, a half dozen white cupcakes and three of the ten-cent pies. "This was a sell out," Elaine sighed as they hefted fifteen empty trays into the rear of Floyd's truck.

Floyd collected the empties, cardboard boxes and a canvas sack of cash, leaving Bill and Elaine to dance at the USO. The latest tune, sung by a finger snapping blond, was loudly played by a local band:

Praise the Lord (Praise the Lord) and pass the ammunition
Praise the Lord (Praise the Lord) and pass the ammunition
Praise the Lord (Praise the Lord) and pass the ammunition
And we'll all stay free...

But the recruits and their mates were not in the mood for war songs. Their stressful soldiering needed a rest, and every one of them had been somehow wounded, even if they had never left basic training. The collective mood of the club became steadier, more comfortably human when the band played, *Taking a chance on love.*

He had assumed that flying would quell his wanderlust, but as soon as Bill got away from home, he missed it. Elaine's existence made home even more magnetic. Consumed by his aviation studies, he would find himself reading his text on physics for pilots, only to be interrupted by the memory of Elaine outsmarting dastardly Butch, the Stroop driver. He would be flying over Catalina Island with his instructor and Elaine's face appeared suddenly in a cloud.

They swayed to aphrodisiac Glenn Miller music, and Elaine led a few dance steps toward the door. Once outside, he took her in his arms and held her, both of them encircled by fascination that was mutual. They drove to nearby Front Street, overlooking the broad Susquehanna River. The moon illuminated the front seat of the car. He took her left hand, saying, "I'm not a good dancer, but tonight I didn't care."

She kissed him and told him, "I love you, I can't even tell you how much."

Bill sighed and said, "Go on! Try to tell me."

After a shake of her long curls, she ventured, "More than Myrna Loy loves William Powell."

He chucked, "That much?"

By the time Bill dropped her at 2232 North Sixth, they were "going steady."

70

Esther Allen crisply made the introductions. "Louise was instrumental in our triumphant July Fourth. It really started with baking pies as therapy and grew into a party for the hospital and Martinsburg."

The visitors were dressed in fatigues and smelled like Brylcreem. "I am so pleased to make your acquaintance. I'm Edmond Witts. This is Colonel Chester Arthur."

"Please make yourselves comfortable here. Louise will spend the weekend with you, explaining how we did the... er... therapy."

And then, Colonel Allen left. She had plans to oversee the tests on a new injection that would aid her fight against infection.

Louise heartily shook hands with the visitors. Chester beamed and then Witts explained carefully that he felt occupational therapy had brought Chester to a functional state, and that he needed to observe Louise working, baking that is, with patients. He proceeded to question her about her training, and simultaneously found himself studying her behavior.

Louise was relieved that thanks to a recent permanent wave, her hair behaved, though she had no intention of behaving. She managed to appear elegant, even in her green nurses' aide uniform. She answered thoughtfully while the psychiatrist made notes furiously. "The work at Lake Erie helped me, but this baking I learned from my grandmother and from being at home in a bakery."

"At home in a bakery," Witts recorded.

"And you taught patients the recipe as well as the

mechanics?"

Louise smiled, "I demonstrated the techniques, but I was *really* intent on them enjoying themselves."

"Miss Stitt, you fostered a state of functional normalcy among traumatized patients."

Louise raised her eyebrows. "That too?"

Witts explained, "Miss Stitt, sometimes it looks as if a patient is bored, but I have seen shellshocked casualties that exhibit impaired brain function, depression or just poor social skills."

Louise replied, "I know all the men who participated, and most of them are back overseas now. The common denominator was boredom, but they were all worried about something."

"Aide identified anxiety," wrote Witts.

Chester boomed, "Hell yeah, war is a tad worrisome."

Witts continued, adjusting his wire rims, "Bear with us, Miss Stitt. I am interested in your baking exercise—and it definitely exercises the mind from an emotional standpoint and a physical perspective."

Louise agreed and handed them white baker's caps. "Why, sure, I'll be happy to help." As she led the way she yelled, "Send me the Marines!"

So they entered the kitchen after the breakfast hour and proceeded to make a few pies. What was it this nurses' aide was doing? Witts pondered as the dough was pinched by Chester Arthur. Even before donning a starched white apron, Louise ascertained he knew nothing of baking and only cooperated out of curiosity regarding this fact-finding mission. But somewhere between the flouring of the rolling pin and the turning out of the dough, Chester became amused. Louise coached him and happened to call him "dahling" and the picture of himself as a "darling" somehow unleashed a reluctant laugh.

Slowly, Chester had healed his mind on his own, possibly through his courageous nature, but now he faced a woman who knew no fear, who had more heart than he did and that helped him take one more step toward wholeness. As he filled the pie, he was somehow more alive and felt like he had regained his old sureness. He chuckled at himself, a warrior baking pies.

Louise did fake magic tricks and tossed a floury dough ball at Chester, who grabbed it from the air. She was fast trimming dough from the pie pan rim announcing; "Now you see it, now you don't!'

Suddenly, Witts also found himself drawn into the scene, stopped thinking, dropped his pad full of sensory annotations, washed his hands and took up Louise's knife, and unceremoniously trimmed the crust. He held the pie pan aloft as though it needed scrutiny. They laughed over his ragged edge and Chester hysterically suggested he "analyze" his dough. Louise threatened to report Dr. Witts to the baker.

Nonsense bred overwhelming silliness. Chester cut crust vents in the shape of the Marine insignia and his laughing caught Witts like a toy boat in a gale. Witts hooted at cherries slurping over the dough, then giggled at the tears running out of Chester's eyes, then he laughed his head off.

As Louise hollered, Witts laughed louder so that the cook came to observe, then he joined in the uproar. Witts could only lean against the worktable and point, trying to get his breath. Louise stopped for a second, then started shrieking again. Everyone in earshot circled into the kitchen, yelling over the din, "What's going on?" The questioning induced another fit of sniggering. The pie bakers had laughed out their war pains. Pain: honorably discharged.

Pies baked while the three sat over cups of hospital coffee. They had entered Louise's realm and been charmed. Chester had the look of a cartoon character just hit with a sledgehammer. The physician appeared to have just seen the hammer strike. Louise owned the hammer. The patient and his doctor were in a state of respect for their new friend and teacher.

Later Witts described her in his notes as an enigma. "Puzzling intelligence with superficial mind, never delving very deep in conversation. Positive emotion flows from her, yet can be sarcastically humorous. Self disparaging. Disorganized, yet surprisingly efficient." She could be fun and serious at the same time.

Louise smiled quietly, "Too bad laughing can't be bottled."

Chester answered, "I'll remember this forever."

Edmond Witts sipped his coffee, still stunned by his own surprise reaction. Now what?

Therapy it was, but what the hell happened? I smelled dough, saw cherries, felt the crust, heard a hundred funny things—all more powerful than tasting of the treat. There was, in that kitchen a determination to have fun and she was as effective as a festival. Heaven, he conceded: brief moments of heavenly hilarity.

Later, years later, Witts told a symposium that the experience of handling dough lends a unique form of security, followed by the enhanced self-esteem that one feels when something good is built.

Chester told Louise, "I feel that I had a lot of mental trash from my life… that went away."

Louise smiled., "That's remarkable."

He continued. "Now I bet what got to me in battle was a truckload of terrible sights."

Witts patted him on the back. "I call it distortion. I think it interferes with cognition."

Distinctly Louise responded, "Yeah, distortion! That's what you get when men go out of control for the love of power over common people!" She sighed, not knowing why she blurted out her thoughts. "I'm tired of the news of the dead, patching people up and wondering about whether the ones I know will ever survive this."

Edmund Witts agreed intoning, "An apt observation."

Louise definitely saw the world through different brown eyes, and made light of her own unique abilities. Was she ever a bit guilty about feeling that fun could reign supreme? Never.

71

E dward Shafer's letters repeatedly indicated that he hoped to marry Louise.

"Cherie, we could honeymoon in Pine Grove. No, we can celebrate in a classy hotel in Baltimore! I long to see you."

Dropping the letter, Louise would not allow herself to think beyond his safe arrival home.

Still, her heart flipped each time she got his letters. Most of the time, a Glenn Miller tune ran on the auditory channel of Louise's mind, while she made a hospital bed, delivered meal trays, walked the injured men. One day she awakened, stared at the dormitory ceiling and sang to herself, "It don't mean a thing if it ain't got that swing," intentionally opening a box of delightful prewar memories. "Eddie, be careful, you'll be okay," she whispered. She daydreamed visions of how he was smart, a good listener and how he covered smoldering lust with his own gentlemanly veneer.

She recalled as how he'd brought her a cellophane wrapped bunch of red roses the day he shipped out. "Think of it! Next time it'll be a wedding bouquet."

"Silly boy," she answered. "Go on, veni, vedi, vici, then get back to me fast."

Sometimes his letters were in transit for a month, and she unfolded these notes to discover a flower pressed into the airmail tissue. This prompted a long return letter, followed by her postscript in the lipstick shade "fire engine red," a kiss print.

"There's no doubt, you're getting restless or getting Army hospital cabin fever," suggested B. Davis as they strolled a lane in Martinsburg.

"Heh, heh, you should talk, sister!" Louise referred to Davis's popularity born out of her inventive nurses' tools. There was the contoured sheet for the hospital bed, the meal tray cover that kept food hot, and the tub with bubbling underwater hose for injured muscles. Her meetings with hospital officials had earned her two suitors from management, each looking for ways to impress.

Louise had been working in Martinsburg for over a year. She had made a contribution and now she felt a calling to some place unknown. She decided that this year she would return to Harrisburg. Her sister Dot suggested Louise stay with her over the bakery.

***

Spring of 1943 and a Saturday off! This was Louise's signal to shop in Martinsburg with her friends, who enthusiastically voted for a drug store lunch. They wore their spring coats with shoulder pads and jauntily warm hats in the spring breeze. Their shoes were quite run down because shoes were rationed. Louise had received a parcel from Clara, with cuttings from *The Patriot News* that served as makeshift envelopes for small sunshine cakes, baked by her grandmother Caroline. Clara had a way of sending darkly foreboding news, which she seemed to see as hopeful. Louise checked Clara's news shorts and read the headlines to B. Davis and Mary Lane.

"Victory Sausages Now Available—a new mix of meat and soy meal."

"February saw Amsterdam resistance group CS-6 shoot Nazi General Seyffardt."

"Soviets Win Battle of Stalingrad—Thousands of German Forces Captured."

"Japanese evacuate Guadalcanal."

"FDR soon to announce end of coffee rationing in U.S."

"German officers plot to poison Hitler with pastry."

Nurse Davis shouted, her hands waving, "Now we're getting somewhere."

"Hmmm, how Nazily creative," Louise mused. "Maybe it was a jelly doughnut laced with rat poison... or Arsenic Apple Strudel."

Mary Lane whispered to Louise, "Why, you could work as a *spy*. You could deliver... cyanide cakes and disarm the SS!"

Louise looked up and seriously replied, "Sure thing, I'll get Mamaw to teach me German."

Then B. Davis ventured, "Americans are eating victory sausage. German officers poison their own leader..."

"With doughnuts, don't forget!"

B. insisted, "Can't you feel the tide turning?"

Louise laughed, "Ha-ha, sure, any day now the Third Reich will collapse! Now if we can only hold on 'til this sausage-doughnut insanity ends."

Nurse B. Davis asked Louise to join her that evening, "So that I won't go crazy," she said with a roll of her blue eyes. It seemed that two men interested in her had managed to convince her to go out to Dino's Grill. She had described the men as Tweedle dee and Tweedle dum, not due to their equally nice appearance, but their immaturity. She could not know that these two had gone so far as to have a violent knockdown, drag-out fight over her. The two men never realized they might alter the course of history that evening.

Sitting at a booth in their Saturday clothes, the four began making small talk that grew into a sort of interrogation because the fellows were increasingly frustrated by B. and Louise.

Sparks flew when B. said that she had no plans for marriage. "I'm twenty-five, and I have been thinking of traveling, seeing the world. The Army will help me with that."

One could see the disappointment and hear it in the man at her side, "Oh, you want to risk life and limb in a war zone?"

B. smirked, "Oh, Louise and I never err on the side of caution."

She explained that she wanted to work for some aid-related cause, and if the Army couldn't provide, then the Red Cross would. After some more nerve frazzling discourse with B., Louise said in an offhand way, "She's gifted and talented."

Then they turned to Louise, who was obliged to say she hoped for the safe return of Eddie. She refused to give many details, although in her mind, the picture was blurred by a wartime veil of fog. Then the man to her left asked the unthinkable.

"How old are you?" he asked offhandedly.

Louise sipped her Coke and said matter-of-factly, "Forty-nine."

Now he raised his voice. "No, I mean really."

"Why do you care how old I am? And why do you question me?"

"Why hide it? I'm twenty-nine. Aren't you interested in my age?"

His friend chimed in, "I'm twenty-eight."

"Hells bells!" Louise growled, "I just said, I'm forty-nine, now drop it!"

The two men muttered to themselves about their acquaintances being snooty, and brought the evening to an early end.

The important thing that "Dee and Dum" triggered was a free form of thinking between Louise and B. They thanked their dates and went to B's room, kicked off their chunky heels, removed their earrings and slipped into a ginger ale schmooze.

They had no more time for what B. referred to as mistreatment. They agreed that Dee and Dum really weren't listening.

"Honey," said B. "They want Betty Grable minus a brain."

Louise added, "I thought I was some kind'a racehorse... all *so* important to know my age. I was braced to have him check my teeth!"

B. went on, "Then there was no sense of humor for the forty-nine-year-old beauty."

"I have never felt so threatened in all my years of concealing my age…"

B. passed the soft drink saying, "And you look grand for a middle-aged woman."

Louise looked down her nose and said, "I like the age, 'over twenty-one.' That's what I put on the civilian defense application for this hospital!"

"I should've told them I'd like to be a nuclear physicist."

"Whatever that is. I could have told them I want to be the youngest woman pool hustler."

They talked about what they had learned, how they needed to learn more, and how much they had been loved.

"You've got to find a man with integrity," B. declared.

"A man who likes women," Louise added.

"A confident man."

"Yes. A respectable, respecting man."

"Keep that in mind when you are deliriously attracted to some Romeo."

B. told Louise that her inspiration was her mother. "She was pushed into marriage by her parents. Her grandmother's marriage was arranged. Women in this world seldom have voting rights. It's because of men like those two tonight, who barely know you, who want control over you."

"We got the vote a short time ago, we can easily work. I guess we women most have to be careful not to be taken advantage of. And I'm not Betty Grable, with or *without a brain.*"

B. laughed, "We're better off because we don't play games. I mean pretending or doing things I don't want to do. I so enjoy being myself, and I want to have time for myself."

Louise sat up on the bed. She was fatigued at this late hour, a little silly and started to think aloud. "I'm ready to leave Martinsburg soon. I feel drawn to something I don't understand. I hope Eddie comes home, but I'm pretty sure it's not about him."

"Back home to live with your sister at the bakeshop."

"Yeah. I'll go back there to live and work… you know last night I dreamed I worked at the bakery in my Playtex bra. I know it was the bakery 'cause I also wore a starched white apron over it."

B. went on, "I hope whatever you're drawn to is fun."

Louise giggled, "Thanks loads, kid, you can count on it!"

72

B ack at the bakery, Elaine endured her desk job. She put down the phone and wrote up an order for a cake. "'Happy Birthday Billy' devil's food cake with milk chocolate icing. Serves 12. Deliver to 333 Green St., May 1. $2.00."

She sighed aloud, "Another year here, and next year I graduate." She thought to herself about how Bill was probably zooming high over the West Coast in his much more exciting assignment of surveillance.

The 1943 Air Corps in conjunction with other service branches was making the oceans safe for ships carrying vitally needed supplies to war-torn areas. Their strategy had reduced the number of German U-boats significantly. Later that evening, Elaine sat next to Dot and daydreamed of Bill, searching out U-boats while the family listened to Roosevelt as he delivered his latest fireside chat.

The enticing Roosevelt drummed out, "It is interesting for us to realize that every flying fortress that bombed harbor installations at, for example, Naples, bombed it from its base in North Africa, required 1,110 gallons of gasoline for each single mission, and that this is the equal of about 375 'A' ration tickets—enough gas to drive your car five times across this continent. You will better understand your part in the war—and what gasoline rationing means—if you multiply this by the gasoline needs of thousands of planes and hundreds of thousands of jeeps, and trucks and tanks that are now serving overseas.

The next time anyone says to you that this war is 'in the bag,' or says (and) 'it's all over but the shouting,' you should ask him these questions:

"Are you working full time on your job?"

"Are you growing all the food you can?"

"Are you buying your limit of war bonds?"

"Are you loyally and cheerfully cooperating with your government in preventing inflation and profiteering, and in making rationing work with fairness to all?"

Dot, wearied of her day-to-day existence, snickered when FDR asked, "Are you working full time...?" She had been having new ideas about bread and about money too. Her father was proud of his ten-cent loaf, and Dot had been exploring the thought of people buying expensive bread. People certainly were hard pressed to make ends meet, but Dot thought if her product were unique enough, the right customers would appear.

Elaine knew Dot had something up her sleeve. Dot had asked Elaine if she would help her decide whether her bread project would be sustainable. If it was initially successful, Dot planned to reveal her idea to Floyd.

73

B. Davis hugged Louise as though she would never see her friend again, and she would be correct. She soon transferred to the nursing division of the Red Cross, taking her innovative ideas about infection control and hand washing with her.

Louise gripped B.'s shoulders and quoted her quoting Betty Davis: "I know, you'd kiss me, but you just washed your hair."

Louise's trip on the bus took less than two hours, and when she alighted toting her suitcase in Harrisburg, she decided to go to the bakery by cab. She was dressed in a lightweight shirtwaist dress and extremely glad to be out of uniform. The very air around the shop was scented with sugar and lard molecules—she was home! She turned her key in the front door lock and smelled the compelling scent of her home: the scent of baking bread.

"Why is the oven going?" she whispered, walking through the cake room, the pie room, passing the cream puff machine, toward the back where the ovens loomed and a crisp saltiness was in the air.

Hearing footsteps, Dot rushed to meet her sister with a big hug as Louise pranced toward her.

"Working? You kid? Alone?"

Dot pulled her over to the hot oven tray, resting on a worktable. There Louise stared at a large tray of strangely shaped pocket breads. There were victory hands with "V" fingers, suns with rays projecting, a "two hands clasping" sculpture, and lastly a reclining nude figure reminiscent of Renoir.

Dot smiled broadly, and offered a victory hand to Louise,

who pronounced it "Swell."

Amidst chatting with Dot, Louise took a closer look at the bread renditions, most as large as a man's hand. The hands were puffy, complete with darker lines on the palms. The sun's chewiness plumped up in its center, and the flatter rays appeared darkly toasty, crunchy. The nude figure was paler because it contained more dough. Its hair had been carefully "combed." She had used a garlic press or a fine knife to get that effect.

"I couldn't stand it, kid!" Dot explained, hands on her hips. "I hadn't made any ceramics *for years*. I was exploding with this idea to use bread dough, like I wanted to do with clay. I couldn't tell Father, so I sneaked in here when I could work alone... and this is my fourth attempt. They came out well, don't ya' think?"

Louise, chewing the "hand," agreed, "You look like you're surely in your element."

"I am in my element. Father should understand because he knows I sacrificed all my artistic tendencies... for paperwork. Now, I'm helping him run the office and getting nutzy-kookoo!"

Suddenly, Louise couldn't contain herself because she knew in her bones that Dot really had something. It was smart, creative and uniquely... special. One of a kind. A product never before seen in Harrisburg. Bread as a canvas. Louise screamed, "This bread is so Stittyian!" She pronounced it again: "Stittyian. Yeah, only Stitt's has it! That's what I was trying to say!"

Dot laughed, and laughing was what she really craved, "My name is Hammaker."

"No," Louise giggled, "you'll always be a Stitt Bakery girl."

***

There was a family gathering, including Clara's brothers' families, at 2232 North Sixth Street to welcome Louise home. They chattered about recent gains by Allied forces in the Pacific, Tinnie talked of the tin can drive and there was more joking than usual over a Sunday dinner of Louise's favorite things.

But while slicing a loaf of sesame seed bread, Elaine confided to Louise that bakery work left her almost as antsy as living with her parents. "I'm chained here, like some kind of short-haired Rapunzel!"

"Your haircut *is* cute," said Louise, changing the subject.

Elaine demanded, "I'm ready to fly with Bill. I can't wait for this stupid war to be over... and I *won't* wait!"

Louise whispered, "Our lives were messed up by this war, but love can't be killed. It goes on and life goes on."

She heard for the first time about the government ban of machine-sliced bread. It seemed that these machines for slicing and wrapping bread in waxed paper required lots of metal replacement parts—metals vital to the war effort. Floyd Stitt seemed to have weathered another storm—once more. He and his competition were making unsliced loaves for victory.

Louise finally headed out to make her new home with Dot when Clara urgently bustled over with a brown paper bag full of recent mail.

Settled in Dot's place above the bakery, Louise opened the first of two letters from Eddie, both written in June.

Dear Louise,

I miss you as always, but I'm getting to be something that's against Army rules. Demoralized, sick and tired of taking orders, the uncertainty, air raids and the food...

I just found out we're moving to Tunisia, which has been pretty active over the last months.

My father was in the first war, now I'm being herded around here, and where does it end?

The flower is a lily that I found at a funeral for some guys in an adjacent unit. Sorry, but that's how it is.

Love,
Eddie

Louise imagined her love trooping on to Africa in khaki formation. She felt his frustration and wished-prayed-intended for war to *end*. The next letter sounded more like Eddie:

Dear Louise,
How are you doing in W. VA? I hope I didn't sound like a fellow ready to desert from these ranks! I have these days when I wonder if it'll EVER end. We smell the end coming though. I'll grit my teeth and sing, the "Basin Street Blues" or "I'm havin' myself a time."

Living with Dot, away from the hospital routine provided some space for Louise to process recent events. She mulled over this while unpacking and later with her two sisters. They all yearned for their partners. Louise hoped to lead a normal life with Eddie. *"Whatever that is,"* she snickered. But she had to admit to an even larger yen. She yearned for the possibility of having her own family, now delayed.

The second morning home, she awakened and stared at Dot's flowered wallpaper, illuminated by a streetlight. Her eyes focused on a rose. In her reverie, she mused first about Eddie, then her brain dismissed him after a while, going to Dot and Elaine. They were now thirty-two, twenty-six and sixteen. Their men were overseas, and they were all working in the bakeshop at the same time. Louise was thinking about her feelings—as though pulled toward something new, yet here she was in the same old place.

She stretched, throwing on her yellow summer dress, staring at herself in the bathroom mirror. *I'm overdue for a permanent,* Louise thought. She lost weight living apart from cream puff land. She found Dot at her kitchen table making sketches of the next edition of breads.

"Good morning. Oh, more victory bread."

Dot giggled, eyes crinkling behind wire rims as Louise poured a cup of black coffee. "Victory? Bread?"

They sat across from each other, sipping in unison. Dot scribbled at the top of her sheet, "Victory Bread" and then quickly sketched hands, index fingers pointing to the words, VICTORY BREAD. Then a short advertisement: "Eat Victory Bread! This unique pocket flat bread is perfect for your sandwich."

They stared at her sketch and Louise said, "That looks easier to sell than hard rolls." She compared victory hands to hard rolls because they had the same sandwich function.

Dot said in a monotone, "'Hard rolls, two cents each, twenty-three cents a dozen.' These hands take more labor and I want to charge more for them."

"Yeah. Hey, let's ask Elaine. She's in Distributive Ed. class today. She'll be here to work in the afternoon."

As the sun rose, Louise and Dot each had a fresh-from-the-oven sticky bun with their coffee. Then Dot worked at her desk in a decidedly better mood than usual and thought to herself, *Victory is at hand.*

Louise went downstairs, where the atmosphere was saturated with yeasty familiarity... *umm. Cinnamon.* The bread wrapping process was done by two young women in summer dresses covered by linen aprons and wearing hairnets. Two- layer cakes were being iced and small blueberry pies packaged in waxed paper. Just as if she had never left, never skipped a beat, Louise greeted all the Fegleys.

"Sarah, that cinnamon is just heavenly!" She noticed that the éclair shells had just come out of the oven. She proceeded to fill them with thick yellow cream and later finished by brushing over the goodies with chocolate fudge icing. She almost felt she had returned from the dead, still it was her upwardly spiraling feeling of renewal the bakery needed. Yes, Louise was back, welcomed as family and valued as one who knew what to do with éclairs. The hand that had only recently plastered a burned arm now applied dark chocolate icing and then she had an unexpected thought: *Treatment is treatment. I have seen burns get well. I have treated shellshock with pie. Now I'll make Victory Bread.* It was simply a new version of the wheat, the dough inspired by Roman goddess Fornix.

"Elaine, we have been wondering about this flatbread Dot's making," asked Louise. She stood in her work outfit, wiping a bit of icing from her arm and sitting at the desk to relieve Dot. The phone rang.

The businesslike Dot steered Elaine out of the office into her apartment, where Dot showed Elaine her bread sculptures. "We have an idea, kid, but it's our little secret—you, me and Louise."

"You mean don't let Father in on it."

Dot shook her short, dark curls. "No one. Not yet."

Elaine smiled at the whimsical bread, tasting a finger that had fallen off one of the victory hands. "These are swell!"

"I'm almost ready to show these to customers, but I want you to help me show it first to some educated people."

Elaine blinked her brown eyes, swallowed, and curiously asked, "Now why would I know any edu-mak-at-ed people?"

Dot laughed, "Ha! YOU yourself are smarter than the average canary[4]!"

Elaine objected, "No. You're the gifted talent in this family."

Dot quipped, "Gifted, talented and getting nutsy, kookoo stir crazy."

"Your Distributive Ed. teacher might be willing to sample my bread. I'd like you to offer one of these hands to him and to the Home Ec. teacher. Ask what they think about the bread and what they would pay for it, if they found it in the grocery store."

"I bet they would pay... more than usual."

"Why?"

"Well, it's so unusual."

Dot adamantly whispered, "No other bakery here makes this kind of bread. Define unusual."

"Well, it tastes good, and it has a pocket for meat or cheese,

---

[4] Slang word meaning woman.

but it's kind of zany too. Like something out of the Three Stooges."

"That bad? It's more than two bread slices, right?"

"You said it! It has... personality."

Dot predicted, "A customer might even feel better by just looking at this." She uncovered her sculpture, the latest victory version. Elaine gasped, running her finger over the small face of FDR, complete with cigarette holder.

"How on Earth...?"

Excitedly Dot said, "I owe it all to the oven and some yeast. No, more than that, I was pregnant *with an idea.*" Dot giggled, arm around Elaine's shoulder, "So now the question is, kid, if Victory Bread went into a grocery store, what would people pay for it?"

Elaine looked up from the array of bread and ventured, "I bet it'd sell best at the USO."

Dot grinned, "The train station." Her eyes glowed with the wildfire of possibility.

"Yeah, people on trips need snacks. The traveling crowd is different than a grocery."

They fairly skipped over to the bakery office to tell Louise.

74

General George Patton marched his troops across North Africa in that spring of 1943, joining forces with the various troops of the United Kingdom in their efforts to stabilize the Mediterranean. Initially faltering against Rommel's panzers, by summer, the Allies controlled the region.

During the spring, news of Hitler's concentration camps became available to the Allies. Though free societies had condemned German anti-Semitism and human rights violations, the freedom of the peoples imprisoned depended upon the intended success of Allied armies. Prisoners could only be liberated by crushing German-controlled areas.

Soon Clara heard a radio account of the overtaking of the Jewish ghetto by the SS in Warsaw, Poland. The Army had been routinely rounding up German citizens as well as those in countries occupied by them. Over one million political and religious opponents, homosexuals, gypsies and especially Jews had already been killed, and millions more were rumored to be imprisoned. Auschwitz was finally exposed.

The Warsaw ghetto was the first civilian Jewish group resisting the Nazis with hundreds of untrained neighborhood occupants plus some armed Polish sympathizers by employing homemade weaponry.

The Nazi occupiers did so poorly in their initial attempt to evacuate the Jewish neighborhood, it was embarrassing. Women and men worked feverishly to collect weapons to repulse the armed soldiers, and the ghetto residents fought to their last bullets. Elders and children huddled in basements, parceling out food stores during the siege. German artillery was repeatedly outdone by homemade grenades and Molotov cocktails. Finally, fires forced out the Polish Jews with an unknown number escaping through city sewers. More than fifty thousand inhabitants of the ghetto were reported killed or sent to camps.

Horrified, Clara tuned out the painful account. She grabbed an empty tin can, threw it at the floor and jumped on it with all of her hundred seventy-eight pounds. "Damn Hitler! Damn Nazis!" She yelled that as if her magical epithets would strike at the heart of the Third Reich. If Hitler had somehow appeared in her kitchen at that moment, he would have been turned into toast carbonise. But charcoal as a way of life would be too good for Hitler, and before her pyrotechnical black eyes, she would have him vaporized!

Caroline stepped into the kitchen from working on the planting in the garden, saw Clara's reddened face punctuated by blazing brown eyes and asked, "What happened?"

"Hitler puts people—civilians—in concentration camps!" she wailed.

Caroline sighed, thinking of her unknown German relatives and said, "He won't get away with it."

Clara stomped on another empty Spam can, then kicked it, propelling grease. "Why, he has! He kills on his whims... thousands of people in a month. I hope this can fights him, whatever they turn it into."

Caroline proceeded to produce a nice lunch as Clara combed through *The Patriot News* and found nothing more about the atrocities in Poland. Byron appeared after his outing, announcing that he had gotten two things, a free loaf of "fresh" day-old bread and a war bond.

This prompted Clara's face to smile with a new determination. "Father, take a seat," she asked, "and offer a prayer for Eisenhower." They touched shoulders, heads bowing over the aromatic steam of freshly picked vegetables.

75

"Hmmm. Fresh. Chewy. Mind if I add a little butter?" Mr. Anthony, the Distributive Education teacher enjoyed the Victory Bread sample while Elaine contemplated him.

He's impressed, she thought.

He asked, "Did you make this?"

Elaine smiled, "No. We're experimenting at my father's bakery, and I just wanted to ask you what you thought of it."

"Very tasty and unusual too. Who thought of representing a hand with a V for victory?"

Elaine explained, "I can't give out any details now. I'm glad you like it, and I wonder if you have any advice about marketing this bread."

Mr. Anthony said, "Ahh, a preliminary test. Were you showing this to anyone else?"

"Miss McKee."

Standing, the teacher said, "Okay, let's look for her now."

Molly McKee was carrying a large flat of eggs into her Home Ec test kitchen when Mr. Anthony and Elaine met her. They introduced the product, and she was, as she said, excited to see it and requested the recipe. Mr. Anthony conferred with her as to market price as well as labor then they encouraged Elaine, promising to keep it secret.

That afternoon Dot, Louise and Elaine put their heads together at Dot's desk. There was Dot giving her impression of the labor required to bake two hundred "hands." Louise injected the sales ideas for the USO as well as the delicatessen that used Stitt bread in order to sell sandwiches.

Elaine reported, "Mr. Anthony and Miss McKee said they

had never seen bread like this, and that they would charge nine cents each. He says a woman buying groceries would probably pay five cents at a grocery store, but the same lady would buy it at the station for nine cents."

"Interesting," remarked Louise.

Dot calculated, "We have to get that much to cover labor and... to get Father to back us. I'll make the hands to sell at the USO on Saturday, and *when* they sell, I'll make some more-complicated versions."

Elaine ventured, her eyes widening, "You'll produce them when the employees leave the shop—to surprise Father. Oh, dear, oh, dear, I hope he agrees!"

"Yeah, I want to spring this on him properly." Dot giggled, knowing her father's mistrust of art, and this was as much art as it was bread. She planned to let the money do the talking.

Louise trusted that Floyd would make the right decision and said calmly, "Dahlings, it'll be Okay."

76

S eabee Christy Hammaker had spent many months on the southern coast of England preparing naval vessels, landing craft and bundling building material. Chemical companies contributed more than parachute material; also tents, ropes and container items for the invasion. They were preparing for a large scale European mission. Christy had access to telegraph offices, and he sent his short messages to Dot:

Dot- thinking of you at your desk stop
Working with metallic alloy from your tin cans stop
Love you can't stop
CBH

Before they could invade Europe, the Allies needed to take control of the Atlantic. One of the many approaches to this was to fit merchant marine supply ships with platforms. This made the ships capable of carrying aircraft to defend their supplies. By July 28th, 1943, U-boat traffic was curtailed, permitting more war material to the fronts.

Louise's latest letter from Eddie was coded:

Dear One,   *June 20, 1943*
I think of you all the time. Good weather, hard work and too many casualties. We enjoyed spaghetti on "leave." I guess it's good you're working at Stitt's again. If—when I come home, I will never take a tour of Europe! Enough right now!
All my love,

Eddie

His division was in the process of invading Sicily then, right at the toe of Italy. The operation took thirty-eight days, and Eisenhower sensed he had made the right decision. Germans were cleared off the island, and Sicilians professed they knew all along that the Germans and "their fat mouse" (Mussolini) could not hold the island. It was clear that the resisting Italians had hoped for this moment. Allied momentum went into higher gear when mouse, Mussolini surrendered, on July 28th.

***

All the Harrisburg Stitt family gathered at home for Louise's twenty-seventh birthday, ending the evening with the group gathered at the giant, maple wood radio listening to FDR's fireside chat. The president thanked Americans for their part in recent victories and urged them to redouble their efforts. He closed, cautioning:

"The plans we made for the knocking out of Mussolini and his gang have largely succeeded. But we still have to knock out Hitler and his gang, and Tojo and his gang. No one of us pretends that this will be an easy matter."

***

Tinnie and Clara shared dress patterns. The dresses were the shortest ones the women had in their lifetimes due to the bulk of U.S. fabric employed in wartime. They wondered if they would ever get another store-bought dress. Clara laughed, "The world isn't ready to see my knees."

Homemade ice cream was in the process, cranked by hand in a small keg. The uncles cranked as if their lives depended on it and Caroline cut the cake but in the cover of chattering voices, the three daughters made plans to sell the bread with the V

278

fingers for victory.

Dot would produce a record number of Victory Bread hands on Saturday when the shop was closed. Louise agreed to deliver it to the USO in the train station.

"It'll be hoppin' Saturday night," Elaine promised. And after her encounter with those intelligent high school faculty members, she felt secretly sure it would be a sellout.

77

"**D**on't sit under the apple tree with anyone else but Bill..." Bill sang a little tune as he put on his uniform. He had two days off, and he had arranged to do a favor for a superior who wanted a shipment to go from Pennsylvania's Olmstead Air Base in Middletown to Williamsport Airport. He asked Elaine if she would like to accompany him on this mission. *That's only about ninety miles,* thought Bill.

Time flew as he picked up the heavy black phone receiver at the home of his parents.

"Hello, Mrs. Stitt, this is Bill. The same to you. May I speak to Elaine?"

"Bill, I'm almost ready to go," Elaine said with a smile.

"Okay! I will pick you up at ten, and we'll drive to the base. Tell your mother we'll be back for supper."

"Swell," said Elaine.

Bill didn't say goodbye, he signed off with, "Hey! Don't sit under the apple tree with anyone but me."

Elaine giggled, "Why, no!" She wanted to look her best and went back to the bathroom to apply make-up, not only to her face. To her legs! A shortage of nylon was responsible for the use of leg make up.

The ride was the first time to Williamsport for Elaine, who made conversation about the mysteries of air travel and then noting the summer green view of rolling farmland in the sunny Susquehanna Valley. Bill was a good driver, and as he drove, described why he enjoyed flying in the Air Corps. He pointed out various landmarks that triggered oohs and ahhs from his date. He admitted that he had missed her, that he often saw her face in cumulous clouds, cirrus, but never in nimbus clouds.

She felt excited in his presence, yet safe, even though he had opened a new world to her. She was losing track of time discussing flying.

She questioned, "How long do you think the war will go?"

"Well, they took Sicily and they got the Germans off guard." He answered. "Japan probably is weakening... I personally think that it will go better in the Pacific once we get into Germany."

As they entered Williamsport, she held out her palm. Bill kissed her fingers. Momentarily, they would enter the small airport. Elaine thought: *The truth is I want you to kiss me.* But she dared not say it. Instead she said, "We heard about the Allies in Italy on the radio, and Mother read it in the paper." Their vehicle pulled up to the cargo hangar.

His cargo crate delivered, Bill led his date to a soda tank in the small airport waiting room. He slid the door open at the top of the tank, peering through blocks of ice into the mass of water. "A bottle of Coke, 7 up or Orange Crush for you?"

Elaine answered, "Crush."

So he rolled up his shirtsleeve to retrieve one of the orange drinks, then opened the metal cap with the opener on the side of the soda tank. He took out a Coke, and shook the cold water from his hand. As he downed the caramel liquid from its green bottle, he noted, "Hey, you know Eisenhower got Coca-Cola to build a few plants in Europe... for the services." He felt pleased that she was enjoying their time together.

They walked to the small concession stand and got hot dogs—they were Victory Dogs—and sat outside under an umbrella-like tree.

Bill said, "I know you don't really enjoy working at your bakery, but what, I wonder, what is your ambition?"

"I like Myrna Loy 'n Zasu Pitts, but I don't want to be an actress," she frowned. "I like to read mysteries, but I don't want to be a writer. I like to drive, but I don't want to be anybody's chauffeur."

281

Bill whispered, "Now I know what you don't want." He took the paper napkin from her hand, dropped it on the ground and kissed her on the mouth politely, then her brown eyes stared at him, transfixed, as though she were a surprised Little Rascal[5] star. He smiled, did not move but she did, kissing him like she wanted to be kissed.

Bill sighed, "You're sharp enough and pretty enough to be an actress! You seem older than seventeen."

She took that as a complement. "You don't say! There was a pleasant kind of meditative silence as they allowed themselves to connect. Let's go home," She said finally, with an enthusiastic smile.

Bill was invited for dinner at 2232 North Sixth Street. It was obvious to everyone that he and their daughter were seriously in love; she seemed to have a permanent blush. The state of the world was discussed, and though Bill wasn't able to reveal sensitive information, Clara worked around this. She sat next to him, interrogating.

"Have you ever seen a U-boat with your own eyes?"

Bill cleared his throat and replied, "I only saw them in movies and photographs. We are working hard to keep them out of the Atlantic."

He could not explain to them the likelihood the U-boats had been dispatched by armed cruisers and aircraft-carrying supply ships. Germany suspected they would better turn their attention to the future invasion of Europe.

---

[5] Popular child actors of the period.

78

Louise's short dress sleeve flapped in the wind because her arm rested in the open window of the Austin Healy truck. Eddie had written to her from Italy, which was now in Allied hands. She wasn't thinking about her fiancé because it was Dot she worried about. Here she was with the "V Bread," Dot's art. Yes, Dot had poured her heart and soul into these forms of edible art, and now it was up to Louise to sell, and sell many. She awakened today knowing it was up to her, and her first thought was to phone Dot's friends. She reached about fifteen people who were customers, some in the church choir, even her own hair stylist. Fortunately, she seemed to have invoked a sense of an *unveiling* of the bread art among those she had alerted, and Father was still none the wiser.

She had decided to set up the goods at the USO stand in the afternoon. Elaine's banner proclaimed: "VICTORY BREAD," then in small letters, "a real winner." As Louise put the banner below the case, people moved through the station, but Saturday evening promised the largest crowd. She was greeted by a few energetic soldiers, who helped her unload trays of V Bread, chocolate lunch cakes, spice cookies and glazed doughnuts. She rewarded her helpers with slices of jellyroll.

When all was in readiness, Louise put on a new yellow, bibbed apron she had purchased for the occasion. It had the same effect a new dress can inspire. Just to move things along, she raced over with a V Bread hand to the deli manager.

"This is our newest," she smiled, handing it to him wrapped in pick-up paper. With that delivery, she felt the ball begin to roll. The train whistle blew and Louise took a seat behind the bakery stand, just in time to serve the incoming passengers.

In strolled mothers with children, couples arm in arm and a motley group of tired Army sergeants. They were not expecting specialized baked goods, but these were—how did Floyd say it—"Better made." The young boys broke away from their mothers' grips and begged for a treat, the couple strolled over and then the hungry soldiers.

They bought as fast as Louise bagged for fifteen minutes. The nine-cent Victory Bread only drew some stares. Then the deli man appeared, took a dozen of the V-fingered art and loudly said, "For twelve cents, come get a grand hand sandwich."

Then a couple of rotund women in mourning black bought some hands, holding them up as though they were twin Churchills.

By the time the USO band tuned up, there remained only one hand, soon snapped up by Sister Theresa Pious, a nun who gave Louise a large order, provided Dot could fashion some praying hands.

***

"Nine cents!" Now it was saucer-eyed Floyd with a Little Rascal face. His brain was playing catch up with his three darling daughters. He comprehended the value of a roll to be two cents.

It was sunset and the light over her desk was trained on her tally. Dot showed him her sales ledger, reflecting an increase of twenty-five dollars over the last USO sale.

Louise handed over her orders from the deli and the Catholic Church. Elaine sat quietly in one of the large wooden office chairs.

Floyd, still puzzling, held a victory hand in his palm. He was trying to take in the bread and how the three had sold it. "Nine cents includes extra labor, Dorothea?"

Dot replied evenly, "It takes about a minute to fashion it, and

284

from there it takes about the same amount of time as a hard roll.

Floyd said, "A hard roll requires all of two seconds of fashioning time." He scratched his balding head and released a hearty laugh. He slapped his left knee with a snap, bending forward to laugh some more, right at the bread. He hadn't really laughed since sliced bread was banned. He was somewhat relieved to be mixed up in this kind of surprise after the arduous sugar shortage. "You spent several hours on that return of twenty-five dollars." He grinned and chuckled.

"Yes," Dot was oddly relaxed and felt secure in her customers' response.

Floyd regarded her kindly, "It's an excellent return… pretty good news. I guess you'll do it again next week."

In unison, Dot and Louise said yes, while their baby sister offered, "I can help Dot until school starts next month."

"You'd best rest up," he cautioned Dot, smirking. "Between this office and the oven, you won't have time to sneeze."

79

The sisters worked like honeybees with their father remaining a skeptic. Dot thought he was a misguided drone. He could not believe they could consistently turn out the bread week after week and find buyers. If it was going to fail, he wanted it to be sooner rather than later. He admitted privately to Clara his pride in their job well done, and she urged Floyd to have Dot supervise the bread baker so she could better work the long hours.

The following Saturday brought rain and fewer customers, but one of them sharply increased the business of V bread. Louise sold a bag of the bread to a Pennsylvania Railroad train conductor, who was a patriotic man with a son in the Pacific naval fleet. He gave some of the bread to his friends in Pittsburgh, and on the same day to some others in Philadelphia.

Dot answered the phone on Monday, to be greeted by a Philadelphia woman who planned to send money by way of her rail conductor friend, to pick up an order of V bread for their own USO. Her voice echoed through the wire like a cavalry charge: "This is just what we need, dear; we must keep up the morale!"

***

Louise returned to the bakery from her weekly mandatory hair appointment. She was wearing a favorite cotton dress she enjoyed in college and the leather shoes with two-inch heels were showing wear, but hair care remained her supreme priority. "It improves brain function," she decided. She picked up the

286

mail and went up to the office, finding no sign of Father or Dot. She selected from the pile of business letters a postcard addressed to Miss Louise Stitt. There was a view of Gibraltar and a man standing on the rock. It was a sturdy homemade postcard. The thin slanting script read:

> *Dear Louise,*
> *This is Gibraltar, a British territory with a nice Navy*
> *base. Very strategic. Hope you are keeping well,*
> *Bud Ditlow*

The picture of the sailor in blinding whites told her the Gibraltar sun was bright as a wind blew strong enough to whip the bellbottoms and lift the sailor's uniform's jumper flap. Suddenly she recalled that Bud had green eyes. All of these men... over in Europe, thought Louise. There was no return address. Louise did not see the postcard writer as an interested party, but as a lonely man stuck on a warship.

Louise knew the Gibraltar territory, positioned on the Spanish border, served to control naval traffic from the Atlantic and in and out of the Mediterranean. Hitler had wanted it, but he had other irons in the fire.

Now, where's Dot? Louise wondered, putting the postcard in her pocket. She found her with Dan by the bread oven, gleefully laughing over her latest in victory art: praying hands for the nun who wanted the hands for a feast day.

"Louise, your hair looks just dahling," then white aproned Dan greeted Louise.

Dot explained, "Father said Dan can help me with the large orders."

Louise exclaimed, "That is remarkable, just remarkable." She was elated by Father's unexpected move, and relieved, as she feared her formerly grounded sister was turning into a yeast-wielding whirling dervish. She did not want to have to witness Father grappling with Dot as a dervish, hell bent on success.

80

Bud Ditlow, USN, was aboard the recently issued aircraft carrier *Wasp*, bound for Trinidad in the Caribbean Sea. Their orders had called the excursion a shakedown mission intended to detect any naval problems before entering a war zone. The crew was not informed as to another purpose for that trip. On arrival, more could be revealed. They put into a few Dutch islands because the Navy and the Allies had a stake in the vast fuel stored in Aruba and Curacao. This treasure trove, an astounding eighty percent of all Allied fuel, was stored in the Netherlands Antilles. Holland had been occupied by Germany since May, 1940 and now the Dutch Island possessions with their secret petrol were crucially vital to the winning of the war. The stored fuel could not be allowed to fall into enemy hands, for it was not only oil they required, but byproducts for tire rubber. Fortifying the islands was now a priority. The naval crew aboard *USS Wasp* joined with island citizens to mount guns at strategic points.

The fuel powering Germany's war machine was from domestic storage originally bought from Russia and later stolen during the invasion into Russia. The Russians had been selling their oil to Germany prior to the war, but the Nazis were about to fail on the eastern front, leaving their gas tank low.

The aircraft carrier *Wasp* continued on route to California by way of the Panama Canal. The Navy waited for various ships under construction that were essential in order to carry out the Pacific strategy against Isoroku Yamamoto's Japanese fleet.

Bud had thought about the Gibraltar postcard intensely before sending it to Louise. Now he thought of Louise as he worked. He had always worked, ever since he could assist his older brother at the family's farm. Since his enlistment, there had been some personal surprises, such as how he was able to think differently. He lived where he worked and out in the ocean atmosphere, personal problems seemed more easily tamed, almost like a lion changed into a calico kitten.

Now he worked in the galley, nearby about two thousand sailors on a floating village of men. It took a crew of cooks to keep the force fed; yet he learned that he was not a cook. The captain, a San Franciscan, chanced to find Bud preparing a sourdough bread of sorts and then approved the finished product by promoting him to ship's baker. Bud claimed the promotion reflected on his timely dependability rather than culinary creativity, of which he did not want any part.

In the aromatic galley air, he sliced sourdough for the midday chow and was satisfied to be of service by producing the simplest thing: bread. His thoughts back in Harrisburg were usually about wages. He had gotten enough work, but even in the steel mill, he had to parcel out the wage to cover each week. Then the war swept away accounting and suddenly he was uniformed, trained and on board a boat the size of Paxtang, Pennsylvania.

As the fat knife handle pushed the blade into a loaf, Bud decided he had to get another postcard to Louise. He had no wartime illusions about the possibility of risking life and limb, but he knew he needed to contact Louise Stitt. Not a woman, not a friend, but exclusively, Louise Stitt. He could not die in war until he made contact with Louise. Another sourdough tray slid onto the workbench, and these loaves emanated the sigh of yeast married to flour. He imagined she was working in the Army hospital, and she was becoming a hopeful mirage on some future horizon of home.

Later, he took out the black and white photographs and found one of himself in uniform at Panama City. He had joined the cooks on shore leave to seek certain staples such as coffee. The photo was of Bud, sun-soaked, posing on a burlap hill of coffee beans and the Kodak paper even had a coffee scent. *This will do,* he thought as he mounted it as a postcard. Now he had to say something interesting.

> *Dear Louise,*
> *Hoping my card reaches you in a good state. Here I am in Panama.*
> *As you see, we went south! We all miss home and want peace.*
> *Sincerely,*
> *Bud*

81

*T*he *Patriot News* ran a photograph procured from *The Philadelphia Inquirer* of an Army outfit standing by the liberty bell. Leafing through the news, Clara gasped at the image of the servicemen holding aloft and eating Victory Hands. She immediately phoned Dot, who laughed and threw Clara another surprise, "Right now, there's a reporter here from *The Patriot*. Yes, they want to feature our bread in the Sunday paper."

Floyd had never had free publicity in all the thirty-five years of his business, and it could not have come at a better time. In short order, Dot was credited with this fascinating form of bread. And that was due to the reporter, a woman and an avid baker, who saw the bread and went on to refer to it as "edible sculpture."

Floyd fielded continual phone calls and had to shut down the baking of assorted rolls in order to meet demand for the new bread. *The Patriot* mailbag was full of appreciation so the family section set up a second feature about sandwiches and asked to photograph the Stitt family.

The photographer meticulously pictured Dot preparing a hand, with close-ups of victory fingers being cut out. He took Elaine to her school in a reenactment of her survey of the teachers and those teachers were animated in their adoration of Victory Bread. Then he set up in the USO, with the bake stand draped in the banner, "Original Victory Bread." Behind the stand were the beaming "Victory Girls" while Clara and Floyd proudly stood out in front of the sign.

The following week, *The Patriot* received one negative letter accusing Mr. Stitt of "putting the squeeze on victory and stuff like that." It was signed Butch X.

Bakeries throughout the state saw the possibilities and wanted a slice of the profits. However, money was motivating them, not victory and not bread. Stroop Bakery spent hours trying to replicate the bread, only to bake up a fat version where the fingers ballooned and popped.

"I saw the version Stroop put out," Louise told Dot, "and the fingers had edema."

Other competitors went too low on yeast and produced crackers. A place in Shippensburg simply stamped "Victory" on their unsliced loaves. A church pancake supper sold lots of victory hot cakes by pouring the batter through a teapot spout.

Floyd took time now to reconsider Dot's talent. He appeared unexpectedly at the early morning preparation of the victory dough and rested his elbows on the floury table.

"Dot," he queried, "what is your secret?"

Dot felt a rush of acquiescence from him after so many battles when she felt forced to listen to his doubts. So often she wanted to leave the shop but felt compelled to stay. She simply needed to create art. In answer, she started to smile and then could not stop laughing, yet trying to hold back, her abdomen ached now.

Floyd raised his eyebrows to his hairline and finally howled along with her. It was an unprecedented scene. Regaining her composure wasn't easy, for her cotton headscarf had come down over her floury nose.

Dot took her father to the refrigerator where she pointed out burlap bags marked "V."

She sighed, smiling, "I let the dough rise in the refrigerator, and add sesame seeds to it, but you know that's not it. Anyone who wants to bake the dough can do it. The sculpting is one advantage, and no one taught it to me. But Father, the answer to your question is I respect this dough. I don't rush it, I get the proper feeling from it and it becomes *alive*. Even after the yeast stops working, it's *alive!*"

She said *alive* the way Dr. Frankenstein had when the monster walked, and her eyes looked widely into his, filled with electricity. The businesslike baker connected to the artisan baker so that it resembled love at first sight.

*****

The following day, Floyd was out to the bank and that was fortunate, as the next phone call rocked over the desk like a quake, warping the ink blotter, unleashing pencils and vibrating the typewriter.

"Hello, Stitt Bakery," Dot mechanically answered.

The line crackled and a woman with a British accent asked for "Miss Dorothea Stitt?"

"Yes, I'm Dorothea. May I help you?"

More crackling. "This is Washington, Miss Stitt. I'm Mrs. Roosevelt's secretary."

"You are?" Dot looked like a Little Rascal who had tripped on a live wire, hair sizzling.

"Yes, my dear, now I want you to speak to Mrs. Roosevelt."

"You do?"

Then Eleanor was on the line, smiling, benevolent Eleanor.

In a lower register, she introduced herself as Dot slapped herself on the back of the neck.

Louise entered the office and Dot held the receiver so both could hear. "Miss Stitt, I want to thank you personally for inspiring us here."

"Well, thank you... Mrs. Roosevelt..." said Dot, flustered but smiling.

Eleanor continued, "I want you to remember that your version of victory as *something to take in* is grand. The people are worried, but this sort of idea has helped people whom you will never meet! I need your help, Dorothea."

"Yes?" Dot had a begging tone in her voice as Louise rolled her eyes, their ears to the receiver.

The First Lady declared, "Now while it is brand new, I feel I need to serve your Victory Bread at a very important dinner. All the Allied countries are to be represented. They are worried people, just the same as you and I."

Dot let it sink in. "Anything for you, Mrs. Roosevelt."

Dinner was to be tonight. There were more words of appreciation for the Stitt Bakery as Eleanor had to take another call, and then the White House baker took the phone, asking if he could address her as Dot.

The baker had made a version of the bread, but his questions were, "What do you think about an egg wash before baking?"

She agreed it would make the bread shine.

"Now, after you sculpt the hand, Dot, how long do you wait before baking?"

Dot answered, "Five minutes."

Dot felt drained of all the adrenalin she owned. She finally had succeeded artistically. Louise shook her hands and head of brown curls like she had to reenter real life, then she hugged Dot.

That afternoon, Elaine had to be briefed on the call. She was excited, but smiling broadly. "THE ER? Oh, dear, oh dear, I hope that her baker knows what to do."

Her older sisters stopped for a laugh break.

Louise said, "Kid, he tried it yesterday, he asked Dot about making the hand shapes."

Dot told them, "I had a conversation about the bread with Father, and I told him I *respect* the dough and let oven timing do the rest. The White House chef understands."

82

The Great Depression had been good for something—sourdough bread. Bud silently thanked his Aunt Janet for showing him what sourdough starter was. He had to make himself take it seriously, even though it seemed not to merit a promotion. The simple components kept him busier than the engine crew. Flour contains enough yeast so that the addition of water will produce something known as "starter," which is a culture. The baker must be patient for at least one day while yeast grows. Small bubbles form on the surface and the mixture will begin to taste tangy. A minimum of eight hours will pass before the baker may incorporate some more bread flour. His aunt liked whole meal flour as it contained more yeast organisms. Bud was patient, as he had seen Aunt Janet ruin a batch by dumping in all her flour at once. He mixed the second addition of flour and set the container, the size of a small canoe, on the counter to season for another twelve hours.

Twenty-five loaves would require over twenty pounds flour, and his dough weighed in at over thirty pounds. Once he had cultured the starter, he could make this phenomenon, loved by the captain. The interesting thing about the starter is: *it never stops.* A culture stores in the refrigerator indefinitely.

Perhaps bread baking would have been just another job for a sailor in 1943, but Bud was happiest when working in a group and the good times rolled. It was no accident that the captain promoted him and secretly valued him above all the enlisted men.

San Francisco was to impact Bud like a bread comet sailing into a wood-fired oven. The city educated Bud and his estimate of himself grew after he visited the port. He had joined some of his signalmen pals on shore leave. They took a cable car and saw some beautiful views that prompted Bud to take photos. As their afternoon started, in a café with a pitcher of Anchor Steam Beer, Bud was tapped on the shoulder by the captain, who had two silk-clad Chinese women following him.

"I want to introduce you to Susan and Gloria Hue."

The Hues looked ageless in their Clara Bow haircuts.

The surprised Bud and his three companions stood and tipped their uniform caps, and the captain, who was a thin, tall man, gripped Bud by the elbow. "Seaman, I hope you will follow along. I want to show you the neighborhood."

"Okay." Bud smiled and handed his beer to the friend closest.

They proceeded walking down a hill that revealed a spectacular sight of the bay and rooftops of a neighborhood where prospectors had tented and then set out with the Gold Rush of 1849.

"Seaman Bud," said Susan. "Captain Carl told us you are the ship's baker."

"No kidding," he laughed into the air as he wondered, *Who the Sam Hill is she?* "Yeah, that's my job, baking."

Gloria interjected, sighing, "It's good to have flour in your life. Gets under your nails too."

Bud saw that the girls were friends of his superior officer, almost like family. "What kind of work are you doing?" he asked.

"Don't tell him," said the captain. "It'll surprise you!"

"Hint, hint," said Gloria and Susan immediately gave one.

"I am good with my hands," she said as she opened and closed her fists.

Then Gloria made a scowl and said, "I am a martial artist. Kung Fu."

Bud had never met a Chinese person, and he was getting mesmerized. "Kung Fool. You don't say."

Susan hinted the work of the Hues had not changed for ninety years. "My great-grandmother started it here when her husband went looking for gold."

Bud asked Carl, "Now you said you live here..." They passed some boat or fishing businesses, a laundry then a fishmonger.

The captain said, "Yes, a few streets away. However, my place isn't as hoppin' as their place. You'll see."

The Chinese women stopped at the double door of a tan brick building and beckoned to Bud. The sign over the door read, "Frisco Sourdough" and the aroma of bread crust blew over his head and settled forever in a segment of Bud's brain. All bread, bread only, all day, six days a week.

There were glass cases brimming with rolls. Behind the servers were shiny chrome bins with assorted loaves, textured with cracks or slashes. The sourdough seemed to broadcast a message: baked today. But there was the captain and his friends leading him, smiling, to where the action was. He had never seen the workings of a commercial bakery.

Skylights lent a great dazzle to the view of the production of the dough. Susan stood by a man shorter than she as he did his version of folding the dough, like a competitive pizza twirler, he did most of it in the air. Two folds in midair, one on the table. Susan explained, "We waste no time here... too many customers."

They moved to another floury table where Gloria, now in a white apron, explained how Kung Fu helped grow the dough. Bud stood back as she slapped her palms against air bubbles. *Pop!* She seemed to be pulverizing the dough then, but in an unusually speedy rhythm. *Blam!* Grow dough! Grow! Her hands moved too fast to follow, like a movie at high speed, and she also appeared to be a small person who grew out of herself, so as to transform a giant ball of sourdough. Bud saw a photograph on the wall labeled Yip Man, who Carl later said was Gloria's martial arts teacher.

Susan smiled and told Bud, "We Hues have the courage, the trust and the loyalty that a bread company requires."

He was dumbfounded further when Susan led him behind Gloria, so he could see the way her legs appeared to be planted, into the floor, yet her muscles moved with ballet precision. Gloria said, "Seaman, go pick out some bread. I hope you enjoy your tour."

He tipped his cap, now guided to the ovens by Carl, where the loaves cooled on wire racks. Carl was already chewing a rye sourdough roll and didn't need to say any more. Bud was mowed down by the chi of the Chinese bakers. They left him humbled by what had taken lifetimes to build. A Chinese gentleman introducing himself as Mike Hue, the girl's father, opened a large refrigerator and showed Bud a starter with a label "1850." They got in a long line to the cashier, and Bud implored Carl, "How could you even compare my bread to this?"

The captain whispered, "I did not do a comparison."

Bud said, "Well, you promoted me after you ate the bread."

"Trust me. It was an appropriate upgrade. Hey, Seaman, you haven't tasted this yet."

He munched. Bud sighed, "The crust is the best I ever ate."

Carl added, "Pretty too," referring to the islands of flour on top. "You taste a difference here in the Bay, sure, but there isn't any doubt you make good bread. Look deeper. I'm talking about psychology."

Carl put his arm around Bud's shoulder. "People are in the war for different reasons, and if you ask five people, you'll get five different responses. Part of my job is to keep the crew ready, full of energy. Good food is one of the keys to that. I tasted your bread, and it was good, but under that taste and smell and the way it sits in your belly afterward, I felt security. That's what you were really promoted for; not the bread but the feeling of security it gives me." Bud was feeling awed by the Hues, then to be informed he was party to some loopy psychology as a way to run a ship... well he was stunned.

Bud decided to get several rolls to sample; he chose rye, walnut, onion and white. He noted the captain had picked rye, so he got a large loaf of rye, which he later froze for a special occasion.

Standing right at eye level on the counter was a framed newspaper article with a shot of bread bakers, but it went unnoticed until Carl whispered, "Harrisburg... hey, aren't you from Harrisburg?"

Bud collected his change and stared. "Sisters Bake for Victory." It was Stitt Bakery, and here was a smiling, framed picture of Louise Stitt—in San Francisco. "Harrisburg's Stitt Bakery has made Victory Bread. The novelty has become a necessity to servicemen as well as families. One customer, a Mr. Gene Elbel is quoted, 'I eat victory. I make a sandwich with this bread. I put greens from the victory garden together with victory sausage.'"

He read later over and over of the Victory V hands, but now he stood transfixed by the sight of Louise. She wore a smile, laugh lines, and laughing wrinkled her nose. Standing between Dot and Elaine, her cheeks were shining, her dark eyes sparkled. He held on to the frame as if he had just stumbled over a treasure. He noted her lipstick and rhinestone earrings. He mumbled, "She's somethin'."

Mr. Hue saw the evidence of some kind of religious experience. He grabbed a newspaper from his desk and gave it to Bud. "It was yesterday's paper, son. Take it with you and Godspeed."

83

At that very moment in Harrisburg, Bill and Elaine sat by the Susquehanna. Bill put an engagement ring on Elaine's finger declaring, "Honey, you are the best thing that ever happened to me." His love was potentiated by the excitement of flying, and that charged him with adrenalin.

She had given thought to his question, "What is your ambition?" Obviously, she yearned to grow and she decided her answer was to live with Bill and build a life together. Everyone knew she wanted nothing more to do with the bakery work.

Bill was a "hellofa" good pilot and enjoyed the machine maintenance it required. His fascination with Elaine had taken him out of that mechanistic one-track mind.

She had picked out the ring, set with a small diamond, at Hoover's Jewelry Store.

They excitedly hoped to wed after she graduated. Bill did not believe the war would be over for years. "Look," he said, "the Japs are so spread out over a large territory. That's what I'm worried about. Common sense tells me the Germans can't last long. They should already be short on planes!"

Elaine wanted it over but didn't want to wait to be with Bill. "I feel like Rapunzel," she muttered. "I'm ready to leave the tower now, no one will stop me."

"Your hair isn't long enough yet," he cautioned.

Soon Bill would be off to the West Coast for maneuvers, to return at the holidays if all went well. She gripped his hand and was thankful that he was not over in Germany. The papers recently reported the bombing of industries in Schweinfurt, where lots of American pilots lost their lives. No, Bill was needed for coastal U-boat reconnaissance.

This focusing of energy had been good for Elaine. The uncertain times bred a different kind of thinking, and teens entering marriage or the service had to take leave of their childhoods, which were dissolving like an Orange Crush soda in the sun. Clara sighed, knowing it had to happen. Elaine was wiser than most teens, so Clara had to content herself and allow the bird to fly.

As Allied commander, Ike Eisenhower was doing everything possible to mount an invasion. Opinions differed among cooperating leaders as to accomplishing the task. Moving mammoth armaments, supplies and forces over to Europe was unprecedented. Ike knew when the troop movement began, it would also end the ongoing ability to practice. He did not want Americans to use equipment they were unfamiliar with, as it might set up accidents.

Everyone agreed that the attack had to decisively overwhelm the Germans, and Eisenhower had to delay. Meanwhile, an Allied conference took place in Cairo that resulted in a demand for the surrender of Germany.

Intelligence gatherers noticed Hitler only surfaced publicly on rare occasions. Thanks to his daily diet of schnapps and speed and the stress of leading Germany on a rollercoaster ride over a cliff, he got very little sleep. There were rumors that generals wished to unseat him before he made any more ill advised, "crack-brained" mistakes.

Louise felt Eddie would be part of the invasion and, as the assault did not seem imminent, maybe he would get Christmas leave! Sometimes, while she put together cardboard boxes, her hands would automatically do all the folding and inserting of the flaps so she didn't even need to think. Often she would stand back amazed at the stack of cookie-ready boxes, teetering six feet high. She went on creating a room full of these containers as she mused about Eddie and how his visit could liven up this holiday.

Yesterday Dot had passed her the latest postcard from Bud. It was the sailor posing on a hill with a view behind him of San Francisco Bay. She wondered if he had violated Navy policy about keeping troop movements a secret, though by the time her mail arrived, the ship was probably elsewhere.

Dear Louise,

Hope you're fine. I guess you are because (surprise) I seen your beautiful picture in the San Francisco Chronicle with your family. You made a lot of newspapers! They displayed your picture in a nice bakery I visited. What's going on in Harrisburg?

Happy Thanksgiving,

Bud

84

Heavy snow fell on Christmas Eve, and the bakery girls finally rested. In addition to all their other holiday chores, they had special orders for V hands. The soft molasses cookies, the cakes inscribed Merry Christmas and fruitcakes sold well, but did not sell out. Floyd donated the leftovers to Harrisburg Hospital. The baker and Dot worked feverishly in the early morning of December 24th to bake V hands for the World War One Veterans' Party. It seemed the customers were in the Christmas spirit and impulsively bought V bread.

Louise played *White Christmas* on the Victrola, and read the newspaper. Caroline, Clara, Dot and Louise planned to attend a midnight church service. Elaine stayed home, hoping for a call from Bill.

The best gifts contain an aspect of the giver combined with a desire of the recipient. Sometimes the exchanging parties like to receive the same gift each year. Others like surprises, and Dot was one of these. The family returned from church in the early hours of Christmas morning with Dot driving Father's car. They shook off the snow chunks in the doorway, expecting to indulge in some hot cider, when Floyd came downstairs in his robe.

"Merry Christmas, girls. Byron went to bed. He said he'll see you tomorrow." Their Christmas stockings were attached to the mantel, and they laughed as they emptied them. Floyd stood and waited—it was long past his bedtime.

The wartime stockings were unusual. Peeping from the top of each winter wool stocking was a tiny rag doll. Caroline had made them to match each of her granddaughters. Dot's doll wore a short Chanel tube and high-heeled dance shoes. Louise's doll amusingly wore a red dress, covered by a white linen apron, on which Caroline had stitched, "Stitts," her hair exaggeratedly curled. Elaine's doll had lighter hair than the other two and wore a lace bride gown made from scraps of an old slip. They shrieked and hugged their darling Mamaw. She sat them down.

"You girls haven't noticed the best part," she grinned as they took a second look at their dolls. Each doll's hand had two fingers projecting in a V. This prompted Dot, Louise and Elaine to wear the face of Little Rascals[6] who had just outrun the Keystone Cops[7]. All three girls were versions of their creative Mamaw—updated. They sighed, knowing they were fortunate. Dot collapsed into an overstuffed chair, holding the artful bakery doll.

Floyd came to her with her stocking, directing, "That's not all!" She peered into the sock.

Indeed, some Santa had put real nylon stockings in the socks, and they all found one orange in each toe—a bit of Florida sun in the snow. Dot also found a Christmas card. She opened the very traditional wreath-decked card and saw only the handwritten line: "Your present is sitting on the stairs." She turned around and saw Christy!

She was laughing, crying and overwhelmed with joy as he lifted her, squeezed her and cried, "I love you!"

Christmas at 2232 North Sixth had never witnessed such festivity. Following midday dinner, Clara's two brothers and their families visited. Tinnie made Clara some homemade soap she scented with lavender. Mrs. Brown, their friend from next door, appeared with a fruitcake, and that prompted Uncle Louis, when he sniffed it, to say the cake was a tipsy cake.

The green and red dressed Mrs. Brown chirped, "Oh no, I only had a quart of Bourbon. Usually I add more."

"Oh," said Elaine, "*That's* her secret for these sweets she stores in the cellar."

---

[6] The Little Rascals were highly inventive child movie actors.
[7] The Keystone Cops were a comically incompetent police force of silent movies.

There were toasts to Christy and presents exchanged. Christy entertained them with a story about how the British confused the Germans prior to invading Sicily. They wanted the enemy to believe they would attack another island, Sardinia, and they made up fake orders indicating this. A dead man, a John Doe whom no one could identify, was dressed in an English uniform and dropped on the coast of a German-occupied area. Mission was accomplished when he was found by the enemy with misleading orders in his pocket.

Louise answered the door for a special delivery. Eddie sent a letter saying he hoped to be there next year, and how much he loved her. Perfume. The tiny box said "Malaga, Spain" and it was a rosy scent from pink rose petals.

"How very exotic," she whispered to herself and held back the tear that stuck for a while in her throat.

85

B ud Ditlow was not about to question a holiday leave, and so he found himself jumping off the Pennsylvania Railroad at Lancaster for a Christmas reunion with his sister, Lois, and other relatives. Bud's father was a Railway Express Night Supervisor and his two brothers, Clarence and George, were in the Army and Navy. Where in the world were they? Bud hoped they were safe and having as good a time as he did in Lancaster. Lois worked in Mechanicsburg at the Naval Supply Depot. She asked Bud about going to Harrisburg, and he said that he wanted to visit Aunt Florence's home and planned to spend the night there. He told her he had orders to be in Philadelphia on December 27th.

Bud held an image of Louise that was expanding like a dirigible about to pop. His was the courage of a man possessed.

At sunset on Christmas night, he phoned her from the Lancaster railway station and the coin falling into the public phone slot was freezing.

"Louise? Louise Stitt?"

"This is her sister, Elaine. Hold on."

Louise had just eaten a ham sandwich and some sauerkraut, which Clara had taken to calling "cabbage" as she did not use the word "kraut."

"Hello?"

"Louise, this is Bud," he said, knees shaking.

"Why, why... where are you?"

His breath fogged the phone booth. "I'm in Lancaster, Louise, I'm here for three whole days!"

She smiled, "Well. I got these cards. Specially designed."

She had propped the cards on her dresser—Gibraltar, Panama, San Francisco.

With anticipation, he begged, "Louise, I'd like for you to meet with me tomorrow…"

There was silence. Louise answered in a neutral tone, "I'm engaged. He's over in Europe."

He insisted, pushing. "I'm not interfering with your, your…"

"Fiancé."

"I have to see you," he coaxed. "You'd be doing a sailor a favor."

Louise sighed as she did not like to be cajoled. "You mean I owe it to my country? Have you been eating too much fruitcake? Why do you insist so… sailor?"

Bud switched hands so to pocket the frozen one. "Well, out in the middle of nowhere I spent more time thinking than ever before. I just want to see you."

She was suspicious of a man who had spent years away from home, a man she really didn't know. Yet she had not been around young men lately—they had all been drafted—and she decided it would do no harm. It had been a Paleolithic eon since she had gone out dating.

***

"Harrisburger Hotel," directed Louise.

They were in the back seat of a barely heated Yellow Cab. As it was December 26, and Bud had no idea where to go, he asked her to pick a "good place for lunch." Most businesses were closed, but Louise, now in the mood for a lunch date, had put on her thinking cap; it matched her mahogany toned mouton coat.

He wanted to make an impression, and thanks to his black wool uniform, he did that. It had style, and he thereby escaped a poor showing in his pitiful civilian wardrobe. Had she seen what he usually wore (jeans with rusted zippers teamed with baggy elbowed shirts), she might have thought she had made a mistake.

But here they were, jumping from the cab at the door of the Harrisburger. The doorman directed them to a dining room that viewed the State Capitol Building, surrounded now by winter whipped trees.

Sun warmed their window, linen-draped table, and the waiter took her mouton. She *had* style. She knew the layout of all the dress shops, shoe shops and hat makers. She wore a white wool dress with shoulder pads. Bud, removing his pea coat, was breathing hard, as he sat facing this woman. Only hours ago she was a mirage. He was so alien to this situation, having never taken many women seriously. It was not that he didn't like women, but work had taken precedence over all, even over Bud himself!

She was pleasantly surprised when she saw him at the door ten minutes before the appointed hour of noon. His white striped jumper flap flipping, his black tie turning in the wind and the white cap contrasting his black Dean Martin hair, were pleasant to her eye. She had remembered his eyes as green, as seen in jewels; Bud's eyes took her in slowly. When she smiled, he felt it in his back pocket.

She scanned the menu while he observed her. For once, he did not worry about the tab and just asked her to recommend something. They sipped eggnog into which the waiter splashed brandy and someone started a rendition of *Night and Day* by Perry Como. He hadn't been on a date since '41, or even out to a restaurant. His word to describe the room was "fancy" and he saw that she was in her element—it was like her home away from home. He needn't have worried about making conversation; she was in the mood to relate her experience of the Army hospital, and that amused him because he had never heard of occupational therapy. Later she realized Bud got occupied with work like addicts take to heroin.

Time flew and now he was explaining his yearning against a backdrop of the war. "When I was out on the ocean, you just came out of nowhere. I never would've had the guts to ask you out back at the garage."

"Why?"

"You know. You're real pretty and you once were going to meet a guy. I didn't think you'd be interested in a car park kid."

Louise smiled; automatically she rejected herself as "pretty" but she was touched by his honesty. "Well, you ain't no kid no more."

This he took as a gem of a complement. Here he was talking to this, I don't know,... cherry pie of a woman! And she looked amused!

They closed the lunchroom, and he needed to get a cab, take Louise back and then he was due to have dinner with Aunt Florence. When they returned to 2232, Louise surprised him by inviting him in for more dessert. Bud had briefly met Floyd once in Broad Street Market, but now they were talking about bread as if they wanted to be consumed by yeast. Bud told the Stitts about the Hue Bakery and of the backbone of the great bakery: perseverance, trust and courage. Dot's eyes widened, Louise gasped and Elaine looked like a Little Rascal in a distasteful school classroom.

Impulsively, Bud asked, "Mr. Stitt, sometime I'd like to see where you bake your bread."

"Flattery will always butter up a baker. How 'bout now?"

Bud laughed nervously and said he had dinner arranged at Aunt Florence's, but Floyd convinced him to call his aunt and tell her he was going to be on time for dinner.

So Bud, Floyd and Louise hopped over to the bakeshop in Floyd's 1939 Ford, which he referred to as "the Fordor." Floyd understood Bud's recent reverence for bread, as he himself had known it like manna from heaven. Entering through the front door, they were greeted by an air recently scented by wedding cakes—light white, three-tiered exuberant cakes. The empty pie workroom lay ahead, with a long table and the machine used to roll out dough. It emitted an extraterrestrial groan as it flattened pie dough. They stepped finally into a high-ceilinged room fitted with ceiling fans over the bread oven. The bread room had to be the heart of the place. Bud leaned against the worktable while Floyd regaled him with the astounding feats of the oven.

"Why, we can produce 300 one pound loaves in an hour! And I guess you heard about the banning of sliced bread." Next, Floyd, sensing a captive audience said, "I grew up on a farm."

"What about that!" Bud related to him more and more.

Floyd said, "I watched a little wheat grow. But I didn't want to be on that end, where seeds sprout. I wanted to be here where humans mix in other ingredients."

"Like love," Louise said.

Floyd patted Louise on the shoulder. "Oh yeah, later come back and meet the baker. He's a genius!"

Floyd found a loaf of poppy seed unsliced bread and passed it to Bud as a souvenir.

"Tell your aunt I said Merry Christmas."

They drove him to Sixteenth Street, the Hill neighborhood, where he would stay until tomorrow's train ride back to reality. Before he left the car, he thanked Louise for spending the day with him, and Floyd for the tour. Then he handed Louise a flat tin from the pocket of his wool coat.

The box contained cookies tinted red and green. "Oh, these look like V cookies!" said Louise, and indeed they were widely made Vs.

Bud answered, "No, look again. They're L cookies." He smiled over his shoulder. This sugarcoated gift took her estimate of Bud to a new place of confusion.

;

86

Christmas was high life for the three sisters, and now they plummeted with a jolt, back to their daily routines. Christy had seemed taller to Dot as he boarded the train, and seeing him leave was almost unbearable for her. Bill flew off on some mysterious mission to Alabama, but Elaine would soon reunite with him and talk about their wedding. Louise felt mixed emotions as she had stepped out on her fiancé, yet she felt so inexplicably good about the meeting with Bud. When Dot referred to the sailor, Louise told her that Bud was "a refreshingly honest person, but too rough around the edges for me."

Historically, women have had to cope with men who "go away." Whether to the hunt, the battle or simply to work—they have had to go. As the war wore on, the bakery girls' men were away, and the three had to find solace in movie going and shopping.

Dot was largely relieved of V bread baking since the bakers had taken that over. At the end of the workday, she read, listened to radio dramas, or Saturday airings of New York opera. She made holiday decorations; now it was red paper valentines with white paper doilies. She could get lost in the cutting, gluing and be shocked how time flew. Her roommate Louise did some experimental egg cookery. It started off with fluffy omelets on a winter's night or possibly an airy cheese soufflé; this was followed by reading novelettes. Elaine was getting tired of the "deadly dull" school routine. She managed to make a little spending money by making cardboard boxes, packing into these "2-packs" of cupcakes and taking Clara's stomp-flattened tin cans to the collection center. She and Clara did some shopping, and she usually visited the Harrisburg Public Library on Front Street, seeking wedding reference books or magazines on the subject.

Shopping in Harrisburg in 1944 meant dressing up. Clara did her gray hair, rolling it into a kind of sausage at the nape of the neck. She put on a nice printed cotton shirtwaist dress and accessorized with a tailored hat, gloves, as well as a decent handbag. Few people could afford new clothes and lots of items were in short supply, but no matter, Clara could make do.

They had a few favorite places to depend on for necessities, and then they ate in the tearoom. The Pomeroy's Tea Room was a sublime retreat on the mezzanine where tired-eyed customers and sales people with aching feet could pause and fortify themselves to proceed with buying or selling; the store knew it was wise to keep the customer inside the store. They scanned the mimeographed menu, typed in purple ink and cased in a plastic liner. A waitress busily took the pencil out of her chignon.

"Hello, ladies, may I put in your order?" She wore a gray uniform with lots of pockets and a cloth tiara.

Clara ordered chicken corn soup as Elaine chanced to see a new sandwich on the menu. "What is this Victory Sandwich?"

"Oh, that's a cute type a' bread with egg salad or a BLT. The bread's cut like a hand that looks like it's making a "V" for victory... twenty-five cents... good bread too!"

"Okay," she smiled. "I'll have the Egg Salad Victory. Oh," she added, "and I'll have a cup of tea since we're in the tearoom."

Clara said, "I didn't know Pomeroy's sold our bread."

Her daughter replied, "Me neither." Elaine gazed down through the window.

An amusing feature of the tearoom was its windows running along one wall, permitting diners to view the entire first floor of the store.

Their orders arrived and, seeing Stitt's own bread, Elaine

exclaimed, "Well I'll be doggone!" The dainty dish bearing the sandwich came with a red paper napkin while a toothpick flag speared the sandwich.

Clara said, "I want you to tell your sisters about this!"

They chose orange ice for dessert, which came to the table in pewter dessert cups to keep their sherbets frosty.

That evening, Elaine called her sisters' bakery apartment and told them to come down to 2232 and have dinner.

"We have to?" Dot joked.

"Yeah this is a command!"

Louise took the phone. "Like going to the White House?"

Elaine said seriously, "Well you don't need to dress up much, but you dahlings can't say no."

Dot sighed, "Okay, six o'clock."

Clara showed everyone their newfound shoes, and then Elaine described a swell green ring, her first credit purchase. When the grandparents, parents and older sisters were seated, Elaine picked up the toothpick flag, and said, "Guess what kind of sandwich this came from?"

"A dangerous one," Louise ribbed, pinching the skin of her neck so it appeared she had swallowed a toothpick.

Elaine frowned and proceeded to describe the egg salad sandwich. There was silence in the kitchen until Floyd said, "They've been ordering those ever since the paper ran the Victory Bread story."

"Why didn't you tell me?" Elaine gasped. She suddenly realized how sanctified the tearoom was in her mind: it was a Harrisburg tradition.

Elaine gave Louise more details of the lunch, while Dot quietly took in what amounted to the ripple effect of her edible art, born slowly out of her yen to create. She surmounted her father's skepticism and once unleashed, it had run all the way to the newspapers, coming full circle to her sister's own plate at Pomeroy's Tea Room.

87

L ouise kept an odd secret to herself. Unbeknownst to anyone, Louise felt she was unattractive. If one were to examine her face, one would note a unique bone structure, a glow that Louise denied. Was it her "unshapely" legs, her recent loss of a molar or a tendency toward weight gain? Somehow, Louise felt she was not being enough or doing enough while the truth is: she usually did too much!

Her attachment to her beautician evolved into therapy, plus Louise did not relish hair care. The "beauty operator" insisted Louise's heavy brown hair was an asset and howled when Louise described herself as "nothing special."

The beautician implored, "Why, Louise, most of my customers would happily trade lives with you!" These compliments only were a momentary reality check. With war as an undesirable distraction, continually wrecking her social life, Louise turned to shopping to fill this gap of murkiness.

There was another helpful woman, another kind of beauty operator, who knew Louise's lack of self-esteem, taking it more to heart than the beautician: the corsetiere. O'Keefe's Corset Shop traded with people who required a boosted body image as well as rescue for a bust gone south. The saleslady-owner was a specialist at fitting and flattery.

Now, women lived in an era, American women that is, that began loosening the trappings of eons, where they had often been treated as chattel. Liberated Louise was an independent sort who prided herself on wearing styles with "oomph," yet due to her sense of low self-esteem, she never could imagine her body as beautiful, and she decided her only hope of being presentable was to wear a girdle, cosmetic for the figure and likened to the permanent wave for hair. She came by this in part having been raised by two corset fanciers, Clara and Caroline. All three women would wear their confining cinchers until their last days.

The bakery girls set out on a Saturday with a plan. Dot and Elaine searched Pomeroy's formal wear for bridal gowns, while Louise went to O'Keefe Corsets, which was located behind the courthouse. She had a girdle waiting there, fitted with new hooks and eyes.

The O'Keefe window display had the usual headless, legless torso wearing a pale pink zippered longline girdle. A filmy blue scarf covered the decapitation. This foundation combined the engineered molding, breast-lifting capability with the restrictive rib-hip binding Louise thought fashionable for ten dollars.

The door squeaked open and the corsetiere smiled from her desk, where she was on the phone. The impeccably dressed and corseted matron had a commanding air about her.

"Yes, we can have it by next week. Thank you for the order, ma'am. Good day."

Louise had been staring at the longline and turned to say, "And how are you, dahling?"

The corsetiere laughed and answered, "Fine and you?"

"Okay. I'm so tired of war. I guess we'll have to hope for the best."

The corsetiere produced a bag marked "Stitt." "We added new hooks and eyes for you."

Louise smiled and asked to try the longline, which she then bought. As usual, Louise stared at herself in the full-length mirror and made light of the saleswoman's flattering complements. She sighed, "It would take a magic wand to get this flabby waist in shape."

The corsetiere put a tape measure around Louise's waist and said, "Hold your shoulders back. You see, you've got a twenty-eight-inch waist and no figure flaws."

Louise was quick to interrupt, "Now don't forget my perfect

thighs!"

But the woman chuckled and said, "For instance, I have a flaw—large hip bones. I correct it by wearing a padded brassiere. You have proportions that could say: 'I can procreate.' I mean the brains of men are simple. They want to merge."

"I shouldn't complain…"

The corsetiere sermonized, "Now then," she declared, in a deep tone, clenching her fist, "we women do not have simple brains. We have minds!"

88

The Third Reich's resources dwindled. Western Allied forces used poor weather and nighttime darkness as a cover in selecting their time to invade; it started with parachute and glider landings. Thousands of people synchronized their watches in the early hours of June 6, 1944, traveling by 2700 ships, making the long crossing to Normandy, France. British, American and Canadian forces endured German shelling from fifteen divisions to bring in their men and material for the invasion.

Eddie wrote a sobering letter to Louise later that week:

D Day was a big damn deal! About 2,000 of our men died, but 200,000+ Allies got control of the beaches. Hours just running and firing, hours setting up guns, hours unloading supplies. But we made it and now you know.

On June 22, the full-scale operation launched with devastating success. Later in the month, the Soviets were successfully breaking through the eastern front. They took whole armies of German prisoners in their rapid advance. The Ukrainian Campaign moved toward Lvov with the Red Army facing 228 divisions of Germans on the five-hundred-mile front.

The Seabee motto was: "The difficult we do immediately; the impossible takes a little longer."

Christy wrote Dot of bulldozing an airstrip while shelling went on in the distance. His Seabees soon advanced to Provence, aided by a French resistance group that had managed to capture a German tank, using it to derail an enemy supply train. She knew her husband was doing well because he asked about

Yankee baseball.

***

The Stitt and Foster families planned for an August 9th wedding. The "festivity" began very early with three list-wielding shoppers powered by adrenalin and Popeye lunch cakes. The wedding dress was Elaine's single-minded focus. She confided to her sisters, "Once I find this dress, the rest'll be a piece of cake." Unfortunately, she had a notion that she required a dress that made her feel how Myrna Loy looked. Clara concentrated on the ceremony and reception. She insisted the event take place at St. Paul's Church, where she was a member. Elaine rejected St. Paul's as a child when the Reverend Judd had chastised her for dropping her donation. Thankfully, he had been replaced.

Dot was driving them down Sixth Street. "There's so much to do and time is short. I need some supplies... I don't want to spill the beans, but I'm making a treat for the reception."

Elaine said, "How nice! Louise and I can meet you at Pomeroy's Tea Room."

Elaine and her sister proceeded to visit several stores, and these trips were disappointingly fruitless. The bride only tried on one dress, and it was a poor fit. Finally entering Bowman's, Louise said, "Did you bring that picture?" She watched as Elaine produced a couple of magazine pictures of wedding dresses.

Louise said, "We have to meet Dot soon, and we're not finding anything. Let's go to look at bridal hats first, then after lunch, we'll look at dresses."

They approached the millinery department as the saleswoman in a black dress popped up from behind the counter. "Oh, Louise Stitt!" she exclaimed. It was Louise's favorite department, partly because the clerk was a high schoolmate, loved hats and loved to shop.

"This is my little sister," said Louise. She said Elaine was in the market for a great hat for her wedding trip. Elaine soon

318

fancied an elegant number that framed her face well, so the clerk planned to hold it for her until she found her wedding dress.

Then Louise showed her friend the magazine dress ideas, asking, "Have you any idea where we could get this kind of... creation?"

Excitement took over as the milliner whispered, "Guess what? We're having a fashion show! Four p.m. Monday. There will be assorted styles in the show, but there will be a designer visiting, and if I were you," she said looking at Elaine, "I'd speak to him before I did any more dress shopping."

Elaine wanted to know, "Why? What's so good about him?"

Authoritatively, she replied, "HE is an expert on dressy dresses... creations as Louise calls them. Uh, one more thing. Don't bring your mother."

With that, they sped to lunch.

***

Clara Stitt shared breakfast with Floyd and Elaine. Byron and Caroline were weeding their backyard garden. "Honeybunch, everything has been arranged for August 9th. What did you find when you went looking at dresses?"

Elaine sipped coffee. "A nice hat, Mother. I put it on hold. Monday we'll continue looking for a wedding dress."

Floyd looked over Clara's elbow at world headlines while the raisin-cinnamon toast popped. "As Allied armies moved toward Paris, Hitler's compound bombed." Floyd murmured, "His own people don't want him."

"He is the biggest liar in the world." Clara read, "Fighting in Pacific at Saipan leaves 16,000 Americans dead, untold Japanese casualties. Roosevelt accepts fourth presidential term." There was no inaugural parade as the troops were marching elsewhere. When faced with grim headlines, there was continuing hope their men remained safe and that peace was coming. Life would never overwhelm Clara: she was fortified by toast.

89

Gilbert Sonora's business card was printed in silver on heavy stock: Gilbert Sonora.

"We honor the bride." He was a tall, slender Hispanic gentleman of about forty and full of surprises. Louise and Elaine were introduced by the milliner.

"Ladies, here is Mr. Sonora."

He whispered something to the milliner and she retrieved a Sonora creation.

"Call me Gilbert." He did not impress Elaine with his plain blue work shirt and matching pants, or his tennis shoes. She thought, *If he's a designer, what does he make? Horse blankets?*

"Louise is a valued customer. Elaine is soon to be married. She is searching for the elegance of Myrna Loy—in a gown that is. I suggested they speak with you."

Louise thought, *So, I'm a valued customer? With customers like me, the store will go broke.*

Elaine extended her hand and the man bowed and kissed it, turned and repeated the gesture for Louise. As he retreated, he winked at Louise. Then Elaine explained what she wanted, and Mr. Sonora seemed charged within his element, eyes flashing.

"I have some photos of my work." He handed Elaine an album filled with professional views of wedding gowns. While she searched the book, the designer told Louise of his schooling in Puerto Rico and years serving the brides of New York.

"Men usually like to undress women," he said, teeth gleaming. "I live to dress them."

This set Louise into a screaming laugh, and he replied surely, "I see you sisters like to have fun, and I warn you, weddings are way too serious. There is tension always. The parents usually want to run the show." He eased into a chair. "The bride has consented to marry and she is at the center of the wedding—or could be. I make the dress only for her, so the bride starts marriage in a good way."

Elaine asked suspiciously, "Why were we not to bring Mother? Is it the price of the dress?"

Gilbert smiled and said smoothly, "You have been living with your mother, but you are an adult. I feel I am empowering the bride when she chooses her own gown. Break away and feel the emancipation!" He was calm yet as excited as an electric eel in his designer vanguard. He checked the price tag on his dress and showed Elaine.

"Twenty-five dollars. It's affordable."

They got down to the business of selecting the ideal gown, but he continued to regale them in a serious tone—to Louise, amusingly incongruous. "I believe the bride deserves more attention than usual church services allow. I believe speaking in ceremonies should be in whispers. Let the congregation sing and have it over in a half-hour. It comes down to the couple's vows, not the minister's speeches! Es verdad?"

Louise said, "Timing depends on the size of the congregation."

He replied, "Well then smaller is smarter. I believe women do not know their own value and your value is priceless. Don't get lost in the crowd."

Elaine listened, and his words were oddly refreshing. He had put her at ease in the land of bridal regalia. At least she knew she would get the right dress and look her best.

"Myrna Loy is quite an elegant person. You should know I made her some stunning pieces for the bond tour. Here is the one I liked most, the most alluring," he pointed to a photo in his album.

"What?" Both sisters were stunned. Their brown eyes rolled—Louise's to the left and Elaine's to the right and they

321

were losing their skepticism. Maybe he could be trusted to provide the "ultimo" wedding gown. He grinned like a Cheshire cat gripping two mice. He was looking at Louise's face as if he had to hypnotize her, all the while delivering another speech on elegance. "Myrna Loy has integrity and confidence. She is not like some sirens, with nothing upstairs that have relied on a pretty face."

Elaine sighed, "She has inner beauty, like a light behind her eyes."

"Ho, ho, cara mia! You have no less inner beauty! Myrna also has a great man lighting her movie sets! She always seems to be in candlelight. Oh, and Miss Stitt, forget all the silly superstitions like wearing old, new, borrowed and blue." He whispered as if it were some top secret: "Good lighting will put you in 'Loy Land!'"

Elaine poured over various necklines in the album, and then Gilbert proceeded to lose his sale. He said licentiously, "Necklines!" and stood behind Louise, his long fingers migrating down over her collarbones.

"Hey!" Louise jumped up and yelled, "Get your honorable hands off the merchandise! What kinda' game are you playing?"

Gilbert shrank back, "Please, cara mia..."

Elaine had dropped the album at Louise's shout. "I thought there was something fishy about a professional who goes to work in tennis shoes!"

Louise now stood looking up at the designer to the stars. "So. You *honor* the brides but treat every other woman like your... your plaything?"

He shook his head no. "No girls, please I meant nothing by it."

Elaine gritted her teeth and said, "I saw you winking, groping and... those pitiful shoes. Three strikes, we're out of here!"

"Es verdad, cara mia!" Louise spat out like poison seed. She stood at the door and stared back at the man who was holding his hands skyward.

"He wants us to buy from him and THEN he takes our dignity!" By the time Louise caught up, Elaine had already filled the ear of the milliner with complaints. She tore Mr. Sonora's business card in two. As the store was soon to close, the milliner, her manager, Elaine and Louise retreated to the manager's desk, where the complaint could be put in writing. Fuming, Elaine signed it and the fountain pen nearly tore through the paper. The manager apologized and promised to remunerate her for the insulting behavior, deemed unbecoming to any salesperson.

Dot was told of the misadventure, but it was kept from their mother; thus in the days to come the bakery girls regrouped.

90

Elaine selected a bridal gown at Pomeroy's Department Store and proceeded to invite the family for the August 9th wedding at St. Paul's Church. The gown was inexpensive, yet a real confection of satin and lace. Clara would be matron of honor, and two friends from school were to act as bridesmaids. Bill had a pass from the Air Corps for a modest amount of time. He wondered how long his aerial reconnaissance would continue and when he would be sent to the Pacific.

The cake had three tiers. The Fegley family baked and decorated. Dot inspected the plaster of Paris bride and groom topper, finding the hair "too blond." She tinted the heads brunette to match those of Bill and Elaine. The Myrna Loy feeling was just about what Elaine had intended, but for insurance, she added more candles to the church sanctuary.

At the last minute, her maid of honor lost her brother to the fighting in Saipan! She had to forgo the wedding for his funeral. The second bridesmaid, in a woeful dilemma, wanted to be with Elaine, but finally chose to accompany her grieving friend. So, Elaine regrouped and enlisted her sisters. Louise enjoyed helping dress Elaine and made a point of complimenting her sister's beauty. Their final look into the mirror revealed a luminous bride in a gown fitting better than Cinderella's slipper. The headpiece crowned her brown curls and was accented by a blusher veil.

Louise also radiated elegance, although in denial. She credited herself for finding a stylish summer suit on short notice, but each morning her blessings went out to the chemist who invented the permanent wave and the designer of foundation garments. Now she beamed at her sister and proclaimed in dramatic falsetto, "Let's go off to Loy Land!"

Elaine doubled over and said breathlessly, "Laugh now! Ha ha ha... can't laugh in church."

They continued purging their hysterical hoots as the Reverend Waggenseller tapped on the door to summon them.

They opened the door straight-faced and commanded him, "Don't laugh." But his look of surprise got them cackling against their will.

Straight-faced Waggenseller mumbled, "Oh, heaven! Where is Loy land?"

Elaine and the groom, polished in his dress uniform, were alert and poised to join each other. The reverend was somewhat delayed by Bill's father, who was the best man. In his excitement to reach the sanctuary, "Dad" took too many stairs and narrowly escaped falling. The minister came to him asking innocently, "Have you seen the best man?"

"Yes," said Dad, momentarily stunned by the excitement. "I know him."

The minister sighed as Dad shook his hand. "I'm best. I'm the man."

The wedding was serenely lovely in spite of the broiling heat. Electric fans whirred as the guests fanned themselves with wooden-handled hand fans that pictured an American flag on one side and on the opposite side the words STITT BAKERY Phone 41990. Love circulated in the wind as the couple exited the church.

The guests filed into the church recreation room, where everyone celebrated with vigor. Years of war, then rationing, even losing loved ones had left people about as stale as a bread crust stuck in a toaster. This reception released them temporarily from that worn state of worry.

Dot had produced a sparkling confection thanks to her dealings with sugar salesmen. She molded pink hearts, also white cupids in flight, out of a hardened sugar solution. Silver trays were set out with the romantic candy, nut cups and, of course, cake, heavy with creamy white icing.

I wish I had a movie camera, thought Dot as she circulated through the group. Here was her dear aunt from Franklin County: "Dorothea dear, you made this candy?"

Uncle Louis and Louise were mixing some punch with a cold cylinder of vanilla ice cream so that it foamed, oozing over the punchbowl edge and he laughed, "They'll think I put beer in it."

Mrs. Brown and some of the church altar guild complemented Elaine on her dress. The sweet confusion went on with some cousins listening to the ball game on the kitchen radio, while some kids hid under the table. *Cluck, cluck, buzz, buzz.*

Urgently, Floyd asked Dot whether she could identify the odd man standing at the table wearing the unsavory white open-necked shirt and plaid pants. He really was a neighborhood lush in search of spiked punch. She could not place him, so Floyd spirited him outside, still holding his cake and punch, asking, "Just what do you think you're doing?"

Downing the punch to avoid it being taken from him, the fellow answered, "Kind sir, always a bridesmaid, never groomed." His breath made Floyd's nose want to leave his face.

Taking the crasher's elbow in a vise grip, Floyd deposited him on the sidewalk and said clearly, "You better groom your ass away from here," and snatching away the glass cup, he pathetically added, "Next time, wear a suit!"

Elaine and Bill emerged in their get-away clothes to head for a honeymoon in New York. She chose a navy dress with puffed sleeves over shoulder pads; it was short and belted. Her hat was appropriate in this heat—a short brimmed straw. Bill, now out of uniform, wore casual clothes plus an air of relief as he brushed the rice from her hat. Secretly, he had dreaded the ceremony more than Me-262 Messerschmitt fire. But now, they could *live!* Her orchid corsage perfumed the interior of the black Chevrolet.

91

N ew York City was a world compacted, its energy continually stirring, humming like a Sunbeam Mixmaster. Yet it welcomed the couple to start their partnership. A tall policeman pointed the way to the Hotel Gotham, where the staff had seen so many honeymooners, they automatically assisted the couple in their quest for *living it up*. Bill waited for the bellman to leave the hotel room, then took his wife out into the hall. He swept her into his arms, and with a laugh of relief, stepped over the threshold toward their room and their future.

The next morning, they wanted to sleep in, but the sound of a siren echoing in the street below disrupted that, followed by the sound of cab horns bouncing off the tall buildings. Manhattan was always awake.

Bill studied the huge black and white photographs on the wall. "Skyscrapers."

She gave him a kiss and said, "I'm ordering breakfast. Room service, dahling, just like in a movie."

Bill smirked. "It is a movie." He held his long arm out as if sighting a camera scene: "Casa-Foster-a-blanca. Hotel Gotham Heights..."

"Honeymoon Hotel!" Elaine gasped. Their laughter reverberated as they envisioned themselves as stars of their own movie.

Over bacon and eggs, Bill pointed to the skyscrapers and said, "Let's go up in a building so you'll have a bird's eye view."

Elaine replied, "A pilot's eye view. Let's go. I'll wear my sensible shoes."

The elevator operator dropped them at the lobby, and while Bill inspected a city map, Elaine asked the Chinese desk clerk where they could go for lunch. He gave her several ideas and addresses, along with the Hotel Gotham business card. He said, "You'd be surprised how many people get lost."

The honeymooners quickened their steps to match the pace of the city. It was a bit surprising to find wartime Manhattan with a similar focus as wartime Harrisburg. They passed a storefront announcing, "Buy War Bonds." In the next block, a movie house marquee shouted, "*Fighting Seabees* John Wayne and Susan Hayward." On the way to the Empire State Building, a dump truck passed bearing a sign, "Win the War! Save Metal Scrap."

Filing into the elevator at the Empire State Building, Elaine noticed three Army recruits with southern drawls. The feeling of freedom pervaded Manhattan—or was it her sense of being able to be herself, free from family oversight? She later said that the trip could be summed up in one word: *liberty.* Now she was even closer to the war, by her marriage. The elevator ride was lengthy, giving passengers time to appreciate just how high they were going and how wondrous the steelworkers were who had assembled the skyscraper. The riders stepped out at the eighty-sixth floor into a heated wind that blew Elaine's hat into the air.

"Ooops!" Bill was tall enough to snatch it out of the rarified air and said, "Next thing you know, that bald man down on the street'll be wearing it."

They had a clear view of the East River, and beyond, the ocean. Arm in arm they took in the Eastside and Westside, a panoramic view of the island. Bill began to think about flying into the clouds and wondered to which ocean he would be traveling. His new bride noticed a Boy Scout troop and their chaperone viewing the East River, then they turned west where three youthful women in black dresses looked down at Fifth Avenue. *I could end up like them,* she imagined. Then she resolved, *I will not be a widow, I'll be a den mother.*

"Hey, you're miles away," Bill smiled.

"You caught me. I was thinking about our future."

He squeezed her and urged, "Don't. Stay right here. We talked about that in the car. Let's have some laughs, love each other and be happy, okay?"

She took a deep breath of Manhattan, and smiled, "Okay. I'll try to be happy now." She felt the odd feeling a guard had mentioned about the sway of the 102-story building.

Her ears popped on the long descent. Bill conversed with the soldiers as Elaine scanned the lunch recommendations. They chose to walk south toward Greenwich Village and noticed that Manhattan residents certainly did like to walk. So much was happening on Fifth Avenue! They spotted a boy juggling small Statues of Liberty on the sidewalk in front of another war bond outlet.

Half an hour of walking whetted their appetites, and they noticed a hot dog vender. He had a lunchtime cue of typical New Yorkers: two freckled kids, a Puerto Rican man in work clothes, a dark skinned nun... all standing in the sun for "Mr. Fatouch's Boloney."

"Can't remember a better hot dog," said Bill, chewing as he got in line for another. Fortified, they were on their way to the part of New York where there were no skyscrapers, Greenwich Village. They arrived at the "Celebrity Entrance" café, a haven for people of the neighborhood. Brownstone fronted, it had once been a home in the nineteenth century. Again, freedom whispered in Elaine's mind as she scanned the customers, abnormal by Harrisburg standards, but average "locals" according to Bill. One appeared to be a working cowboy, another wore a Zoot suit with a black beret. Elaine thought his suit was out of place. It consisted of an oversized Billet, wide lapels, broad shoulders, and low crotch. The pant legs of the suit narrowed towards the ankles.

A young woman entered in a polka dot dress, but she wore a knapsack that she carefully unshouldered to reveal a smiling baby. As she was a regular, the waitress came to her bearing a tray for café au lait, and a few ginger snaps for her teething partner. Elaine imagined what a life the baby would have here in a cultural Mecca that was full of noise and auto exhaust.

The welcoming waitress then brought menus and recommended the iced drinks to fight the heat. The clientele chatted or read newspapers, but Elaine eyed the framed photographs nearby.

"These aren't celebrities," she observed.

Bill said, "Frank Sinatra is over at the entrance, by the sign that says 'Viennese Coffee.'"

Their red-uniformed waitress, who had an Irish accent and long red hair, informed them, "We hung these shots of people we know. They're mostly actors who want to be celebrities."

They sipped their cold, charming beverages named "Ladies Gossip"—iced tea with lime and "Chocolate Dust"—a malt with nearly frozen milk. They drank in the quaintness surrounding them and found their second wind. On the way out, a strange young man in a sort of Thomas Jefferson costume passed them. Elaine could no longer contain herself and shouted, "Let freedom ring!" The chap turned and saluted them vigorously.

Next, the couple sprang into a Checker Cab and went back uptown to relax in Central Park. Elaine's sensible shoes came off. She walked on the grass and then soaked her feet in the lake. Bill searched for another hot dog while Elaine sat against a tree. She relaxed into a reverie, smoothly consolidating her past with her future. The oak seemed to hug her reassuringly. She let go of her war-related angst and felt like sleeping, but she was simply still, against the tree's coolness. She realized she was in just the right place in her life to make a difference. Women were working in factories, Louise had treated the war wounded, Dot created Victory Bread, now it was time for Elaine, a pilot's wife, to support the cause of liberty by supporting Bill. He sat next to her and handed her a large soft pretzel.

"You're so gorgeous," he complimented.

Resting her head on his shoulder, her side moved into his chest and she answered, "I'm happy that we have each other."

New York had surprised them again with a pastoral view from an old tree that had seen many couples, and they sat and steeped themselves in the afternoon's light.

Perhaps it was Elaine's mood, or perhaps the phase of the moon. That evening she objected strongly to her cake. The hotel dining room had served a fine, romantic meal, followed by a slice of chocolate cake.

"This cake is too airy. It's so flimsy that soon the icing will collapse on it."

Bill took a taste and agreed, "Not as good as your dad's. Your first cake impression was your grandmother's homemade cake. Next, you had lots of cakes made by George. Cake that's better than most homemade."

She had had a steady diet of great desserts all right. "I bet they used the wrong flour. Well, since we agree, maybe Stitt's slogan, "Better made," is correct. It's not just Father's claim," she nodded adamantly.

92

The following day was more leisurely, but their time for living it up was winding down. They rode the boat to the Statue of Liberty, where they viewed Manhattan from the windows in Miss Liberty's crown. They had lunch in a French bistro, and all was well until Elaine tasted the peach tartlette.

The peaches must have been trucked in from France."

"Honey, the war stopped exports."

She moaned, "I guess I'm just realizing how very lucky I was to have great desserts for so long!"

Bill arched his brow. "I hope you can eat southern cooking when we go to the base in Birmingham."

Elaine said, "Then it'll be my cooking... but it'd be great to have bakery pecan pie..."

Now what puzzled our heroine was the possibility that two "highfalutin" city bakeries could be outdone by her father and his bakers. "I'll have to tell Father about this. A hotel chose the wrong flour or... some cake mix... that's it! George never buys a mix. He uses his own recipes."

Bill replied, "Well, were those peaches in the tart canned?"

"Hmmm. They were a bit watery. Hmmm. No, I'm guessing that this pie was under baked. The filling didn't consolidate. George buys his peach filling from a great farm in the Dutch country, but he adds lemon juice. Makes it zingy." She wore that laughing-eyed smile that came out of sleuthing.

***

Hotel Pennsylvania was the place where they spent their last evening as well as the last of their dwindling funds. Elaine wore her sassiest dance dress. It was red satin, V-necked and calf-length. Bill helped her to attach a pearl choker that shone elegantly in the dusky light of evening. She looked up to help him straighten his tie; surprisingly printed with sketches of the Grumman XP-50 Skyrocket. Soon they would be dancing cheek to cheek, swing dancing and Charlestoning their way into the night as they "forgot their troubles and just got happy." The ballroom itself was destined to become one of Elaine's brilliant memories. The room had a high ceiling, yet was half as spacious as the Hershey Ballroom. Crimson draperies matched the stage curtain, the decorator being true to the Café Rouge's name. And oh, the lighting! The dancers appeared to be illuminated by candlelight, when it really came from art deco electric wall sconces and lights installed in the floor perimeter. Les Brown's renowned band always had a great vocalist and the audience was electrified when she appeared, wearing a blue sequined evening gown that complemented her dark blond hair.

The bandleader pronounced, "Welcome, ladies and gentlemen, to the Café Rouge! This is the band you've all been waiting for and I'm Les Brown. Now, a salute to Glenn Miller." The band loved to play *In the Mood*, and when they took off, a charge of excitement went out to every person in the room. Instantly everyone was dancing as if they were addicts for the sound, and even the waiters were unable to keep from humming along.

First I held him lightly and we started to dance
Then I held him tightly what a dreamy romance
And I said "Hey, baby, it's a quarter to three
There's a mess of moonlight, won't-cha share it with me"
"Well" he answered "Baby, don't-cha know that it's rude
To keep my two lips waitin' when they're in the mood to be
kissed

The young singer left the mike, beckoning to a toe-tapping sailor who was standing alone, and she let the band finish the tune. They swung with the power of a couple of whirling dervishes, inspiring the crowd to whistle, to yell, "go man go!" The feeling drew people from all over the hotel, even from the street, inspiring more dancers. Finally, there was tumultuous applause with a few tipsy whistlers standing on their chairs and then, mercifully, the band shifted into the mellow *Shine on Harvest Moon*, the next of a whole gang of songs Elaine loved.

Elaine and Bill would remember that evening of pure joy for the rest of their lives. They felt synchronized with the woman who stood and snapped her fingers while belting out tunes like Strayhorn's *Take the A Train*.

Bill sighed, "It's such a great song—and to think it's about taking a subway ride."

She added, "Sounds like a real shakin' train ride, dahling."

They chatted with "the world" that night: a caffeinated Brazilian couple on vacation, a gum-snapping Cuban dancer on her day off, other visitors from North Carolina, who had dropped out of college, and New Yorkers who loved Swing music.

The charismatic singer closed by slowly crooning *Lullaby of Broadway*. Her sequins still sparkled, but she drained her throat of melody and was glad to bid the audience farewell. She introduced herself and the band: "The Café Rouge enjoyed serving you this evening. I'm Doris Day."

93

B ill's black Chevy moved on a two-lane highway south of Pennsylvania, packed carefully with Air Corps uniforms, Sherlock Holmes mysteries, summer dresses and wedding gifts. The honeymoon had gone into phase two on this hot August morning as the two set out on a road trip to Alabama's Maxwell Air Base. Bill's orders specified for the couple to be based in Montgomery. Elaine basked in the thought of their future domesticity.

Bill moaned, frustrated, "More training? But I'm ready now!"

Elaine quipped, "Maybe the war isn't ready for you. I just wish it were over right now, before there's any more suffering."

Yes, Bill was champing at the bit, a workhorse ready to enter the ongoing fray that already employed Eddie, Christy and Bud.

***

Millions of citizens throughout the world in 1944 agreed with Elaine. They wanted to end the war in Europe and with Japan, but the Allies knew they had to win, and win in the best possible way.

The Allies had been building feverishly toward a likely battle in the Philippine Sea, the U.S. sending a fleet from Hawaii. However, Bud Ditlow, baker first class, was not in either of these battlegrounds. His aircraft carrier—*Wasp*—had been assigned to escort supply ships to Europe for the invasion of Germany. There was a lengthy trip west to Hawaii, and then a return to Panama. The ship was part of a military strategy to insure the continued safety of the Allied fuel storage in the Dutch colony Curacao; a Caribbean island located fifty miles north of Venezuela.

The enlisted men read newspapers bought in port or old hometown papers mailed by their families. The naval crew murmured about ongoing military activity and most were of the opinion that Hitler was a madman and Tojo a power-crazed loose cannon. Given Atlantic U-boat activities, some felt an attack on the U.S. East Coast a real possibility.

Bud heard the talk but immersed himself in his work, living from one day to the next. He would punch down dough and sense the activity of bread in its infancy, thinking automatically, *Maybe Louise is doing some baking, right now.*

Since the start of the year, he thought of her all the time, reviewing their meeting and thanking himself for going to see her. He had written a few notes, careful not to offend, and finally he had received a letter, neutral in tone, describing her sister's wedding. Louise's letter sent him into a state of hopeful euphoria and convinced him he just might be worthy of her, even though she had more education. The memory of meeting her family sent a glowing flashback. He would write and visit again, being sure to act like her equal.

***

Louise rarely baked anything; why, she would laugh at Bud's image of her running a commercial oven. She had earned extra money this day by making specialty cake deliveries in the Austin Healy truck. She was not worried about the war because now she worshipped General Dwight Eisenhower. Every time she heard his voice over the radio, she whispered, "That's the stuff!"

Elaine had left a gap in Louise's world, and she imagined that she might eventually marry also and have children, though by then she would be an ancient thirty! She thought about Eddie and dutifully wrote him to maintain his morale. Bud Ditlow was somewhat a nuisance, but she wrote to him as a friend, not wanting to encourage him, though she had to compliment him on his "L" cookies.

> *Dear Bud,*
> *Thanks for your letter and the written tour of exotic Panama City. I know you can't reveal secret military activities, but by what they say in the news, I'd say you are in (1) Europe or the (2) Pacific. Hopefully, you are safe—as safe as a man on a large warship can be. I hear now about neighbors, in the Army, who have been wounded fighting in Belgium.*
> *The bakery is doing more business since my sister added Victory Bread to the menu. We have survived in spite of the tasteless sugar shortage, and there is the banning of sliced bread. I have been driving a bread route to various grocers in Dauphin County.*
> *For fun, I saw "Philadelphia Story"—a great show.*
> *Thanks to you and those you serve with,*
> *Louise*

***

Some sailor was having a birthday, so Bud spent the morning baking a large sheet cake after the bread had gone into the other oven. As he had reread Louise's latest letter, he wondered how to respond.

The captain greeted, "Hey, sailor! You're sure quiet these days."

Bud explained he had a crush on Louise. "I want... need to get to know her—to know her as a friend. I'm kinda afraid of her boyfriend, and I don't even know him."

The captain sat down with Bud on some deck piping.

"Well, good for you. We love the gals, don't we?"

Bud answered, "Yeah, I do love her."

The captain pondered, finally saying, "Confidence, man. Confidence is the magnet. Courage is attractive. Don't concern yourself with the guy she's dating."

Bud mused, "I want to write that I love her."

"Don't worry. Tell'er about yourself, but focus most on questions about her. Love comes through and love is strong. No room for fears." He slapped Bud on the back.

Bud took a deep breath, grinned and exhaled, "Con-fid-ence."

94

The air carried the cool afternoon scent of autumn leaves as the Chevrolet delivery truck motored down Third Street; here it was, Friday. The diminutive woman driver wore a plain white dress, accented by printed flowers on the cuffs and belt. Louise felt as though she needed a break before returning the truck to the bakery and settling accounts, so she pulled into a parking space in front of the restaurant owned by Eddie's family.

She sat at the bar and ordered a lemon Coke, presented in a Coca-Cola glass, on a saucer, with a wheel of lemon hooked onto the glass.

Her eyes wandered from the bar to the empty tables. She mentally conversed with the absent Eddie. "Wherever you have been, wherever you'll be, come home!" She sighed. She was not one to buckle under but, *Gee zooey*, she thought. Her eye strayed to the latest *Patriot News* on the bar. It foretold of the advancing Allies—British, French, Americans, Russians and others who opposed the Third Reich, marching toward Germany. She heard some talk by town shopkeepers that Hitler had lost the confidence of the German people through his tactics of force, and it would only be a matter of time until the Allies prevailed over the Axis.

She took one last swallow, "To Eisenhower," she toasted, grinned at the waiter and took the bar tab. The paper was pulled out of her hand. She looked up to see two soldiers, about her age. One held her bill and beseeched, "Please, miss, we're shipping out, both of us."

The other man, holding his hat and bowing, asked, "Yeah, won't you have another one?"

Louise answered, "Well, it isn't every day I'm treated by two such charming, handsome fellows."

So she downed another small lemon Coke while listening to the two from Steelton, who were home on a short leave. They told her they were bound for the Pacific, where they would be stationed indefinitely, and that it was great that she joined them. She would be an image of home in the wartime tasks of the future.

She came home to mail from Elaine, addressed to Dot. The envelope was postmarked Montgomery, Alabama.

Dear Louise and Dot,   *Sept. 10, 1944*

We got into Montgomery safely. 900 miles at least! The weather is hot and humid. We are in base housing and learning our way around. I met a few women in town, and one invited me to go roll bandages at the Methodist Church. We rolled hundreds to send overseas.

Bill is training on a four-engine plane. There are several flight schools here.

We expect to go west after the training, but things can change at the drop of a hat. Thinking of you.

Love,

Elaine

Dearest Louise,

You know how much I love you! I am not able to say what's next, but what's passed is safe to say. We went into Paris Aug. 24th, to assist the French and drive the Germans out. Many of them just waited unarmed in the eastern part of Paris. Many fled out of the city knowing the "jig was up." So Aug. 25th, the French regained control and the church bells went crazy!

A priest passed out gallons of aged wine to our outfit.

Thanks loads for your letters—they mean the world to me.

Love,

Eddie

Dear Louise,
As I attended to my usual chores, preparing the bread
dough and making some cookies, I was reminded of the
visit to you and how it has sparked my imagination. I felt
like an engine with new spark plugs!
I wish we could meet again, but the Navy is my life
now.
Here I close with my first poem

Please LOUISE

Please Louise, accept my thanks
For meeting you was the greatest gift!
Please Louise, see me again.

Sincerely yours,
Bud

Sighing, Louise forcefully kicked off her white oxfords. She
reread the letters from Eddie and Bud. "How did this happen?"

She went to the small white refrigerator, took out yesterday's
leftovers to warm, then ran a tub bath. She stewed herself in the
tub... and she was only sitting in water a foot deep. It had to do
with conserving water. She added Epsom salts, a drop of
perfume and stirred it with her toe. Louise ruminated.

Hearing Dot come home, Louise emerged wearing a bathrobe
and a half-smile. Dot was not in a good humor. Floyd had added
extra work to her overflowing inbox.

Louise sighed, "I have had a... a flabbergasting
development."

Dot laughed, astonished, out of her bad mood. "I'm coming."

As she changed, Dot told Louise that Father was anticipating
war ending and wanted her, Dot, to approach an acquaintance in

the Pennsylvania Senate about rescinding the ban on sliced bread.

Louise soothed, "I couldn't do your job."

Dot smiled, her brows moving. "Time's like these, I wish I'd been born a boy. Well, spill it, sister."

Louise showed her Bud's poem. She speechlessly looked up, allowing her head to fall back like a bowling ball had rolled it over.

Louise went on to say she had met two men at the restaurant who had bought her drinks, then about the letters.

Dot mused theatrically, "It was like a sign, meeting two men, then two letters come together. Love letters. I know you didn't lead Bud to believe you were interested in him."

"Right. But I had a part in it. I didn't *have* to park at City Parking."

"Oh, when you met?"

"Yeah. Now what? I have to set him straight. He didn't take my engagement seriously."

Dot set out squares of baked macaroni surrounded by bright red tomatoes from Broad Street Market. She was depleted by the day as well as near starvation. "Hey kid," she snapped, "Just think! They may not survive! What if neither one comes home?" She glanced at a picture of Christy and herself.

Louise sobered, agreeing, "That does put a different light on my problem!"

They did delight in Dot's cheese creation. They read Elaine's news and missed her intensely, wishing she could go with them to a Saturday matinee. Except for wartime newsreels, the movies were still a great escape. Louise smiled, remembering a recent showing of Casablanca. But wait, it was also associated with war.

"We will," Dot replied, "carry on, yes to go on in spite of... of our trials!"

"I could answer this letter, but I'm so tired."

Dot offered, "We can change, we could get to the drug store

for ice cream before they close."

They walked briskly to Loper's, then came strolling home, somehow revived, and it had nothing at all to do with eating tutti-frutti cones.

Louise mumbled about her need for distraction until Dot created another distraction. "You do a good job of muddling through whatever you have to do, and seem happier than me. You seem able to lose yourself in the task at hand."

"I've got a grip on things now," Louise said, "and I don't dread the letter writing."

Dot stopped. They were on Jefferson now, and only a few people sat on their front porches in the twilight. "Enjoyment leads to endurance."

They moseyed along. Louise grinned, "I bet enjoyment even builds endurance."

Dot continued, "With enjoyment we endure."

Stepping away from some skipping children, Dot's tone emboldened. "Well, dahling, now you can imagine how you will 'enjoy' writing to Bud Ditlow."

Louise breathed in the grassy aroma of the ball field as they approached their apartment. Louise mused, sarcastically, "I'll enjoy the heck out of it."

95

It was September, and Montgomery, Alabama had welcomed the newlyweds. Elaine and Bill lived nearby the Maxwell Air Base, where Bill trained on the B-24 Liberator aircraft. Elaine was initially busy setting up the apartment, knowing they would likely be reassigned, happy that she and Bill were together. She, flourishing at eighteen, was the most youthful of the wives of the airmen and the lone Pennsylvanian. She only mentioned that she was formerly a bakery girl, one time, to a neighbor.

Now, she entered Montgomery Grocers right behind Montgomery native, Veronica Francis, wife of a base mechanic. "Elaine," she said, drawling, "Might you he'p me w' somethin'?" Veronica was thirty, slim, and appeared to have copied Veronica Lake's hair allure, but Elaine thought the woman behaved "too much like a spoiled brat to be a middle-aged woman." She habitually stood pigeon-toed and fidgeted, arms folded, like a spoiled kid whining for a lollypop.

"Veronica! How are you?"

Veronica smoothly took her by the arm. "You ever made cornbread?"

"No. There was no need for me to bake." Elaine went on to tell her about Stitt Bakery and that cornbread was not on the menu.

Veronica giggled, "Do tell. That is a durn shock. Why, in these parts, cornbread's a big fav-o-rite," said Veronica as she fidgeted on toward the flour shelf of the store. "Hey, you gonna haf'ta advise me about bakin' fer the State Fair."

"Hah!" Elaine chuckled darkly. "Let me repeat, Veronica. I'm not a baker, and I cannot help you bake. Heck! I never even tasted cornbread."

"Oooheee!" But the imprudent Veronica remained convinced a baker's daughter had to be full of wisdom, if only by association. Then there was the matter of the cash prizes.

Elaine gripped the handle of her woven market basket saying, "If you'll excuse me..."

But noooo. Veronica launched into explaining her mission: winning the state fair baking contest and the coveted cornbread blue ribbon. She then followed her annoyed acquaintance into the produce section, begging for a tip, a hint, some precious kernel of Yankee baking creativity! But Elaine had tuned her out, way back in jams and jellies, and when Veronica blocked her path, Elaine bellowed, yelling loudly enough for the grocer's ears, "Put corn in it!"

Veronica was nearly floored by the force of Elaine's response and gaping, shouted after her, "Oh my stars! Fresh corn! I will! I will do it!" She skipped out of the store with gayety, waving flirtatiously to the grocer.

Veronica miraculously proceeded to take a three-egg cornbread recipe, add corn she had cut off the cob and pray. Oh, she won every judge's vote, to the dismay of last year's reigning bake-off winner, Polly Thigpen, a veteran baker who had been nicknamed "Pone" because of her reverence for the chewy yellow stuff.

Elaine's face dropped when she read in the morning paper, "Novice Francis Wins Blue."

"Oh, my!"

"My what?" said Bill, imagining some shift in the European war status.

Elaine read, "Veronica Francis' recipe captured the judges' interest. Her secret ingredient: corn." There was a photo of Veronica, grinning widely, holding up a ribbon.

"And that's just what you said to her in the store, 'put corn in it.'"

"Oh! I just wanted her to back off! Now there'll be hell to

pay," sighed Elaine.

"Why?"

Elaine dropped the paper. "Because she's confused about me as a baker and my so-called advice. She won, but she would've won without adding corn."

Mimicking Veronica's accent, Bill shrilly responded, "Do tell!" Then in a low tone, "How do you know?"

"Well, I really don't know. I guess the extra ingredient helped her believe in herself as a baker."

"And," said Bill, with a grin, "she got the idea from a baker's daughter."

96

Veronica indeed planned to enter a contest in another county, but she had also a commitment to two neighborhood church bake sales in September.

Veronica reproduced the recipe, now dubbed "Maizey Cornbread." She was up most of the cool night prior making enough for the two sales, her intrigued neighbors and her husband.

Never a great student, Veronica barely passed high school Home Ec. She had a difficult time learning to focus on the mixing bowl before her or the burner flame. During her egg cookery lesson, she failed to tend the fried egg in her pan, so it overheated and exploded yolk on her long blond hair. She felt she would rather look out the window at the boys' intramural football team trooping by the window.

Now she had redeemed herself personally by her win at the fair, and Veronica was riding high on cloud nine until noon that Saturday.

Things were bustling in the recreation hall at the Baptist church bake sale. The Women's Auxiliary had made well over twenty dollars. The cornbread table was flanked by Arminda, busily selling biscuits of pure white, displayed on a large pink turkey platter; and by Dorcas, the minister's wife. She sold crescent rolls, egg rolls, poppy seed rolls, and they were yeastily aromatic.

"Well," said Veronica, standing at her table. "I do believe my 'Maizey' has all been sold, y'all."

She wandered outside at the same moment a black Chevy sedan tooled by transporting Bill and Elaine. "Hey, is that

Veronica?" Bill mumbled. He pulled up to the curb and Elaine waved to her. She decided that Bill would finish the errands, then collect her at the church.

"I have sold out of cornbread!" Veronica said proudly.

Elaine congratulated her and said, "I'd like to go into the sale." Elaine had trouble interpreting Veronica's drawl-- at times it drove her wild.

Veronica sniffed, "Holey moley! Cimamon!"

"That's Cinnamon."

Veronica looked over speckled cookies, "Cim-mon."

Elaine breathed, "Cinn- a- mon. Can't you say it?"

The stir of the sale interrupted the tongue twirling. She found an array of baked items; many seemed to be a southern rendition of Stitt's Bakery. Giddy customers were sampling as they socialized.

Looking about the room, Elaine spotted her old favorites, white bread, vanilla sugar cookies and layer cakes of chocolate and yellow, here sprinkled with peanut topping. Veronica introduced her to a few elderly women, who beamed over their pies.

"It takes a heap o' horse sense ta bake like Effie here," Veronica swore. She displayed crusty apple, berry and peach. Her cakes were piped with icing decoration that reminded Elaine of the woman's red lipstick.

The next baker was Lula Mae, who volunteered, "While I'm bakin', I'm 'bout as happy as a Bluetick Hound after a squirrel!" Her cherry custard and coconut custard pies looked happy too.

Veronica said, "I had a lady tell me something positively heart rendin'."

"What?"

Veronica whispered, "See, her husband was killed las' year. Since then, she has grieved, but she said she stays alive by comfort food."

Elaine nodded, thoughtfully digesting. "Sweets?"

"No," Veronica assured. "She swears by biscuits and gravy."

By the time Bill arrived for Elaine, she had learned enough to fill a cookbook about Veronica's "Granny," who had inspired her to cook. She used her grandmother's cast-iron skillet for baking success. The pan could withstand incredibly hot temperatures, leaving the finished product's exterior crisp while tender inside. Veronica entertained Elaine by describing an iron skillet with wedge sections.

"That'n really gives ya crunchy ol' bread."

She had a few iron oven pans that were molds of ears of corn. "The chunks of cornbread out'ta that'n are sticks shaped like ears of corn."

Elaine learned something else about baking that day. She saw how proud the bakers were of their culinary art. She noticed that it brought the community together. She also had to admit that Veronica *was* a good baker. She made plans to meet her two weeks later at a nearby soda shop.

***

Inspiration attacked Elaine! The bake sale women were to blame. There she was with her sticky utensils alone, looking into the ancient oven. She had never baked a cake before and here she was, about to assemble a "red velvet" cake.

She fortunately knew about baking parchment and had lined the cake pan rounds with that so the cake didn't stick. She peeled the paper off, then proceeded to match two spongy circles of red.

Her icing was simple and pure white; it smoothed over the bottom layer like thick sugary paint. She adjusted her wire rim glasses…studying. Now the part she ecstatically enjoyed—the rapture of aligning the two layers—they matched to perfection!

I made a two layer red velvet cake! She was in festive mood vanguard now, washed her hands and dug out a wedding gift. It was a glass pedestal cake stand! So she proudly set the cake there, finished applying icing and set it in the middle of the kitchen table. She had joined the club. She had been inspired by the women of Montgomery to create beauty. Fornix the Roman bake goddess approved and appreciated it all.

***

Sipping Cokes, they sat at the counter on swivel stools and Elaine did the talking.

"I really was glad I stopped at your sale."

"Okay! You got some homemade bread there."

Elaine hastened to say, "A nice loaf. But you taught me something even better... about comfort food. Remember?"

"What? About how it's so home style, like a peanut butter and jelly sandwich."

Elaine answered, "That's right. Comfort food tends to be easy to make and reminds us of childhood. But what I learned from that bake sale is bakery food is comfort food."

Veronica whistled in amazement. "Folks call it 'treats' an' Elaine honey, it's a reward for sure."

"Veronica, the strangest thing is I've been right on top of a comfort food factory all my life. I was saturated with it. I had to escape from being another cog in the wheel of the factory."

"Well then, girl, you had to move on—out of comfort."

Elaine squeezed her shoulder in parting and said, "Moving on! Now my husband is set to go to Riverside, California. I have some packing to do."

Veronica sighed, "Well, sister, you'd best leave 'fore I start cryin' jus' like a pine knot in a sawmill."

Sooner than expected, Bill transferred to California. He and Elaine left Montgomery with enriched memories as Elaine hummed a traveling tune about wandering. Meanwhile, Bill drove like his life depended on it and the Chevy had a mind of its own.

Elaine declared as they left Montgomery, "I am saturated with bakery thoughts and baked goods! I don't feel I can even look at another cookie or cake. Enough!"

Bill said, "I know, you've lived with it for years and worked around it."

"I'm taking a vacation from... from anything bakery related."

"Okay," he answered. "I'll have your toast tomorrow."

"Hmmm."

97

Harrisburg was a canopy of red autumnal crispness. Stitt Bakery had continued producing a delicious selection from their ovens. Sliced bread was still banned, losses had been covered by the introduction of Victory Bread and soon Stitt bakers would make pumpkin pies for Thanksgiving.

During October, Clara searched *The Patriot* for good news and found advances by the Allies. Previously she had been relieved by news that Parisian landmarks were saved by self-styled conservationist, German General Von Cholitz. He had blocked directives by Hitler to leave the city in ruins, stopping the setting of explosives at the Eiffel Tower. The Soviet Army had begun to enter German held Hungary and Czechoslovakia.

"Look here," she noted to her mother. The latest news was accompanied by a shot of MacArthur, which now caught Clara's toast crumbs.

She read that after some setbacks, the Allies took Okinawa in the Pacific. Now Douglas MacArthur made good on his promise to return to the Philippines at Leyte; with him were the president-in-exile, Sergio Osmena and General Carlos Romulo.

In the bakery apartment, Dot held on to hope that Christy might be home from the Pacific for Christmas. She listened to a ballet on the radio: Bernstein's Fancy Free, pirouetting with a feather duster as she did some Saturday housework. Later, she and Louise would tune in *Ozzie and Harriet*.

Louise had posted her reply to Seaman Bud Ditlow. Bud had not written since he opened Louise's letter:

Dear Bud,

Understand, I had a nice time with you, but you forgot something. I am unavailable to you.
I am engaged, or in bakery lingo, "Off the market."
Louise

Bud chuckled and thought, *She's really somethin'.* He had gotten her attention, and he wanted to continue to contact her because a Christmas leave was imminent. But how? He thought as he stood for his turn at night watch patrol. His *USS Wasp* was stationed off the coast of Florida, and when he got to Miami on shore leave, he knew what he would do.

***

Louise returned home from the farmers' market bakery stand, helping to close and cash out, and now she was tired, her long brown hair fresh looking, tied in a snood. "You're very industrious, dahling," she greeted her sister and set down a market basket with some late-ripening tomatoes, fresh greens and half a chicken, rotisseried.

"We have dinner."

Dot smiled, pointing the duster, "Your mail's on the table."

There were a couple letters and a large, brown envelope, no return address, and it bore a Miami postmark. Opening the wrapper, she slid a 78 rpm record out of its sleeve.

Louise laughed heartily, "A Nat Cole record!"

She went straight to the player, and spun it, mumbling, "Who sent this?"

Then as the liquid vocal melodies of King Cole flooded the room, she saw a note.

It was really a gift card:

Louise dear,
You're the cream in my coffee,

Sincerely,
Bud

Then, on cue, Nat Cole delivered Bud's latest go at winning Louise's attention.

Dot was amused. Did Bud guess or did he know Louise enjoyed Nat Cole?

Louise was also tickled to have such a preferred recorded tune; however, Bud obviously did not wish to hear the word, her latest "no."

Louise kicked off her shoes and while the record played, reckoned she would have to get her message across some other way. She and Dot split a quart of cold cider. "He ignored me! He's ignoring that I'm engaged."

Dot quipped, "I bet you met with him because you were taken by his uniform."

"Well, it wasn't from loneliness."

Dot chuckled, "I never did see you pine away over a guy."

"No and you never will. Bud here, is way off base. I can't very well return a record to him... out on the bounding main." Louise relented, "Oh, I know, war does funny things to people."

Dot added, "*You are* helping a fellow countryman..."

"War, humph!" Louise continued matter-of-factly, "All I have to do is accept a hit record, and then when he comes back and puts his foot in the door, I step on it... the foot, I'll keep the record. But shoot! Who do I think I am?" She spoke now with mock seriousness. "I'm so very charming and attractive to these military supermen! Why I'm so swelligant, I have two beaus!" Now she adopted her cinematic Scarlett O'Hara stance, and snickering, Dot couldn't stand it any longer, and laughs blasted through the room, rattling the hand- thrown ceramics on the wall. They had difficulty getting a breath for a moment, but they had desperately needed a good laugh.

They listened to the radio while having dinner, savoring also a letter from dear Elaine. She wrote, "Bill says he's enjoying the

Air Corps and I've been learning about southern style baking."

In November, Americans elected Roosevelt to an unprecedented fourth term. The same week Louise received another record, *Imagination* by Glenn Miller; she knew it well from the radio. Just the name Glenn Miller sat well with Louise, and it hit her like good medicine. She really didn't care where the tune came from, she just played it over and over. It was a tonic she needed desperately but had been too busy to give herself.

The earnest Bud had told the owner of the Miami record shop that he wanted to serenade a girl who was something special. He put fifteen dollars in his hand in exchange for three hit records to be posted monthly.

December 1944 was a terrible month for news. On the 16th, Louise gasped while driving the truck to deliver a cake, for the radio announcer reported, "Yesterday, Glenn Miller, the famous band leader, disappeared as he flew from London to Paris." A medley of his famous hits played sadly into the night. Louise thought of the dances she had attended, steeped in amazing Miller swing, and she mourned as though a family member was taken.

The same day, Allied infantry was in the frozen Ardennes forest of Belgium, advancing toward Germany, when they were surprised by the Fifth and Sixth Panzer Armies. It amounted to a last desperate attempt by Germany to hold off the invasion. The Battle of the Bulge, as it would come to be known, claimed 120,000 Germans and 81,000 Allies by the time the Germans retreated on January 21st.

December 16th the third record came from Miami with a note enclosed.

98

L ouise was one of three women working at a machine, wrapping browned molasses cookies, when the postman opened the front door. There was a parcel too large for the mailbox. After the run of cookies, Louise took off her white apron, washed the sugar off her hands and took a break. She took a chair in the office opposite Dot and opened what she knew was a record.

Dot was on the phone with a woman who wanted Christmas sand tarts.

"Yes, December 23rd. I got that. One hundred red and a hundred green. Thank you. Bye."

"Another record." Louise looked up. "It has no note and it doesn't have a label."

Dot giggled, saying, "Go play it!"

Louise went to the apartment and applied the needle to the 78. After a few seconds of crackling, she recognized Bud's own voice. He was smiling, as if holding back a laugh. "Hello Louise. Merry Christmas. This is Bud. I hope you enjoy the holidays. I know you would prefer that I keep my distance from you. I want to let you know I spent my happiest time ever with you. I guess I needed a kind of girl back home, and I tried to recruit you. Ha-ha. Poor Louise! Well you helped me through many tough days, even though you don't know it. Get ready to win the war next year. And then I promise not to interfere in your life—well, not much!"

At that point, the record began to skip and it repeated, "not much! not much! not much!" until Louise adjusted the needle. "So I'll say farewell."

Louise exclaimed to herself, "Geez, Louise!"

***

Christmas arrived as Byron, Caroline, Clara, Dot and Louise stood in candlelight at midnight at St. Paul's Church. Carols floated out through a crack in one stained-glass window out over the crusted snow. Many silent prayers for servicemen circulated in the minds of the congregation, though Louise's prayer was extraordinary. She prayed for Eisenhower, for the future safety of all service people, especially Bud Ditlow, that he would find a "girl back home." Feeling much more spirited and free from his unwelcome courtship, Louise forgot about Bud.

Dot drove the car and sang, "Christmas Bells are Ringing" as they made their way home. The gift of two telegrams assured that Christy was at a base in the Pacific where an evergreen tree cheered the Seabees; Eddie had weathered a few grueling European campaigns, saying he would come home soon.

Christmas dinner with Clara's brothers' families had a very optimistic outlook, saying, with an enthusiastic eggnog toast, "Next Christmas we'll be back together!"

Louise retreated to a corner with a book and a chocolate-covered pretzel. Later she got up and put on her winter boots and coat. She said, "Goodbye" to her family, walked to where the truck was parked, and drove to the home of her friend Ginny. She found Ginny home and invited her to take a walk in the remaining sunlight.

The stroll was an immediate tonic. Louise seemed to Ginny like a snake shedding her old skin. They jumped from the auto, walked north along the old, wide Susquehanna, a good river to gaze upon.

Louise announced, "I've got a pee-culiar notion."

Ginny asked, "What would that be?"

Louise stared and said in a monotone, "I feel out of place, stuck and in need of an overhaul."

"Well, join the club, kid! That sums it up for me. Everyone's sick of the war. Only thing keeps me goin' is my husband is alive."

Louise went on, "This is me that's turned around and not much about the war. Yeah, maybe in other circumstances I'd be with Eddie and not complaining, but we're looking at New Year 1945, and I don't want to go into it in this frame of mind."

"What? You want a new you?"

She looked down her nose, "That's really not possible."

"Hoo hoo! Don't mess around with perfection," laughed Ginny.

"Ginny, I have a mind not to get married."

A terrified look came into Ginny's eyes. "You don't say, Louise. Now what brought that on?"

"Seriously, I woke up today and felt like a new car engine with a bad frame. I can't explain it."

Ginny put her arm through Louise's.

"I need to bust out of this. I really know I'm changing right now, just gotta figure out how. Before it takes over."

Ginny said emphatically, "My classmates from high school... some were recently killed in Belgium. You have madmen running Germany, a suicide squad in Japan, and if that's not enough, you haven't seen Eddie in years. We've been working to make peace happen, and it takes a toll from you. No wonder you lost the spark."

They walked faster in the dim light with the river's wind beating their faces. They pulled their wool hats over their ears and pushed on. A mile later, they felt less tired, lighter and turned around, keeping up the speed.

"You know how rocks have layers?" Louise puffed.

"Stratum?"

"Well the strata have moved from solid to more mobile. All the permanent waves, girdles, new hats... they are trappings. This is a newer kind of me. I'm cutting myself free from Eddie... as his intended."

Ginny said finally, "Louise!"

Louise laughed her self-deprecating laugh, saying, "I'm outta breath."

The lights on the river bridge reflected onto the water. Ginny said, "Let's just remember to play it out like a game. Let's not get down in the dumps, girl, just because you've changed. Everything has!"

***

When Louise awakened on December 26th, frost coated her bedroom window. Rising rapidly, an energized Louise made hot cocoa in two large cups, topping them with ground cinnamon. Then she went into Dot's room and blew the chocolate steam toward Dot's nose.

"Ag ogg… is this a dream?" Dot whispered in the voice of a four-year-old.

"Yep," said Louise, thinking of the aroma of the chocolate factory. "You've woken up in Hershey."

Louise handed her the mug, and they sipped. "How would you like to run away for a day?"

"Ohh! That is a nice idea."

So they took Dot's car, motoring to the tiny village of Duncannon, which was named after an Irish hamlet. Just a short hop over the river, it was far enough to expand their minds. They pulled into a space near a clapboard house with a sign hanging over the door: "The Garden Seat Café."

They passed a rusted potbellied stove in the yard. It was now a pedestal for a potted pine tree. They entered and found themselves alone with a jovial cook who made them feel right at home. She wore a cross-stitched apron, that read: "I'm melting… melting!"

"Ladies, welcome. Surprise! You have one choice on the menu—leftovers."

"Okay, we are adventurous." Dot nodded to Louise.

The cook played a Victrola recording of *Frosty the Snowman*. There were four tables in the café, and each was decorated with garlands made of construction paper rings and glittered stars suspended from a plastic chandelier overhead. Framed photos on the wall included Eleanor Roosevelt, Shirley Temple as a child, and Harvey Taylor, who was a Harrisburg politician. Whimsy had taken over the room as though a few dedicated fairies had decorated.

The cook bounced back with a gelatin fruit salad, mint green and topped with a crimson cranberry. The main attraction was a warm glass baking dish lined with stuffing, filled with turkey and smothered with mushroom gravy. Dessert was eggnog custard.

"Isn't it wonderful how gravy and a change of scenery can affect me?" Dot wondered.

Louise nodded as she sat swimming in holiday sedation. Riding home over the snow dusted streets, the two felt a sense of hope as Dot planned to produce pocket bread shaped like hearts. She anticipated Valentine's Day.

Back home, Louise began to iron some clothes and contemplated her uncertain future in the flattened wrinkles. Dresses neatly hanging in the closet, Louise put away the ironing board and got her stationery box. She was going to write a "Dear John" letter to Dear Eddie.

She told him she had had a change of heart, insisted it was a change not brought about by him; she was calling the engagement off. Louise wanted to cry. Instead, she sighed and finished the letter with appreciation for all the memories and hopes for his future. She set it aside, to reread it before putting it in the mailbox.

99

Throughout the war, leaders on both sides used potent words to describe the conditions in the hope of inspiring the people they led. The eloquent Eisenhower said in 1944: *"The tide has turned! The free men of the world are marching together to Victory! I have full confidence in your courage."* Another general, Anthony McAuliffe, answering an enemy demand to surrender: *"Nuts!"*

"Aw, nuts!" Bud exclaimed when he heard there would be no holiday leave. An intelligence report indicated that the *USS Wasp* was needed near the Netherlands Antilles. There were no naval incidents after all and business went as usual onboard. The enlistees were treated to warm winds daily, unlike the icy winds in Pennsylvania. At this point of the war, the Allies left nothing to chance, while the Germans threw their entire stock of planes and Panzers at the front in Belgium. Eisenhower and his cohorts were exhausting Hitler so that he had very little appetite for more than amphetamine, flatulence remedies and sleeping pills.

Bud was a frugal man who did not waste his monthly salary of $250., but he had become adept at the game of poker, so much so that he had to put his winnings in the ship's vault.

He knew he needed more than cookies to get Louise's attention.

Fortunately for Bud, leave to Pennsylvania was granted, just as his birthday rolled around on January 27th.

Tracking her down at 2232 North Sixth Street, he arrived by motorcycle with a sidecar. Louise went to the vestibule's glass door when she heard the doorbell, but she recognized him and sped away from the door with a gasp.

"Don't answer the door!" she told her mother, "It's Bud. Again."

But Bud was sure someone was home as a truck was parked in front of the house. He could not see into the huge front window—it was too high. He tried jumping a few times, but saw no one. Louise tiptoed to the window to see if he was gone, and she noticed his unmanned motorcycle. Bud reappeared with a small stepladder, and Louise watched as his hatless head of black hair looked into the living room. The first thing she saw were his green eyes connecting with hers and the green eyes smiled.

"Go away," said Louise seriously. She was frustrated more than threatened by him.

Then a piece of paper was placed on the cold glass. In pencil it read: "Happy to see you! I want to take you to a birthday party!"

"No." She barked in disgust, muttering, "Why me?"

She went out the front door, taking her sweater. Gasping again, she tripped over a large gift-wrapped package. The sight of him on the ladder with the note was slightly disarming. "Just what are you up to?"

He wore a nice suit, leather boots and his Navy pea coat. His demeanor was somehow calmer and more confident. He stayed on the ladder, which allowed him to tower over Louise. "I'd like to take you to a party at the Harrisburger."

She leaned against the brick front. "You are out of your ever lovin' mind." Her face stared.

He grinned, "Thanks. A lot. I waited a whole year to hear myself called 'ever-loving.'"

He had changed, maybe the war aged him. He had laugh lines, and his eyes were extremely green.

Louise shot back, "I wanted to return your records."

"You could have sent them to the store, but you didn't..."

Louise added, "The truth is they helped me. I played them a hundred times."

"You don't say! I did something good."

"Yeah," Louise relented, invited him in and he came, after returning the ladder to the garage next door. When he entered the kitchen, he found Caroline pulling a sunshine cake out of the oven and Clara making glasses of milk with sugar and vanilla extract. "How 'bout some vanilla milk?"

Bud was feeling treated, like a conquering hero, while Louise was uncharacteristically silent.

Clara listened as Bud told the story of Anthony McAuliffe of the Glider infantry, how in Bastogne he refused to surrender. "'Nuts!' Is what he told the Germans only one month ago."

Clara drank her milk while drinking in the story, seemingly more authentic than any newspaper. "I'm glad you're not on the front line," she reassured.

Bud shifted in his chair. "I don't think I'd last very long in the trenches. I've been happy to serve under my captain, and now we just hold on. Hitler stopped his tirades and we're closing in on him. When he goes, all our attention will be on Japan."

Bud and Louise went to the living room. He was in a childishly playful mood that had become foreign to her lately. He pointed out to his motorcycle, "Go on, get warm clothes, I don't want to be late for the party. I'll bring you back whenever you say."

She agreed, and as she changed, she admitted to herself she felt infected by his good mood.

The weighty package on the kitchen table contained confections from the Blue Swan candy store. Clara and Caroline were pleased.

She found the sidecar to be a hysterical experience in the winter's sunset. He was burned by the wind, wearing no hat, but could care less because now he was in his element—driving her and driving fast. Bud thoroughly enjoyed work, so much that he was on his way to becoming a workaholic. Now he had gone out on a limb, created pure playtime, and Louise was part of the fun!

Louise followed a restaurant manager to a small private

banquet room and noted it was empty. She asked, "What about the party?"

"It's coming." Bud laughed. "It's only five o'clock."

Louise quipped, "I guess the important people are already here."

Bud giggled, "Those lucky people."

They ate Italian specialties, seated by the window, by the light of a double candelabra. In January, the place was clock tick quiet, and Bud had decided he needed a birthday celebration. If he had played his previous cards right, he decided now to bet his winnings on Louise. That was what accounted for his confidence; he felt like a winner as he tossed cashews into his mouth.

Louise thought highly of birthday parties and sensed this to be a big deal. In fact, she was the deal. The peculiarly large undertaking wasn't what she was accustomed to, but it felt safe with Bud, so she enjoyed his party. She took off her navy wool Billet, revealing a pleated cotton blouse with a necklace of large pearls; her earrings matched perfectly and were complementary to her dark hair and eyes. She had done her make up with a little rouge and a lot of Helena Rubinstein "Chile" lipstick. It tasted of cloves.

Louise asked, her head tilted to the right, "When was the last time you had a birthday party?"

He reminded her about his baking duties and said, "I'm baking cakes nearly every day, so I don't lack for celebratin'."

"But I mean when you were at home."

He thought for a moment, and it seemed so very long ago.

"That would be back on the farm before Mother died."

Louise whispered, "Years ago." Her heart went out to him.

"Right. Today I'm twenty-four."

Louise never told her age, but now as a ploy to discourage Bud she said, "And I'm twenty-eight ..."

Bud would not have minded if Louise was forty-eight, so he ignored the age statement. "But tell me what you're up to. I'm tired thinking of the ship."

She rehashed her post Christmas escapade, the loss of Glenn Miller, and she carefully avoided revealing her recent unleashing from Eddie. "I'm making deliveries, working at Market, sometimes I fill in as a route... woman."

She had not really taken Bud seriously before and not been relaxed. Now her wit began to surface.

"I'm so important they can't even turn around without me!"

Bud ordered champagne and the party got silly.

"Ya' don't even *know* how..."

Louise finished his sentence, "trivial I am, and my work is so secret, even I don't know what I'm doing."

Bud shook his head, "Ya' don't get..."

She did it again, "...my significant insignificance."

He sighed, but he was thrilled. He guessed that probably he would not see her again. She spooned chocolate mousse onto her tongue, like she was intoxicated by cacao, and would never in her life eat it again. His overindulgent birthday was foreign to depression-raised Bud, but he savored every moment, this moment. Two hours sped by.

They visited the piano bar for a brandy, which triggered some inane stories, mostly about baking failures.

"When a cake falls, it can be turned over and disguised..."

"When the icing runs..."

"When the cookie crumbles..."

They were having such a good time that patrons at adjoining tables were watching them. Louise finally ended the party and laughed all the way home, though she had to demand he slow down. She felt her pent-up anxiety was expelled like a poor student from a good school. Joy was moving throughout her face, contorting her cheeks, out to her ears. She felt an earring fly off. Bud circled around the vacant Sixth Street and scooped it up, out of the trolley tracks. The clownish effect of a motorcycle with a sidecar was not lost on Louise, now in an irrational rapture, but the earring rescue pushed Louise toward death by laughter.

The bakery was beginning to wake up as the neighborhood retired. Light spilled from the bakeshop windows. Louise loosely got out of the sidecar and came around as Bud turned off the machine.

She could see her breath. "I haven't had so much fun in a long time."

"But you don't want me to come back."

Louise answered in surprise, "What? Well, I don't know. My mind isn't very sharp now. But I owe you."

Bud said, "Naw."

"You brought me to my senses. I needed to laugh. I didn't know how much I needed to laugh."

Bud smiled, placing his cold hand on hers.

"I will write, okay?" She wanted him to realize she was back in her own element, but she just did not have any clarity. She was feeling infused, steeped in such a pleasant array of emotions, yet so unclear.

Bud smiled, "Swell!"

"Thank you." She kissed his ice-cold cheek. He didn't move.

He followed her with his eyes as she disappeared behind the bakery door.

100

L ouise slept like a hibernating bear, but when her eyes opened, she had sharper senses. She dressed with the speed of a fireman and grabbed the phone book. She found Bud's aunt, Florence Huber's listing, and dialed.

"Hello, Ditlow speaking."

"Bud, this is Louise."

"Why, Louise! What a surprise."

"I know you're due on the train. I wondered if I might come over just for a minute."

Bud did a dance. "Sure. I leave on the noon train."

Louise tried to put some order to her thoughts as she drove the truck to "The Hill" neighborhood. She whispered, "Be true to yourself!"

Brushing lint from his black sailor's uniform, Bud was ready. He made a call to the Blue Swan candy store. "Mrs. Thomas? This is Bud Ditlow. Remember me from yesterday? Yes. I'm leaving, but my friend will pick up her package. Louise Stitt. Right. Thanks."

Louise came in, and he made coffee for her. Aunt Florence was a diligent banker working downtown, so Bud was alone. The house was spotless. They sat in a high-ceilinged dining room that suddenly filled with sunlight, reflecting off a chandelier. A portrait of an unknown ancestor observed the two from across the room. He was jovial. She was pensive. Would she be able to get her message across? And what in the name of peace was that message?

Louise began with authority. "I want to make the right choice... I'm at a crossroads, and not because of you, if you had not come, I'd be doing... well... my life anyway. I was moved yesterday to a good... feeling, and I have you to thank for it. I'm wise enough to know I need to do something... important in my life. I feel like I know the right information that'll help me do it..."

He leaned over and kissed her reassuringly on her Rubinstein lips.

She took a breath, "I know you are a good person."

"You don't want me to... own you?"

"Yes... that's part of it. You have been warned."

"Ha, ha. I don't have any plans to own anything but my motorcycle. Louise, I already know you're unusually... unusual."

She smiled. "I don't believe I can be domesticated... by anyone."

Bud noted, "Like some heifer?"

"That's right. I don't want to be tied to anything, fenced in or taken for granted."

"Well now. What brought you back from hospital work? There you were free."

Louise thoughtfully explained, "I had had enough of battle-maimed youth. I hurt for them. I got almost shell shocked when they patched them up and sent them back to battle. I like bakery work, and my family creating it. Cupcakes are peaceable and our casualties in baking are minor."

This was good. She did not reject him. Bud leaned toward her, saying, "Let's write."

His eyes were so green; she got distracted by them. When they stood up, Louise took his neck in her hands and kissed him. He kissed her hair, rushing over it to her neck. He noticed a cinnamon scent, and he hugged her like a long-lost friend, rocking right and left. She felt excited by the urgent confession of her feelings, and he gripped her cinched waist, wishing there were more time.

Louise offered, "I'll run you over to the train station."

Bud took her hand with his right, keeping his left hand on her waist. "I'm no kind'a dancer, but I feel like dancing."

So they fox-trotted toward the door, moving against each other all the way. Louise hummed *Imagination*, but Bud did not recognize it as the same tune he had sent in November. He was looking at her, memorizing a dozen views to keep in his head.

She stopped her truck at the station entrance. He jumped out with his small satchel, came to her window and gave her his last best wettest kiss. She was on an emotional merry-go-round, elated, purged and wanting his combat-free safety.

He handed her a card. "I hope you miss me because I'll miss you. Go to the candy store next month. I left you a valentine." He had laid it on as thick as icing on an éclair. Yet he used candy and other refreshments as a vehicle for his adoration, and that was genuine. He felt increased excitement as he took a seat and the train rhythm took him back to reality.

101

"**D**epress the clutch, change gears, now give it gas," urged Bill, his head bobbing.

Grind screetch... Elaine was getting the hang of manual transmission. Her New Year's resolution for 1945 was to learn to drive.

Elaine had been given a few driving lessons by Bill already, but now they were practicing on a private road ending at a dilapidated barn. This was not far from their apartment down a dirt road. The old black Chevrolet was behaving, but Bill was about as patient as a whirling propeller. Elaine guided the car into second gear, down the road, but as she manually shifted into third, she found herself on the road shoulder, grazing the wire fence.

"Stop!" Sweat ran down Bill's cheek as he leaped from the passenger seat to check the fender.

"Out! Get the hell out, enough of this!"

Elaine stepped out. There was a small scratch on the old car. Bill got behind the wheel and zoomed ahead as Elaine stood in the breeze with arms crossed, her cotton-print dress flapping. Dust flew, birds scattered and he went on down the lonely road to ruin. Elaine watched incredulously as he tried and failed to make a u-turn. She laughed behind her hand. He hooked his fender on the doorway of the barn. A loose board clunked, bouncing off the hood, to the ground. She turned away and laughed into the wind. There was only injured pride as he puttered back to her. She would drive on a learner's permit for the time being.

California was an abundant agricultural area, and the

Riverside apartment they rented bordered on a fragrant orange grove. She spruced up the rooms they let within an old Spanish colonial mansion. She liked its comfortable furniture, although most of the Mission pieces weighed more than a granite boulder. Elaine concentrated on making their house a home. He was one of 100,000 troops in the area of March Field and was eager to help win the war in the Pacific. Bill believed Hitler was doomed because he had exhausted all of his ammunition during the Battle of the Bulge.

They enjoyed exploring the new residential area in their free time. The agricultural area known as "Coachella" farmed acres of grapes. California proudly grew the most grapes in the nation—that and dried grapes, raisins.

One Saturday in late January, Elaine and Bill attended a grape exposition in a town called Lancaster, at the Antelope Valley Fairgrounds. There were a hundred folks strolling among trellises banked with grape vines, magnums of wines and endless bushel baskets of raisins.

"How festive!" Elaine said.

Bill quipped dryly, "We're surrounded by raisins."

The grape growers sold lots of wine that day, and Bill purchased a bottle of Chardonnay. Small paper bags of raisins were handed out to children by women in white dresses with starched red sunbonnets. Elaine sampled every imaginable dried fruit. She was impressed by some Army home economists who displayed K rations developed for wartime needs.

Their sign read: "Our Army Travels on its Stomach." Not surprisingly, the dietitians had produced a ration that provided high energy in a small package. Elaine took a sample and amazed the experts when she correctly identified the ingredients.

"This is the best K ration I ever had... and the only one. This tastes like a cookie. Raisins, oats, chocolate, peanut butter..."

"One more?"

"Cinnamon."

The dietitian said, "We had complaints back in '42 about the taste. We invented a cookie you can live on."

Her associate added, "It's not so simple to make K rations that will last through plane rides, swamps and cannon fire. The raisins pack lots of energy!"

Elaine conversed about Stitt sticky buns—light on raisins, heavy on the sugar.

Bill had wandered to the ice cream stand and now produced a cone of rum raisin. Elaine tried it and laughed, "That's a great use of the raisin."

They wandered by a country and western band, diversely manned by a seated slide guitar player who was Polynesian, a mulatto mandolin player/singer and a drummer of Cherokee origin. Bill tapped his toe. The band launched mournfully into, *I go from Grapes to Raisins*. And it was sung to the tune of *I Go from Rags to Riches*.

In spite of Elaine's intended vacation from baked goods, she had wandered into another sugary village at the fair. The raisin growers were eager to show people how to use the fruit because it was nutritious, abundant and inexpensive. Dried fruit provides sweetness and moisture for a baker's dough, so naturally raisins were highly visible in Riverside markets.

***

Elaine had hot cereal for breakfast as the air became cooler. She rejected "sweet stuff" for weeks, but now craved Waldorf salad with crisp seasonal apples and raisins. She enjoyed ham and learned to make raisin sauce to accompany it.

Her husband snickered about her attitude toward all bakery things, "You can break your hunger strike any time."

"I'm not striking, and I'm surely not hungry for sweet stuff." She ate bread occasionally, but when she shopped, she instinctively stayed away from the shelves of cellophane wrapped dessert items. Elaine was attracted to a saltier, more astringent diet. She entertained herself lately by browsing through groceries for cheese, bacon, nuts and anything related to tomatoes. These were her luxuries. It seemed to Elaine that California food was the best she had ever had, maybe because sugary things had had no appeal for months, even when Dot mailed her a tin of assorted Stitt cookies. Bill, however, gratefully engulfed them as though he was in the throes of a religious experience.

Bill trained to fly over the Pacific, and Elaine practiced cooking. He was flying up the coast for a few days when she took a vacation from cooking. One day from the far reaches of her brain came a distinct craving, though she was not prone to longing for special foods, she went shopping.

She enjoyed joking with the shop keeper, a Chinese woman who once stumbled over the word "almond" and Elaine explained, "The L is silent, dahling."

She shopped the small neighborhood market for three items: strawberry jelly, peanut butter and bread. She selected a loaf of sourdough because it was unsliced. She liked the escaping doughy aroma brought out by slicing.

Elaine made a sandwich and sat outside on her front step to enjoy it. To nobody, she said, in grammatically fractured words she would never tolerate, "This is the bestest sandwich I ever eated."

She soon blamed cool weather for her next dessert, served by a neighboring military wife having a birthday. It had a resemblance to Stitt shortbread and had a biscuit-like texture. The hostess topped the shortbread with baked apples and whipped cream.

102

Harrisburg of February 1945 was like other cities in America and other small towns: people were edgy. The armed services were giving their best to the war effort. At home were men and women over induction age, elders, children and young working women, who often performed jobs formerly held by males. Now there were more "gold star" mothers, widows who had lost sons or husbands to the war. Everyone seemed to age faster in this whirlwind as energy transferred into the war effort. The average annual U.S. salary was $2400, the cost of a new home was $4500 and a gallon of rationed gas went for fifteen cents.

Dot continued to run the office with her father, who had to admit her Victory Bread had increased overall sales. Her letters from Christy, in the Pacific, sounded upbeat. Her roommate sister had weathered the winter doldrums largely through Coca-Cola addiction and regular hair appointments.

Now Louise hung up her mouton coat and took a seat in the styling chair. It was the end of the strangest workday due to a sick call, Sarah's toothache and resulting bad mood. Louise had filled three hundred éclairs, wrapped five hundred lunch cakes and had put together over a hundred cardboard boxes to hold them.

"I feel wild and wooly!" Louise stared at herself in the beauty shop mirror, riveted. The white uniformed hairdresser rubbed her hands together gleefully, like a wizard with secret magic. Her own hair bounced a long sausage curl down her neck.

"Shall we go red again? A tighter perm? Bangs perhaps?"

"Silly girl," Louise sneered. "Oh just make me look like Donna Reed!"

The beautician replied, "I already heard that five times this week. But *you* are about the only patron I have who has any chance of imitating Donna Reed."

"From a back view."

Forty-five minutes later, Louise got out of the chair with her long brunette tresses in a pageboy on her collar. The stylist was pleased and generously applied some new eye make-up samples to complete the new look. Louise clipped on her rhinestone sapphire earrings and said, "All dolled up and no place to go."

The stylist said, "Well a happy valentine to you."

"Hey!" said Louise excitedly, "I do have some place to go, dahling; Blue Swan Candy!"

***

Arriving at the candy store, Louise saw people filing into the store as if they were sweet "tooths" homing in on the sweet. She stood outside looking at the window display—a gigantic, glass pedestal compote full of homemade candy. She looked up at a poster; ironically, there was Donna Reed eating Whitman's Chocolate with a dimple and a smile. Briefly, Louise checked her hair in the glass reflection—it was not identical to Donna's do, but it *was* close. Reverting to the candy display, she slipped into a mental flavor reverie: first milk chocolates, vanilla lavender cream, peanut chocolate cluster cup, even oval crackers dipped in chocolate, in a fan-like arrangement. The dark chocolates shown were mocha melt-away truffle, dusted with cocoa powder, chocolate-covered pretzels, a stack of nearly black nonpareils with pink sugar beads and lemon jellies with marshmallow stripes. She appreciated the display for she knew edible art all too well.

Still hypnotized, she heard a man's voice say, "You meet up with the nicest people at the candy shop."

Returning from marshmallow world, Louise looked up, "Harold, Harold Simon!" Her beau of years ago. Still stylishly impeccably groomed in his business suit; a red licorice whip was incongruously clamped in his teeth. He was married with at least one child, she knew.

He asked how she was, then said, "Good thing I didn't go to war."

Louise replied, "Alcoa needed you here?"

Harold said, "Yeah, but I'm not tough enough to be in those trenches. In Europe, I would've died in the cold, and in the Pacific, mosquitoes would've got me."

Louise recounted a little about the Army hospital and declared about soldiers, "It's not the 'mountain' they had to climb, what did them in was the 'stones' in their shoes."

He patted her arm, hefted a large Whitman's Sampler under his wool sleeve and bid her good evening.

She entered, hearing the familiar creak of hardwood floor and decided to wait her turn, sitting on an old bench from a church. A slightly built Negro boy of about ten came in and joined her on the bench. He removed a homemade wool mitten that matched his cap, then rattled a tin of coins.

Louise asked, "Do you have a valentine?"

"No, ma'am, I'm buy'n fer Mother. It's my money from the newspaper route."

Louise smiled, "Well, that's swell of you."

The boy added matter-of-factly, "Father's dead, died in Guadalcanal."

Louise gasped. She could only get out, "I'm sorry, honey." Her mood was shattered now. She tentatively patted his small cold hand.

The store emptied and they saw the sprightly owner, an elderly woman with a gray knot of hair, staring, "May I help you?"

Louise gestured for the boy to order. She jumped up and placed a five-dollar bill in the clerk's hand, pointing to the boy, who was counting his nickels onto the counter.

"Mints fer my mother," he said, pushing the coins toward the cash register.

The candy lady took a large heart-shaped pink box and carefully loaded it with every conceivable mint then looked at the child saying, "I sure hope your mother enjoys this. Now you can pick out something for yourself."

"I don't have enough," he answered thoughtfully.

The woman laughed, "Yes, you do!"

"'Is'mus' be my lucky day..." said the boy as he took a small cellophane bag of malted milk balls. "Hot dog! Wait till Mother sees this!" He left with a grin on his face.

"Now," said the candy lady, with excitement, "I remember you and your sisters."

Louise produced the card Bud had given her. The woman paged through her ledger book, seeking instruction while Louise tried to read upside down. "I remember. What would you like, Miss Stitt? He said you could name it. He took care of it."

For the second time she gasped, eyes wide, but her mood was lifting at the prospect of chocolate. Louise was taking in the truth of Bud's words, and for once in her life, she was without any words. She sat on the bench, and the candy lady realized Louise was stunned. The man had said it with candy all right!

The proprietor preached into the quiet store, "I've seen it before, child, when a man is at a loss for words but needs to communicate. That Mr. Ditlow was not the sort who buys luxuries. But because he... loves you, he arranged this gift."

She watched the proprietor taking another pink heart box with a few sections inside. Louise said, "I will have..." and she went on a recital of the display window, "plus candied ginger."

The woman complied, adding a cellophane bag of nonpareils, with an attached note from Bud. "LOUISE, *You have no equal. Love, Bud.*"

***

377

Louise picked up Dot and went home to 2232 North Sixth Street. Everyone was home—parents, grandparents—but they missed Elaine. Louise laid the box on the kitchen table, sat down and watched Caroline stirring a pot of chicken corn soup with a long wooden spoon while Clara tossed in some carrots. The resulting steam had a cozy effect that balanced Louise's feelings.

Dot said excitedly, "I guess your valentine sent this."

Louise explained how he had done it, in an unusually quiet tone. "I tried to avoid Bud for the longest time." She opened the box to the amazement of the onlookers. "Today I have come to know he loves me, and my heart, I guess, wants my mouth to stop saying no."

Floyd sighed and remarked, "I'm proud of that fella," as he gingerly selected a candied strip of ginger.

Louise thought intensely of one of her favorite quotes: amantes sunt amentes—lovers are lunatics.

103

"**I**got my driver's license," wrote Elaine. She did not go into detail, but said she had driven numerous times on her learner's permit. They had moved again, and out of necessity, Elaine packed their possessions by herself and drove the car for hours unlicensed. Bill was expecting to fly out to the Pacific on the B-29 Superfortress bomber any day.

She explained the joys of Riverside and talked of living there when the war ended. She admitted she was mostly on vacation from baked goods and enjoying it.

Clara quizzically asked, "No bread? No desserts?"

Caroline said, "Imagine that!"

But they could not guess how she lived without baked goods.

***

The early April temperatures were cool, but the crocus and forsythia were blooming. Louise noticed them as she drove the truck into the Stitt garage, then reported to Dot, dropping off cash from some cake deliveries.

Dot stood up for the first time in an hour and stretched. "There's a gentleman waiting for you by the front door."

In a dark tone, Louise asked, "Who might that be?"

"Go down and be surprised!"

Louise sighed, "Do I need combing and lipstick?"

Dot giggled, "I believe it would be a good idea."

She ran down the stairs, peering around the door. A man was sitting in a 1940 Dodge, sleeping.

She walked to the driver's window. Eddie! She laughed with

joy. He was home. He threw open the door, saying loudly, "You're the most beautiful sight I've seen yet!" and she hugged him right there, in the middle of two-lane Jefferson Street. He had a haggard face for a young man, but it was a genuine Eddie smile radiating down at her. His left arm was in a plaster cast from wrist to elbow. This had been his ticket home, Louise guessed.

He was careful not to kiss her as she pulled him into the aromatic bakery, where two-layer chocolate cakes were decorated now to the tune of Doris Day's recording, *Sentimental Journey*. Louise was ushering him into the apartment kitchen.

"I'm starting some coffee, and what would you like with it?"

He settled back in his maple cane-back chair. He had a new haircut, combed back and wore a white shirt covered by a lightweight white sweater. Civilian clothes, how strange after years of fatigues.

He was delightfully amused. "A Stitt cookie would be heaven."

Louise was so excited by the sight of her friend, she couldn't think straight. She grabbed a linen napkin, put it in front of him with a molasses, a sugar and an oatmeal cookie right on the cloth. As she poured two steaming cups, she thought, *I'm not* acting *like a woman who wrote a Dear John letter.* She questioned him about the injury so he related his war story.

He broke all the cookies in half just to catch the homemade aroma. "Here's what I fought for." He dunked the sugar cookie in black coffee, smiled and said, "I have to say, being here with you, alive and having this... " he paused, again recalling deprivation, "...moment. It was worth the fight."

He had spent most of his time in England, North Africa and Italy, but he had been part of the Ninth Army that crossed the Rhine to invade Germany. Simultaneously, the Russian Army advanced toward Berlin from the east. He told Louise a deeper tale than those superficial ones in the news. The Germans tried to burn their own bridges as they ran from the Allies, yet on

March 7th, 1945 one bridge remained at Remagen, southeast of Cologne. The Ludendorff Railroad Bridge. Americans commanded by Omar Bradley came upon the bridge and observed from above enemy soldiers on it, setting up explosives. It became a race to save the bridge, the only remaining avenue over the Rhine. The time was so crucial: 3:50 p.m. From the time the Americans set foot on the bridge, there was machinegun fire to dodge as the Germans attempted to delay the coming invasion. They timed the explosives for four p.m.

Eddie's group was behind the U.S. demolition unit. Quickly a few experts cut wires to fuses, one man, a Lt. John Mitchell of Pittsburgh, kicked dynamite off the bridge into the river! Eddie and his unit moved dozens of crates of explosives off the bridge. The Germans did set off a charge, weakening the structure, but not enough to make it impassable. GI's moved Germans off the bridge and fired a tank gun on a troop train on the other side. Next, engineers covered the railroad tracks with timber, making way for tanks and other vehicles. The bridge salvage certainly gave the Allies momentum with the rapid transport of troops and materials.

"They shot you on the bridge?" Louise asked.

Eddie nodded. "I had a crate of TNT, holding it in front of me, and I was shot in the forearm bone. It was set by a good medic on the other side, in the town of Remagen. Our commander bet the war in Europe is ending and got a detachment in from somewhere and sent home about twenty-five of us who were injured. But that wound was worth the effort 'cause eight thousand of our guys got over the bridge in the first day."

Louise said, "Well I'm glad to see you and glad you made it home in one piece."

"It's been years!" He had lost his 'babyface' look thanks to years of rigorous Army schedules and wartime uncertainty. "I'm getting used to a safe place real fast."

He hadn't been able to tell anyone about various prisoners of war or friends who had been killed. He said, "I have cried for Europeans—even the German citizens, the ones who were killed or duped by Hitler. Now, they have a big mess on their hands."

Louise smiled and soothed, "Rest is important now, see that you get it."

She felt like a kid again, though she held on to her own agenda in order to sidestep the unknown chaos of romancing an old love.

His eyes widened. "Remember the night we got caught in my Ford out on Route 22 in a bad, bad snowstorm?"

Louise slowly recollected, "Yeah?"

"Well, Louise, I was really worried when we slid off the road. I was shakin' so hard I thought I'd never get warm. But you weren't scared at all and you said, 'Don't worry, now we'll have some traction.' You drove it out of that snow bank."

Louise added, "With you pushing, or was it pulling?"

"Doesn't matter, I want you to know I thought o' that, that way you have of going through things without fear. You can cut trouble down. When you have a hard time, the trouble will not outlast you."

Louise laughed, but it was a breathy, knowing laugh. He went on with a tear in his eye, "Every time I found myself disgusted by… soldier stuff, I went back in memory to when you said, 'Don't worry, Eddie, now we'll have some traction.'"

Louise, touched exquisitely by these emotions, lost her voice. He looked so serious because he was remembering a much-loved man he had served with who had not survived his war injuries.

He went on, "I wondered what it was about you that made me want to be around you. I thought about it when I shipped out, when I'd be marching to God knows where, and one night alone on guard duty, I finally figured it out!"

Louise smirked, smoothing her perm, "Do tell, dahling." She was unconsciously ready to deflect the complement.

He leaned over the table toward her and said softly, "Here's what makes you so human. Louise, you are funny… and

382

serious... at the same time."

Louise had no comeback and could only work at frowning while rolling her eyes like brown marbles, about to cross. Eddie looked at her as he chewed the oatmeal cookie. He refused to allow her to change the subject.

"I love you now, and I always will," he continued. "I know you broke up with me. That's okay. Find your best way. I need a rest, I need to relax. I'll go back to Penn State in the fall to get educated. You call me if you're in the mood." He sighed and gazed at her. "I won't expect anything... expect you to marry me, remember that," he said kindly. "But if you decide to get married to some new guy, don't invite me to the wedding."

Louise knew how much Eddie respected her, and it induced her to think again of the future. She wanted to be friends with him. Why, they were like two peas in a pod... and the possibility of running straight to his arms now seemed such an inviting idea. She felt no obligation to Bud—no, that was still an unknown something...like gratitude. She was so grateful to Bud for bringing her back to herself.

Just knowing Eddie was in town made a strange improvement in her life. Yes, it was delightfully like winning the war before it was over. She could allow Eddie to go his own way. She could wait until the war ended, when Bud returned and then decide. However, she would have to come to terms with it someday. But didn't her history teacher tell her that "some day" was not a day of the week?

Her thoughts of freedom were continual now, just like when she had informed Bud about her wariness of domestication. A fleeting vision suggested she see both suitors! Then she could decide on her choice. This was far worse than choosing between milk chocolate and devil's food. Mae West would have thought "the more the merrier." Louise did not want to juggle two men simultaneously, or did she? She would think again.

104

D ot and Louise were taken by a photo appearing in the paper in the spring, one symbolic of the Allied win in Iwo Jima. It showed five marines raising the American flag on Mt. Suribachi. It was a desirable image for Allied morale because more men were lost in taking Iwo Jima than in the Battle of Normandy on D-Day. It was an important advance, as Tokyo and the Japanese mainland were 650 nautical miles to the north.

Dot mused, "I'm sure Christy's in the Philippines."

"And thank goodness for that," Louise replied.

***

Bud had no idea of Louise's dilemma; however, he began a new communication campaign to assure her that he cared. He felt he needed to send reminders to that effect. What would he use in order to find a place in her heart? Telegrams! He had begun with photo postcards, then letters, finishing the year 1944 with recordings. The telegram had a certain punch, probably because it was used for fast transmission of important messages. It was more expensive than any special delivery, but he could afford it, thanks to his continuing poker winning streak. The *Wasp* did make occasional stops in port towns where telegrams could be created.

LOUISE
THINKING OF YOU stop
YOU ARE THE LIGHT OF MY LIFE stop
LOVE,

BUD

Bud soon attended the wedding of his sister Lois and her husband, Dick Landis, a Navy tail gunner, who was stationed in Jacksonville, Florida. Bud gave away the bride, as his father couldn't make the trip. It was such a festive break from the usual, to celebrate nuptials—to laugh and to hope the next party would happen in peacetime.

Bud's telegram had the effect of a mental Whitman's Sampler, for Louise and was as stunning as the valentine treat had been. Though she realized the gravity of her situation, she was thankful for a clear mind as she quickly threw herself into work. To get clear, she made no calls to Eddie and wrote no letters to Bud. If she awakened with the problem, she whispered to the air whatever insight she had gathered from her dream.

Staring out at the street one story below, she said, "I'm not going to hurry into a wrong decision, no matter how old I become. If either of you dare to pressure me... watch out, buster!"

If she had too many of these unwanted thoughts, she asked Dot to drive someplace to get ice cream therapy or to the movies—or both. On April 12, sitting in the middle of the Senate Theater, the audience was heartrendingly surprised by the manager, who ascended the stage to make an announcement.

"Ladies and gentlemen, I have cancelled the newsreel in order to inform you of some tragic news. President Roosevelt has died."

There was such a grievous reaction, some people wept and some left the theater. All children and teenagers knew no other president in their lifetime, for he had taken office in 1932.

The manager added, "He died of a massive stroke. We will show a news reel of him; this was four years ago, the Four Freedoms speech." Soon a black and white image appeared of FDR delivering his famous speech, punctuated by the dramatic signature tossing of his head:

In future days which we seek to make secure, we look forward to a world founded upon four essential human freedoms.

The first is freedom of speech and expression—everywhere in the world.

The second is freedom of every person to worship God in his own way—everywhere in the world.

The third is freedom from want—which translated into universal terms means economic understandings which will secure to every nation a healthy peacetime life for its inhabitants—everywhere in the world.

The fourth is freedom from fear—which translated into world terms, means a worldwide reduction in armaments to such a point and such a thorough fashion that no nation will be in a position to commit an act of physical aggression against any neighbor—anywhere in the world. That is no vision of a distant millennium. It is a definite basis for a kind of world attainable in our own time and generation. That kind of world is the very antithesis of the so-called new order of tyranny which the dictators seek to create with the crash of a bomb.

– Franklin D. Roosevelt, excerpted from the State of the Union Address to the Congress, January 6, 1941

This night felt heavy with the shadows of the times that lay ahead of them. They sat through the movie knowing well that tomorrow things would be different. Louise realized FDR left her pondering her own freedom. Then in the car she thought: *I have freedom and will always be free, no matter who I choose to share my future with.*

They drove to Loper's drug store, and Mr. Loper kept the store open until they drank ice cream sodas. He was speaking of his admiration of FDR. He acted as though he knew the president personally.

"Your father intended on producing ten-cent loaves of bread. Well, I tried to keep my prices affordable too, and FDR helped create jobs and helped people like us stay in business. I will miss the man."

Mr. Loper pushed the two frosty glasses toward Dot and Louise. The glasses had metal casings and large handles. The druggist smiled, "And FDR helped us win this war. Now things look better in Europe. The troops'll soon come home."

"Yeah?" Dot sighed. "Christy's in the Pacific. But I guess it is a matter of time."

"And Louise? Do you have a special person overseas?"

She was surprised that he asked. "At the beginning of the war I did, then last year I didn't. Now I do... have one overseas."

Mr. Loper was much too tired to inquire about a soldier who perhaps had returned from the dead.

Louise stepped outside and looked at the full moon. Mamaw called it the "pink moon," the nickname for the April full moon. "Ahh." She leaned against Dot's car.

Louise looked up and told Dot. "You know, I'm a free woman. FDR reminded me today."

Dot sat on the stoop to view the moon and said, "I am afraid for Christy's safety. I can't freely express myself in Father's presence. Therefore, I'm not free."

Louise added, "I see your point, kid, but I'm thinking most of freedom is a state of mind. You know Christy's activities are beyond your control, and he is helping to insure freedom in the future."

Dot agreed, "That's right."

"And... you just don't jive with Father, but that doesn't mean you can't express your mind to me."

Dot was silent. Louise said, "It feels good to me to realize that these kind of worries have to be temporary."

"Go on," Dot was listening as the moon emerged from a cloud.

"I wasn't used to the feeling of having two men interested in me. I guess I didn't take them seriously."

"You?" Dot said, knowing Louise all too well. She took

nothing seriously.

Louise had to laugh, which infectiously triggered another shrieking giggle from Dot, and the unison of laughs reached the smiling Mr. Loper as he headed home, waving.

Louise inhaled the night air and said, "I'm... going into the future one step at a time. I like both Eddie and Bud, and that is kind of like choosing between two of anything that is good. One day... I'll know the answer."

105

Eddie had now been convalescing for one month in Harrisburg. His arm burned a bit, but the doctor had removed the cast—a huge relief. He awakened May 7th, turned on his radio and made a light breakfast. He had benefited from a few weeks of rest. As he had not heard from Louise, he dropped into his habit over the last few years of wondering what she was up to.

A frantic radio announcer interrupted his program to scream, "Ladies and gentlemen, the war in Europe is over! The Germans have surrendered!"

Eddie had no close male friend in Harrisburg—they were all overseas. He awakened his mother, who was overjoyed. He phoned his father, who was listening to the broadcast.

Eddie had spent too many days and nights toward this end. He just could not contain his relief as joy was percolating rapidly in his bloodstream. He dialed 41990 and Dot answered.

"Stitt Bakery," she greeted him with surprise. "Thanks loads, Eddie! I'll spread the word."

His mood grew more expansive by the minute. He held the receiver to his shoulder in order to tie his shoes. "Dot, is Louise working?" *Damn it,* he thought. *I'm going to draft her to celebrate this with me!*

Dot answered, "Yes, she's downstairs."

"Well, tell her to turn on the blame radio! Don't tell her I'm coming. I'm going down to our restaurant and getting a few bottles of champagne."

"Whoop de do! I'll tell Father," Dot chuckled.

"Forgive me if I get the bakers smashed."

The line went dead and Dot jumped from her desk. She found Floyd in his office on the phone. Dot took a pencil and wrote left-hand, upside down on the desk blotter: "WAR OVER."

Floyd smiled and nodded. She guessed the caller had already shared the news.

Eddie burst into the front door of the bakery and yelled up the stairway, "Dot!"

She and Floyd helped Eddie to tote a dozen glass tumblers and his champagne and the party started. Louise and Sarah were slicing jellyrolls when he entered.

"Louise," he said, "I'm in need of a celebration!"

Louise smiled and said, "Look who's here!" They did a little jig as Floyd turned off the wrapping machine.

Eddie hugged her and every other woman present, though Sarah protested his aerial embrace saying, "Now put me down!"

Neatly suited, Floyd went to get his mechanic from the garage, who followed him past the wrapping machine and layer cakes toward the sanctum sanctorum, or the bread room. The large room held the temperature of molten lava, even with fans going full tilt. High on the whitewashed brick wall was a sign: "From the womb of the Earth to the mill—and beyond—the seed that makes bread is a living creature." – H.E. Jacob.

This sunny room held the largest oven; at the moment baking cakes so the bakers worked in an atmosphere of vanilla steam. Everyone had heard the news of Victory in Europe Day, the lemon meringue pie makers, the cupcake decorators and wrappers joined the bread bakers standing around the bread table. The buzz died down as Floyd looked at his employees.

"The damn war is *over.*"

There was an extensive cheer and a few tears. He shook each employee's hand. "Thank you for everything you did to help us get through it. These last few years were hard on us all. Now I know we still have it going, still in the Pacific, but that will end too. I just wanted to personally say thanks. Now a bit of business news. I just got word from the capitol that sliced bread is back! I hope that means more income and, if so, you'll see better paychecks." This was met by much louder applause punctuated by a whistle from the mechanic. "Now here is Sergeant Shafer, back from Germany to give us a toast."

Eddie and Dot popped the cork while George Fegley passed out glasses. The fizzing popping cork allowed emotion to flow and humor to reign. Eddie said with conviction, "I'm just so glad we can look forward to peacetime in the place I love. I've come home and I'm really happy to be a loyal Stitt customer." Glasses clinked.

The group wandered then into the brightness outside, where the neighbors were also in a mood to say good riddance to war. Passersby in cars waved. A few cars had people riding on their roofs, horns blaring. The bakers debriefed Eddie about the crossing of the Rhine River. One of the neighbors played a record over and over all afternoon in front of an open window about flying into the wild blue yonder.

Louise sat on the steps leading to the store. Thanks to a group of elderly women, the party intensified. The six were merrily walking downtown. They wore sensible shoes but were tired of sensibility. One skipped and the other five waved hats and scarves. White gloved, they patted Sarah on the back and shook hands with other employees.

"Do you know them?" Floyd asked Sarah.

She smiled, "Never saw 'em in my life!"

Eddie and Louise danced on the sidewalk to the neighbor's wafting music. Cheering and car horns drifted through the air. It had turned into a festival born of the vacuum-packed angst of separation, strife and loss building since before the war.

Eddie and Louise sat on the steps to the store, recovering their breath. He told her things went as well as he expected. He remained traumatized by horrible images, but his wounds were mending. He told her of the recent high points, he babbled how his mother was glad to have him home, how he had read old newspapers of the campaigns he had been involved in.

He chattered with gaiety and admitted if he felt low, he took a shower as an excuse to sing off key. "I've scrubbed off lots of sad times that way."

"I feel how painful it must have been," Louise said, "Don't forget that we at home have made many sacrifices too and," she sighed, "how we wished for this day. Why, Mother should be here! She salvaged so many tin cans…"

They found themselves alone when the oven timer went off, dragging the bakers back to reality. Louise studied her friend while her oxford-shod dancing feet cooled. She was not accustomed to the complex feeling that had descended upon her. Her gut told her she would love him forever, yet her heart did not wish to pledge or align itself to him.

So after pouring out the recent events of his life and having satisfied his desire to end VE Day in a good festive way, he hugged Louise, one arm newly cast- free, smiled and said goodbye.

106

No sooner had the Germans surrendered than Bill was transferred—not west as he hoped, but east! It was not clear why he was transferred east, but here they were, motoring east on Route 66. In order to take the oil-guzzling black Chevy, their parents sent them gas-rationing coupons. Before crossing the state line into Arizona, they blew one of the balloon tires in the town of Needles.

The newlyweds were not amused. "We could be on a sleeper train halfway home by now," Elaine moaned.

Sweat trickled down Bill's forehead. "We have to have a car anyway when we get to Virginia," he said as he changed the tire. "Nobody was very interested in buying an aged Chevy."

She handed him bolts while he twisted them in place. "I'm glad I brought extra water."

He smiled. "Well, I'm glad I brought you! Hang on, dearest. I'm hoping we'll make it deep into Arizona by tonight."

Already they missed Riverside with its friendly people and orange-scented air. Elaine had promised to keep in touch with her friends from the base. If the couple looked anxious, they came honestly by it because the Chevy was about as reliable as a rattlesnake. It puttered along at first, burning some oil, then they were treated to that agonizing popping sound as the rear left tire blew on Bailey Avenue, meaning they had to buy another spare.

Before wending their way toward Arizona, they stepped into a diner where the food energized them, and they didn't mind waiting for a large white bowl of pinto bean soup accompanied by corn fritters, warmed by mild chili peppers.

They motored over the Arizona state line bound for

Kingman. The land of red clay hills contrasted nicely with the cerulean blue sky. They found accommodations at a boarding house owned by Sara Wilson. She had lost her husband to the First World War and a nephew to the current war. She wore her swinging gray hair like Clara Bow, and she had reading glasses perched on the tip of her nose. For a person with losses of loved ones, she was highly optimistic.

They slept gratefully in her last available room, in bunk beds, which were surprisingly comfy. They both shared the lower bunk, spooning.

Next morning found them drinking glasses of cool aloe juice and having the "cowboy breakfast" of hash brown potatoes, heavily peppered, and eggs.

Sara overheard Elaine and Bill planning their next stop— Flagstaff.

"Young 'uns, if you want to go to Flagstaff, you must be headed east."

"Yes, we are," Bill answered.

"Are you military, by chance?"

"How did you know?" Elaine asked. "Does it show?"

Sara laughed, "Oh, it's not a guess, honey. There's been quite an exodus passing through since April. A slew of Hispanic Marine recruits, a Negro flyer, a WAC. I even met a Navajo Cipher expert."

This disturbed Bill as he thought he should be in the Pacific action.

"Now don't miss out on the world of sights you're going to be driving through."

Elaine asked, "Okay, what could we see?"

The woman whipped out a new map of Arizona that had space on the opposite side for notes. Sara penciled in some Xs, looked up and said, "Picture yourselves wherever you intend to be. If you map it out, you'll get there and hey, if you hit delays, relax, relax. Travelers don't relax enough."

Elaine saw her markings. "What are these points?"

She smiled, pouring coffee for the three men who were now taking seats at another table. "The first," she said confidentially, "is the ravines, covered by mesquite and tumbleweed, the second is a very windy lookout point where I've been lucky enough to get rained on. Beware of dust storms though, when they hit, you just sit for a bit till it blows away."

"Natural sights," said Bill sounding a bit condescending.

Sara placed her hand on Elaine's wedding-ringed left hand, which held Bill's hand, and whispered, "Look up at the moon. It looks different in these parts than it looks in the city you'll be stationed at. Look at it tonight."

They moved toward their destination, warmly dressed, well rested, both amused by their hostess and both not in any mood to tarry. However, they underestimated their tour adviser because the ravines were breathtaking against the cloudless sky. The red soil contrasted against all the variations of cactus, desert trees and a few longhorn cattle. They reached the lookout and decided to stop for a picnic of sandwiches and pickles. A large black Raven politely snacked on a few crunchy bugs.

They breathed in the view of a number of mesas—table-like rock structures—and the wind whipped wickedly through their travel outfits. Bill wondered if he was to be part of some European post-war peace-building plan. Elaine really was not looking forward to relocation but happy to spend this time in this way, as she dreaded the day he would be deployed.

They went on to find a clean "motor hotel" in Flagstaff and while Bill did some auto maintenance, Elaine decided to moon gaze. She strolled down a side road where she came upon a pond, took a smooth back-resting boulder as her seat and stared as water reflected the white moon, waxing toward fullness. She was awed by the light and its watery reflection. Sara had advised well; the simple pleasure of the moon calmed all of the travel stress and uncertainty. When the hooting call of an owl signaled she needed to return, she moseyed to their motor hotel. Tomorrow they would be in a new state.

***

Gallup, New Mexico was having a celebration. Elaine saw a group of destitute Creek Indians sitting outside a gas station and felt heartsick. Then there were stores with American flags, some with signs. Indians made strong tea and sold fry bread stuffed with onions and tomatoes. A woman in rainbow colors wearing a beadwork necklace mixed the dough with her hands while another wrinkled elder popped dough into sizzling oil. Blankets were stacked high and elders organized a group of laughing children. Several men gathered in a cluster of gnarled trees in the median of the paved street, each carrying a large drum.

"This looks like a good place for lunch, dahling." Elaine said. So they promenaded down the row of street booths, floating on a creative current, a mixture of bright sun, turquoise stone jewelry, and spicy aromas. After lunch, Elaine was attracted by a woman, who looked to be about twenty-five, sitting in a booth with an attached umbrella. There was a sign saying "Fortunes Told." Elaine could not resist because the young woman bore a strange resemblance to herself.

She paid with a fifty-cent piece for a reading and was instructed to get a piece of fry bread. The bread was to be "read," not by the seer, but by the customer. The bread she selected was plate size, plain and puffy. Elaine took a seat on a stack of woven blankets and studied the bread for images while the Hopi woman sang a soothing native chant.

Her eyes discovered an X, then a cross hatching, and on the opposite side, three circles. Elaine said, "Okay, I see an X." The seer glanced and agreed.

"X—You are not ordinary, but an extraordinary woman."

Elaine grinned, "You probably say that to everyone."

She shook her head slowly. "No one before," she replied solemnly.

"Extraordinary." Elaine continued, pointing to the bread. "I take this to be a fence."

Again the seer verified the image.

"You will have your fences. But you will jump fences, as you have already done, and break through the gates which hold you."

"Gates." This time Elaine was listening closely. "And here I see three circles."

The woman's face lit up now so that her glow spilled out to Elaine.

The seer directed, "What are these images? Look again with your mind's eye."

Elaine ran her index finger over the bread, seeing caramelized dots and not circles... ovals. "These could be eggs. Three... eggs, children, maybe?"

The Indian said quietly, "Maybe. It is your choice. I must say I am glad you came along because as I prepared for this day, Spirit sent me a token. I now hand it on to you."

Elaine was touched when she handed her a small birds' nest the bird builder had fashioned with weeds, feathers and a corn shuck. The woman said, "It will be a reminder of your abilities as an extraordinary person."

Elaine smiled and thanked her, but the Hopi seer had something more. "This is a sign with depth. On another level, I see three balloons. Spirit says look closely now at the image of three."

Elaine sighed. She waited, wondering. "I wonder if the circles might be... tires..." *There!* It popped out, and it was as though these words spoken by Elaine came from an unexplored cave.

The Indian woman held her palms up, then clasped Elaine's hands as she murmured a Hopi blessing.

107

Balloon tires—what a strange comment from a fortune teller. It was as if the information had dropped out of nowhere. Elaine first thought it was a fluke, but they already had blown their left rear. She knew Bill would merely laugh it off, but the tires now occupied her mind.

The Chevy chugged over a mountain pass that in the twilight appeared to be lavender against a yellow sky. They were zooming along at fifty miles per hour, well into the Texas leg of U.S. Route 66, followed by a Texas Ranger. They seemed to be hypnotized by a newscast related to food rationing. Most of the bread consumed by Americans was commercially baked, not the case during the Depression years. Floyd Stitt's friend, M.S. Hershey, was in declining health and had willed his fortune to underprivileged children. He was pleased to see the Hershey Bar recently used in Europe as a medium of exchange. He celebrated VE Day by increasing the size of the nickel chocolate bar.

Bill saw headlights in the rear-view and then heard a whining police siren, so he came to a stop. The officer was an older, roly-poly man.

"Headed east?" he asked with a tip of his officer's hat, revealing bloodshot eyes.

Bill was all business. "Yes, sir, I've got orders to Newport News."

"Oh! Yer one of our brave boys. What branch?"

"I'm in the Air Corps, sir."

The ranger sighed, "Well, sir, you got a flat in de makin'."

"What? A flat-- in the making?" Elaine shrieked. She knew now the seer's vision was accurate.

The ranger said smugly, "I's sure it'd blow when I saw that tire, but now ah see's it's some kinda defect in de inner tube. Go on up to the town ahead, Sageville. You'll find help at the garage, the ESSO station." And the officer drove off.

Bill and Elaine scrambled out to examine the right rear balloon tire, which now looked as if it had a sphere of black bubble gum growing out the side. Bill moaned, "Tires tire me out. I'll drive and hope it holds until we get help inside the town."

On the way down the road, Elaine knew they absolutely must avoid any more of this tire trouble. They had a long road ahead before reaching the East Coast. "Bill, when we get to the gas station, I want you to check the front tires."

"Okay, if we find this helpful station," he said through gritting teeth.

***

The Sageville ESSO was open, and they followed the sounds of a radio into the garage, a woman's voice singing, *Life is Just a Bowl of Cherries* combined with the mechanic's off-key duet: "so live and laugh at it all." At the sound of footsteps, the mechanic's disheveled head emerged from under a car's hood.

"Hey, folks!" he grinned.

Bill ignored his grease-smeared fingers, shook hands and asked for an assist with his inner tube, now bulging like a black cantaloupe. While the men studied the herniated tire, Elaine took a steel penny from her purse and inserted it into the treads of the pair of tires on the front of the car. She had learned from her father that if the penny went into the tread, it had less wear, and if the tread was worn, the penny would not insert. Her mind's eye examined the tires. One was balder, and she sensed imminent danger.

The mechanic set about repairing the defect while Elaine set about persuading Bill. "Dearest, I realize you've had a long day, but I've found something here," she said, crooking her index finger. "These front tires are worn. I did the penny test, and I can see all of Lincoln's face."

Bill frowned. "So you think we should get all new tires? We can barely afford this repair."

"We at least need a trade on the baldest one."

"A trade?"

"We've come halfway and blown two tires, and we'll probably not get there on this one," she said, pointing to the balder tire.

Bill had to agree it was bald but bit his nails over their travel budget.

Elaine said, "I intend to get to Virginia safely. Think how much you'd pay for a tire in Chicago. That's coming up."

The repairman came over and soothed, "Airman, there won't be a charge on the inner tube seein' as you're on the way to makin' the world safe."

Bill smiled with relief at Elaine and said, "Why, I guess I'll ask you if you'll trade on this right front while we're here. My wife says we need another tire."

Helpfully he said, "I'll tell you what! I've got a nice used tire I'll trade you even Steven."

This time Elaine sighed a well-earned breath of relief. And she hadn't had to reveal her source. *Well*, she thought, *I do believe I jumped that fence.*

108

L ouise was not the only one who revered Dwight Eisenhower. There had been a warm reception for the general in London, where he said: "My most cherished hope is that after Japan joins the Nazis in utter defeat, neither my country nor yours need ever again summon its sons and daughters from their peaceful pursuits to face the tragedies of battle. But—a fact important for both of us to remember—neither London nor Abilene, sisters under the skin, will sell her birthright for physical safety, her liberty for mere existence."

Louise was prematurely ejecting herself from the privations, such as rationing, loss and separation. The farmers' markets usually operated on Tuesday, Friday and Saturday. On this spring Saturday, Louise presided over the Stitt market stand at Broad Street Market. She had been there early to arrange the endless variety of baked goods, from toasty sesame loaves at her right to aromatic cakes, pastries and cookies on the opposite end of the long glass-covered stand, sunlit from a window overhead. She promoted the cherry custard pies because they were new and "scrumptious." Sparkle oozed from her pores even more than from rhinestone earrings hidden by shoulder-length brunette curls.

Her enjoyment of the markets mystified her sisters, who noticed that Louise never tired of working in that hectic environment, often standing for an hour without a break, waiting on customers and making change. One day, she realized her average sale amounted to thirty-six cents.

Louise had become a master at balancing frugality with frivolity. She made up for years of only window-shopping after the war with a Pomeroy's credit card.

She joked lightheartedly in her white linen apron over pink spring frock with everyone from basket-wielding housewives, farmers, businessmen out for their sugary doughnut breakfast, even a pair of black-habited nuns craving cream puffs. She replenished the medium brown paper bags and settled herself on a stool with a paper cup of black coffee. Soon, three green-uniformed Army men converged on the stand, seeking a cake for upcoming Memorial Day, and two soldiers chomped oatmeal cookies while the other one flirted unmercifully as though Louise owed her attention to him.

He was insistent. "I've got tickets to the swellest dance in Harrisburg," he grinned.

He was sharp in appearance and wit, but when he tried to ask her number, she replied flatly, "Sorry, soldier, I'm spoken for."

After the men walked down the aisle, she said to herself, "I am?" Then she realized she somehow expected to pick up where she left off with Bud Ditlow. Unconsciously, Louise expected Bud, vaguely imagining their reunion. His ploys to garner her attention were unique to say the least, and Louise had been obliged to change her opinion of this man, nearly four years her junior. His unassuming nature appealed to her, and she had to admit, he impressed her with his postcards featuring himself, friendly letters, 78-rpm serenades climaxed by the recording of his own voice and now telegrams!

He had kept his telegrams coming, waxing poetic, and since these transmissions were expensive, he was short and snappy. His Spartan poetry had a good effect on her—better than any flowery verse. Louise opened the telegram, picked up the sincerity, then laughed to herself for the whole day long. It had the effect of a gourmet meal, leaving her to yearn for a bit more.

I look out northward
Where Harrisburg holds you Louise
You, seeing this same moon

She replied without referring to his poetry. Her news was of Stitt sliced bread gobbled up by happy patrons, rationing lifting, and her deliveries of "welcome home!" cakes. She signed her letters: "Until you return," "Awaiting your arrival," or "Safe sailing."

He replied:

Awake but dreaming of you
Hoping you've found a place for me in your heart
Lost in love

***

His ship lingered on the East Coast, preparing to ferry the servicemen home, but then the captain had to deal with proposed action in the Pacific, where there were to be more air raids over Japan involving aircraft carriers. Bud spent long hot days over his oven, some windy nights on guard, and little in the way of shore leave. He dreamed of getting his feet back on solid ground, yet he had become an expert at immersing himself in work, just as his hands immersed easily into a batch of sourdough.

He became poetically emboldened, daring to refer to the Wizard of Oz and ending with a whistle:

Longing to see her
Ruby Slippers take me home to her
Wheep weoow!

109

"A year of important happenings, both sad and glad, lies behind us, but the year ahead is an unwritten page and much that will be written on it depends on the way our hearts feel, our minds understand and our hands work for the good of the world as a whole."

– Eleanor Roosevelt

Louise sensed correctly how Bud balanced his work ethic with nonsensical humor, and that he wanted to work long hours without interruption. He interacted well with most people, especially elders. He appeared to have enjoyed traveling in the line of duty but could not have justified travel otherwise, as it was a luxury. He possessed a sense of being an outsider who enjoyed observing people and surroundings while not pondering about much. He could not be expected to be a seeker of insight while occupied with a torrent of work activities. Now, his poems had, in effect, caught Louise in a thrilling web of love she found amusing. A naturally formed charisma made Bud a welcome suitor, possessed of unexpected magnetic qualities.

Louise was relieved by Floyd for lunch and walked across Verbeke Street to Alsedek's Restaurant, where she sat at the counter, ordered the lunch special and dreamed, staring into the glass cupboard. She was mindful that Bud might not survive the war, but subconsciously she began preparing for him.

110

The bug-splattered black Chevy pulled into Harrisburg with Bill at the wheel, and he had driven it through the night. The ravenous car had consumed six quarts of oil, numerous tanks of rationed gas and two balloon tires. Elaine greeted her mother and grandparents while Bill went to the bakeshop garage to beg his father-in-law for a tougher tire.

Clara clucked, "Oh, my darling honeybunch is here!" Caroline had not expected her granddaughter but had been working at her stove like a maestro cuing two vegetables and a stewing chicken in the pot.

Elaine feasted at the kitchen table and gave her elders a taste of her travel adventure in return. Caroline was most amused by the description of the sizzling fry bread, as she had a special place in her heart for Native Americans. Clara was entertained by her daughter's California memories of living near orange groves. Always neighborly, Mrs. Brown surprised Elaine with a strange "Spring Fruitcake" she described as springy, and Elaine was too tired to resist.

Then Elaine felt the overdrive of maps and lumpy mattresses and road dust and yodeling, so she craved a tub bath. She wanted to revitalize herself prior to the next day's driving marathon. Clara drew a bath and added a cupful of Epsom salts to ease away the stress of the road. Elaine sank herself into the steaming bath feeling the singular joy of being home.

Bill and Floyd found lightly used tires to refit the car, so there would be no more blowout incidents. Along the way, Bill welcomed himself to the bakery by eating a whole eight-inch Shoofly pie, still warm from the oven; it went down well with a cup of black coffee. He visited his parents and soon was looking anxiously at his watch.

So, time waited for neither traveler, and before you could say "Newport News" they were motoring down the East Coast clutching a pack of gas coupons. They had noted the mood of Harrisburg's workers and neighbors to be hopeful and better than the somber local media accounts of the Pacific front. The green hills of Penn's Woods floated by, and soon they were in Virginia's mountains. Elaine was glad to have had the opportunity to accompany Bill, even through these uneasy days when they awaited orders to the Pacific. Perhaps the war speeded their courtship, but they counted themselves lucky to be together.

They reached a woodsy lookout in the vicinity of Spotsylvania, and it was time for a break, so Elaine turned off the main road. A sign read: "Spotsylvania Battlefield of 1864." *Oh dear*, she thought. *Why did I pick a darn battlefield as a lunch spot?* They passed a marker commemorating the 28,000 Civil War victims who died at Spotsylvania battlefield.

"Well, Hon," Bill said. "We're certainly hungry enough to eat and take the surroundings as we find them."

They chose a space running wildly with daffodils. Here were two rock "chairs" and a table of high grass. They put down *The Patriot News* as a tablecloth and opened a clean flour sack, packed by Caroline.

"Ohh," Bill sighed. "Nothing like a picnic with Mamaw's home cookin'."

Indeed she had thought of everything; a jug of lemonade, chicken soup in a thermos, egg salad sandwiches, sour pickles, a pint of strawberries and then the Stitt desserts. Through cellophane, they saw a pair of strawberry iced vanilla cupcakes. In the bottom of the sack, they found more desserts with longevity: spice cookies also wrapped for freshness. While lunching, they scanned the view from their lookout spot.

Sipping lemonade, Bill said, "The battle happened here

because the Union wanted to take Richmond, south of here. But Lee and Grant were equally good leaders, and I think the battle was a draw."

War-weary Elaine did not want to know *an- y- thing* about the bloody business of eighty years ago, but she patiently heard that although Lee had lost fewer men, it was the beginning of the end for the Confederate South.

All the lemonade caught up with Bill, and he went to relieve himself. Elaine sat quietly in her blue and white spring dress. She glanced at the paper, almost shouting war headlines, and it was then that a strange sense came over her. The birdcalls were so calming that her ear perceived an inner voice. It was the reassuring sense that Bill was safe from the war, that he was inside a mysterious bubble of protection.

111

Summertime arrived in Harrisburg, and with it, a letter from Christy Hammaker.

> *Dear Dorothea,*
> *I'm missing you so much that sometimes I sing "to you" opera arias in the camp shower. I do get a lot of wisecracks from my buddies. As you probably read in the paper, we're in the Mariana Islands for now. We have worked night and day to clear an airfield in a cloud of mosquitoes. We're constructing a building now for incoming freight.*
> *I so look ahead to coming back home to our normal life. I lost all the weight I put on since I learned how to make pies. I haven't been injured, and my football knee is working better.*
> *We had so many good trips to Silver Lake! I think of you when you went in that new white bathing suit, with the one strap behind the neck, and you Dorothea, are my mental "pin-up girl."*
> *Yours, X O*
> *Christy*

What Christopher Hammaker did not know was that the building he constructed was for the express purpose of assembling a mysterious new weapon. This bomb was transported via his base airfield. Select people had designed it, Americans and some German defectors, and then President Truman approved what came to be known as the atomic bomb.

August 6th and then August 9th were trying for America and devastating to Japan when two cities, Hiroshima and Nagasaki, were destroyed.

However, prior to these attacks, the military continued preparing to invade Japan. Christy believed he would be part of the invasion. Instead, he was assigned as part of a reconstruction team in post-war Japan.

Bill, as an aviator, was being coached for the invasion in Newport News. Bud Ditlow, as a seaman onboard an aircraft carrier, was expecting to be sent to the Pacific. Both servicemen indeed would soon be sent west; Bill by train to the West Coast, while Bud moved to the Pacific on the *USS Wasp*.

112

The Newport News air base provided apartment housing for Bill and Elaine. There they became acquainted with other couples poised for separation by the war, many of them Navy recruits on maneuvers in the bay. Bill eagerly awaited his calling west and barely tolerated his training. There were some warm idyllic weekends spent at Virginia Beach under an umbrella with friends who picnicked, swam and played gin rummy as the waves moved in and out. With all its deep tan sand, tall grass and serene sea birds, the beach served to ease the tension of women who did not want to be left at home.

Elaine tried her hand at baking more and more; she had amassed a recipe file she labeled "sure to please." Bill applauded his latest birthday cake, a towering stack cake of five thin moist layers. These levels were separated by fruit filling made from apple "schnitz." One may be assured mathematically how precisely the layers matched.

Elaine's precision was rewarded at a beach picnic where a dispute erupted—related to cake cutting. There were two women who had baked a cake together and wanted to divide it in two pieces. The tiff came about because one baker liked the icing roses while the other preferred the maraschino cherries which dotted the top. Neither wanted to disturb these decorations.

Elaine ceased her sun worship with, "Pipe down a minute!" She directed the cherry queen. "You cut the cake and then *She* will choose the half she wants."

She referred to the icing lover. They had to surrender and with sighs and smiles, saw to an equitable division of the cake.

In July, Bill was finally called to the coast, leaving Elaine to pack up and go to Harrisburg. The two shared their breakfast, prior to his departure. She stared at his face, her head in hand, as though she needed to memorize it.

He said, "You take your time on the road, Hon, and don't take any chances." He grabbed his bag.

She replied, "I could say the same to you, Flyboy. And don't take any wooden nickels." She knew how much he wanted to fly—some solace that was. He encircled her waist and lifted her off the ground.

They held on to each other, absorbing the moment, not thinking of the coming conflict. "I will be in Mountain Home, Idaho in a few days, and I'll drop you a line."

She watched as he walked down the street to headquarters. Disconnecting was difficult. She whispered the words, "He will be safe," as she set about cleaning their place and then went to find some groceries for the week, as she was planning to get some work done on the Chevy prior to departure.

She proceeded to Harrisburg, where her mother had some travel plans of her own.

***

Louise Stitt had been channeling much of her energy into the decoration of wedding cakes. Stitt's Bakery had a tremendous backlog of orders for wedding cakes because brigades of service people were returning home to walk down aisles with their intended.

Baker George Fegley was also the master decorator, the man with the hand steady enough to pipe, with a pastry bag, perfect garlands on a succession of three-tier, white-iced creations. Louise applied silver sugar balls and attached toppers. She had been tapped by George to run out for extra toppers, while Dot worked on another topper for customers of color. She took a basic topper with a white couple and tinted the skin appropriately. Finally, Louise assisted with the order for candied

411

flowers, a most expensive cake decoration. The next week's orders demanded cake toppers with the usual brides, grooms in uniform, standing under an arch that held a tiny American flag.

George had been talking to Louise, Dot and Elaine forever about cake. They had learned that the egg was responsible for the ability of cake dough to rise. Baking soda and baking powder came along in the mid 1800s, and then with modern regulated ovens, the more delectable cake became indispensable for wedding receptions. George was an authority on everything, down to the size cake pan for anyone's guest list.

Icing is dependent upon sugar for texture and flavor. Dutch traders and other explorers moved cane into the Caribbean in the 1700s, and with its wide production, sugar became less expensive worldwide. Confectioners' sugar, the sisters observed, produces a creamy cake icing. It is ground with a small amount cornstarch to avoid stickiness.

A number of Saturday weddings were delayed because George, Bill and the cake team could only engineer two of these larger cakes per day. One bride ordered a small cake for display and several sheet cakes to serve guests.

Louise was standing before a four-tier cake, placed on a lazy Susan in the cake decorating area. She applied the topper with extra icing for stability. This topper was specially ordered, as it had a soldier couple—a WAC of the Women's Army Corps paired with a soldier! They must have met in the line of duty, Louise decided. As she assisted George in mounting the second and third tiers, she found herself blessing the nuptials for her unknown customers. She stood nearby in order to help George center the tiers properly. Then he inserted small straws to stabilize the cake tower.

The black Chevy pulled up to the shop and a travel-weary Elaine entered quietly, exclaiming, "Pretty cake!"

Louise circled icing-smudged arms around her, and George and Sarah welcomed her with surprised faces.

"I'm here for a couple of days, then I drive to Bill's post in

Mountain Home, Idaho," she announced.

The three sisters convened for lunch. Elaine entertained them with her memories of the beach and living in Newport News. Elaine explained how she had sworn off desserts as she simultaneously cut a slice of plain angel food cake.

"Umm!" Elaine giggled.

"Mother wants to go out west with you," Dot warned.

"Holy moley," Elaine groaned. "I hope she can stand to ride in that wacky car of ours."

Louise observed, "Since you went so many thousand miles, why worry about a little trip to Idaho?"

"*Little!*" Elaine couldn't resist mimicking Louise: "Per aspera ad astra." Through difficulties to the stars.

113

L ouise felt she had entered a new realm, as if she had thrown off the tattered wartime skin she had worn like a figure in a still life. She worked tirelessly, had evening dinner with Dot, except for Sundays when they ate at 2232 North Sixth Street. Her focused mind strayed to Bud, who never failed to get one of his penetratingly poetic love notes transmitted every week. She had to admit he was intriguing. Her spirit felt like a kid called to come out and play.

Louise sensed Bud's simplicity and knew how much effort went into his messages of commitment. She stopped questioning her inclination to retain her freedom within marriage. Her spirit would never be contained—not ever! She somehow realized that her identity was on the line, but now she wanted nothing more than to get immersed in a family of her own.

She forgot to wonder about his whereabouts and instead wondered if she was nuts to wish she could lose herself in his green eyes. She yearned to taste his kiss; she was transported by her imagination to a vision of him braiding her hair like fancy gourmet bread and her arms pulled like young dough, his hands kneading her back muscles like making bread, Louise becoming elastic, more pliable in his hands.

She fantasized about their reunion, when she hoped to find him as engaging as she imagined. She spontaneously built her fantasy around chocolate, inspired on Third Street while shopping in Woolworth's Five and Ten. The variety store lighting was dim at day's end, and only a few schoolgirls shopped for paper dolls. She was looking for a new shade of nail polish and found one: "milk chocolate." It was marked five cents because it was an unpopular shade.

As she awaited the cashier, she spotted a rich-looking, white-dotted, brown velvet headband, for which she paid ten cents. "Humm," she mused, now with a dress the shade of chocolate, *I'd feel delectable!* The thrill was not so much in owning a chocolate outfit, but the very idea of "being" in chocolate transported and delighted her. The headband bore a resemblance to the candy known as "nonpareil," which translates as "without equal." Nonpareils were Bud's favorite candy.

As she was riding this flowering, blooming feminine tide, Louise soon happened upon a free summer fashion show at Bowman's Department Store. She was seeing the world through "chocolate glasses," like no other person at the fashion show, and found her dress through mix and match. She purchased a fitted top the color of café au lait and a silken fabric skirt the shade of a Hershey's semi-sweet bar. On a whim, after shopping, she went to a late afternoon movie, *They Knew What They Wanted*, starring Gable and Lombard.

That evening she bathed in the "low-tide" bathtub to conserve water and manicured her overworked hands. Observing the effects, she applied her carved wooden "chocolate" ring and painted her nails. She whispered to herself, "Upstanding chocolate... I'm like a good truffle," and laughed uncontrollably over it, so Dot called her "nutsy."

She became part of the mass wedding march mentality, and this seemed logical after years of wondering about marriage in those uncertain war years. "Perhaps I've been around sugar too long," she giggled to herself, as now she fancied herself a living confection to be consumed by her intended.

114

Elaine headed west by car with Clara, who couldn't bear the thought of her out on the open road alone. Clara meant well, but her daughter definitely did not need a chaperone. Luckily, the Chevy behaved, and Clara left Elaine with Bill in Mountain Home, Idaho, then took the return train east. Before Elaine knew it, Bill was transferred to Oregon. Portland Columbia Army Air Corps Base was where he was to join a crew to fly to the Pacific; however, that base was as far west as he would go.

The creation of the first atomic bomb was top secret. So much so that most people in contact with the weapon had no idea what it was or what it could do. Congress was not informed and Truman—as vice president—was not informed of it by Roosevelt. Now, Truman directed a targeting of the Japanese military. Twenty-nine-year-old Paul Tibbets, the pilot of the B-29 who flew that mission, only had a vague idea of what he carried. The most visible authority for the use of the bomb seemed to be a General Thomas T. Handy.

***

On August 7, 1945, Clara reached breezy Chicago by train and proceeded to walk briskly toward the exit to remove herself from the blackened atmosphere of the train's exhaust. She adjusted her navy blue dress, secured the small straw hat and her gray hair coiled beneath it. Her wide feet had become swollen in her tightly laced dress shoes. She had an hour to visit the ladies' room and get her lunch. She questioned a policeman, who directed her to a small shop outside, where she found the

Chicago Special—a hot dog and a beer.

"Make that a root beer," she ordered. The small shop was buzzing, and the server with an apron, proclaiming himself "hot dogger," hardly looked at Clara. She took a seat under a rotating fan and consumed her lunch. She listened to the buzz.

Two men in work clothes waited in line. "Does this end the war?"

They seemed anxious. "Don't know, now we have to wait and see. Never been a bomb like this."

"But now we don't have to go into Japan to end it."

Clara hustled to her train, stopping to buy a newspaper extra and yes, she needed to read all about it. The man in the adjoining seat on the train was deep into the same paper. He smiled and went back to reading. Clara absorbed the story as how recently, July had seen a number of air raids by allied aircraft on Japan. It appeared Japan would not submit, so the atomic bomb was dropped on Hiroshima, a city noted for its schools, trade through railroads and port, and a significant military presence. Clara opened her mouth to air the excitement over a possible end to World War II, but silenced herself when she noticed her seatmate was reading lingerie ads.

Clara began to wonder about the involvement of her sons-in-law. Bill was to stay on U.S. soil, Christy had been tapped to help with post-war engineering in Japan, and then Louise's friend, Bud, onboard a carrier, now in Pacific waters bound for Hawaii. Everything and everyone held their collective breath, including the president, who intended the A-bomb to end a war that needed ending.

No sooner had Clara gotten settled in Harrisburg than news of another explosion in Nagasaki reached the world. A ceasefire went into effect, and by September second, Japan formally surrendered.

115

The B-29 bomber's crew had assembled for take-off, and Bill was signing out. Recent years of his life he had built around this flight to Japan. Before he exited the hangar, his mission cancelled due to the eminent surrender of the Japanese. He was stunned; his adrenalin level was on overload, and suddenly the peace, so hard won, flooded the air base. Bill was like a blazing fire smothered unexpectedly by peaceful rain.

Elaine was home, industriously sweeping the living room floor to the strains of big band music. Pausing, she turned down the radio. She suddenly had a strange string of clairvoyance, beginning with a vision of happy Stitt Bakery employees, then the lovely southern women of Montgomery, and the faces of friends she had made this year. She heard them all cheering. Loud noises too, seemed to be coming from distant car horns. Through the front door screen, she saw a car go by sounding its horn, with a man waving a flag out the passenger window. She turned up the radio and heard the news, sighed, "yay!" and certainly knew now Bill really was safe. She put on her favorite lime green frock, a rose scented perfume and knew the celebration was about to begin.

***

The pictures of Japanese leaders signing for surrender dominated the newspapers. Aboard the *USS Wasp*, Bud baked lots of sourdough bread, "Celebrate!" cakes, and then poured a bottle of beer down the back of an unsuspecting signalman's pants. Their aircraft carrier halted in its path west, turning back toward California. The captain informed his crew the world was officially at peace, that they were ordered to Norfolk, Virginia by way of San Francisco, and in due time, discharges would go into effect. A roar went out over the sea, sonoric enough to drive away a school of fish.

Bud sent Louise his telegram from San Francisco Bay:

Dearest Louise my love
I cannot keep quiet—WAR OVER!
See you in October

***

That night Louise concocted a romantic drink composed of welcome, energy, relief, and hope. Really, it was another of her chocolate compositions with warming spices and coffee-flavored cream she had whipped. She located martini glasses in Bowman's to serve it appropriately.

Dot watched in amazement at the organized ingredients going into a cocktail shaker, for Louise usually threw things together without a plan. They sampled it.

"Oooh!" Mocha mellowness. Dot pulled a bottle of coffee liqueur off the shelf and added a hefty slug to her glass. Two drinks were toasted... "To us!"

"This'd make a good ice cream." Louise preferred the nonalcoholic version. Now she had a unique libation to offer Bud as a toast.

Louise turned on the radio and heard the sound of Doris Day. This record was entertaining thousands of service people wending their ways home at that very minute.

Louise frivolously sang along, "Gonna take a sentimental journey, gonna set my mind at ease..."

Dot had instantly become slaphappy and warned, "He'll get landed, see you in your finery, take a sip o' this elixir an' ee won't know what hit 'im."

"I think you've seen too many Walter Brennan movies," Louise retorted.

116

Two weeks later, Bud's friend, the signalman, drove him from the train station to the bakery at about one in the afternoon. He could hope she would be receptive, but he was unsure. He had some bright pink roses tied with a red ribbon.

Louise had guessed he might soon arrive and had her hair done two days before. She carefully pulled together the chocolate outfit, now eagerly waiting in her room, but presently she was working in the storage at emptying a small, cotton sack of flour into a large, wooden rectangular bin. She wore a white apron over an old dress—the apron splattered with cherry pie filling. She shook the bag crisply and was humming to herself, soon to be surprised, phenomenally shocked by Bud.

He emerged from a Ford sedan smiling widely, standing in the sun, shouldering his sea bag, and waving at his ride with the pink bouquet. He then moved quickly through the garage, catching sight of her as he headed for the work area. She was focused on the bin, bending forward. He walked toward her as he had longed to do for years.

In white uniform, he was quiet. He stood to her side, snickering. His sudden appearance unbalanced her! Diving forward, she dropped the sack and her head wound up like a white mop against the flour bin wall, the flour filling eyebrows, ears, caking her lipstick and her resulting shriek had Bud rescuing her to a standing position while Joe, the mechanic, appeared to investigate.

Louise shook her hair, saying, "Gee-zooey!" Billowing flour dusted the room as she swiped flour over her shoulders. "I'm okay, Joe."

Bud wiped her face, then hugged her floury chest to his uniformed one. "Oh Louise, Louise, Louise." He had tears in his sea-green eyes. She looked racoonish with flour-whitened eyebrows, but her eyes shone merrily.

The two white figures went outside, clasping each other's waists, kissing, shaking, licking off the flour and stepping blindly toward the bakery's main entrance. They stopped in the second floor office, finding Dot typing at her desk.

"Hi, Dot," greeted Bud.

Dot came and took Bud's arm as he gave her a jubilant hug. "Am I glad this war's over!"

"Christy in Japan?"

"Still in Japan, helping them reconstruct," she sighed. Then inspecting Louise she said, "You look like a poor little match girl in a snow bank." She spurted out, hissing laughter.

Rolling her eyes, Louise said, "I'm done for the day. We'll be upstairs."

Dot whispered to her sister, "Hey, don't forget your special drink's in the refrigerator."

***

Following fear, separation and death, there must be an opposite. The opposing state must affirm life and empower the survivors of war. Love in its many forms gave hope to the people of 1945. Louise and Bud found themselves together, and from the moment the flour settled, their marriage began.

The third floor apartment had been unoccupied for some time, but Louise had chosen the small place for her reunion with Bud.

He stood in the kitchen waiting for Louise to return with her refreshments. It fairly echoed, it was quiet, sunny and Bud felt so relieved to have returned to his beloved. His spine tingled as he placed his sea bag on the floor. He arranged his bouquet into a Mason canning jar. A recent newspaper with photo of Eisenhower was propped on the table model radio at the kitchen table, where she had read about his speech in London. He picked up The Patriot News and saw the reverse side, where a crossword had been completed and he noted something circled with fountain pen ink: "Leo—the lion. Planetary influences will find you purring. Your whiskers may twitch at sudden irritations, but keep those claws sheathed, and the lion's share is yours." Bud had no idea what sign he was or what was meant by planetary influences.

He toured the apartment, finding a bathroom with a claw foot tub, a small living room with an old Victorian couch, and the bedroom. It was shaded by the only new item in the place—a flowery pink curtain. The bed had a headboard and footboard with wooden spooled rungs. He did a double take when he saw the assorted postcards on the wall surrounding a mirror. They were his cards from the rock of Gibraltar, Panama City and Frisco! He had a photogenic face, the cards reflected, for which he was now grateful. He dreamed when he sent his photo cards that he would be accepted—welcomed by her.

He took a kitchen seat as Louise, made her entrance, looking like she had escaped a Gold Medal hurricane. She toted her drink accoutrements. "How do you find my digs?"

"Louise, I wouldn't care where I had to go to get to you!"

"I hope you appreciate all the horrendous *cleaning* that had to be done here," she declared.

Bud opened the kitchen window, with difficulty as it had been closed since 1940. "Yeah, sure is clean," he chuckled. Robins trilled in their nest on an oak limb.

Louise pleaded, "I'm really not ready to be a good hostess." The flour in her hair now mimicked dandruff.

He tilted his head and chuckled, "You're doin' okay, even if you look a little white-ish."

She was clownishly funny. She whirled from the counter where she had poured spices into a mixing bowl.

"Get this straight, kid, I'm glad you made it back, but I carefully planned to be a fashion plate..." Now she wore flour lipstick, an ancient girdle plus the disgusting state of her hair...

"And instead you look like…"

She cut in, "Hell! I look like hell!"

Bud continued, "I thought you looked like a sight for sore eyes," he answered, then added, "just like a cream puff."

She raised her steel eggbeater in mock attack.

He took the beater gently away and asked, "Tell me how and I'll help you with this."

He beat up a cloud of fresh sweet cream. "Topping?"

"That's right. It ain't the Harrisburger Hotel, but it ain't bad." They licked froth off the beater.

Bud looked into her flour-flecked eyes, "I'd rather be right here. I'm not much for fancy places."

She shook a cocktail shaker violently and soon the famous cocoa drink was a reality, being poured into martini glass stems. She inhaled, and her nose calmed a bit to the waves of cinnamon, ginger and coriander.

"What's this? Cold coffee? My, that is fancy!"

She carefully spooned cream over the chocolatey libation, grabbed a grater and shaved a small aromatic semi-sweet bar over the two drinks. Appealing to her as a willing playmate, Bud was mesmerized by Louise. "It isn't every day a man returns from war," Louise observed.

Bud replied, hefting the stemmed glass, "You didn't need to go to any trouble."

Shifting to movie-star lingo, she shot back, "Trouble's my middle name, dahling. You did the war thing! Live a little, why don'cha?" The concoction they sipped contained no alcohol, but the two were so high on each other they were flying.

Louise gave up on the chocolate outfit; in fact, she needed to get completely out of her clothes. She said, "Bud, I simply have to take a bath to get this flour off. I'll be out after that." She pulled her chair closer, took his hand and planted a caffeinated kiss on his mouth. He gripped her waist too late; she was up and headed for the tub.

Hell's bells! Louise thought to herself. *I have to wash my hair!* A task she had long ago assigned to her beautician. She had only a cake of Ivory Soap in the tub, and that would have to remove all the white stuff.

She had flicked the art deco radio on low, and it hummed the song of the moment: *Sentimental Journey.*

While she was working on her hair, Bud leaned out of the screenless kitchen window and viewed a new green delivery truck, "Stitt's Better Bread" painted in yellow, parked on shady Schuylkill Street. He had never seen such a shiny delivery vehicle, and he visually inspected it. What he could not know was that he himself would soon be spending his time in that very truck. A couple of kids could be seen playing around the truck. A customer exited the shop carrying a "welcome home" sheet cake.

"Bud," Louise called out with uncertainty. She needed another towel, as her hair was now wrapped in her bath towel. "Please take a towel for me... from the closet."

While Bud searched, Louise decided it was time to be brutally honest. She wanted Bud, he wanted her, and they were behaving like horseshoe magnets on the loose, flying toward each other. Why, she had no intention of putting on her new outfit now, and certainly not the discarded, powdered work dress. She let the water out of the tub.

"Bud," she said again. He thrust a towel through a crack in the door, and in the tub, she fearlessly stood, steaming.

"Go on open it," she said.

He came slowly forward, through the steam, holding towel before him, blocking his own view. She clasped his uniformed arms, and his smiling face became visible. He wrapped her in the towel, and her body gave up its shame along with rivulets of floured bath water. He dried her skin with electric scrubs, pats, squeezes and she glowed with anticipation.

He whispered, "It's hot in here—mind if I lose my laundry?"

She kissed him as she emerged from the tub.

"Be my guest... darling."

His body had been seasoned by his years out on the sea. His hair had often been washed in salty seawater. His eyes were the green of rough emeralds. He was built compactly, toned by the lugging of bread dough, heavy milk canisters and sacks of Panamanian coffee beans.

Louise was beauty-contest beautiful. Her figure showed lissome curves compounded by a world of desserts. Bud never realized that Louise belittled her body because he thought she was superior to every pin-up girl, can-can dancer or marble statue he had ever seen.

Wordlessly, they made a trail of steam to the bed, a springy set of coils topped by a cotton mattress. The sheets were cool and ventilated by autumn air.

He was a bit stunned. "I missed you... so much!"

"Honestly, I've hoped you would come," she said, plumping a pillow. "I want you here, and now I need to be with you."

The holding force of the two elastic magnets generated energy beyond anything either one previously imagined. Sounds of mating animals echoed down on Schuylkill, for they denied each other nothing. They made noise, pleased each other; they made whoopee, and euphorically made love. The apartment breathed itself back to life. The windows rattled, the wallpaper peeled and the spools on the headboard hummed. Robins quizzically cocked their heads in the oaks by the open window.

Dot heard none of this because she worked over the noisy adding machine. Two floors below the apartment, Sarah paused, her stainless steel icing-loaded spatula poised above her naked devil's food cakes and said, "George, I think I heard howling wolves... did you hear that?"

George said no, but was shaking his bald head as he stared at a three-tier wedding cake. He had just witnessed the cake levitate. He rubbed his eyes, cleaned his bifocals and stepped back. He believed his own eyes because some of the icing had shifted. But he said nothing and quietly went about his decorative repairs.

Upstairs, the lovers felt the magnetic charge loosen, like an anchor falling into the sea. Nothing more could have been desired—nothing at all, not even sleep. Tired they surely were, and after years of war-related tension, here was the incredible peaceful warmth of love. Louise noticed then, Bud's irises had changed to hazel. He had no explanation for the color change.

They talked while propping palm to ear. She wanted to hear his accounts of wartime travel. He told her everything he could recall about his stop in Italy. He had liked the "Eye-talians," he told her, and he had no difficulty understanding the people he met. The captain, who spoke some Italian, had escorted him to the nicest museum of weapons. He learned all about prehistoric weapons!

Excitedly he repeated of Italy, "The place is old!" He mentioned a puppet show he saw, food he had never before eaten—eggplant in tomato sauce, zucchini flowers and squid. After Louise spoke of coffee rationing at home, Bud had to tell her, "The Eye-talians had the strongest coffee in such tiny cups—my, it was strong!"

"They call it espresso," she informed him. "They have it here too at Shafer's."

"Here in Harrisburg?"

Louise added, "Why sure. Italians travel." The woman was so refined!

Then they embraced like an encoring honeymoon couple, planning their wedding between kisses. *Per aspera ad astra*, thought Louise, through difficulties, to the stars.

They laughed about that first time they met in the garage, how he hoped she would return, how she had wished to avoid him, and after all how they needed to be together; she thought like peanuts in the shell, he thought like nuts and bolts. She was not expecting to hear that Bud was now in the Naval Reserves... but there would never be another war, with talk of her revered Eisenhower running for president. Finally, after a couple of sandwiches, they slept, lost in love.

117

Late in 1945, the returning service people referred to Europe as half graveyard and half junkyard. Reconstruction had begun in Japan, and there was a U.S. presence in the Philippines. The economy was shifting to accommodate the population. Bud had shared his ship with men who were going to stay in the service, some who were bound for the dormant auto industry and one radioman who had an idea for "the radio of the future." It would need batteries. Bud was mainly focused on Louise, and he thought she was focused on the bakery.

Now that he had returned, Bud wasted no time idly wondering how to earn a living. There would be no sentimental journeys for this man! "Uh- uh! No sir-ee Bob!"

Clara invited him to Sunday dinner. There the Stitts soaked up his stories of bread baking on board ship. They paled at his remarks of bread as a European commodity of exchange, a black market item and of children begging for stale bread.

Floyd responded, "What would you like to do with yourself now, other than attend Navy Reserve?"

Bud hopefully answered, "I hope you like this idea. I really want to marry Louise."

She was quiet, drinking her October cider.

Floyd said, "Louise and Bud, you have our blessing. Now we will start working on the cake! Bud, you were out there on that ship baking—that was what you did. I wonder if you still want to do bakery work."

Bud ventured, "Yeah, I do need a job."

Floyd explained, "My bakers have been on the job for years and years, you see, so I don't have that kind of work for you, even though the demand for sliced bread is growing. However, I need a man to organize the delivery truck routes, and I need a driver. How does that suit you?"

"Ha, ha, I can start tomorrow."

Floyd agreed. And so began an association that lasted until the bakery closed its doors in 1968.

The following week, Bud and Louise rendezvoused in their apartment, and Bud was told adamantly, "You know your eyes have changed back to green."

He had forgotten when he was with her the previous week that his eyes were hazel. Louise was soon to discover that his eyes changed to gray then blue in succeeding weeks. Years later, when her children asked what brought their parents together, she answered, "I thought I was under a magical spell, but really, I saw my children in his eyes."

118

Elaine and Bill had pondered their situation out on the Oregon coast. They enjoyed Riverside, California, now teeming with servicemen searching for work. Then Bill was offered a chance to work as an ambassador in Venezuela. But after pondering, they finally found themselves homesick and motored back to their home state in their Chevy.

Dot and Christy finally reunited in 1946. He returned home with lovely Japanese ceramics he said had the look of Dot's pottery. The Seabees labored long hours in Japan and were informed reconstruction efforts would help to preserve the peace. Dot finally had to admit that the bakery could be a source of creativity after the success of Victory Bread. The Fifties brought with it massive bakery factories selling "air bread." As Floyd observed, the bread was devoid of nutrients, flavorless, and mysteriously successful along with air dessert cakes. This made competition difficult, so Dot decided to close the shop after the death of her parents. Before she closed, she created a special cake for one of Louise's daughters. Due to the miracle of freezing, it was consumed after Stitt Bakery closed, evoking many peaceful memories.

Peace is a pleasing benefit of eating bread. It is a frugal method of feeding the belly while calming the mind. Lots of effort by the bakery girls had created peace in the hearts of customers while depression depressed and war raged and uneasy parents sent their children into battle. Dot and Louise continued this work with their associates. Elaine, who became their customer, was happy to nurture her family and three children free of the bakeshop.

The Stitt girls lived to ripe old ages and never congratulated themselves at all for their profound ability to be catalysts in the production of food and fun. They did indeed create the fun and helped so many others to bake, ice, wrap, truck and sell what founder Floyd Stitt referred to as "Better Made."

References to Popular Music

Maple Leaf Rag – By Scott Joplin. Copyright 1899.

Shan't Have any of Mine – Old camp song, composer unknown. Included in *The Franklin Square Song Collection*, 1881, New York.

Row, Row, Row Your Boat – Traditional nursery rhyme, composer unknown. Published by *The Franklin Square Song Collection*, 1852.

On Top of Old Smoky- Traditional folk tune, composer unknown. Recorded by The Weavers 1951.

On Top of Spaghetti – On Top of Old Smoky parody recorded by Tom Glazer 1963.

Ain't Nobody's Business if I Do – Words and music by Porter Grainger and Everett Robbins. Performed by Alberta Hunter. Copyright 1923.

Down By the Old Mill Stream – Words and music by Tell Taylor. Copyright 1910.

Basin Street Blues – Written by Spencer Williams. Copyright 1928.

Begin the Beguine – By Cole Porter. Copyright 1935.

A Tisket A Tasket – Traditional song of late eighteenth century. Words and jazz version by Ella Fitzgerald and Al Feldman Arranged by David J. Elliot. Copyright 1938.

Cheek to Cheek – By Irving Berlin. Copyright 1935.

The Sheik of Araby – Words by Harry B. Smith and Francis Wheeler. Music by Ted Snyder. Copyright 1921.

Pack Up Your Troubles in Your Old Kit-Bag and Smile, Smile, Smile – Words George Henry Powell. Music by Felix Powell. Copyright 1915.

Moonlight Serenade – Music by Glenn Miller. Lyrics by Mitchell Parrish. Copyright 1939.

Night and Day – By Cole Porter. Copyright 1932.

Every Little Breeze Seems to Whisper Louise – Music Richard A. Whiting. Words by Leo Rubin. Copyright 1939.

Praise the Lord and Pass the Ammunition – By Frank Loesser. Copyright Famous Music 1942.

Pennies From Heaven – Words and Music by Arthur Johnston and John Burke. Copyright 1936.

Don't Sit Under the Apple Tree – Music Sam H. Stept. Lyrics Lew Brown and Charlie Tobias. Copyright 1939.

It Don't Mean a Thing (if it ain't got that swing) – Music by Duke Ellington. Lyrics by Irving Mills. Copyright 1931.

In the Mood – Words by Andy Razaf. Music by Joe Garland. Copyright 1940.

Take the A Train – Music Billy Strayhorn. Copyright 1939. Words Joya Sherrill. Copyright 1944.

Lullaby of Broadway – Music by Harry Warren. Lyrics by Al Dubin. Copyright 1935.

Rags to Riches – By Richard Adler and Jerry Ross. Copyright 1953.

Shine on Harvest Moon – Written by Jack Norworth and Nora Bayes. Copyright 1909.

The Army Air Corps – Written by Robert MacArthur Crawford. Copyright 1939.

You're the Cream in My Coffee – Music by Ray Henderson.

Lyrics by Buddy G. DeSylva and Lew Brown. Copyright 1928.

Tangerine – Words by Johnny Mercer. Music by Victor Schertzinger. Copyright 1940.

Imagination – Music by Jimmy Van Heusen. Lyrics by Johnny Burke. Copyright 1940.

Sentimental Journey – Music and lyrics by Ben Homer, Les Brown, and Bud Green. Performed by Doris Day. Copyright 1944.

Bibliography

Books

Ambrose, Stephen E. *Citizen Soldiers.* New York: Touchstone, 1997.

Barton, Michael and Dorman, Jessica. *Harrisburg's Old Eighth Ward.* Charleston, SC: Arcadia Publishing, 2002.

Churchill, Winston S. *Closing the Ring: The Second World War (volume v).* New York: Houghton Mifflin Co, 1951.

Dunnigan, James F. and Nofi, Albert. *Dirty Little Secrets of World War Two.* New York: Harper, 1996.

Ellison, Mark and Ellison Eli. *Dear Mom, Dad and Ethel.* Lincoln, NE: iUniverse, 2004.

Gross, Margaret Geissman. *Dancing on the Table: A History of Lake Erie Collage.* Burnsville, NC. Celo Valley Books, 1993.

Hamelman, Jeffrey. *Bread: a baker's book of techniques and recipes.* Hoboken, NJ: John Wiley & Sons, Inc., 2004.

Jones, John Bush. *Songs that Fought the War.* Lebanon, NH: New England University Press, Brandeis University Press, 2006.

Wiseman, Ann. *Bread Sculpture.* San Francisco, CA: 101 Productions, 1975.

Internet References

"1942" [Online] Available at: http://www.thepeoplehistory.com/1942.html. April 8, 2008.

"1944 Europe and the Battle of the Bulge" [Online] Available at: http://www.thejucketts.com/ww2website/1944-europe.htm. August 9, 2009.

"AVWeb" [Online] Available at:
http://www.avweb.com/news/profiles/Paul
Tibbets_StudsTerkel_EnolaGayInterview_2002_196499-1.html.
January 22, 2010.

"Damn Good Vintage" [Online] Available at:
http://damngoodvintage.com/WWllSewingPamphlet.html.
March 18, 2007.

"EyeWitness to History" [Online] Available at:
http://www.eyewitnesstohistory.com/w2frm.htm. July 12,
August 2007.

"German Fuel Shortage of World War 2" [Online] Available at:
http://vanrcook.tripod.com/Germanfuelshortage.htm. March 23,
2009.

"Henkels and McCoy" [Online] Available at:
http://www.henkelsandmccoy.com/Timeline/Pages/TL1945.aspx
. October 2, 2008.

"Jitterbuzz" [Online] Available at: http://jitterbuzz.com.
December 8, 2010.

"Lisa's Nostalgia Café" [Online] Available at:
http://www.angelfire.com/retro2/lisanostalgia1/40slifestyle.html.
March 7, 2007.

"Miller Center of Public Affairs" [Online] Available at
http://millercenter.org/scripps/archive/speeches/detail/3329.
January 16, 2009.

"The Letter Repository" [Online] Available at:
http://letter.ie/0015/0017.html. June 5, 2009.

"The Road Wanderer" [Online] Available at:
http://www.theroadwanderer.net/route66.htm. October 29, 2009.

"The War" (Ken Burns and Lynn Novick) [Online] Available at:
http://www.pbs.org/thewar/about_site_credits.htm. January 24,
2009.

"Timelines of History" [Online] Available at: http://timelines.ws/20thcent/1943.html. April 19, 2008.

"Welcome to the USS Wiseman DE 67" [Online] Available at: http://www.sunwestmonograms.com/wiseman/duty.htm. August 22, 2009.

"Merriam Webster's Online Dictionary" [Online] Available at: http://www.merriam-webster.com. February 14, 2011.

"Word History" [Online] Available at: word-origins.com. November 24, 2010.

"World War Two Timeline" [Online] Available at: http://history.howstuffworks.com/world-war-ii/world-war-2-timeline.htm. November 7, 2008.

Suggested Topics for Book Clubs

The novel focuses on the lives of women born coincident with the rise of women's equality in work and the right to vote. Discuss their tasks set against the Roaring Twenties, the Great Depression and wartime.

Dot is associated with what product? Does this fit her personality?

Creativity is usually not associated with bread baking, but Dot makes bread a creative vehicle. Did you agree that victory bread was art? Have you ever used baking in a creative way? If so, what was the item you baked?

Louise is associated with what product? Does this product lend itself to research, or occupational therapy? Did you feel any fun occurring as her byproduct, or was the fun created intentionally?

Elaine is associated with cake. Is this consistent with her personality? How did you feel about Elaine's attitude toward the bakery?

Is finding fun an important pursuit in wartime? Discuss how the three women incorporated humor, play and enjoyment into their lives.

Do you as a reader feel the metamorphosis of women's lifestyles happening in the span of *The Bakery Girls* early years; 1911–1946?

Acknowledgements

To those who assisted with information and photographs: Jim Ditlow, Cindy Sobkowski, Mike Sobkowski, Ellen Carter and John Grove.

The technical support team: Genady Filkovsky.

Those who advised prior to publication: Genady Filkovsky, Judy Gire, Micky Reindeer, Lois Landis and Catherine Van Wyck.

The superior Editor: Mark Hooper of Angel Editing.

A special thank you to Aunt Elaine for devoting her time to numerous interviews that prepared me to tell the tale.

Made in the USA
Charleston, SC
21 September 2012